About the Author

Geraint V. Jones lives in north Wales. He has had several works of fiction published in Welsh, ranging from tales of mystery and suspense to political espionage and historical novels. *The Schidoni Pentacle* is but his second publication in English

The Schidoni Pentacle

Geraint V. Jones

The Schidoni Pentacle

Vanguard Press

VANGUARD PAPERBACK

© Copyright 2024
Geraint V. Jones

The right of Geraint V. Jones to be identified as author of
this work has been asserted by him in accordance with the
Copyright, Designs and Patents Act 1988.

All Rights Reserved

No reproduction, copy or transmission of this publication
may be made without written permission.
No paragraph of this publication may be reproduced,
copied or transmitted save with the written permission of the publisher, or in
accordance with the provisions
of the Copyright Act 1956 (as amended).

Any person who commits any unauthorised act in relation to
this publication may be liable to criminal
prosecution and civil claims for damages.

A CIP catalogue record for this title is
available from the British Library.

ISBN 978 1 83794 030 1

This is a work of fiction. Names, characters, businesses, places, events and incidents
are either the product of the author's imagination or used in a fictitious manner. Any
resemblance to actual persons, living or dead, or actual events is purely coincidental.

Vanguard Press is an imprint of
Pegasus Elliot Mackenzie Publishers Ltd.
www.pegasuspublishers.com

First Published in 2024

Vanguard Press
Sheraton House Castle Park
Cambridge England

Printed & Bound in Great Britain

In loving memory of Máred (1990 – 2013). Forever in our thoughts.
In loving memory of
Máred
(1990 – 2013)
Forever in our thoughts.

My sincere thanks to the following for all their help and advice – Gareth T. Jones, Delyth Lloyd Jones and Debora Morgante

YEAR 2002

Prologue

The scene was spectral, the ruined ramparts bleached eerie white by the Pyrenean moonlight. The last of the tourists had long gone and night was once again laying claim to the ancient citadel, dispatching its squadron of pipistrelles to patrol a warm star-studded sky.

The tall phantom like figure, stepping out of the shadows, paused but briefly to cast a final look around. Then, satisfied that all was well, he turned to depart, knowing that he would be back again tomorrow night, and every other night until the threat had passed, or been removed.

Not since his grandfather's time had there been need for such a vigil and the threat then, as now, had come from men of considerable power; selfish men who coveted nothing other than personal glory or prodigious wealth.

Kukes, northeast ALBANIA near the Kosovan border

Exiting the tunnel and without breaking stride, he stooped to snatch the Uzi SMG out of the reluctant grasp of one of the dead guards. Their corpses still lay there, spreadeagled across the tracks, mouths gaping, empty eyes mirroring the cold light of a wintry Balkan sky. Behind him, in the blackness, the bobbing flashlights and the yelling and the shrieking were getting ever closer. He had maybe two minutes to make good his escape. Previous surveillance had proved that the site was heavily guarded during the day but he had no way of knowing how many patrolled at night. There were these two, whom he'd already taken out, and the other one at the entrance to the second tunnel – the one who'd spotted him and raised the alarm before taking a bullet – but there had to be quite a few others as well, judging from the level of cursing and shouting now coming up behind.

A quick glance at the black Mercedes parked near the tunnel entrance confirmed that it was locked and offered no means of quick escape, so he sent a salvo into each of its front tyres and watched it collapse, like a wounded animal falling to its knees.

The sub-machine-gun's stutter momentarily silenced his pursuers and their caution now gave him precious extra seconds. A glance at the night sky told him not to expect any favours from above. Full moon! No clouds! He'd be a sitting target if they got within range. Desperately, he fired several rounds back into the tunnel, smiling ruefully as he listened to the cacophony of dull thuds, whining ricochets and chorus of warning screams. Then, swivelling on his heels, he began haring down the dirt track towards the rented car, hidden in undergrowth a good half mile away, his breath preceding him in constant puffs of white vapour. As he ran, he had but one thought, other than making good his escape. Contacting London! After that he'd have to think about getting out of the country, out of Albania. It wouldn't be easy. Far from it! Not after tonight! By morning, every port and airport would be closely watched, with little chance of his escape route to Italy being still open to him.

As he listened to the weight of his own body pounding the frozen track, he felt a desperate need to glance back over his shoulder, but resisted the urge, for fear of tripping over his own feet and being sent sprawling. A distant crack now gave warning that a shot had been fired and instinctively he ducked, at the same time realising that the bullet must have fallen short or else he'd have felt its searing heat in his flesh by now; either that or heard the whine of a near miss.

Eventually, he let out a sigh of relief as he spotted the little Fiat, parked off-road where he'd left it, in the shadow of windswept scrub and stunted pine trees. He still had the Uzi automatic in one hand, the Beretta with fitted silencer held limp in the other. Hurriedly, he placed the Uzi on the car roof and, with his free hand, delved deep into his pocket for the car keys. A quick glance confirmed that his pursuers were getting ever closer. He could make out four... five dark shapes in the distance, heads bobbing up and down and catching the moonlight as they ran.

It took an eternity for the car door to swing open. Then, as he reached for the Uzi off the roof.

'Don't touch gun!'

The whispered command in broken English and the menacing dark form emerging out of the shadows to his left caused his flesh to creep and the sweat on his back to turn to ice. One of the guards, arriving late for night shift, must have spotted the parked Fiat and then lain in wait for its driver to return. In which case, he was done for! Another couple of minutes and they'd be swarming all over him. Capture, torture, execution! These guys, he knew, never took prisoners.

'Move away from car!'

The stranger, cautiously circling, had a gun pointed directly at his head. 'When I say, you get in car and we …'

He glimpsed an extended arm reaching for the semi-automatic on the car roof. That meant slight distraction, split concentration! No time for caution, he argued. This had to be his only chance. The Beretta spat three times in quick succession from hip height, catching the startled stranger full in the chest and sending him reeling backwards into the undergrowth. But it also brought an instinctive response from the man's dying finger, one that erupted in a wild flurry of bullets. A dull thud in his solar plexus and searing pain along his left temple was all that he felt but they were enough to send him staggering backwards, desperately clutching at the open car door to remain upright.

The drumming of feet was getting ever closer but he couldn't hurry, no matter how hard he tried. His arms, his legs were heavy… numb… too leaden to do anything except in nightmarish slow motion. Painfully, he half-fell half-dragged himself into the driver's seat and prodded blindly with the key, frantically seeking the ignition.

The car door was still open, but out of reach. Did it matter? No, nothing mattered anymore. All he needed was sleep; deep, sympathetic, all-consuming sleep. The car key, despite its bulky fob, was slipping slowly through his fingers. He needed to clutch at it but couldn't. Vaguely, he wondered how one side of him was so wet and warm whilst the rest of his body was getting colder by the second.

The pounding was still there, more in his head now! Heavy panting filled the air; animal noises, belonging to another world, another life. It occurred to him that if he kept his eyes tightly shut, they might not see him. If he could remain perfectly still, they might not realise that he was there. If he could stop gasping for breath then they might…

Only his right hand, with its vice-like grip on the steering wheel, kept him from toppling out of the car. His left, still gripping the Beretta, hung limply at his side. From afar, and yet close by, unfriendly voices filled the air, harsh against the silence of the night. Questions were being asked, answers being demanded. But not of him, he realised. Could that mean that he was, indeed, invisible to them? The idea pleased him and he forced a little smile.

Suddenly, heavy hands wrenched the heavy gun away from him and he felt his heavy body being dragged out of the little Fiat and allowed to drop heavily to the ground. Everything was heavy. He felt pain but it didn't matter. Nothing mattered except the pleasant caress of hoar frost on his cold face. Spectres stood over him, their cackling laughter polluting the clear night sky. What could be so funny? Maybe they expected him to laugh too!

'Haha!'

He mouthed the laughter but no sound came, just the briefest puff of frozen breath. A sudden kick into his side brought excruciating pain and he screamed, eyes now wide open and momentarily aware. There were faces looking down at him, sneering faces against a beautiful cobalt sky full of winking stars.

'It is good, is it not?' The gloating in Tosk was fuzzy and distant. '…MI6 kill Mossad, Mossad kill MI6!'

An explosion of crowing laughter was the last thing that he heard.

Ealing Common, WEST LONDON (6 weeks later)

'Off you go, Red!'

As it felt the clip release on its collar, the setter needed no further encouragement. With great loping strides it set off across the Common, each pounding paw bringing up its own little shower of heavy morning dew. Tom Mackay remained in his crouched position to watch it go. Then, with appreciable effort and audible groan, he slowly straightened, pressing as he did, the knuckles of his right fist into the small of his back, by way of support for the aching weakness there.

The pain was a legacy; the legacy of a skirmish, years ago, when he'd had to leap off a night train as it steamed out of Sarajevo. Quite literally a leap into the dark. He'd leapt because he'd had little choice. Risk breaking his neck or take a bullet! As simple as that! He'd opted for the leap and had landed heavily on his heels. Early X-rays had shown no damage but the pain had persisted and he, foolishly as it turned out, had been too stoic – or too busy – to submit to the problem.

'Old complaint, obviously!'

Years later, the osteopath in Ealing, after much fingering along the spine, had grimaced as though the pain had been his own.

'Compacted vertebrae, base of spine! That's the cause of your stiffness and pain. Should have had it seen to before now, you know. Had you come to me earlier...! Still, I'm willing to give it a try. It'll mean a number of appointments over the next few weeks.' Tom had smiled ruefully, paid through the nose for the initial consultation and diagnosis and had left without bothering to explain why he couldn't possibly commit the time. Next day, stepping gingerly off a plane at Tirana Airport, he was back in the Balkans where he was stationed with MI6's Eastern European Controllerate.

Now, leash in one hand and the other, his left, clutching the morning's tabloid *Times,* he began walking after his dog, inhaling deeply as he went. Nothing pleased him better than the smell of freshly mown grass and the rustle of a warm breeze in the tall elms surrounding the Common. Spring had come very late this year; March had been wet and windy, April had given unexpected hail and frosty nights, but the warm weather had arrived at last, much to the relief of Tom Mackay's ageing and aching joints.

Red had already disappeared between the stationary cars on the Warwick Road and onto the Northern Common beyond, where the mower was still at work, judging from the gnashing of cutters, harsh against the drone of traffic on London's North Circular.

The solitary park bench, when it came into view, was occupied, as Tom Mackay knew it would be. The man had his back to him, seemingly engrossed in his Saturday morning newspaper, also a tabloid *Times*. The usual supplements were strewn on the seat next to him.

The years have taken their toll, Tom thought, noticing the thinning hair and the rather scraggy nape above the black astrakhan collar of the overcoat. Instinctively, he looked around before taking his own place on the bench, at the same time realising that such caution was unnecessary because the man waiting for him would already have made doubly sure that they weren't being watched. Casually, after checking that his dog hadn't wandered too far, he placed his own *Times Supplement* on top of the one that was already there and raised his paper, to read.

'Good to see you, Tom, after all these years.'

'Good to see you, Jimmy.'

Mackay's accent was unmistakeably Scottish and offered stark contrast to the other man's refined tones. Neither of them looked in the other's direction. To any casual passer-by – and there were but few of those – they were just two strangers sharing the same park bench to read their morning papers.

'How long is it? Five?'

'Nine, come next September.'

'Good God! That long?' The younger man didn't dwell on his surprise, though. 'Time flies! You were too young to retire when you did, Tom. You know that.'

'Not much choice, had I?'

Sir James Oldcorn, director of operations at Vauxhall Cross, was quick to detect the hint of bitterness and recalled that his old colleague had had to retire early to care for his terminally ill wife.

'No, of course not. Sorry about Carol. You should have phoned me, to let me know, Tom. I'd have come to the funeral.'

Tom Mackay remained silent. It was almost seven years since his wife had passed away. He had expected his old colleague to at least send his condolences, but he hadn't.

In an attempt to relieve the pressure on his spine he adjusted his sitting position. 'You've done well for yourself, Jimmy. Or should I call you C, now? Sir James even!'

'No need for it, Tom. Not you of all people.'

The older man smiled ruefully. *I wonder?* he thought.

Sir James Oldcorn wasn't a man to dwell too long on pleasantries. He'd come here with just one objective. 'You sounded pleased with yourself on the phone, according to my wife. Caught three fish, you said? Pretty good catch in such a short time, I'd say.'

'I've thrown two of them back, actually. Pages eight and nine!'

Casually, MI6's director of operations folded his newspaper and laid it aside, at the same time reaching for the colour supplement that now lay on top of his own. He thumbed through the pages until he found what he wanted. Page eight had three photographs carefully pasted onto it; page nine had two. The set of three were of a muscular and ruggedly handsome young man in his mid-twenties. He'd posed for the camera in two of them—one on a beach, in crotch-tight black bathing trunks, the other on a concrete ramp by a river, dressed in light blue vest and shorts and proudly propping up a vertical oar. In the third photo, the camera had obviously caught him unawares as he emerged from The Wild Boar, wherever that pub might be.

'No names, Tom!'

The Scotsman nodded briefly. He knew the drill.

'You threw this one back, then?'

'I gave him some serious thought, Jimmy. Cambridge blue and all that! Fluent in German and Italian. Works in Whitehall, actually.'

'Hm!' Sir James, obviously respecting his old colleague's decision, nodded sagely. 'Too traceable. Too risky. And the other?'

Of "the other" there were two photographs. A woman in her early thirties, at pistol practice in one, sharing a joke with colleagues in the other.

'Special Branch! Highly thought of in Scotland Yard, I'm told. Service of some distinction in Northern Ireland and Kosovo. Speaks a wee bit of

Tosk, of the textbook variety. More fluent in Italian, though, which is your first requirement, or so you said.'

'But?'

'Well, at a pinch, either of these might have fitted the bill.' As he spoke, the Scot casually turned over another page of his newspaper. The charade of playing strangers had to be maintained. 'The third I came across quite by chance, a week ago, thanks to my son, Eddie. Sixteen and seventeen!' He waited until his companion had found the relevant pages and the five photographs pasted onto them. The first, in grainy black and white, was of a boy and girl aged ten and eight years, respectively. Both were thin and gaunt, the boy looking surly and apprehensive, the girl tear-stained and frightened. 'Front page of *The Observer,* sixteen years ago. Father Sicilian, mother, Albanian. Orphaned in Kosovo an hour or two before that photograph was taken. A middle-aged childless couple living in Peterborough saw the picture and immediately put in for adoption. Must have had some clout at the foreign office, I'd say, because their application was fast-tracked and the kids were here in England within a few weeks. Hell of a good move for the kids, as things turned out.'

Sir James now studied the more recent photographs. The girl didn't feature in any of the others, but there was no mistaking the young man in them; some of the gauntness remained but the fear and the mistrust were gone. One showed him jogging on the Thames Embankment, long, dark curly hair held in check with a crimson bandana, thin face set and resolute. The next had him dressed in loose karate dress, facing up to an opponent in the gym; eyes fixed and with a disturbingly hypnotic glint, whilst the mouth held a confident sneer. In the fourth, he was sitting poker-faced astride a powerful Kawasaki Z750 bike, in front of a block of luxury apartments. His whole demeanour exuded confidence and arrogance. The fifth and last photo, taken with telephoto lens, showed him exiting the HSBC headquarters in Canary Wharf.

'And he's the one, you reckon?'

'I know it, Jimmy! I know it!' Mackay could barely hide his enthusiasm.

'Thin as a rake, though! Would he be up to it?'

'Doesn't look the part, you mean? Just as well, don't you think? You weren't looking for hero material, or so you said.'

The head of MI6 sighed with some resignation. 'That's true. So, tell me more about him.'

'Last week Thursday I'd arranged to meet my son Eddie at the KKK in Bermondsey. He's a member there…' Out of the corner of his eye, Tom glimpsed a sudden concern on his friend's face. 'Kennington Karate Klub!' he explained with a chuckle. 'Not the KKK you were thinking of! Why Kennington rather than Bermondsey, though, I wouldn't know.'

'So?'

'As I said, Eddie had asked me to meet him there. Wanted to take me out for a meal, afterwards. I don't see him all that often, Jimmy, and I wasn't going to let the chance slip by, was I?'

'So?' The single syllable now sounded more like *Get on with it!*

The Scotsman turned yet another unread page of his newspaper. 'Anyway, I got there early enough to see him perform. Surprised me how good he was, actually, considering that he's now in his mid-forties and that he hasn't been a member of the club all that long. Already a brown belt, you know…'

'And?'

'Then these two came onto the mat. Him…' Mackay was alluding to the slightly built young man in the photograph. '…And another black belt, seventh dan. Seventh dan! They don't come any better than that, Jimmy.'

'So?'

'I've never seen anything like it. They squared up to one another and then… Well, I must have blinked or something because the next minute… next fraction of a second, rather… the other guy was flat on his back on the canvas, looking absolutely bemused. He got up, only to be thrown again, just as quickly. I'm telling you; I've never seen anyone move like that guy! He was absolutely phenomenal. Greased lightning, believe me!'

'Okay! So, he's good at that sort of thing.'

The Scotsman chuckled. 'Good is a bit of an understatement, my friend.'

MI6's director of operations frowned impatiently. 'But what makes you think he's the man I'm looking for?'

Tom Mackay was doing his best to curb his enthusiasm. 'Look! I think I've struck gold for you on this one, but I can't be sure, can I? At least not until you tell me what it's all about. All you said was that you wanted to send a new face into Albania, out of Italy… an outsider who wasn't too vulnerable… but that you couldn't go through the usual recruiting channels. After three weeks, and from a list of about thirty names, I'd come up with just two possibilities, neither of which I was a hundred percent happy with. But then, a few days ago and by pure chance, I came across our friend here and I instinctively knew that I'd found the ideal candidate for you.'

'Just instinct?' Again, a hint of scepticism or even reproach.

'Instinct together with what I suspect you want him for and what I've found out about him since. It's not a lot but it's pretty significant I think. I'm doing my best here, Jimmy.'

'I realise that. So, what have you found, Tom, other than that he's a martial arts expert?'

After checking once more that his dog was still within hailing distance and shifting his sitting position yet again to ease his aching back, Tom Mackay turned another page of his newspaper and carried on talking into it, whilst Oldcorn continued to gaze at the photographs in front of him.

'Not much, but bloody interesting.' The older man allowed himself a self-satisfied smile. 'He and his sister did reasonably well at school in Peterborough. Then the brother decided to study economics at Bangor University in North Wales. Why there, you wonder? Well, probably because the family owned a holiday cottage in Snowdonia and because the lad, whilst staying there, had developed a passion for rock climbing. Anyway, he got his degree. Then, four years ago, his adoptive mother died of cancer, his adoptive father of a heart attack ten months later. Left the brother and sister with quite an inheritance, believe me. The father – senior partner in a firm of building consultants here in London – must have been a pretty shrewd businessman. Years ago, off his own bat, he bought some derelict property in the Docklands area before there was any talk of the proposed development in that area… or at least before anything was made public… and when land was still reasonably priced there. Had inside information about what was to come, I'd say. Anyway, he subsequently developed the site. Luxury apartments. Private venture on his part. Nothing to do with his firm. Owned the lot, he did. Four blocks, three storeys high, six apartments per floor. So, when he died a couple of years ago, the brother and sister inherited everything—the flats in Canary Wharf, the house in Peterborough and a sizeable bank account to boot. How's that for a slice of luck? What do you reckon the apartments are worth nowadays, Jimmy?'

'Tell me.' The man from Vauxhall Cross wasn't going to be drawn into discussing irrelevancies.

'At least four hundred thou apiece, which means that this guy and his sister are virtual multimillionaires. Looking at him, you'd never tell, would you?'

'How does he fit the bill though, Tom? Is he what I'm looking for?'

'He's probably the ideal candidate for you, Jimmy. If you gave me another six months to look, I can't imagine finding anyone better.'

'Convince me.'

'Qualifies through his real parents. As I said, father, Italian… Sicilian actually, with Cosa Nostra connections… and the mother native Albanian. The boy is fluent in both languages, Italian and Tosk.'

'Mafia? You're one hundred percent certain on that, Tom?' At last, MI6's director of operations was showing genuine interest.

'I contacted the *Observer* journalist who wrote the article that goes with that picture. She had no trouble recalling the incident. Says she found out later that the parents weren't victims of the war in Kosovo at all, at least not directly. Seems that they were killed in some kind of mafia vendetta.'

'Hm!' Oldcorn remained thoughtful. Then, as if thinking aloud, 'Cosa Nostra! What would their interests have been out there if not…'

'Gun-running! Of course!'

'Ye… e… s!' C, Head of Vauxhall Cross operations, seemed convinced. 'And what else do we know about him, Tom?'

'He's currently a Trader for HSBC at its HQ in Canary Wharf, buying and selling shares, currencies… that sort of thing. And since he lives in one of his own luxury apartments – the ones that I've just told you about – then I'd say he's probably the only bank employee… and there are eight thousand of those sharing the same building as him, who can actually walk to work every day. The surprising thing is that he bothers to work at all, considering his assets.'

The younger man remained pensive, reluctant to commit himself.

'So, what do you think, Jimmy?'

'Hm! I'd normally need to know a hell of a lot more before deciding.'

Mackay could sense the tenseness and the frustration that accompanied difficult decisions. 'As I said, even if I kept looking for another six months, I doubt… no, I know that I won't find a better candidate for you.'

'I can't afford a month, leave alone six! I need someone out there now. To hell with it! I'm going to rely on your instincts, Tom. So, recruit him!' A sudden worry creased Oldcorn's forehead. 'I take it that you'll be able to manage that. How will you do it?'

'You don't need to know, Jimmy.'

'No, I suppose not. So just get on with it. I've already set up a slush fund and I don't have to tell you, of all people, how to go about getting the necessary papers for our friend, do I?'

Mackay shrugged his shoulders. 'No problem there. So, are you going to brief me?'

Sir James Oldcorn sighed and took several seconds before answering. 'I've been losing agents out there, Tom. Two in the space of as many months. One in Albania in February, another in Rome three weeks later.'

'Good God!'

'After which I decided to contact you. Then, last week, another was killed … in the Languedoc of all places.'

'South o' France?' It was an expression of surprise more than anything else.

'Don't ask me what he was doing there because I don't know myself. He was supposed to be in Rome at the time. I can only assume that he was following some kind of lead. Anyway, he got done when his car plunged into a ravine.'

'Accident?'

'No,' Oldcorn's reply was unequivocal. 'Evidence suggests that the car was pushed off the road.'

The Scotsman frowned long and hard. 'But why come to me, Jimmy? Can I ask you that?'

For the first time that morning, Sir James Oldcorn, head of MI6, glanced at his old colleague, in order to witness his next reaction. 'I'm convinced that some of my personnel have been got at.'

The surprise was immediate. 'Bloody 'ell! Are you sure?'

'Money buys loyalty, Tom. You know that. One or more of my people at Vauxhall Cross have been bought. I'm convinced of it. Information on my agents abroad is being passed on to somebody or other and I'm losing men because of it. The one killed in Rome had only just got off the plane. He was obviously expected. Someone had been warned and that could only mean one thing—a tip off from Vauxhall Cross. I'd had my suspicions before that, mind you, so it merely confirmed my fears.'

Mackay sat in stunned silence.

'I could well be a target myself, Tom... A target for surveillance, I mean... Which explains why we're meeting like this. I wouldn't take the risk otherwise.'

'Three agents lost! That's serious.'

'Yes. And we're not the only ones. The Mossad have also lost two of their best operatives in the region.'

'Good God! Mafia? al-Qaeda? Iran?' Tom Mackay was listing the usual suspects.

'Who knows? It could be any or all of them.'

'So, what was their brief? The agents you lost; I mean.'

'Huge... and I mean really huge... sums of money are being poured into Albania to fund the purchase and the manufacture of military hardware. The business has been going on for years, we all know that... you as much as anybody... but recent developments suggest a massive escalation, with a hidden agenda. Tell me Tom, have you heard of the CTR Programme?'

'The Co-operative Threat Reduction initiative by the Yanks in the nineteen nineties you mean? Yeah. To help Russia rid itself of the chemical weapons that had been stockpiled during the Cold War. Old news now, surely!'

'Not just Russia, Tom. A sixteen-ton cache was found in Albania alone when the Marxists finally lost power there... all of it illegal, of course, and a violation of the country's commitments under the 1994 Chemical Weapons Convention. Anyway, last year, in 2001, the Yanks, through their Nuclear Threat Initiative, authorised twenty million dollars to have them destroyed. But if the US, or the UN for that matter, imagine for one minute that it's all done and dusted, then they'll have to think again. Our Intelligence suggests that there's still a hell of a lot more of the stuff to be found and that it's been finding its way into the wrong hands.' He took a deep breath and sighed. 'And as if that wasn't enough, some of the allies' own ammunition has been disappearing in large quantities, and I don't just mean the conventional stuff. Just listen to this, Tom! It seems that during Desert Storm our troops were using ammo… missiles, bombs, shells, bullets… made with depleted uranium.' He paused briefly. 'And can you believe that NATO forces did the same during the Balkans conflict? And it now turns out that our own lads, as well as their victims, were radioactively contaminated. Can you believe it?' Oldcorn sounded genuinely aggrieved.

Mackay expressed his own astonishment with a clicking of the tongue.

'…This is bloody serious stuff, Tom. We have good reason to believe that somewhere or other in Albania, conventional and unconventional arms are being stockpiled for shipment. Destination as yet unknown to us. I can only assume that our agents came too close to the truth and were killed because of it.'

'What sort of conventional arms are we talking about?'

'Custom-made AK47s, Uzi SMGs…'

'The spray and pray.'

'That's right…' Oldcorn was also aware of what gangsters called the Uzi sub-machinegun. Spray and pray because the weapon was capable of firing up to six hundred rounds a minute. 'The Uzis come in self-assembly packs these days. Then there are the rocket launchers, grenades and grenade launchers, plastic explosives… You name it!'

'And the Italian connection? You mentioned Rome.'

MI6's director of operations fell silent for a few seconds. 'There have been a few pointers to the Vatican.'

Mackay drew an audible breath. 'P2? Opus Dei?' He knew something of the Holy See's underlying currents.

'Knights of Malta… Solar Templars… Take your pick!'

'That means the CIA can't be too far away either. Or the mafia! So, what's the connection?'

'Signs are that the Vatican Bank is funding the illegal arms production in Albania but we're very much in the dark as to what the agenda might be. Hopefully, your man will be able to find that out for us, just by being there and keeping his ear to the ground. That's all he needs do. Simple, straightforward brief. No undue risks. No need for heroics. What do you think, Tom? Will he do it?'

Tom Mackay gave the question some thought. 'He'll have to be pushed into it.'

'And can you do that?'

The smile was a rueful one. 'Do I need to remind you of my record in the Dirty Tricks League, Jimmy? Anyway, you don't really want to know, do you?'

'Fair enough. Just one more thing. Recent surveillance suggests a lot of extra hush-hush activity in the Vatican itself these days. Whether there's a connection between that and what they're up to in Albania I can't tell but feathers have certainly been ruffled in the Holy See of late. Not only there but in the Knesset as well. Which probably explains the Mossad's increased involvement. There might be a connection with the Albanian business, but again there might not. There may be no link whatsoever between the assassinations in Albania and Rome and the one in the South of France. That's something I have to keep an open mind on, for the time being at least. This is serious stuff, Tom, so tell your man to be careful.'

'Listen, Jimmy! It's all very well for me to recruit this lad for you... brief him even... but you don't expect me to run him as well, do you? It's been nearly nine years, for God's sake! Things have changed. I've lost touch. Lost confidence too, probably. Not to mention the fact that I've got this crippling back and that I'll be seventy-two next birthday.'

Sir James Oldcorn was prepared for the argument. 'I've thought long and hard about this, Tom. Fact is, I need someone from outside the agency whom I can trust implicitly. And you fit the bill as well as anyone I know. We spent years together in the field. Remember?' He turned to smile briefly. 'I learnt a lot from you. I know your strengths. If anyone can come up with the goods on this one then it has to be you, Tom. I can't put you on the official payroll, of course, for obvious reasons, but you'll be generously reimbursed by other means. You could do with the extra cash, I take it? Your service pension can't be worth all that much, these days.'

Tom Mackay chuckled briefly as if to agree. But it wasn't the monetary rewards as much as the thought of relieving his daily boredom that appealed to him now.

'Okay, you've convinced me, Jimmy. I'll give it a go.'

'Good. Now listen, Tom. I'm not going to give your man any contacts in either Albania or Rome, in case he's compromised before he even starts. All you can tell him is this—The arms are being manufactured in or around Kukes. That's a town up in northern Albania, not too far from the border with Serbia and Montene …' Oldcorn stopped in mid-sentence and smiled. 'I forget, Tom! You know that area as well as any of us.'

The older man also smiled. 'I should, shouldn't I? And if things haven't changed all that much, then I have a fair idea, too, where one of the production centres might be. I've nosed around the place often enough in years gone by. By the way, that's the area where this lad's parents were murdered, sixteen years ago. Their bodies were found in Prizren, in Kosovo, not far from the Morini border. The family were actually living in Kukes at the time.'

'Well! Well! It seems that you really have struck gold on this one, old friend.' At last, MI6's director of operations sounded genuinely pleased.

'Och aye, I think so too, Jimmy. Anyway, during my time in Albania, the arms were being shipped out of Durres on the Adriatic, most of them finding their way, eventually, to North Africa.'

Oldcorn nodded. 'Not anymore, though. As I said, signs are that there's been a significant escalation in activity of late but, as far as we can tell, the arms aren't going anywhere at the moment. They're certainly not being shipped out through any of the ports. I need to find out what's going on, Tom. My main concern is the agenda behind all this. If your man can find that out for us, then we'll be really indebted to him. It's up to you to decide how he should contact you. If he goes into Albania, then there could be a problem. You don't need me to tell you that. In Rome, though, my sister's girl could be useful. She's out there freelancing as a tourist guide. Does a lot of work for Thomas Cook and Thomsons, so I'm told. But that's all I can give you, I'm afraid, except that her name is Sally Jeffers. Haven't seen her or her mother in years, not since Sally was in her early teens. She might be able to help your man get some coded messages relayed to you, but I don't want her otherwise involved, nor in any way compromised. Make damn sure of that, Tom. And I certainly don't want her to hear my name mentioned. Is that clear?'

Tom Mackay nodded. It was the cue to change the topic of conversation. 'By the way, Jimmy, I haven't congratulated you on your promotion, have I? Nor on your knighthood. I've got to hand it to you! You've come a hell of a long way since those hair-raising days in the Balkans in the early nineties. But now that I'm in your employment, so to speak, maybe I should be showing you proper respect, and start calling you Sir James.'

The younger man smiled briefly, carefully brought the covers of the magazine together and laid it on the bench between them. Then, casually rolling up his own newspaper, said, 'If you, Tom, of all people, start doing that, then I'll set my wife on you!'

The Scotsman laughed. 'And how is Janet, anyway?'

'Things being different, you could ask her yourself. She's sitting in the car, behind us. Who do you think has been our lookout for the past…' He glanced at his watch. It was dead on ten o'clock '…Thirty-five minutes?' Slowly, he got to his feet. 'Anyway, good to have talked again, old friend. I'll look forward to developments.'

Mackay listened to the receding rustle of feet in the grass behind him and waited to hear an engine start and then fade into the distance. Casually, he tidied the pile of papers at his side and called Red back to him, to be leashed.

Snowdonia, NORTH WALES

'There it is!'

The rock face was coming into view above the ridge in front of them. 'Clogwyn Du'r Arddu.' The pronunciation was laboured. 'Means Black Rock something-or-other. Some of the best climbs in Britain on that.'

The other two felt a mixture of excitement and trepidation. Unlike their companion, they'd never attempted anything as difficult before.

'Well named, don't you think? Never any sun on it. I've been up here a few times and it's always been in shadow.'

The cliff face, blackened by centuries of running water, did indeed look intimidating.

'Well? So how do you feel now, Roy? Looking forward to it?'

The youngest of the three didn't answer. Something had caught his eye and he was now staring open-mouthed, in awe. 'God!' he muttered. 'He's doing it alone!'

It took a second or two for the others to follow his gaze and to spot the lone figure, high up on the cliff wall. Then they too gasped.

'Hell! He's going for the overhang!'

The three of them stood transfixed.

'... A fuckin HVS! And the stupid bugger's goin' solo.'

They watched the solitary climber, camouflaged against the rock by his dark grey clothing, inch his way towards the final overhang, just a few yards now from safety. The westerly breeze had an early morning bite to it and the heavy cumulonimbus clouds threatened rain before the morning was out.

'He'll never make it!' The breathy whisper was more out of concern than disrespect. Then, 'My God! He's coming down!'

The three caught their breath in unison as they saw the body swing free from the rock face and, for what seemed an eternity, dangle by a single arm. Then, still gaping incredulously, they watched the climber's other hand grope upwards for a hold, a leg being swung sideways... once... twice... to reach a foothold and suddenly the overhang had been conquered.

'What the hell happened there?' Young Roy's question was full of relief.

'Not many good holds up there...' The appointed leader of the group had regained his composure. '...But I know there's a little fissure there. He must have jammed his fist into that. Goin' solo, it's about the only way to tackle that overhang. He may be a fuckin madman but he knows his stuff, I'll give him that.' The expletives underlined the relief that he, too, was now feeling.

'Who is he, though?'

'Buggered if I know!' Then a penny seemed to drop. 'Unless it's that mad Italian they've been talking about! Heard him mentioned in the Pen-y-Gwryd, last time I was here. That's the pub I've been telling you about; the one where Hunt's Everest team used to meet when they were training here in the early fifties... We'll be going there for a pint, afterwards... He's up here most weekends, they say, climbing solo. Never uses ropes or pitons or anything. Il Ragno they call him. The Spider! Has to be him, I reckon.'

*

Gus Adams stood on the very edge to survey the climb that he had just made. The adrenaline still pumping in his veins mixed sweetly with the sense of exhilaration and achievement that he now felt. With a flourish, he whipped the crimson bandana off his forehead to let his shoulder-length hair hang free in the wind and then looked at his watch. Twelve-fifteen! It had been worth coming early.

Far below, three figures stood looking up at him, their voices faintly wafting up on the breeze. Briefly, he wondered what route they would tackle but he wasn't really that interested. They weren't in his league, he knew that.

'Ciao!' he muttered arrogantly and then, taking four deep breaths, he turned to follow the well-worn path down to where the bike was parked.

These visits to Snowdonia always brought back memories of his university years in nearby Bangor. Not that he'd enjoyed the academic end of his stay there, nor the company of immature students whose only idea of a good time was a communal pub crawl. He hadn't even bothered joining the uni climbing club, since he already knew the area better than any of its members and since he preferred to climb alone, anyway. Always had done, ever since he'd started coming up here as a boy, to stay at the cottage. Preferred his own company at other times, too. He knew that he hadn't been popular with other students; knew that they regarded him as a loner and a snob, amongst other things. Fair enough! To Hell with them! He'd merely retreated further into his shell by pretending to understand very little English, a deception he'd often used since then, when he needed to be left alone. His only haunts in the tiny city of Bangor had been the two Italian restaurants, where chats with Carlo and Stefano, the respective proprietors, had helped restore his fluency in the language. Otherwise, he felt indebted to no one, no one except the Uni karate club for introducing him to that particular martial art.

As he picked his way down the rocky path, he cast one last glimpse over his shoulder at the climb he'd just accomplished and felt some of the exhilaration returning. Tomorrow morning, just as early, he'd take a different route, then lunch at the cottage before the return trip to London.

The thought of going back to the city instantly dispelled his euphoria, as if a hot shower had suddenly gone cold on him.

Rome, ITALY

Through tear-filled eyes, Sally Jeffers looked at her naked suntanned body in the bathroom mirror and felt her misery give way to embarrassment and then disgust and anger. His casual "Ciao!" still rang in her head with a finality that now incensed her. He had used her! For three months, he had fucking used her! Hiding behind a pack of lies whilst being married all along! The bastard!

'Married with God knows how many kids!' she snarled. 'Bloody fool! I've been a naïve bloody fool!'

She stepped under the cold shower to wash all scent of him away and waited there for her blood to cool.

'Never again!' she sobbed angrily. 'I won't get caught like that ever again.'

Canary Wharf, LONDON (three days later)

It had been another bad session of trading for him, recording maximum losses on his currency-holding for the second day running. He had arrived at seven-fifteen a.m. as usual, hair glistening and trouser bottoms uncomfortably wet with the heavy morning drizzle. Then, more despondent, more listless than usual, he'd begun his working day by flicking through the papers on his desk, then scouring a choice of commentary screens – Money Market Services, Capital Management, the Reuters news services *bets, gags* and *gurn* – in time for trading to begin. Morning had been a headache, having to deal with more brokers than some other dealers had had all day—Tullett, Marshalls, Bierbaum in Dusseldorf... The list seemed endless. Then, at lunchtime, the persistence of the rain had added to his gloom by denying him his usual jog around the docks. It did cross his mind once to go up to the gym on the fifth floor for a workout but he'd thought better of that. The place was too popular. Today, as most other days, Gus Adams preferred his own company.

Afternoon had been an even worse headache, what with the rush of trading on sterling and the Japanese yen exchange rate. Tomorrow had to be better, he thought. It couldn't possibly get any worse. He'd lost count of the number of times that he'd glanced at the clock during the past hour but now, at long last, it showed three minutes to five o'clock and he could agree his closing position with the back office before leaving the building for the day.

As he tidied his desk, he tried not to listen to the usual end-of-afternoon chatter all around him.

Voice one: 'Bloody long day! Fancy a tipple?'

Voice two: 'Why not? I need a couple of g-and-ts to put my life back in gear.'

Voice three: 'Yeah! Just the job! Tube's crammed this time of day anyway. No point rushing.'

It surprised Gus how many of these dealers and brokers, facing long journeys back home and with families waiting there for them, made beelines for the nearest watering hole at the end of the day, to do nothing other than talk endless shop. He'd been lured a couple of times himself when he'd first started working here but the conversation had been nothing-more-nothing-less than an extension of the day's tedium and the day's problems. By now, he'd cried off so often that no one bothered asking him anymore. That suited him fine. He didn't like them anyway, and they probably didn't think much of him. To hell with them!

'Gus Adams?'

As he turned to confirm his identity, he was surprised to see two of the bank's security guards facing him.

'Yes?'

'Will you accompany us, please?'

'Accompany you? What do you mean, accompany you? Accompany you where?' Aware that others around him had fallen silent and were now all ears, he felt a sudden unease.

'You'll soon know, sir. Come now, please!' There was no element of choice in the request.

In full view of treasury department staff, he felt as if he was being frogmarched in the direction of the FX manager's office. The fourth floor had suddenly become a vacuum in which sounds reverberated and voices were amplified. He picked up the occasional hushed whisper – 'What's going on?' 'What's he done?' – but the dominant sound was the rhythmic rubber clump of his escorts' feet on either side of him.

After an age, they crossed the treasury department floor, and the door to the manager's office opened before them, as of its own volition. Templeton, the FX manager, was standing behind his desk, flanked by two men in dark suits. There were others present as well but Gus Adams' eyes were fixed on Templeton's scowl.

'Adams, these gentlemen are from Scotland Yard. They'd like to ask you a few questions.'

Gus let his eyes take in each stranger in turn.

'Gus Adams?'

'Yes?'

'Of Adamshouse Apartments, Limehouse?'

His brow became more creased and questioning.

'Yes?'

'Alias Guiseppe Maratta?'

Gus' eyes suddenly narrowed. What the hell was going on? He was being cross-examined and had no idea why.

'That's not an alias.'

'So, what would you call it, Mr Maratta?'

'Look here! My name is Gus Adams, and has been for the past sixteen years, ever since I was brought to this country for adoption. Guiseppe Maratta was my name before that.' He glanced towards Templeton, his boss, but the FX manager's face remained stony and full of suspicion. 'What's all this about, anyway?'

'And where would that have been, Mr Maratta? Italy?'

'There and Albania. My parents were killed in Kosovo.'

'Hm! And do you know how they were killed?'

'Not really. There was a lot of fighting, lot of killing, going on there at the time. I was too young to understand all of it.'

'Isn't it true that they were executed?'

Gus took a threatening half-step forward and saw the security guards move to intercept.

'What the hell are you suggesting?'

'Wasn't your father Giovanni Maratta?'

'Yes.'

'Sicilian born.'

'Yes. So am I.'

'With mafia connections.'

Gus was taken aback. 'Who the hell told you that?'

'So, you don't deny it?'

'Of course, I deny it.' He turned to look at Templeton. 'What's all this about?'

But his boss wasn't inclined to interrupt the cross-examination.

'We'd like you to accompany us back to your apartment, Mr Maratta. We have reason to believe that you are involved in terrorist activity. We do have a search warrant.'

As they exited the building, a number of paparazzi rushed forward, cameras at the ready.

Kennington Karate Klub, Bermondsey, LONDON (the following evening)

Eddie Mackay smiled ruefully as he got up off the mat. He'd just been thrown three times in succession, each time with some considerable force.

'My fault for thinking I could take you on.'

He sounded apologetic, especially since he'd personally asked for the chance to face Gus Adams.

'...Should have known better, shouldn't I?'

His opponent also smiled, but coldly and without humour. More of a sneer than anything else. 'Came down rather hard that last time, didn't you. It happens!'

Eddie Mackay fought back a scowl. The guy didn't endear himself, he thought.

'I'll put it down to experience,' he muttered somewhat brusquely, and then forced a smile. 'I'll buy you a drink at the bar.'

Gus Adams paused, as if to think up an excuse. After the bad press this morning, he hadn't intended coming to the Klub at all tonight, but then he'd argued that he wasn't going to let some stupid mistake by Scotland Yard or Special Branch or whoever make him a prisoner in his own apartment. 'No. Don't think so.'

Eddie again tried to ignore the young man's rudeness. He'd promised his father a "chance-meeting" with Adams, so he had no option but to bite his tongue and try again.

'Come on! I owe you! And maybe you could give me a few tips on how not to be thrown so easily next time. I'd appreciate that. I'm too old to be bouncing too often on any mat, these days.'

Gus Adams gave it some further thought before agreeing with a shrug and a grimace. 'Yeah, okay then! Glass of wine. Just one.'

Twenty minutes later, the two of them had showered and changed and were sipping wine and making idle chat about martial arts in general when Tom Mackay walked into the bar to join them.

'Dad! I didn't expect you this early.' Eddie's surprise sounded genuine.

'Well, you know how it is, son. Rather than kick my heels at home, I thought I'd come and see you displaying your skills on the mat.'

Eddie laughed. 'You've got to be joking! Had you come earlier you'd have seen me bouncing all over the damn thing, courtesy of this young man! Dad, I'd like you to meet Gus… Gus Adams.'

As they shook hands, Tom Mackay's face suddenly showed enough hesitant recognition for his new acquaintance to grimace.

'My face familiar, I take it?'

'Well, yes… I think.'

'You obviously read your tabloids! Front page at least!' The brusque tone bordered on rudeness.

Eddie now cut in, sounding surprised, 'So it was you, Gus? I'd noticed the resemblance but I didn't want to embarrass you by mentioning it. Got the name wrong though, didn't they? Mistaken identity?'

'Yeah! Could say that.' He was making no attempt to hide his bitterness.

Tom Mackay and his son remained silent, waiting for him to offer an explanation, to exonerate himself. It came with some reluctance.

'After giving me the third degree, they then kept me in a cell overnight!' The tone of voice was caustic. 'Said they'd been tipped-off that I'd been involved with some terrorist cell. Bloody stupid!' he muttered, again sounding genuinely aggrieved. 'First thing this morning they handed all my stuff back and told me, in as many words, to bugger off. Turned out that they'd arrested the wrong bloke.'

Tom Mackay shook his head in a mixture of faked sympathy and disbelief. 'It happens, I suppose! Damn sloppy, though!'

'Sloppy? Criminal, more like it!'

'The paparazzi were damn quick off the mark though, weren't they? Tipped-off beforehand most likely?'

Gus Adams scowled at the thought. 'Still haven't cleared it with the bank, though.'

'Who?'

'Scotland Yard. My Nedcap security pass was taken off me yesterday, so when I tried to report for work a couple of hours late this morning, security told me point blank that I no longer worked there.'

Tom Mackay grimaced sympathetically. On the one hand, he felt some guilt but on the other he was inwardly satisfied with the way things had gone, thus far. Eddie had done well to arrange this meeting, he thought.

'They'll take you back, surely? Legally obliged I should think.'

'Don't put any money on it. Don't bet on my wanting to go back, anyway.'

As if on cue, Eddie excused himself to go to the toilet. Tom Mackay shuffled somewhat uncomfortably in his chair and swirled the little that was left of the beer at the bottom of his glass. He knew that he had to tread carefully. The lad wasn't stupid. He'd very quickly smell a rat if the matter wasn't approached properly.

As it turned out though, Gus Adams made things easier for him. 'So, what line of work were you in?'

The ageing Scotsman struggled to curb his enthusiasm as the opportunity offered itself. 'I'm not sure I should be telling you, Gus.'

His roguish smile made Adams raise a quizzical eyebrow and ask, 'Why? You haven't got mafia connections as well, have you?' It was probably meant as a bitter joke but the thin young man seemed incapable of smiling.

Tom, however, laughed. 'Worse, I'm afraid! MI6 actually.'

'Spy? You're joking!'

The hint of interest gave Mackay some heart. He laughed, 'Spy sounds so mundane, Gus. Don't you think? I prefer secret agent. More like *James Bond* than your run-of-the-mill spy.'

'You joke about it. You're saying that the work wasn't interesting?'

Tom laughed briefly. 'Well, I've had my moments, I suppose.'

'Such as?'

'Nothing much I can tell you, really.'

'Oh!'

Sensing his companion's waning interest, Mackay now added, 'You know! State secrets and all that!'

'If you were MI6, then you didn't work here, in the UK, did you? I know that much. So, you travelled a lot?'

'Aye. That's true. Became involved with some interesting characters, I can tell you.'

'Oh?'

With a knowing smile, like a fisherman feeling another little tug at the end of his line, the silver-haired Scotsman once more gave the impression of relenting. 'In fact, I can look back on some pretty hair-raising times and a few narrow squeaks. But I'm well out of it now. Or at least I thought I was.' He waited a second or two for the question to form in the other's eye. 'It's a young man's job, Gus. Great whilst I was single and carefree, but once I became a family man… I missed out a lot, after that. Eddie will know that better than anybody. Hardly knew his dad in those days.'

'So, when did you retire?'

Tom laughed ironically. 'That's the point. I thought I had, nine years ago! But now they want me…' As if suddenly realising that he'd said too much, he clammed up.

'Another assignment?' Adams was still sipping at the bait.

'Aye, you could call it that I suppose.' Then, with an apologetic laugh, 'But I talk too much.'

Things were moving far too quickly! Tonight's contrived meeting had been for a mere introduction, nothing more. He had to tread carefully, take things slowly, or else the lad was bound to smell a rat. He wasn't stupid. But having said that, it was Adams himself who was pushing the conversation along.

'You think I'm prying!' The unpleasant curtness was there again. 'None of my business, is it?'

The Scotsman laughed briefly. 'Don't apologise. How did the subject come up, anyway?'

'My fault. I asked you about your work.'

'So, are we going to have just one more drink before we go?' Eddie was back, now standing behind Gus' chair and looking directly at his father for a sign that he was satisfied with the way things were going. The smile and the insignificant nod of the head confirmed as much.

Tom delved in a pocket for his wallet. 'It's my shout! Gus and I haven't finished our chat yet.'

'No, I'll get these.' Gus Adams leapt to his feet. 'Same again?' And to confirm the order in his own mind, he muttered '*Due bicchieri di vino rosso e una birra*' and was gone before Tom Mackay could feign surprise at hearing Italian being spoken.

Eddie waited until the young man was out of earshot. 'Well? Satisfied, Dad? Is he what you were looking for?'

'Aye. I think so. I really think so.'

'He won't be put in any danger, will he? You promised me that. I don't want his blood on my conscience.'

'I haven't offered him anything yet.'

'But you intend to?'

'Aye. I think I do.'

Eddie's face became suddenly serious. 'That business in this morning's papers. Tell me that you had nothing to do with that.'

His father looked away, to watch Gus at the bar.

Adamshouse Apartments, Canary Wharf, LONDON

He hadn't been home an hour before the phone rang.

'Gus Adams?'

'Who's asking?'

'Tom, here. Tom Mackay.'

The few seconds silence that followed was a question in itself.

'...You'll be wondering why I'm calling.'

Still no response from the other end.

'...Got your phone number through the Klub.' A brief laugh, now. 'Wasn't easy, I can tell you! Had to tell them a few wee fibs. Hope you don't mind.'

'What is it, Mr Mackay?' He could tell that the ex-MI6 man was walking and talking at the same time.

'Couldn't bring it up in front of Eddie... Um! Just something you said, that's all.'

'Something I said?' Gus' tone suggested some surprise but not much interest.

'You said something in Italian.'

'Did I? So?'

'You speak Italian?'

'Yeah. So?'

'How fluent?'

'I speak fluent Italian, Mr Mackay. No big deal. I was born in Italy.'

The silence now came from the other end of the line as Gus waited to be told the reason for the call.

'Can we meet, Gus? I mean now?'

'Depends. Where are you?'

'Adamshouse Apartments are directly in front of me as I speak.'

'Hm! That close?' But the younger man's tone didn't suggest any undue surprise or suspicion. 'I don't know if it matters but I should warn you that this place could still be under surveillance. They could even be listening to this conversation right now.'

'I'll take my chances, Gus.'

'Then you'd better come straight up.'

*

'Rome?' The young man, now dressed in an olive-coloured tracksuit, reclined his chair a little further. He'd listened to Mackay's proposition with hardly an interruption but now he was expected to respond. 'Let me get this straight. You want me to work for MI6 in Rome?'

Tom Mackay smiled inwardly, sensing the growing interest and confident that he'd sussed his man out well.

'Unofficially, yes. That was the idea. You wouldn't be expected to take any undue risks, of course... that goes without saying. It's just that we need a good pair of ears out there, ears that understand Italian.'

'Why Rome? You said that the problem was in Albania.'

'Couldn't send you there, obviously. Too dangerous. You'd be out on a limb. But my hope is that you could get some information for us on the grapevine in Rome. Our intelligence tells us that things are being run from there, anyway.'

'How would I do that? Where would I find your so-called grapevine?' Gus Adams was making no attempt to hide his cynicism.

'Well, we would obviously suggest where you could start. Give you a few pointers. Not contacts as such, just some individuals to keep an eye on, see who they meet... That sort of thing.'

'And if I can't? Get you the information, I mean.'

'Well, that'll just be too bad. At least you'd have tried.'

Gus remained silent for a few seconds, then, 'You said you'd retired years ago?'

Mackay was ready. 'Aye, so I did. But as I said, Vauxhall Cross approached me with a proposition for this one job... It's just that I've spent years working for them in that part of the world... and my smattering of Tosk is seen as an extra qualification, I suppose.'

'Tosk? You speak Albanian?'

Since the sacked banker was making no attempt to hide his surprise, Tom Mackay responded with an apologetic laugh. 'Not really. Just a smattering,' he lied. 'And what little I had is pretty rusty by now anyway.'

He half expected Gus to confirm his own fluency in the language, but he didn't.

'...Still better than my Italian, though,' he added with a mirthless chuckle. 'Anyway, I told them I'd do it, but only if they couldn't recruit someone else for the job, someone younger but just as competent and reliable. But they're not prepared to send a trained agent out there, to be nothing more than a pair of ears on the ground. They say that that would be a waste of MI6 manpower. Anyway, after the chat we had earlier, it occurred to me...'

He laughed briefly, again without humour, and slowly got to his feet.

'...Look, Gus! Maybe I shouldn't have come here in the first place. Actually, I don't know what made me do it. I know that you're damn good at martial arts, and pretty competent at your banking job too, I imagine, but as far as this cloak and dagger business is concerned... well, I'm afraid you'd be a wee bit out of your depth.' He forced another embarrassed laugh. 'But I've now made the offer and it's too late to take it back.' He paused briefly, then, nailing the young man with a cold stare, he spoke quickly, 'Yes or no, Gus? If no, then I'd be obliged if you forget all about the proposition.'

The stare was returned. 'I'll think about it.'

'I'll need to know soon.'

'Give me your number. I'll ring you.'

Rome, ITALY (ten days later)

'Curioso?' The eyes glinted threateningly and the skin on the fleshy face coloured. 'What do you mean, snooping around?' There was no denying the harsh Sicilian accent nor the instant suspicion in the voice.

'He is asking questions about our cousin Giovanni Maratta.'

'*Bugiardo*! He lies! My cousin Giovanni Maratta was killed many years ago, in Kosovo.'

Maurizio Bonnano, the *capo dei capi* of the Cupola, turned pocket-laden eyes towards the other mafiosi in the room, as if daring one of them to argue otherwise. Two or three of those sitting at the long, mahogany table nodded sagely but without conviction, the others merely wrinkled their lips in cold sneers as if the topic of conversation was beneath contempt. Maurizio sensed as much and, feeling the need to show more authority, turned again to the man who had just interrupted their meeting to bring him the news.

'Who is he, Luca? Is he a secret operative? Mossad? CIA? What? Because if you have led him here, to me, to the Cupola...' With a brief sweep-of-hand he indicated those sitting around the table with him. '...Then I swear it is you who will pay dearly.'

The burly Luca, of the fixed stare and emotionless eyes, didn't seem particularly intimidated by the threat. He had thought twice about interrupting the meeting but had then decided that what he had just heard on the streets could not wait.

'He is asking about the family. Your family and mine, Maurizio! He says he is looking for his relatives. But I do not trust him. I think he lies.'

'Then get rid of him, Luca! It is what I pay you to do. If he is a threat, then let him be food to fish in the Tiber.'

Tired heads were seen to nod, as if to suggest *get on with it!* The Cupola, otherwise known as *La Nuova Alba* – 'The New Dawn' – had more pressing matters to discuss.

'*Si,* Maurizio! It shall be done.'

But, as Luca turned to leave, 'Wait!'

With great deliberation and a pompous show of authority and self-importance, the *Capo* got to his feet, his considerable bulk being squeezed against the edge of the heavy table in front of him.

'...This man! You say he is Sicilian?'

'*Si,* or so he says, Maurizio.'

'And he asks about my cousin, Giovanni?' There was an edge of wariness to the voice, now. 'Where did you see him?'

'I have not seen him but I have heard that he is asking his questions here in Roma, in the Archivio and the Biblioteca, in the cafés and *ristorantes*, out on the streets. Always he asks about Giovanni Maratta. But he will ask no more questions, Maurizio. I will silence his tongue.'

'You say you do not trust a man you have never seen? You are an idiot, Luca. You check first before you deal with him, because if you cause harm to one of the family...'

As he straightened his shoulders in a further show of imperiousness, Maurizio's braces grew taut.

'...Then I shall personally flay you alive and drape your worthless skin over the vines on the hills of Roma.'

One or two of those at the table sneered inwardly. To them, Maurizio Bonnano was just being his arrogant self, full of bluster and empty words. But he was the *capo dei capi* – the boss-of-bosses whom Aiello had personally selected to oversee the work of the Cupola – and they had no choice but to live with that fact; at least for the time being.

'Si, Maurizio!'

The swarthy Luca didn't look particularly troubled. He was used to Maurizio's bluster and idle threats but the harsh warning hurt him just the same. What if he, Maurizio, was boss-of-bosses of the new Cupola here in Roma, with Luca himself just a common foot soldier, it didn't give him the right to humiliate his old friend in this way, not in the presence of some worthless Camorra vermin freshly out of the gutters of Napoli and still smelling that way, or to impress the 'Ndrangheta swine of Calabria. Wasn't he, Luca, blood family? And wasn't he therefore, like Maurizio himself, a man of honour, Sicilian by birth, and a proud member of Cosa Nostra? Had they not grown up together in Corleone? In the old days, had they not stood side by side on the cobbled streets of Viccuria Market in Palermo and sprayed bullets at those who had tried to prevent them muscling in on their protection business? The greedy riff-raff – amateurs by comparison – who thought they could prevent men of honour from Corleone from collecting protection money from the city's wealthy traders? And hadn't Maurizio promised him that when he, one day, became *Capo*, then Luca would automatically become his *consigliere*, his adviser and second-in-command? But Maurizio had gone back on his word. Two years ago, when a messenger from the Holy See had sought him out in Sicily, to bring him here to Rome to be *capo dei capi* of a new Cupola – to be boss of bosses of a group of representative mafia leaders from across Italy – Maurizio had reneged on his promise and had told Luca that he already had a chosen *consigliere* but that he had important work for him just the same. 'You, Luca my old friend, will be my personal aide and bodyguard, answerable to me and to me alone.'

But he, Luca, had been neither impressed nor pleased. He now shrugged, to dispel the nagging memory. 'I will check on this man personally, Maurizio, and bring you more information on him. Then I will deal with him, as necessary. Come Tommaso!'

Struggling to hide his hurt pride, he motioned to his sidekick, who had been leaning patiently against the door frame, to follow him out.

'Luca is Family,' Maurizio offered the explanation as he lowered himself back into his chair. 'Not much in the head but a good servant. I only have to…' He clicked finger and thumb. '…And Luca obeys.'

'Is he an organ monkey?'

Maurizio Bonnano, although inwardly seething, chose to disregard the derisive comment from the other end of the table and also the smirks that it so readily produced. 'Let us get down to business,' he rasped. '*La Nuova Alba* is meeting today because Aiello has demanded an up-to-date report on the Albanian situation.'

'He demands?'

'Yes, Bernardo. He demands!' He glared at the questioner. There was no way that he could allow his authority to be further undermined. 'Do you have problems with that?'

Bernardo Pellegrini from Calabria, the most senior of the three 'Ndrangheta mafiosi in the room, looked around for support but all others avoided his gaze. Aiello might be just a name to them – an alias even – but they knew that his demands could not and should not be challenged, because he represented a higher authority than even the mafia themselves. Aiello's authority came directly from Il Vaticano and to challenge him would be to challenge the wishes of *Il Papa*, no less.

'*Mi scusi!*' Salvatore Provenzano, appropriately sitting next to Maurizio as his *consigliere*, his second-in-command, was now leaning forward in his chair and looking directly at Maurizio in a show of underlining his own role in the scheme of things.

'…Before we proceed, before we discuss Albania as Aiello asks, perhaps we should know more about your cousin, the one who is now being sought by Luca.'

Provenzano was Neapolitan Camorra through and through and had been Aiello's specific choice as the Cupola's second-in-command. In contrast to Maurizio who was overweight and ponderous of body if not of mind, Salvatore was small and wiry, his features pinched and sallow. What he lacked in corporal presence was more than made up for in his cold, calculating eyes. Luca called him Rat Face, to his back; to others he was known as *Il Pallottola* – The Bullet – a sobriquet that he had more than earned, in his native Napoli.

Maurizio's tired eyes showed some respect as they turned towards his second-in-command. 'It is well that you ask, Salvatore. It seems that the person whom Luca is worried about has been enquiring about my cousin Giovanni Maratta. You will not be remembering Giovanni of course.' He let his gaze wander around the table, so as to include everyone else present. 'He was gunned down in Prizren, in Kosovo. He and his wife Agnesa.'

'Why? You must explain, Maurizio!' By seeking to have the situation clarified, the Camorra man was again reminding everybody of his status within the Cupola.

'Some said CIA, others said al-Qaeda assassins.' Maurizio had regained his composure, and now spoke with more authority. 'CIA?' He wagged a dismissive *finger*. 'No! I spit on CIA, but Giovanni and CIA worked for the same cause, if for different reasons. Al-Qaeda? No! Islamists had some cause to kill my cousin but they had more to gain by keeping him alive. Some suggested renegade mafiosi.' Again, he paused. 'Probably not. Giovanni Maratta was a man of honour and had it been renegade mafiosi who killed him then Cosa Nostra would have avenged his death before now.

My friends, enquiries were made at the time and the family concluded that my cousin Giovanni and his wife Agnesa – Agnesa Kadare, who was Albanian – had been assassinated by the cursed Israelis.'

'And why would the Mossad want to kill *your* Giovanni?'

The *Capo* sensed the sneer in Salvatore's tone. 'You think our mission in Albania today is greatly different to my cousin's mission so many years ago?'

The question, rhetorical as it was, was aimed specifically at his *consigliere*'s lack of understanding of what had been going on for years in the Balkans, and Salvatore Provenzano duly looked away.

'…So now can we move forward and discuss our next report to Aiello on *La Crociata Finale?*'

Il Vaticano

Had he known of the covert association between a faceless Aiello within the Vatican and the mafia's so-named *La Nuova Alba* in Rome, then the pontiff would indeed have been doubly worried. As it was, though, he had more than enough to concern him, which was why he had again today, the eighth time in as many weeks, called for a meeting with the commander of the Swiss Guard who was head of Vatican security, and Padre Leonardo Messina, guardian of the Vatican's secret archives.

Today, rather than seeing them in the L'Ufficio del Papa as he normally did, he had chosen the Borgia Courtyard as a meeting place, simply because he felt the need for open air to soothe his tired brain. For eight weeks he had prayed for the safe return of the missing papyri; today he hoped to hear that those prayers were being answered.

When the loss was first reported to him, he hadn't been unduly worried, since it was common knowledge that books and manuscripts were often mislaid and later found. After all, the Vatican Library, not to mention the secret archives, contained hundreds of thousands of items and the occasional mistake was inevitable. The library alone, it was said, had over thirty miles of shelving, all heaving under the weight of rare and priceless volumes. But the pontiff was also aware that books were not just being accidentally mislaid but occasionally stolen as well, by unscrupulous readers, which was why one of his predecessors had authorised a new system of tagging all Vatican books, manuscripts and artefacts by having microchips pasted onto each and every one of them—1.6 million items in all. It was a process that would take years to complete but, once in place, the librarians would then be able to keep track, via a radio transmitter, on all misplaced volumes and thus have the means to retrieve the stolen ones.

What had surprised the pope to begin with, though, was the fact that these latest disappearances had been reported to him at all, because it certainly wasn't standard practice to bother the pontiff with such trivialities. But this incident had been deemed serious enough. An ancient map, he was told, attributed to a certain Comte de Razès of the Languedoc in Southern France and dating from the seventh century, and another ancient manuscript from the Nag Hammadi collection, had been found to be missing from the secret archives.

'I believe the theft has to be very recent, Holy Father.'

Despite putting on a brave face at the time, Padre Leonardo Messina's embarrassment and great concern had been plain to see.

'...As your Holiness knows, not many readers have right of access to the archives, and all who do are carefully screened.'

'But not this time?'

'No, it seems not, your Holiness.'

'So, Padre Leonardo, you consider the incident more serious than most? Tell me why you think it necessary to bring the loss of these particular parchments to my notice and why you believe the theft must be recent.'

The curator had then lowered his voice, as if to confine his shame. 'The other day, one of my staff reported that the Schidoni Pentacle had been carelessly left on one of the reading desks, so I naturally checked the map and manuscript archives. My worst fears were realised when I found that the map of the Conte de Razès had gone missing.'

The pontiff, however, had failed to see the connection. 'You say naturally? Why naturally, Padre? What is the significance of the missing document? And what is its connection with this... this Pentacle, as you call it?'

The curator had then gone on to explain that the Schidoni Pentacle was an ornate copper imprint, by a Scottish artist and engraver called Sir Robert Strange, of a pentagram originally drawn by a seventeenth century Italian painter called Bartolomeo Schidoni. The fact that Schidoni's drawing had later been destroyed by fire in a Naples art gallery meant that Strange's engraving was the only surviving copy of it.

'The engraving is on a larger scale than the original, Holy Father, but is true to scale in every other sense, if you understand my meaning. 'According to tradition, the pentacle can reveal where, on the map of the Comte de Razes, the Treasure of Solomon's Temple is hidden.'

'But you say that the pentacle was not stolen, Padre. The loss of the map, such an ancient relic, is of course deplorable but is not in itself so worrying. Is it? Tell me it is not!'

'Most Holy Father, we suspect that whoever took the pentacle onto the reader's desk to study it, may also have taken a brass rubbing of it, and possibly a photograph as well. If that is so, then it is as concerning as if the engraving itself had been stolen.'

'Hm! And the Nag Hammadi document, Padre? What is the significance of its loss?'

The guardian of the secret archives had winced at having to answer this question.

'It pains me to tell you, Your Holiness, that it is documented in our archives as the *I Jesus epistle*. I have seen it but once, many years ago, and I can best describe it as three pieces of papyri that were thought to have been crudely ripped off what would once have been a larger scroll, probably to be sold at exorbitant prices on the Cairo Market. Since no one seems to know what became of the rest of the scroll, then we can but assume that it has been lost for all time. I recall that the writing on them is badly faded and, for the most part, impossible to read. However, I was reliably informed at the time that the words *I Jesus* can still be identified in three different places. But even though the parchment is old, and dates back to the days of our Lord, it can but have been written by a false prophet.'

'Explain why, Padre.'

'Because it is said to contain references, Your Holiness, to things that took place after the Crucifixion.'

The pontiff had blanched at the curator's revelation and the past two months had, for him, been laden with anxiety and sleepless nights.

*

The guardian of the secret archives and the commander of the Swiss Guard, now waiting for him in the Borgia Courtyard, were so engaged in serious conversation that they didn't hear his approach until he was almost upon them. Then, as if they'd both been stung or touched with live electricity, they jumped apart to greet him.

'Your Holiness!'

'Most Holy Father!'

With a sign of the cross, he led them to a shaded corner of the courtyard, where there stood an ornate marble bench, and gestured them both to sit.

Reverently, they stood aside, waiting for him to do so first. Despite his years, the pontiff was surprisingly nimble.

'You have news, I hope?'

It was the commander who answered, 'I only wish that I had more to relate, Your Holiness. It pains me to tell you that we have had reports that the missing parchments have indeed reached the Languedoc but as yet we have not been able to discover who possesses them. Our agents tell of increased activity in the region and I fear that other parties, apart from ourselves, are also seeking the documents. However, I assure you, Most Holy Father, that we are keeping a close watch on the place of *Il Tesoro* and will thwart all attempts to recover it.'

'*Il Tesoro*? You say that we know the location of the treasure?' The pontiff made no effort to hide his surprise.

It was Padre Leonardo, the curator, who now answered, 'It has been the Vatican's closely guarded secret over the years, Your Holiness.'

'Is there a reason why it was guarded from me also, Padre?'

The guardian of the archives became flustered. 'Forgive me, Most Holy Father, but the information wasn't deliberately kept from you. It is just that the need to keep the documents secret has meant that they had become forgotten over the years. There are so many ancient and important manuscripts in our keeping.'

The pope waved a dismissive hand to suggest that he wasn't laying any blame. 'But you say that the location of *Il Tesoro* is known to you?'

'There is no written record within our archives… at least as far as I am aware… of any reference to where the Treasure of Jerusalem actually lies. I only know, Your Holiness, what was passed on to me by my predecessor, many years ago. He maintained that, according to ancient oral tradition, *Il Tesoro* is hidden in or near a hill fort in the French Pyrenees but that the exact location is not known. He also told me that the place is virtually inaccessible and that the Treasure of Solomon's Temple will never be found.'

The pontiff had hoped for more positive news but at least his worst fears hadn't yet materialised. 'In the name of Our Lady, I hope that your story is well founded, Padre. But my greatest concern is for the Nag Hammadi papyrus. If that should fall into the hands of our enemies…' He didn't feel the need to elaborate.

Piazza Venetia, ROME

Less than a mile from where the so-called La Nuova Alba had been meeting, Gus Adams sipped at his coffee outside the Café Vittorio on the Piazza Venetia, well shaded from the midday sun by an expanse of faded maroon awning. Deaf to the incessant drone of traffic and the angry tooting of horns as heedless pedestrians risked life and limb to cross the busy square, he gazed vacantly across at the Vittorio Emanuele Memorial, his mind mulling over the events of the past week.

Only twelve days had passed since he'd last reported for work in Canary Wharf! It seemed an eternity. Twelve long days since he'd been stupidly accused of plotting acts of terrorism and then taken into custody, albeit for just the one night.

The nightmare of it all was slowly ebbing. What still grated though was the fact that the bank had refused to re-employ him and that Scotland Yard, rather than apologise for their mistake, had let him off with a warning that he would be under surveillance for some time to come.

Tom Mackay's offer, a day later, couldn't have come at a more opportune moment. Or at least that's how he had seen it at the time. In retrospect, though, maybe it had been a little too opportune. Could there have been a connection between the sacking and the quick offer of a new job? Mackay was MI6, after all, and the long arm of Vauxhall Cross influence was nobody's secret.

'To hell with it!' he muttered. Mackay's offer had appealed a hell of a lot more than returning to the humdrum world of trading in Canary Wharf.

He placed his cup back on its saucer on the red-and-white-checked tablecloth and absentmindedly fingered the calling card in his other hand. Three days he'd been in Rome. And before that, three days in Mackay's company, being briefed and then discussing what plan of action to take. They'd both agreed on one thing. There was neither time nor need to create a new identity for him. He would arrive in Rome as Gus Adams, evacuee to England from Albania sixteen years ago but now a naturalised Briton, to begin a quest for the families of his real parents now that his adoptive parents had passed away. Paternal relatives here in Rome, maternal ones in the port of Durres, Albania. And if checked, records would confirm that he had already made telephone enquiries to Corleone and Palermo in Sicily to corroborate the fact that he, Guiseppe, and his sister Gina Maratta had both been born in Corleone to a Sicilian father, who had undisputed Cosa Nostra connections, and Agnesa Maratta neé Kadare, ethnic Albanian from Durres. Authorities in Sicily would also, if asked, confirm telling a certain Gus Adams that the Maratta family had moved to Rome soon after he had been born and that if he wished to make further inquiries about them then he should look to the Italian capital.

'We know... that is, I've just found out...' Mackay's self-correction at the time had been Gus' first clue that MI6 had set him up. '...That one of your distant relatives is currently an influential mafia member in Rome, known to be somehow involved with the proliferation of arms production in Albania over the past couple of years. Our surveillance suggests that the business is being run and monitored from Rome and that the group responsible is answerable to someone or other in the Vatican; someone who represents an organisation that has access to unlimited amounts of ready cash. That much we know, but that's also as far as we've been able to go. They're obviously keeping their cards very close to their chests.'

Gus hadn't been unduly surprised when Mackay told him about his mafia connections. Hadn't Scotland Yard made similar revelations when arresting him? And didn't he have his own childhood memories about the sort of company his father kept whilst they lived in Rome and then in Kukes in northern Albania? But he'd scowled incredulously when Mackay had mentioned Vatican involvement.

'You're not suggesting that the pope?'

'Of course not! Look, Gus! For your own safety, you're in this on a purely need-to-know basis, so the less you know the safer you'll be.'

But his frustration had got the better of him. 'For God's sake, I'm not flying blind out there. You'll have to fill me in on the Vatican angle. How does the Holy See stand to gain by this illegal proliferation of arms? What makes you think that it does deals with the CIA and the mafia? Bloody farfetched if you ask me.'

Tom Mackay had smiled wryly before continuing, 'It seems that you know very little, Gus, about the Vatican's wheeling's and dealings over the years. You realise, I take it, that the place is a law unto itself; that it's self-governing and with a massive amount of clout worldwide?'

'Yeah, I realise that – smallest country in the world and all that – but you make it sound corrupt.'

'So, what do you know about it? Do you know, for instance, how and when it became fully autonomous? Do you know why?'

'So tell me.'

'Benito Mussolini's fascist government arranged that. Check it up! It's history. Lateran Treaty 1929 got Mussolini the agreed support of the Catholic church on condition that the pope be given full control of the Vatican State, with Catholicism becoming the official state religion in Italy.'

'So, it supported a fascist government. I've known worse.'

'Yes, I know. Supporting Hitler's Third Reich, for instance.'

'The Holy See never did that.'

'Didn't it?' Mackay had smiled at his naivety. 'Take it from me; the pope at the time was involved in that decision, as well. Choice of lesser of two evils, of course. Hitler's fascist regime offered some sort of future for Catholicism; religionless communism didn't. Have you ever considered what would have happened to Christ's Vicar on Earth and to the Vatican state if the communist block had swallowed them up before 1945? Have you any idea at all of the Holy See's assets, Gus? Priceless art treasures and sculptures, a museum full of invaluable artefacts, secret books and archives long hidden from the world. Make no bones about it! The commies would have stripped the place clean. What hope for the future of Catholicism after that, do you reckon?'

Gus wasn't convinced. 'Hitler would have done the same. That's history too!'

'Yes, he would have, in time, and the pope and his bunch of cardinals knew the score as well as anybody, I imagine. Which is why they humoured the Fuhrer throughout the war, to postpone what was hopefully not inevitable. Believe me, Gus, the Eighth Army landings in southern Italy, when they came, must have seemed like manna from Heaven to Pope Pius XII – Hitler's pope as he came to be known – and to every devout Catholic worldwide.'

Gus sipped some more coffee and reflected on Tom Mackay's words and on his next question to him. 'So, if it's funding arms production, who does the Vatican see as its enemies today? Communism is dead. So is fascism… in Europe at least.'

The MI6 man had smiled sagely. 'Same old enemies, Gus. The ones that have always been there. Israel and Islam. The rival creeds. Enemies for close on two thousand years… Well, Islam for a little less than that of course, seeing that Mohammed wasn't born until sometime in the sixth century.'

Gus took another sip of his coffee and looked at the card that he'd been fingering in his other hand. *Gus Adams* it said. HSBC *trader of stocks. Adamshouse Apartments, Limehouse, London E14.* And written in ink, beneath, the address of his hotel on the Via Cavour, about half a kilometre from where he was now sitting. He'd made a point of telling the receptionist where he would be all afternoon in case someone wanted to contact him. His time in Rome so far – getting on for three and a half days – had been spent visiting places where he would have expected to get information on his family during their brief stay here in the Eternal City, all those years ago. He'd made a big deal of wanting to find his missing relatives and, working on the strategy that if Moses couldn't find Sinai then the mountain would have to come to him, he had made a point of leaving calling cards everywhere he went, similar to the one that he was now fingering. He'd even quizzed the waiter who had just brought him his coffee. But three days had now gone by and his confidence was beginning to grow thin.

The idea for making the mafia connection had come from Gus himself. 'What can be more natural?' he'd argued. 'After all, I am interested in finding my family now that my adoptive parents are dead. Not only that but I also have copies of tabloid headlines to prove that there's gangster blood running in my veins.' He'd smiled wryly at that and although Tom Mackay hadn't been too eager in his response, Gus had persisted because, if truth be told, the MI6 offer had appealed to him from the very start. Which was why he'd argued for a freer hand.

'Listen, Gus! And listen carefully! Your brief is to keep your ear close to the ground. Nothing more than that. We've got hard evidence on the arms production in Albania, Kukes up in the north east in particular. What we need to know is why there's such a huge – and I do mean huge – arsenal being amassed in the region and, more importantly, where it might be destined for. In other words, what new plot is being hatched there? The Balkans have been a hotbed of insurgence over the years; today is no different. You'll be dealing with remorseless people, make no bones about that. Don't underestimate any of them. Killing comes as naturally as eating to them, so keep your head well down, for God's sake! I don't want your blood on my hands, or my son will never forgive me.'

Tom Mackay had sounded genuinely concerned and Gus had taken to the man because of it.

'Yoo are Goos Adams?'

The voice in his ear startled him out of his reverie. The words were English, the accent unmistakably Italian. *Bingo!* he thought. *At last!*

Remaining seated, he looked up as the burly stranger came around the table to face him. He was also aware of an accomplice standing directly behind his chair.

'Yeah! I'm Gus Adams. Who are you?'

'Yoo know what a Magnoom ees, Meester Adams?'

Gus felt his limp hair curl at the roots and his nod was barely perceptible. Tom Mackay had spent hours showing him pictures of various weapons, from hand guns to missiles and rocket launchers. He tried to sound as casual as possible.

'If you mean a Magnum, yeah I do. It's a gun.'

'*Bene*! Beecose there ees a Magnoom pointing at yewer... yewer...' The stranger was momentarily lost for words. '...*Timpano*, and Tommaso has a... how you say? *Dito nervoso.*'

Having his eardrum blown away, together with the rest of his head most likely, just because a certain Tommaso had a nervous finger, wasn't a picture that Gus wanted to dwell on for long, although he suspected that what he was hearing was just an empty threat and that there was probably no weapon in sight. No one, not even a mafioso, would be stupid enough to display a gun in full view of other customers and innocent passers-by.

'*Parlo Italiano*,' he muttered.

'Ah! *Bene*!' The uncompromising Luca, dressed in white shirt and black trousers and wearing heavy rimmed sunglasses, seemed relieved. It meant that he no longer had to struggle with what little English he had. '*Ora camminiamo!*'

Walk where? Gus wondered but after leaving a five euro note to pay for his coffee he did as he was told and, following instructions from behind, he headed for the black Mercedes that was parked on the corner of Via San Marco a short distance away.

Fortnum & Masons, LONDON

'Is it really you, Tom? After all these years?'

'Janet? I don't believe this!'

They hugged, kissed one another on the cheek, smiled with genuine pleasure and shook their heads disbelievingly at such a chance encounter. Only it wasn't a chance encounter at all. Fortnum & Masons as a venue might have been Janet's idea, but the meeting itself had been secretly arranged at the behest of her husband, Sir James Oldcorn, head of MI6 operations.

'Good God! You look well! Do you have time for coffee and a chat?'

The act was convincing though hardly necessary since none of the other customers took the slightest bit of notice of them.

'For God's sake, Tom, tell me you have some news for him. He's been running around the house like a headless chicken for days.' They'd just been served their coffee. 'Not that I see much of him at the best of times.' She spoke in undertones.

'Pressures of work! Yes, I can imagine!'

'No, not that. He's usually up to it. But I tell you, this business that you're involved with has him on tenterhooks, simply because he doesn't have a finger on the pulse. Apart from a couple of useless diplomats, your man is now the only operative that Vauxhall Cross has in Rome.'

Tom Mackay shrugged dismissively. 'Nothing to report so far, I'm afraid. My man, as you refer to him, will send word once he's made any sort of contact out there. So far, I've heard nothing.'

What he didn't add was that Gus Adams had insisted on more involvement than Oldcorn had originally intended. 'How the hell do I go about getting the sort of information you want, Tom? Once I start asking the right sort of questions then I'll be drawing the wrong kind of attention to myself, and if the mafiosi in Rome are half as ruthless as you make them out to be, then I'll just be making myself a sitting target for them, won't I? What's the point of that, when I've got a perfectly legit reason for contacting them in any case?' At that point, Gus had gone up in Tom Mackay's estimation. The lad not only had his fair share of common sense but a lot of guts to go with it.

'As soon as I hear anything from him I'll find a way of letting you know.'

'Discreetly of course.'

'That goes without saying.'

They talked for a while longer, finished their coffee and said their farewells. 'Nice to have seen you again, Janet. Give Jim my regards.'

ROME

The black Mercedes crossed the Ponte Palatino and took a left along the west bank of the Tiber, stopping after a hundred metres or so. Luca, as he climbed out, glanced up at a third-floor window, half-hoping that Maurizio, boss-of-bosses, would be there to witness their arrival. In fact, it would be good if the whole damn Cupola were there to see, but he knew that the meeting would have ended long before now and that the Camorra rats and 'Ndrangheta swine would long since have retreated into their respective sewers.

He signalled to Tommaso and then watched as Gus Adams emerged from the back seat, being prodded by the tongue-tied Tommaso. Then, at a further signal from him, the Mercedes slid away.

'*Presto!*' he barked and the three made their way towards the door directly beneath the window that he had just been looking at.

Gus was surprised at how calm and rational he felt, considering the risk that he was running. During the brief journey from the Via San Marco, Luca – a mafia mobster if ever there was one – had mentioned the name Maurizio. Now if he and the Maurizio Bonnano, *Capo* of the mob in Rome, whom Gus had heard mentioned by his Scotland Yard interrogators a week ago, were one and the same – and he hoped to God that they were – then there had to be some family ties between himself and the mobster. That, surely, should guarantee his safety, at least in the short-term.

Two frowning guards stood inside the door of the building, the taller of them having a badly pockmarked face. Like Luca and Tommaso, they too wore white shirts and belted black trousers and the scene brought back more childhood memories for Gus. *Standard mafia uniform,* he thought. Many of his father's friends used to look like this.

The spacious lobby, with its marble floor and walls, was nice and cool but the same couldn't be said for the lift that took them up to the third floor. Here, they barely had room to stand and Gus was sickened by the strong smell of garlic on Luca's breath. Tommaso's fidgetiness didn't help either, especially since he now did have a gun in his hand, having brought it out of a bag that he'd been carrying over his shoulder.

When they exited the lift on the third floor, two other mafiosi stepped forward to intercept what could be a possible threat, but Luca and Tommaso were known to them, and they relaxed.

Maurizio Bonnano, *capo dei capi*, faced them as they entered the room. He was alone, sitting at the far end of a highly polished mahogany table. Behind his chair, a large picture window looked out over the Tiber. In front of him lay a tray of dirty dishes, the remains on which suggested that he'd partaken of green pasta salad. The pile of black seeds and a crescent of dark green was proof that he'd had water melon to follow. Above him, the air conditioning fan rotated lazily. Maurizio Bonnano, boss-of-bosses, looked as if he was ready for his siesta.

As Gus was ushered into the room, the mafioso did little more than move tired eyelids and waited for Luca to speak. He was clearly unimpressed by the skinny-legged stranger who now stood before him, dressed in a creased blue shirt and knee-length khaki shorts.

'This is the man I was telling you about, Maurizio. He is the one who has been asking questions about our cousin.'

With a sharp turn of head, Gus glanced at Luca. Cousin? Was it possible that this dolt was also a distant relative?

Maurizio answered the question for him. 'Giovanni Maratta was my cousin, Luca, not yours. Do not forget that you are only part Cosa Nostra.'

Luca's shoulders drooped somewhat. He had again been put down in front of Tommaso. His pride had again been hurt. But Maurizio was in no mood to notice. Throughout, he hadn't taken his heavy eyes off Gus.

'You are the one who has been asking questions about Giovanni Maratta?'

'Yeah.'

'Why? Who are you?'

Gus had thought long and hard about this moment, about what attitude to take, on coming face-to-face with the mafia. Should he show fear and plead for the Capo's help in his search or would it be more fitting to show a bit of defiance? Any show of weakness, he'd decided, would only meet with disdain from a hardened criminal like Maurizio.

'It depends on who's asking.'

That stirred the Capo to open his eyes a little more and to grasp the wooden arms of his chair.

'You answer my questions, you skinny dog, unless you want your feet in cement at the bottom of the Tiber!'

Gus felt the additional threat of Luca and Tommaso behind him.

'I will only answer the questions of Maurizio Bonnano, man of honour and boss-of-bosses here in Roma. This fool...' He gestured back towards Luca, 'calls you Maurizio but there is more than one Maurizio in Roma. Only one Maurizio Bonnano though, and he is Cosa Nostra, like me.' His last words suggested a show of great pride.

If the Capo wasn't fully awake before, he was now. He snarled. 'You lie! You are secret police and Luca here will whip the truth from your lying tongue.'

Gus heard another snarl from behind, to endorse the threat, but he was reading things clearer now and feeling more relaxed because of it.

'I am no fool, Maurizio. Do you think I would have let these two buffoons bring me here like a little lamb to the slaughter if I wasn't who I say I am?'

At that, he felt Tommaso's gun again prodding his back and Luca growling, '*Idiota*! You came because you had no choice.'

The decision was spur of the moment. In one movement, Gus fell on his haunches, swivelled on one heel and with the other extended leg took Luca and Tommaso's feet from under them, at the same time wrenching the heavy Magnum out of the latter's hand. In another instant he was back on his feet and stepping clear of the two writhing bodies.

Maurizio's jaw fell, surprised by the lightning speed of the attack and frightened by what the outcome might now be. His first thought was to call in the guards but the sight of the Magnum in the young man's hand tied his tongue.

Gus glared into Luca's lustreless eyes as the embarrassed mafioso struggled to his feet.

'Who says that I had no choice?'

He then turned to Maurizio and slid the gun along the full length of the table's polished surface until it came to rest against the edge of the tray that had held the Capo's lunch.

'If you are Maurizio Bonnano, man of honour and boss-of-bosses here in Roma, then it is you whom I will speak to, because you are family, you are Cosa Nostra, like me.' Rather than give the big man another chance to challenge him, Gus continued: 'My name is Gus Adams…' He pulled a calling card out of his shirt pocket and took it over to Maurizio, who, in turn accepted it in his large fleshy hand and cast a cursory glance at it. '…But my real name is Guiseppe Maratta, son of Giovanni and Agnesa Maratta who were killed in Kosovo sixteen years back.'

The cogs of Maurizio's brain were seen to turn slowly. 'Giovanni had three children.'

Gus knew he was being tested. 'You are wrong, Maurizio. There was only myself and Gina who is two years younger than me.'

'Ah! But there is nothing of Giovanni about you.' The words were spoken without any real conviction.

'Then you did not know my father. When I was a boy, everybody said that I was the spitting image of him.'

He reached for his wallet out of the back pocket of his shorts, withdrew from it a folded newspaper cutting and passed it on. Without any apparent haste, Maurizio unfolded it and smoothed it out on the table in front of him, then took his time in studying the old black and white photograph of two orphans in Kosovo. There was no mistaking the resemblance between the distressed boy in the picture and the young man who now stood before him. Maurizio, however, wasn't easily convinced. Eventually, he raised his puffed eyes and for the first time Gus detected the depth in them. That one glimpse told him that Maurizio Bonnano, despite his languid appearance, was not one to be taken lightly.

'Giovanni was born in Sicilia. He was killed in Kosovo. Why do you look here in Roma?'

'Because I no longer have family in Sicilia. I have checked. I came to Roma because this is where we lived before going to Kosovo and because I have heard that you were my father's cousin.' With a dismissive shrug of his shoulders, he turned, 'But if you do not wish to help me, so be it. I shall go to Durres.'

As he turned to leave, Maurizio raised a hand to stop him. 'Durres? Why Durres? Durres is in Albania.'

'Because that is where my mother was born. Perhaps if I find relatives in Durres then they will be more willing than you to help me.'

'Help you? Help you do what?'

'To find out who killed my parents. That is all the help I will need.'

'Then what?'

'I will not need help to avenge their deaths.'

Maurizio's heavy lips tightened into a cold smile. 'Luca!' he called. 'Bring us some wine, then you and Tommaso leave us. I wish to talk more with the son of my cousin Giovanni.'

ROME (two days later)

Gus spent the next two days sightseeing, knowing that Maurizio had ordered a check on his story. He also sensed that he was being watched wherever he went; not that that particularly worried him, as long as the tail, whoever it was, presented no immediate threat. It was no surprise either to find that his room had been searched. He wouldn't have noticed only that his passports – his British one in the name of Gus Adams and the forged Italian one in the name of Guiseppe Maratta – hadn't been put back in exactly the same position as he'd left them, in his case. The hotel proprietor had obviously been either threatened or bribed to unlock the room.

One of the first things that Gus had done on his arrival in Rome had been to phone his sister Gina, back in Peterborough, to let her know that he'd arrived safely. Prior to leaving London, he had contacted her to tell her of his intention to trace their parents' families and she had shown a lot of enthusiasm for that. He had also, at Tom Mackay's request, spent some time on the internet, getting information on subjects ranging from the Cosa Nostra, and the mafia in general, to wartime Italy and Vatican involvement. He'd then printed off some stuff on Albania and Kosovo and had been surprised at how little he knew about those countries, considering he'd actually spent time there as a boy. The website that fascinated him the most, though, was the one that dealt with the powerful fringe organisations that allegedly had footholds within the Vatican. One of them was, or had been until recently, a rogue masonic lodge called Propaganda Due, better known as P2, established in the late 1960s by a master mason called Licio Gelli and, if the website's author was to be believed, with the backing of the Italian Premier Guilio Andreotti. Also involved with P2 were the CIA and another organisation known as Opus Dei, not to mention the Gambino Mafia in America and some shady characters like ex-president Nixon and right wing South American dictators.

Gus had read it all with a great deal of cynicism. Conspiracies, especially CIA conspiracies, were being seen everywhere these days!

P2 had been formed specifically to combat the spread of communism in Italy. Similar lodges – P1 and P3 – had been established in other countries, with the same objective. The article made a lot out of the murder of someone called Roberto Calvi, a Vatican banker whose body had been found hanging under Blackfriars Bridge in London in 1982. It claimed that P2 had had him eliminated. In addition to its own bank, the Vatican also had part ownership of a Swiss bank, and Calvi, often referred to as *God's Banker*, had allegedly been involved, in one way or another, in money laundering and other financial misdemeanours. Other powerful organisations mentioned were:

(a) Opus Dei—a politically and economically powerful Roman Catholic right-wing organisation with some 70,000 members worldwide, described by a former member as sinister, secretive and Orwellian. In other words, the Vatican's MI5 and MI6 rolled into one!

(b) The Knights of Malta, another Vatican intelligence agency fighting communism and promoting Catholicism, and

(c) a shadowy group calling itself the Order of the Solar Temple.

Opus Dei apparently saw itself as a reincarnation of the ancient order of the Knights Templar and was suspected by some of having "arranged" the death of Pope John Paul I in 1978, simply because the pontiff had ordered an audit of Vatican finances. Gus had had to smile again at that.

'Conspiracies, conspiracies!'

Whoever had been rummaging through his things would have seen the printouts and studied their contents. No sweat! He could justify having them. They would also have seen the adoption papers and Somerset House confirmation that Guiseppe and Gina Maratta would henceforth be known as Gus and Jeanne Adams.

La Nuova Alba (The New Dawn) ROME

On the third morning, the faithful Luca called for him whilst he was still at breakfast. 'You are to come now. Maurizio Bonnano demands it.'

Gus' response was something between a grin and a scowl. 'I will come when I have finished eating.'

The conversation was again in Luca's preferred language. 'Maurizio says now.'

Rather than provoking him by being too obstinate, Gus decided to pour some oil on the troubled water between them. After all, it was better to have the mafioso as an ally rather than enemy. And he might even turn out to be a useful source of information.

'Sit for coffee, Luca. I wish to apologise for what occurred the other day.' He offered his hand, but without getting up. 'I felt threatened and because of that I was less than civil towards you and Tommaso.'

The Italian looked unsure. Once again he'd been caught unawares and because of that he was reluctant to offer his hand in return.

'Come now! Did I not hear you say to my cousin Maurizio that we, too… you and I… are family? Come, cousin! Let us start again, as friends this time.'

Slowly, Luca brought his hand forward to have it shaken and, interpreting the firmness of Gus' grip as a mark of his sincerity, he ventured the ghost of a smile and took a chair opposite his erstwhile adversary. He was even heard to mumble *'Grazie'* when Gus called for a coffee for him.

'I take it we're going to the same place as yesterday?'

A reluctant nod was his only answer and it was enough to remind Gus not to appear too inquisitive too soon. He needed to tread carefully.

'Our cousin is an important man, Luca. How long has he been boss-of-bosses here in Roma?'

The Italian shrugged as he sipped his coffee. 'Two years… A little more perhaps.'

'Pardon my ignorance in these things, but what does the boss-of-bosses do? Is he perhaps like the captain of a team?'

He particularly wanted to appear naïve in such matters.

Luca thought a while about the word captain before accepting it. '*Si*! He is captain of La Nuova Alba.'

'Ah! That sounds good. And The New Dawn is important? Is it a business… a company… here in Roma?'

Luca sneered at that. He was beginning to think that his newfound cousin wasn't such a threat after all. '*La Nuova Alba* is another name for the Cupola and Maurizio is its boss-of-bosses.'

Gus finished his coffee. 'Ah! I understand. You and Tommaso, and the guards I saw yesterday, are the Cupola and Maurizio is your boss-of-bosses.'

Sensing that Luca was about to give up on him, he quickly continued, 'So if Maurizio is captain, then you, Luca, must be vice-captain? His… how do I put it? his second-in-command… his *consigliere*.'

'Come! We go!'

*

'I have had you brought here because we must talk.'

Maurizio had waited for the door to close behind Luca. Again today he sat with his back to the window but now the morning sun was in Gus' eyes and the big Italian was nothing more than a faceless silhouette to him.

'You say you wish to avenge Giovanni's death?'

'Also, my mother's.'

'*Si*. But how will you do that?'

'I am hoping that you, my father's cousin, man of honour and boss-of-bosses here in Roma, will help me.'

'What help do you wish from me?'

Although the face was silhouetted, Gus could well imagine the calculating look in Maurizio's eyes.

'I wish you to help me find their murderers.'

'And then?'

'Then I will exact my revenge.'

'How?'

'It matters not how, Maurizio. What is important is that I reclaim the honour of my parents. Will you help me?'

The big man remained silent for some seconds. Then, 'You will find work here in Italia? Or perhaps Albania?'

'Work? But I have work back in England.'

'Ah! But you lie!'

Without warning, a pile of English newspapers was pushed across the table. Gus recognised himself on the front page of each of them. Maurizio obviously had every intention of being thorough.

'Ah! That was a stupid mistake by Scotland Yard. I am not a terrorist.'

'But is it not true that you no longer have a job?'

Gus allowed his shoulders to sag a bit, as if he'd been caught out. 'You don't miss much, do you cousin?'

'I miss nothing, which is why I want you to explain this.'

Maurizio now pushed another sheaf of papers over the table and Gus recognised them as photocopies of his notes off the internet. He pretended to be lost for words.

'…Why do you carry information on Il Vaticano?' The voice had a distinct edge to it now.

'Because I remember.'

'Explain.'

'My father had dealings with someone from the Holy See. I know because I heard him talk to my mother about it.'

'Dealings? What dealings?'

'Guns.'

'Explain.'

'My father was a businessman, Maurizio. He bought and sold guns. You, of all people, should know that.'

The silhouette remained unmoved. 'From where did he buy them? Who did he sell them to?'

Gus knew that his answers were being carefully scrutinized. 'I have no way of knowing that. I was only a young boy. I only know that someone from *Il Vaticano* was involved.'

'His name?'

'I'm not sure that I ever heard it, but I was hoping that this information…' He indicated the photocopied notes. '…might jog my memory. That it would help me in some way.'

'And did it?'

'No. There is no name there that I recognise.'

Maurizio slowly got to his feet and moved out of the glare so that Gus could now see his face. 'When you leave Italy, what will you do?'

'Back to Britain you mean?' He shrugged. 'I'll find something, don't worry.'

'Worry? Why should I worry, cousin?' There followed a pregnant pause and then, 'How would you like to work for the Cupola? For me, Maurizio Bonnano?'

Bingo! But Gus assumed a look of surprise, nevertheless.

'Depends what sort of work? Don't expect me to have anything to do with banks.'

Maurizio smiled without humour, to show that he understood the inference. 'You would carry on your father's work in Albania.'

'My father's work ended sixteen years ago, cousin. I will only go to Albania to avenge his death, and the death of my mother.'

'So be it! You are most likely to find their killers in Kukes, up in northeast Albania. That is where your father was operating.'

'Then that is where I shall go.' He made to get up.

'And that is where I would want you to work for me.'

Gus slowly sat down again, eyeing Maurizio, boss-of-bosses, with a show of suspicion. 'You are having me on.'

'You agree to work for me and for the Cupola in Kukes and I shall point you in the direction of your father's killer.'

'You would not deceive me, Maurizio?'

'Deceive you!' The rasp was back in the big man's voice. 'I am a man of honour, cousin, as you will be. Cosa Nostra are all men of honour. Remember that!'

'I ask your pardon, cousin. I did not mean to suggest otherwise. I value what you have told me. Does it mean, then, that I was wrong when I said that someone from Il Vaticano was also involved in my parents' death?' He prodded at the sheaf of notes in front of him.

'Perhaps. I will make enquiries.'

*

He had very little to say to Luca on the way back. There were too many important things on his mind to give way to idle conversation. Yes, he had reason to feel pleased with how things were developing but he had to guard against being complacent. It would be rash, for instance, to try any sort of contact with Tom Mackay in London. MI6 would have to wait.

Arch of Titus, Roman Forum

'Everybody out!'

A number of the American tourists groaned out loud, hoping that their young courier would reconsider and allow them to stay in their air-conditioned coach. For the past two and a half hours they'd been shuttled like cattle from one end of Rome to the other, visiting historic site after historic site. They'd walked, they'd listened, they'd questioned and they'd taken no end of photographs. By now, however, the relentless heat and the surfeit of culture were taking their toll. Most of them were dead on their feet.

A complaining voice was heard to say, 'We only just got back on.' Which was true. No more than five minutes had passed since they'd exited the Coliseum to board the coach, which had then merely circled the Arch of Constantine and crossed the busy Via di San Gregorio before coming to a halt again. Now they were all expected to disembark once more. 'We could have walked that.'

'Not through all that traffic,' someone else reasoned.

'Chop, chop! Out you come! Last call. Then it's back to the hotel.'

'Thank God!' they muttered, almost in unison.

The pretty young courier smiled with some degree of sympathy. Not only were they all the wrong side of pensionable age but many of them were also seriously overweight. But they'd paid for this guided tour weeks in advance, as part of their package holiday, and however tired they felt now, she knew that the complaints and demands for reimbursement would surely come later amid claims that the excursion had been incomplete. She also knew from experience that the more bone-weary they all were, then the greater would be their relief at getting back to their hotel. Ergo, the more generous their gratuities!

'Gather round folks!' The tail end was just getting off the bus. 'Here we are, at our last stop. Last but not by any means the least important. Directly in front of us on the Via Sacra is the Arch of Titus and beyond that the famous Roman Forum. As a matter of interest, the Arch of Titus was Napoleon's inspiration for building the Arc de Triomphe in Paris.'

Sensing the lack of real interest, she decided to offer her tired flock a compromise. 'Given that the sun is so unbearably hot and your throats, no doubt, well and truly parched...' To which there were murmurs of assent. '...And since your itinerary notes contain all the relevant information about the Forum anyway, then, rather than listening to me blabbing away for another hour, would you rather wander around on your own for thirty minutes or so, just to get a feel of the place, and then return to your hotel a little earlier than scheduled to catch up on your notes over a nice cold drink?'

More murmurs of assent. 'Best suggestion yet, young lady! I'll be waiting for you all on the bus.' The burly Texan waved his cane in the air, pulled at the peak of his baseball cap and began waddling back towards the coach, his substantial rear end rocking heavily from side to side.

Sally Jeffers smiled sympathetically as she watched him go. Then she turned towards the others as they began wandering listlessly in the direction of the ruins.

'The arch directly ahead of you on the Via Sacra,' she called, knowing that she was repeating herself. 'is the Arch of Titus. Make a point of studying the engravings on it. Your notes will explain their significance.'

She paused, glad of the few minutes' breather herself. She'd been prattling away for over two hours, and that for the second time today. Same itinerary as this morning's tour – same content as well – but a different *lingua franca*. Her morning's work had been in French, accompanying a group of students from Narbonne University. In one respect, those two and a half hours had been more demanding, simply because the questions had been far shrewder, more testing. A disappointing tour in terms of tips, but intellectually far more rewarding.

She now found a block of stone to lean against.

'Excoose please!'

The harsh bass voice startled her.

'You tour guide?'

She looked up. A man in his mid-twenties, casually dressed in a faded denim shirt and jeans, stood there expectantly. He had thick black hair and a three-day stubble on his chin. His eyes were hidden behind dark sunglasses. She struggled to place his accent. It certainly wasn't English. Greek? Turkish? Middle East, she finally decided. Arab most likely. Quite good-looking and even vaguely familiar.

'Yes, I'm a guide but I'm afraid that I'm otherwise engaged.' She indicated towards her group, none of whom had wandered very far.

'I wish for help, please. I pay.' He drew some notes out of a wad of euros that he held in his clenched hand.

Sally Jeffers was suitably impressed. 'I only have a few minutes, mind you.'

With a slight bow the stranger expressed his gratitude. 'I wish you to explain pictures on… How you say? Arch of Titus?' He was holding out a fifty euro note.

She promptly got to her feet. 'That's too much.'

It was a weak protest though, so when the man made no show of offering her less, she took the money without further reluctance or hesitation. *Beggars shouldn't quibble,* she thought. *There's rent waiting to be paid!*

'Shall we go over and look at it?'

When they got there, a few of her group were already studying the engravings on the underside of the Arch and consulting their notes. Sally heard one of them reading.

'Erected in AD81 by the Roman Senate as a mark of honour for their general Titus and his legions.'

'Gee! He sure must have been some general!' The American was clearly impressed. 'We never gave Ike anything like this, did we? And look what he did to the Jerries!'

She smiled, not without some pity. 'But you did make him president, if my memory serves me right?'

At which the man's face lit up. 'Yeah! I guess we did make it up to the old guy, didn't we? But this…' He was still pointing up at the arch, 'Is something else though, ain't it?' At which, he began wandering away from the group.

A quiet cough from the Arab reminded her of his presence.

'I'm sorry! You wanted to know about the carvings. Well, the truth is that back in those early days the Roman Senate had every reason to be grateful to Titus. Not only had he and his men claimed Jerusalem for Rome but they also brought back with them the treasure from Solomon's Temple.' She pointed upwards. 'There you see a depiction of it being carried by them, probably along this very road, the Via Sacra.'

Since no one appeared to be taking the bait, she continued: 'The Temple of Solomon in Jerusalem was a fabulous place and Titus and his men carried tons and tons of gold and silver from there. There is speculation that they might even have pinched the Holiest of Holies, the Ark of the Covenant itself, but that's not likely.'

'Gee! That's quite a legend.'

'More than legend, actually. We have an eyewitness account. Maybe you've heard of Josephus, the Jewish historian?' Her question was met with blank looks. 'Well, Josephus was actually with the Roman army when they sacked Jerusalem and in his writings he lists a lot of the stuff that they carried away with them. No mention of the Ark though.'

After studying the engravings for a few seconds, the Americans began to drift off in the direction of the Forum ruins. Sally Jeffers, tourist guide, turned expectantly towards the olive-skinned stranger, as if to ask, "What else do you want to know"?

'You say story is true?'

'Looks like it. As far as I know, nobody disputes Josephus' account.'

'And treasure? What happen to treasure?'

Sally laughed. 'Wish I knew! I could do with some of it myself.'

'No Ark of Covenant?'

'Stolen by Titus you mean? No, I shouldn't think so. I'm sure that Josephus would have mentioned it. He mentions a lot of other things. A heavy gold table encrusted with precious stones, for instance. Dozens of gold lanterns, urns of gold, diamonds by the score...'

'And that?'

Sally followed the direction of his pointing finger. 'Ah! You mean the Menorah? The seven-branched candelabrum. Yes, Josephus does refer to that. Huge thing, apparently, and made of solid gold. Probably adorned the altar in the Temple.'

'You say it was in treasure?'

'Part of the treasure brought to Rome, you mean? Yes, I believe it was. Almost as important as the Ark of the Covenant to the Israelis, some say.'

'Explain, please.'

She looked at him for a second or two. 'You're Arab, right? Moslem?' She took his silence for an affirmative. 'You will know, then, that your Al Aksa Mosque in Jerusalem stands on the site of Solomon's Temple. It is holy ground for you, but it is holy ground for the Israelis as well and they would dearly love to claim it back.'

She thought she heard a muted grunt from him, as if choking on his anger.

'Anyway, that's where the Ark of the Covenant was being kept, until it went missing. But that was well before Titus' time, of course. Imagine what it would mean to the Jewish people to get it back!'

'Not possible.' With a hint of a sneer, the Arab again indicated the scene engraved on the arch. 'Not on there.'

'You're right. It's not on there.' She couldn't imagine what the man expected from her. 'Probably lost for all time, I'd say.'

'But...' His hands, fingers apart, curved outwards and upwards to form the shape of the candelabrum depicted on the stone. '...That is there.'

'You mean the Menorah? Yeah, that's there. As I said, according to Josephus it was part of the treasure that Titus brought back with him.'

'Where now?'

There was such an intensity about the man that Sally Jeffers felt a sudden apprehension but she just as quickly laughed it off. 'You've already asked me that, but there's no way of knowing, I'm afraid. All that history tells us is that later the Visigoths helped themselves to the treasure, after they sacked Rome... sometime in the fifth century if my memory serves me right.'

'Visigoths? They take it where?'

Good God! she thought. *This guy's really serious!* 'Who knows! They went west from here. Spain most likely.'

'France?'

She looked at him askance. 'France? Not to my knowledge, but they could have, I suppose. I'm no historian, remember, just a poor tourist guide trying to scrape a living. Which reminds me! I've got a busload of tired Americans waiting to be taken back to their hotel. So, unless you have something else to ask me, then I'll have to be off.'

'What you know about Schidoni Pentaclé?'

Sally's forehead became creased with astonishment. 'I've no idea what that is, I'm sorry. I suspect that pentacle is another word for pentagram, in which case it's a five-pointed star, similar I suppose to the Star of David, only that's got six points to it...'

The comparison brought another scowl to the stranger's face but she barely noticed.

'...What the Schidoni bit can be, I have no idea. Now, I'm afraid I must go.'

Without a word of thanks, he walked away, leaving her wondering whether he felt he'd had his money's worth or not. Then suddenly, from his gait, she realised where she'd seen him before. As recently as yesterday, in fact. Dressed differently then, which explained her belated recognition of him, he'd spent some time standing on the fringe of another of her tourist groups, listening to her expounding about something or other. Had it been in St Peter's Square? Yes, she was sure of it.

Suddenly, an unease gripped her. What if there had been other times but that she hadn't noticed? What if he was stalking her?

Despite the hot sun beating down on her, Sally Jeffers felt her skin crawl.

ROME—The Cupola Decides

He hadn't expected things to move so quickly. Within two days of his agreeing to work for the mob in Albania, Gus was now on a flight to Tirana. From there he was booked on an internal flight to Kukes, in the north east of the country, where there would be someone waiting for him. Courtesy of Maurizio, he now carried a third passport, in his mother's maiden name of Kadare.

'It is best that no one in Kukes knows that you are Giovanni's son,' had been the Capo's advice. 'In the meantime, I shall ask my contact in Kukes to make enquiries about how my cousin Giovanni was killed.'

Even though the initial offer of a job had come from Maurizio himself, the Capo had still insisted that Gus be cross-examined by the Cupola before a final decision could be made. 'The others must also give their blessing, cousin. You will answer all their questions truthfully.'

The Cupola, otherwise known as The New Dawn had met the following day to decide Gus' fate, and he had immediately sensed the rift between them; between Salvatore Provenzano and his henchmen on the one hand and Maurizio and the Cosa Nostra on the other. Salvatore and his Camorra mafiosi from Naples could not be trusted, he realised. Nor the 'Ndrangheta members of the council, for that matter. His so-called cousin had good reason to watch his back.

'You have religion?'

He had already answered several questions put to him by Salvatore and he now recalled that Maurizio had asked him the same question earlier.

'Religion?'

'You are Catholic?'

'I am a lapsed Catholic. Why do you ask?'

But the second-in-command had ignored the response. 'You are not Moslem.' More of a statement than a question this time.

'Moslem? Of course not.'

'You have friends in England?'

'A few. Why?' The questioning had taken a bizarre turn.

'Jewish friends?'

He carefully considered his reply. 'Not as far as I know.'

'What is your opinion of Jews and Moslems?'

'Opinion? I have no opinion. But the killing is stupid. Moslems kill Jews, Jews kill Moslems. It proves nothing. Solves nothing.'

Salvatore and the others had looked long and hard at him then. 'You have a problem with killing?'

'Yeah. I'll do your work for you in Albania but don't expect me to do any senseless killing.' He'd wanted to make that clear from the start. 'I will only kill to avenge my parents, but to do that I must go to Kosovo.'

In retrospect, the conviction with which he'd said those words surprised him now. The thought of seeking revenge hadn't seriously crossed his mind before that; had never been a considered option. Now, though, twenty-two thousand feet above the Adriatic, the possibility seemed to be taking root.

At that point, Salvatore Provenzano had ordered him out of the room and the discussion without him had gone on for another fifteen minutes or so. Meanwhile, in the corridor outside, with two mafiosi gunmen for company, Gus had listened to raised voices and sounds of disagreement until finally he'd been recalled to be told that the Cupola had given its *benedizione*, its blessing, and that Guiseppe Maratta was now a recognised mafioso, just like his father before him. He'd learnt later from Maurizio that the strongest argument in favour of giving him the job had been his fluency in Tosk, Albania's official tongue.

'When you arrive, you will be briefed on what is expected of you. Do not disappoint me, cousin.'

Gus Adams now closed his eyes, hoping for an hour's sleep before landing in Tirana, the Albanian capital.

*

For the past two days, Sally Jeffers had been on her guard. Wherever and whenever she stopped with a group of her tourists, her first reaction was to search the fringes of her group for signs of the intense-looking Arab. To her relief, he hadn't reappeared and she was now beginning to put her fears behind her.

ALBANIA

Sleep wouldn't come so he reached into his hand luggage for the internet notes on Albania. He'd scanned them more than once since leaving London, but now he needed to refresh his memory, particularly on relevant points of interest. He knew that the country would have changed a lot since his time here as a boy. After forty-six years of xenophobic communist rule, the regime had relaxed its hold in the early 1990s, giving way to a multiparty democracy. This, he now read, had led to disruptive politics and widespread gangsterism. His father, Giovanni Maratta, would no doubt have been part of all that and had ultimately lost his life because of it.

Gus read on. No longer a communist state, Albania had opened its borders to more trade, especially with Italy. Three quarters of overseas trading was with its Adriatic neighbour. He looked at the list of Albania's industries—food processing, textiles and clothing, lumber, oil, cement, chemicals, mining, basic metals, hydropower. Nothing significant there, he thought, unless the "chemicals" also included "chemical weapons". Imports listed were machinery and equipment, foodstuffs, textiles and chemicals. What kind of equipment, he wondered. Chemicals for the production of what? Exports were textiles and footwear, asphalt, metals and metallic ores, crude oil, vegetables, fruits, tobacco.

'From what I know that list should also include military hardware!'

Lek was still the national currency, which meant that his euros wouldn't be of much use to him. But the mob would take care of that, once he was on the ground.

A paragraph on religion took his eye simply because it brought back memories of Maurizio's and Salvatore's line of questioning. May 1990, he read, had seen a lifting of restrictions, not only on freedom of worship but also on the right to travel abroad. Both decisions had brought repercussions. Before the end of that year, five thousand refugees had crossed into Greece, with thousands more taking the same route soon afterwards. And in May alone of the following year, eighteen thousand Albanians had crossed the Adriatic to seek asylum in Italy.

'Most likely fleeing the war and the ethnic cleansing,' he muttered. December 1992 had seen the country becoming part of an organisation known as the Islamic Conference. That snippet surprised Gus. Although he'd spent time there as a child, he'd never thought of Albania as being Islamic. He soon found corroboration of the fact now, though. According to the statistics in front of him, 70% of the population was Muslim, 20% Albanian Orthodox, with only 10% Roman Catholic. Hm! So why had the Cupola warned him against fraternising with Jews and Muslims? Were they afraid that he'd collaborate with them in one way or another? If so, collaborate on what? One thing was for sure, he'd have to watch his step when he got there. It didn't need any guessing to know that the new kid on the block would be put under the microscope from day one. He had asked Maurizio what would be expected of him in Albania. The answer had been brief and unequivocal.

'You will do as you are told when you get there.'

Far below him he could see two ships ploughing the Adriatic in opposite directions, their wakes like white furrows on an azure field. In the distance, the coast of Albania was doing its best to hide in a smoky haze. *What else lay hidden there,* he wondered.

LONDON

'Bring another one, please.'

Tom Mackay was sitting at a window table in Garfunkels, looking up towards Leicester Square where people were scattering for cover as a sudden shower broke through the swirling mist. A cup of cappuccino had just been placed in front of him.

'…I have a friend about to join me,' he explained, in answer to the waiter's enquiring look.

He had just spotted Lady Janet Oldcorn coming from the direction of the Charing Cross Road, dressed in a calf-length black raincoat and with her umbrella held low over her head. Even scurrying through rain and splashing through puddles, she still managed to retain her elegance.

She smiled at him as she entered the café and he watched her take off her damp coat and hang it on a peg by the door. Underneath, she had on tight-fitting black sweater and black slacks.

'Hi!' He struggled to his feet and pulled a chair out for her. 'I've ordered a cappuccino. Is that okay for you?'

'That'll be lovely, thank you Tom.' The quality of her smile again surprised him, as did the kiss on both cheeks that she gave him before sitting down. 'My husband's idea,' she whispered, sensing his bewilderment, as her hand now reached for his, across the table. 'Thinks we should appear to be more than friends; in case anyone's followed me.' She laughed lightly. 'Prefers us being seen as having an affair than discussing matters of national security. You know how paranoid he can be.' Again, she smiled at him. 'So put your hand on mine and pretend that you fancy me.'

There was mischief in her eyes and Tom Mackay flushed with embarrassment, but he did as he was told. Her skin was cold and wet.

'I've never known him so worried, Tom. He thinks he's failing the service, that he's no longer up to the work.' Her smile had now given way to a look of some concern. 'Pressure from Whitehall, not to mention Downing Street. Rumour has it that Tony Blair is less than happy with what

Vauxhall Cross is up to. James is half-expecting to be called to Number Ten to be questioned at the next COBRA meeting. So, I hope you have some good news for him?'

The arrival of the coffee brought back her forced smile but it also gave her reason to pull her hand away.

Tom Mackay waited for the waiter to retreat. 'Afraid not, Janet. I haven't heard a word from my man. I don't even know where he is... but I'm still hopeful.'

'James feared as much. Look, Tom! He doesn't like to ask this of you but do you think you could fly out there yourself, to try and contact your man? Yesterday, James was called to Downing Street to discuss the situation and the meeting turned out to be a bit of an embarrassment for him. Apparently, he didn't have enough answers for them about what's really going on in Albania.'

Tom Mackay said nothing. He had a fair idea of the pressure that Jimmy Oldcorn would now be under. His job as chief of the secret intelligence service at Vauxhall Cross would be at risk.

'Well, Tom?' She again reached for his hand across the table and held it with genuine feeling this time. 'Will you do it?'

'No problem,' he muttered at last. 'Anything for Jimmy!'

'Thanks, Tom.' She sounded truly grateful. 'And now that you've agreed to fly out there, there's one other thing that he wants to ask of you. It seems that there's a lot of other activity in the Vatican of late.'

'Yes! Jimmy did mention it when we first met. So, what's the problem?'

'Apparently it's to do with some missing documents. That's about all that he knows, except that the Israelis and the Arabs are also interested.'

'Interested or involved?'

'From what I gather, the one seems to be leading to the other. These documents could or could not have something to do with this business in Albania. James is keeping an open mind for the time being. He particularly wants you to keep your ears open for any reference to something called the Schidoni Pentacle.'

'Schidoni Pentacle?'

'Yes. According to surveillance, it's a name that has cropped up quite often of late, together with references to a missing map.'

The Scot nodded sagely. He knew that MI6 would have taps on certain lines out of the Vatican, so choice bits of information were bound to be picked up from time to time.

'Apparently the map relates to some part of the Languedoc in the south of France.'

Mackay now recalled that Jimmy Oldcorn had told him about an MI6 agent being killed in that part of the world recently. 'And Jimmy reckons that this Schidoni Pentacle is, in some way, responsible for ruffling the Papal feathers?'

She nodded.

Ten minutes later, having seen her off home in a taxi, Tom Mackay trudged through the rain towards Tottenham Court Road station, from where the Central Line would take him back to Ealing Broadway. He was already regretting his further involvement but it was too late now. He'd given his word.

NORTHEAST ALBANIA—Kukes, near the Kosovan border

As the helicopter approached Kukes, Gus Adams alias Guiseppe Maratta alias Guiseppe Kadare, leaned forward in his seat to gaze at the grey mass of concrete buildings that was getting ever closer. In the distance, beyond the sprawling town, the waters of the Drin shimmered as the river snaked its way westwards into the Ligenzi i Fierzes reservoir and on from there towards the sea. In terms of population, Kukes was not big – twenty-five thousand at most, Gus knew – but the vast area of buildings that he was now looking at, belied that fact.

He patted the pilot on the shoulder. 'It's much bigger than I expected,' he shouted, competing against the deafening throb of the rotors.

'Empty now!' came an equally loud reply.

It was only when they got nearer that Gus realised the sad state that many of the buildings were in and that they couldn't possibly be inhabited. As far as he could make out, the town proper was cocooned within a shell of roofless, windowless prefabs and a network of dusty roads.

'...In 1999, because of the troubles in Kosovo, a quarter of a million refugees crossed the Morini border into Kukes.'

'Because of the Serbs?'

The pilot nodded. 'Milosevic pigs!' he spat.

'So, all these empty buildings were part of a refugee camp?'

The Albanian again nodded agreement.

'And the refugees? Who were they? Kosovars?'

'Albanian Kosovars. Kosovo rightfully belongs to Albania but the Serbs said "No" and the KLA said "No".'

'KLA?'

'Kosovar Liberation Army.' Again, the pilot made a spitting noise. 'They, too, killed Albanians in Kosovo. Islamic pigs!'

Gus suddenly appreciated how little he really knew about Balkan politics and how much less about the religious problems within the region.

He had only a child's recollection of his time here, and his printout off the internet was obviously far from adequate. Of course, he remembered the Kosovo troubles of a few years back. He'd regularly listened to news reports at the time, as well as reading the occasional article in the newspapers, and he knew that Slobodan Milosevic would soon be facing charges of atrocities before an international court in The Hague, but he had to admit that his own interest in events, during his time with HSBC, hadn't been all that honourable. He'd been concerned not so much about the atrocities being perpetrated in the Balkans as about how the market would react to each day's events in the region. Rather than taking in the horrors of the war, he'd been eyeing the Dow Jones and the Nasdaq and the Footsie. That realisation now brought on a momentary twinge of guilt.

To the right of the town and its maze of dusty roads, Mount Gjallica rose majestically to over eight thousand feet, its peak in the distance bathed by the warm rays of a late afternoon sun. The chopper banked towards it, following a flight path that skirted the inhabited centre of Kukes, gradually losing height as it did so.

Gus peered down, without really knowing what he was searching for, if anything. Somewhere below, he reminded himself, he and his family had lived for the best part of two years. Would he go searching for the house? Did he want to find it? He had but few memories of his life here in Kukes, none of them pleasant! He could still recall the misery and the forlornness of those early months and the friendless atmosphere of the place. What he remembered in particular was the wretched school that he'd been sent to. The bullying, that he'd had to suffer there, still lingered like a festering wound. Little wonder that he had withdrawn into his shell, inflicting upon himself a loneliness that he had become accustomed to by now. Most vivid of the nightmares was the day that he and Gina were orphaned when strangers with very little compassion had come to take them away.

'You have to come with us,' they'd said. 'Your parents are dead and they won't be coming back with you from Kosovo.' Gina had cried for "Mamma"; he himself had bit a stoic lip and sulked.

'You cannot see your mamma,' they'd answered, without pity. 'She is dead. Your father is dead. They have been shot. They will be buried here, in Prizren.' Thinking about it now brought back to Gus the memory of a cameraman rushing forward to take their photograph. That picture might well be the one in the newspaper-cutting that Tom Mackay had given him and that he now carried in his wallet. There'd also been a kindly lady offering comfort and asking questions. There was only one image that he wanted to hang on to, though, and that was of his mother's pallid face and her sad little smile as she drew him to her in a sympathetic hug. But even that picture had become blurred with the passing years. His father's face, on the other hand, remained as clear as ever in his mind. The irony of it! His mother had always been there for him, his father hardly ever.

They'd left the town behind by now and straight ahead he could see a huge crater in the mountainside. This, as they approached, turned out to be a rock quarry, with clearly defined galleries along one side of it. In the few seconds that it took them to fly over, Gus glimpsed a railway line crossing the crater floor and disappearing into tunnels at each end. Further north it reappeared again, on its way down towards an extensive web of railway sidings in distant Kukes. That was the direction that the chopper now took.

Eventually, they landed on a raised helipad in front of a complex of huge sheds and warehouses and the pilot brusquely motioned him to climb out, that they'd arrived.

Then he raised his voice, 'Any time you people need my services, just call me. I can be up here from Tirana in an hour or so. Remember now, any time! My number is…' And he repeated it once… twice.'

For a second or two, Gus stood on the concrete landing area, looking around and wondering what surprises awaited him, but he soon had to move when the whine of the engine again became deafening and the downdraught from the rotors announced the chopper's intention to leave. Safely out of the way, he looked up to watch it go.

'Guiseppe Kadare?'

Two Italians were striding out to meet him. They had mafiosi written all over them.

'Yes, I am Guiseppe Kadare.' It was the name that he and Maurizio had decided on. 'Who are you?'

Their only response was to sneer. 'You carry a gun? Or a knife, perhaps?'

'No.'

'We will check.'

And he had to stand still, legs apart, whilst one of them frisked him. Finally, they seemed satisfied.

'You go in!'

He saw little point in arguing and so made his way towards the nearest door.

Languedoc, SOUTH OF FRANCE

Rennes-le-Château, a little hilltop village in the Pyrenean foothills, had never seen so many tourists this early in the holiday season. Three coaches had just snaked their way up the narrow winding road and were now disgorging their enthusiastic passengers onto a dusty car park, the perimeter of which was already full of cars, baking in the hot afternoon sun.

'Look! That has to be the Tour Magdala!' Wearing a wide-brimmed straw hat, she was the first off the bus, her camera at the ready.

The elderly guide on the coach smiled. He'd seen it all before.

'Where should we start?' asked another.

Patiently, the smiling courier waited for the whole group to disembark, then he too climbed down and began pointing, starting from his left. 'Tour Magdala... Villa Bethany...' They all craned to hear what he was saying, since the soft French voice no longer had the advantage of the coach's microphone. 'Beyond the open-air restaurant, you'll find the church and beyond that the cemetery with Saunièré's grave.'

'And his housekeeper's!'

He smiled benignly. At least they'd been listening to what he'd been telling them on the way here. 'That's right. They're buried next to each other, by the wall at the top end of the cemetery.'

'And the treasure? Where will I find that, then?' This question was coupled with a deep chuckle.

There's always one! thought Claude Boudet with a sigh. 'It's around here somewhere, sir. You'll just have to find it on your own, I'm afraid.' Then, as they all began wandering away in twos and threes, he reminded them, 'You will have to pay to visit the villa Bethanie, the museum, and the tower but I recommend that you do so. The museum, although small, is particularly well worth a visit.'

Then, after standing for a second or two to watch them go, he reached under his courier seat on the bus and took out a bag, nodded to the coach driver, as much as to say, "I'll see you later", and wandered towards the lookout point, to sit on its low stone wall and to pour himself a cup of coffee from his thermos. The afternoon sun was unrelenting on his blazered back.

Behind him, the parched hillslope fell away steeply to join the farmed fields below. Drowsily, he looked around at the familiar surroundings. To his left, the tower of the Magdalene stood perched on the very edge of its twenty-foot-high cliff. Berenger Sauniéré's Library with a view! A poor priest's folly! Claude Boudet smiled. 'Poor? Hardly that! So where did you get all that wealth, abbé Sauniére?' Countless others had asked the same question over the years and no one, as yet, had been able to provide a credible answer.

A leafy garden stood between the tower and the villa Bethanie. Today, the place was a hive of activity, with tourists from far and wide milling around; if not promenading along the Belvedere, then peering over the tower parapets or peeping out of the villa's many windows. In his years of coming here, and despite it being so early in the tourist season, Claude Boudet couldn't recall seeing so many visitors. People did indeed love mysteries!

Beyond the walled garden restaurant, hidden from him now, stood Sauniéré's little church, also dedicated to the Magdalene, and beyond that, the Calvary Garden and the cemetery where the priest and his housekeeper lay buried. To the right of the walled restaurant, a few terracotta roofs shimmered in the heat. From where he was now sitting, it was all he could see of the village. The rest of Rennes-le-Château, with its narrow, cobbled streets, clung to the hill's eastern slope.

Closer to him, little more than a metre or two away, people were queuing to look through the public telescope that was provided there and, while they waited, they were able to study the panoramic skyline map, laid out on a tourist stand close by. On this were arrowed all the distant peaks and places of interest to the south.

'Over there! That must be Bezu!' The man looking through the telescope was pointing into the distance. 'Didn't she say that that was where the templars minted their gold coins?'

Claude Boudet smiled as he unscrewed the top of his thermos flask and poured himself another coffee. *We couriers must be doing a grand job,* he thought.

In the blue above, a skylark chirped tirelessly whilst thirsty bushes, on the slope below, crackled in the heat. Cars were arriving, cars were leaving, all having to manoeuvre around the coaches that now claimed centre stage of the parking area.

As the minutes dragged by, Claude Boudet began to feel uncomfortably hot and his eyes grew heavy. He allowed his mind to wander. When he retired eight years ago, his intention had been to write an authoritative history of the Languedoc – a classic study to surpass all other books on the subject – a goal that had been greatly encouraged by his colleagues.

'With your scholarship, Claude… with your years of specialised study, who better to take it on?' And he had thrown himself into the work. Ten months and just two chapters later he'd had to abandon the idea, not because of his lack of knowledge on the subject – if anything, the reverse was true – but because he didn't have the organised, compartmental mind for such a task. The failure had resulted in a bout of depression that had lasted for several weeks and he had even contemplated suicide! But then, out of the blue, had come the offer of work as a tourist guide, visiting ancient sites of Cathar and Knights Templar interest, and the job had been his salvation.

He leant back to receive the warmth of the sun on his ascetically handsome, albeit rather effeminate face; a face that belied its seventy-three years. It pleased him to hear the endless chatter all around him, in so many different tongues. For years, the tourist trade of the Languedoc had been in decline and the region's economy had suffered disastrously, until someone in authority had had the vision to promote the area's wealth of history. Signs had been erected - *Le Pays de Cathare*. 'This is Cathar country,' they proclaimed—and much literature had been published on Cathar castles and Cathar history, and on the Knights Templar's association with the region. He himself had been commissioned to write some of it.

Boudet now found himself wondering which, of all the places that he visited with his tourist groups, was his favourite? It had to be either Montségur for its historic majesty or this place, Rennes-le-Château, for its mystery and romance. He had yet to bring a group here that didn't love hearing the story of Berenger Sauniérè, the impoverished priest who had arrived in the village in 1885 and had suddenly come across untold riches from a mysterious source. He had used some of the wealth to refurbish the local church, albeit in a somewhat unorthodox fashion, and to build his Villa

Bethanie and his Tour Magdala. He had also paid to renovate many dilapidated buildings in the village, an undertaking that had endeared him greatly to the local people. And when Sauniérè died in 1917, his housekeeper, Marie Dénarnaud had compounded the romance and the mystery by promising to reveal the secret of the treasure on her deathbed. Years later, however, a heavy stroke had left her paralysed and speechless and the secret had followed her to the grave. The irony of it all!

It was a story that never failed to enthuse his listeners and Boudet smiled to himself now as he recalled the questions and answers that always followed the telling of it: "If there was a treasure, then where did it come from"? It was a question that he loved to answer because it guaranteed a rapt audience.

'Some say it's the lost treasure of the templars, others think it belonged to the Cathars. Some even claim it to be Visigothic gold, in which case a lot of it would have come from the Temple of Solomon in Jerusalem. And personally,' he would add mischievously. 'I wouldn't discount the possibility of it being the crown treasure of France because history tells us that Queen Blanche of Castille, who ruled France whilst her son Louis IX was away on crusade, brought the crown treasures with her to Rennes-les-Baines for safe keeping... and Rennes-les-Baines isn't all that far from Rennes-le-Château.'

'But what do you think, monsieur?'

With tongue-in-cheek, he'd always answer: 'It could be all of them.' Then he'd go on to tell them how Sauniérè and his brother, as boys growing up in the area, used to spend days on end searching the old mines in the surrounding hills. 'Gold mines,' he'd add, just to see their faces light up even more.

'Did Sauniérè ever admit to finding treasure?'

'No, but he didn't repudiate the claim either. Marie Dénarnaud, his housekeeper, made no bones about it, though. She is recorded as saying that the people of Rennes-le-Chateau have untold wealth beneath their feet.'

'But how did Sauniérè find it?'

'Ah!' he'd answer teasingly. 'That story will have to keep because we have no time now. But I will tell you this much—In 1891, soon after he arrived here, Sauniérè brought workmen in to do some work around the church altar, and in the hollow altar rail they found the Hautpoul archives, documents written in Latin and said to have been hidden by the Abbé Bigou a hundred years before. My friends, two of those documents are still missing.'

'Really? And what were these Hautpoul documents?'

'Too long a story, I'm afraid, but it's possible, don't you think, that they might hold the secret of the hidden treasure.'

He'd always end with a reference that never failed to raise a few eyebrows. 'But listen to this! Sauniérè is said to have taken the parchments to a local linguistic scholar to decipher, and his name was... Henri Boudet!' At which point he invariably made a show of placing a hand across his own chest to playfully suggest that he, Claude Boudet, was a descendant of that same linguistic expert who had been given access to the mysteries of Rennes-le-Château.

With a wry smile, Claude now finished his coffee and got up off the wall, to return his mug and thermos flask to the coach. Surprisingly, not one of today's group had asked him why Sauniérè had dedicated his tower to the Magdalene. Would he volunteer the information on the return journey? It was, after all, another good story! Another thread to the mystery!

He'd hardly got halfway across the car park to the coach when a terrifying scream ripped the air, to be followed by another... and another. He froze, as did everyone else around him. The scream was one of pure terror. Had someone fallen off the Belvedere? Or even worse, over the parapet of the Tour Magdala? That was the direction from which the screams had come. Were still coming!

People stood motionless, looking at one another in shock, whilst on the other side of the car park bewildered villagers began appearing one by one. And the screaming continued.

Claude Boudet shook himself out of his trance and began striding purposefully in the direction of noise. Others were also hurrying to investigate the chilling screams that were still being heard.

A path ran with the base of the cliff on which the Tour Magdala stood, a path that followed the slope around the hill, to eventually reach the village from the other side.

Below the path, the hillslope here was just a thick mat of stunted blackthorn and briars.

They'd passed beneath the tower of the Magdalene and the Belvedere beyond it before they saw the cause of the disturbance. Two women stood there on the narrow path, staring wide-eyed into the jungle of thorns beneath them. One of them had her arm around the other's shoulders in a half-hearted attempt to silence her screams. As she heard their approach, she raised her free arm to point, at which point her companion finally stopped screaming.

It took a second or two for Claude Boudet and the others to realise what they were looking at, and then they, too, let out a collective gasp. Through a narrow gap in the thick undergrowth, a pair of eyes – dead eyes in a blue and bloodied face – stared up at them out of the thorny shadows. A bare arm resting at an awkward angle across an abundance of black hair suggested the presence of a second corpse.

Claude Boudet reached for his phone and dialled. *'Police, s'il vous plait. Urgence!'*

Cappella Sistina, IL VATICANO

'And when a pope dies, you say that this is where they choose a new one?'

Sally Jeffers smiled at the lady who had whispered the question in her ear. 'That's right! This is where the Conclave meets.' She, too, spoke in hushed tones since visitors to the Sistine Chapel were expected to maintain a respectful silence at all times. 'The Cardinals are locked in here until they come to a decision on who the next pope will be.'

'Locked in? I never knew that before.' Then, with a quiet word of thanks, the executively-dressed woman wandered after the rest of her group, to do as her guide, Sally Jeffers, had just suggested, which was to study at will the marvellous frescoes that adorned the walls and ceiling.

Sally had given them her Capella Sistina spiel before entering the chapel itself; her task made easier by the fact that her group today was small and exclusive; all of them company executives visiting the Eternal City for the very first time, to attend a conference. Only six of them had taken up their corporate host's offer of a two-hour guided tour of the Vatican, a fact that pleased their courier no end, especially since today's tip would come in the form of a generous sum on top of a higher-than-usual fee. Gratuities were always welcome, of course, but that didn't mean that she actually enjoyed accepting individual handouts from people as they left the coach at the end of their tour. It always felt as if she were standing there, cap in hand, expecting charity. It was demeaning. Today, though, things would be done differently.

The mere fact that she'd been asked to lead the group was pleasing in itself, especially since the Vatican offered its own variety of guided tours. 'Show them as much as possible without bogging them down with too much detail.' That's what the company rep had told her over the phone. 'Just a general idea of what the Vatican is all about. And' he'd added as a joke, 'if you can get the pope to bless them, and especially to bless the work that they'll be doing for this company, then there'll be an additional bonus in it for you.'

Sally smiled now at the recollection. It had been a good tour, she decided. She had earned her money. They'd all been good listeners and had smiled politely when informed that they wouldn't have time to see all one hundred and six acres of the Vatican State but rather a selection of the Holy See's most interesting features.

The tour had begun with a coach ride to the museum's entrance on the Viale del Vaticano. There, she had shown them the Leonine Wall and had pointed out the tower from where Vatican Radio broadcasted daily in twenty different languages, worldwide. She'd also explained to them that the Holy See, with a mere five hundred residents, had its own judiciary system and post office, not to mention its own bank and currency and even its own daily newspaper.

'It may be the world's smallest state,' she had told them, 'but it has powers and assets far greater than most of the world's largest countries. You'll get some idea of what I mean during the next couple of hours!' Then, she'd added, 'Rome may be known as Caput Mundi but to all Roman Catholics, the Vatican is the world's capital, and the Bishop of Rome, the pope, has probably more authority worldwide than any other world leader, the president of the United States included.' They'd reacted with astonishment and disbelief to that claim. 'Bear in mind,' she'd added by way of proof, 'that there are over nine hundred million Catholics worldwide. Imagine the impact of those on any political elections. If he so desired, the pope could hold sway in many countries, just at the drop of a hat, so to speak.'

She had then listened to them "Oohing!" and "Aahing!" their way along the galleries, marvelling at the magnificent tapestries and ancient maps, through to the Raphael Rooms and finally the glorious Capella Sistina. The chapel never failed to impress, and what breath they still had left by then was taken away by their very first sight of the Sistine.

Now, at Sally's invitation, the group was milling with other appreciative sightseers, to take a closer look at the wonderful frescoes that surrounded them—Michelangelo's ornate ceiling with its stunning scenes from the book of Genesis, his masterpiece Last Judgement on the altar wall, breathtaking wall panels by the likes of Botticelli, Signorelli, Perugino and others. No matter how often she came here, Sally Jeffers never failed to marvel at the wealth of art in this one relatively small corner of the Vatican.

Eventually, they all trooped out into the warm sun and she now led them towards the Basilica of San Pietro, stopping but briefly on the way to point out the two Swiss Guards, dressed in their distinctive uniforms of blue and yellow, guarding the entrance to the Papal Palaces.

'So what pantomime are they doing this year, then?'

Sally smiled politely. 'The pontiff's personal guard!' she explained. 'By today, there are only a hundred of them. Used to be five times as many, years ago. And yes, every one of them has to be a Swiss citizen… and Roman Catholic, of course. They must all be aged between nineteen and thirty. Another requirement is that they must have attended military school in Switzerland. Which is why you shouldn't be fooled by the way they look. They are all supremely fit and capable soldiers. By the way, I've heard it said that the uniform was designed by Michelangelo himself, but that's debatable.'

They then spent half an hour in the Basilica, marvelling at Michelangelo's Pieta and Bernini's wonderful creations and a further twenty minutes in the crypt, gazing at the final resting place of so many popes before finally calling it a day. Now, as she watched them leave, she was glad of the few minutes alone. It gave her the chance to mull over what she'd overheard earlier. Two priests, coming from the direction of a cordoned-off library wing, had been speaking in hushed tones. Not that that in itself was surprising but rather something that she overheard one of them saying as they walked by. '…*Il segreto del Pentacolo di Schidoni…*' That was all! A reference to the secret of something called the Schidoni Pentacle. It wasn't as if the words meant anything to her but they had rung some sort of bell in her head. Schidoni Pentacle! She'd heard it mentioned before. Recently! She was sure of it. Someone had asked her a question that she hadn't been able to answer. But who? And where?

It would be nightfall, alone in her apartment, before the penny finally dropped.

Kukes, ALBANIA

Excelsior Steel was a mafia-run if not mafia-owned company specialising in the manufacture of steel scaffolding. Or at least that was the public face of things. Anyone remotely connected with the firm, though, knew that the factory's main production was precision-made gun barrels and rocket launchers. Gunstocks were also manufactured on site but all the firing mechanisms had to be imported. All of it illegal, of course, under international law! But UN inspectors, despite a number of unannounced visits in the past, had never been able to find evidence of arms production on the site, simply because warnings of their intentions had always preceded them.

After his acceptance by La Nuova Alba, the so-called "New Dawn" in Rome, Gus had tried to keep an open mind on the sort of work that would be expected of him. Anything would do, he'd thought – anything other than killing – as long as it gave him access to the sort of information that MI6 wanted. What he hadn't bargained for, however, was to be cooped up in a tiny office, day in, day out, being nothing more than a glorified wages clerk for Excelsior Steel and a neighbouring firm called Kukes Plastics. The two mafiosi who'd met him at the helipad six days ago, after outlining his duties for him had then disappeared, leaving him to fend for himself and to find his own way around.

Boring as it was, however, the job did have an upside, in that it gave Gus some access to information. He came to know, for instance, that goods and materials were being illegally imported under another name, though he had no way of knowing how they were being brought into the country, or from where, since what little paperwork was available to him showed only legitimate addresses of legal suppliers. Were they smuggled over the border into Kosovo from Serbia or Macedonia, and then on from there? Or did they originate in Greece, or maybe beyond? Or perhaps they were being shipped in across the Adriatic? For the time being, he'd just have to keep an open mind on that. The only thing he could be sure of was that the final stage of delivery to Kukes was by rail. Another thing that baffled him was the fact that Excelsior Steel was paying well over the odds for the amount of raw material that it was importing. It just didn't make sense. Since when did the mafia get involved in anything that might be termed "mere peanuts"?

What he hadn't as yet been able to find was evidence of the sort of weapons that Tom Mackay had been worried about. As far as he could tell, no chemical or radioactively contaminated weapons were being made or stored within the complex. At his earliest opportunity he'd taken a tour of the two factories, knowing full well that he was being watched, probably on the orders of Maurizio in Rome. But getting to know his workplace was surely expected of him, so his walkabouts shouldn't raise any mafiosi eyebrows.

First of all, he sought out the manager at Kukes Plastics, only to be told that no such official existed and that he, Gus, was solely responsible for both sites. A quick look around the factory showed him why. The business was obviously on its last legs. At one time it had thrived on supplying plastic mouldings for Skoda cars but that was before Volkswagen bought up the Yugoslav car company. Now, with a workforce of just eight men there was very little going on here.

'So, what are these for?' He pointed to what could only be described as large plastic trays, coloured dark grey, neatly stacked one on top of the other. Each, he reckoned, was about thirty feet by twelve in size, with a depth of around ten inches. A rough count told him that there were about forty of them in all, set out in two piles.

The Albanian being questioned looked at him long and hard. Gus could tell that the man's guard was up, that he was being wary. Eventually, the answer came: 'Paddling pools.'

'Paddling pools?' Gus made no effort to hide his incredulity. The mafia making and selling plastic paddling pools? The very idea was nonsense. The guy was having him on!

'They are in great demand in Italy.' The man's brazen grin now confirmed the lie.

'And those? What are they for?' Gus turned to point towards the other side of the extensive warehouse, where tons and tons of small and medium-sized rocks had been dumped along the whole length of the building, again almost to roof height.

'Hard core.' There was extra mischief in the man's grin this time. 'Good material for building new roads.'

Sensing again that the Albanian was having him on, Gus scowled, shook his head in impatient despair and turned to leave. As he did so, he trod on a stray lump of stone and automatically kicked it aside. The speed and the hollow sound with which it sped across the warehouse floor took him by complete surprise. It wasn't a stone at all but a lump of grey plastic, made to resemble a stone. His questioning look was again met with a knowing grin.

As he left Kukes Plastics and headed back towards neighbouring Excelsior Steel, he had to cross a set of railway sidings. This was Excelsior's link with the main railway line less than half a mile away, from where goods could be transported down to the main railway depot in Kukes and on from there to whatever market they were destined for.

His tour of Excelsior didn't spring any great surprises either. Yes, armaments were being manufactured there – there was little doubt of that – but on a far smaller scale than he'd expected. Roughly a third of the workers on the factory floor were engaged in the legal production of scaffolding poles and accessories, the rest were manning lathes and diamond saws or standing at long workbenches that ran the length of both walls. A cacophony of screeches and squeals assailed Gus' ears as cutters and files came into busy contact with hard metal, and showers of sparks here and there showed grinders and welders at work. Despite his inexperienced eye, Gus knew that he was seeing a highly skilled labour force of both sexes at work. He also knew that the level of production was relatively low.

Hardly any of the workers looked up as he walked by. They were too engrossed in their various tasks. Even so, Gus knew that he was still being watched. Security cameras were recording his every movement, of course – that was something everyone in the factory had to put up with – but Gus could sense other eyes on him as well. Probably on the orders of Maurizio Bonnano! *If that's the case,* he thought with a cynical smile. *Then the great man of honour back in Rome doesn't trust even his own cousin.* The frustrating aspect was that the close attention he was getting was making it difficult for him to get the information that Tom Mackay required of him, thus giving him no other option but to bide his time, and to hope.

He had been given lodgings on the outskirts of Kukes. There, he shared a dormitory with an Albanian and two Kosovars who, by now, were just about the only friends that he had in Kukes. Friends in the sense that they were at least willing to talk to him, which was more than could be said for most of the other workers. Even so, lying in his bunk at night, listening to the three of them snoring and farting in the dark, made him feel particularly lonely.

*

When he repeated his tour of the machine shop a couple of days later, he was surprised to see a stocky, balding priest chatting to a group of the workers before moving on then to another group that was coming together to greet him. Gus stood by to watch. In a few minutes, the priest continued across the shop floor to be met by yet another newly formed group. Eventually, however, the man of God caught sight of Gus and, with a broad smile, strode purposefully towards him, arm outstretched to offer a hand of friendship.

'You must be Guiseppe Maratta. I am Father Galileo. Welcome back to Kukes, my son.'

He had a florid face, not ascetic by any stretch of the imagination. To Gus, he looked more like a man of the world than a man of the cloth. And the name! Hadn't the church once branded the original Galileo a heretic?

'Kadare,' Gus corrected him, though he wondered to what purpose. 'Guiseppe Kadare.'

'Of course!' Father Galileo grinned a knowing grin. 'Guiseppe Kadare! I knew your father, Giovanni Maratta. And your mother, too. Agnesa Kadare.'

Gus gawped disbelievingly. 'You knew them?'

'I remember them well. As I remember two little children called Guiseppe and Gina.'

Gus breathed deeply to get over the shock. He looked around. 'Can we go somewhere to talk?'

The priest smiled as if the request had been expected. 'Somewhere quiet.' Then, with another knowing grin, he added, 'I have just the place.'

Taking Gus' sinewy arm, Father Galileo led him out of the noise and into a quiet corridor that Gus hadn't yet had the chance to inspect. The priest was obviously well-acquainted with the building and he was soon ushering Gus into a little box room that was cluttered with cardboard boxes and filing cabinets. There was also a stack of chairs, two of which he now pulled clear before inviting Gus to sit.

'We will have peace here.' Then, with a wink and yet another knowing grin, he began rummaging in amongst the boxes and eventually produced, like a magician pulling a rabbit out of a hat, a part-full bottle of ruby port wine. A quick delve in the top drawer of one of the filing cabinets yielded a couple of plastic mugs and the ruby port was soon gurgling out of its bottle.

Explains the complexion! Gus thought. He'll be telling me about his gout, next.

'You visit the factory often.' More of a statement than a question.

Another grin and another swig. 'I must visit my sheep, must I not?'

'Your sheep?' The reference momentarily confused Gus.

'My flock,' he explained, waving a casual hand in the direction from which they'd just come. 'And I trust that I can now regard you, too, as being in the fold.'

'Ah! I see. Your church is in Kukes?'

The little man grinned again, but without humour this time. 'My church? This is my church, Guiseppe.'

Gus let the comment go unchallenged. 'But what do the others think, Father? Do they mind you coming here?'

Now it was the priest's turn to look confused. 'Others? What others, my son?' He drained his glass and helped himself to a refill.

'I mean the... the...' *How shall I put it?* he thought. 'The non-Catholics.'

'Non-Catholics?' A look of amusement creased the jovial face. 'In God's name, who would they be?'

Gus recalled what he'd read about the religious background of Albania. What had the figures been? Seventy percent Muslim, only ten percent Catholic. 'Some of the workers have other beliefs?'

Father Galileo laughed out loud, then snarled. 'Muslim, you mean. Don't even think about it, Guiseppe! Not one Islamist pig dare show his heathen face in this place.' There was a ferocity in the way he now gulped the ruby port.

Gus felt his mouth fall open. What he'd just heard were hardly the words of a God-fearing man. But if his face showed disapproval, the priest made no show of recognising the fact; either that or he was choosing to disregard it.

'Only those of the true faith are employed by Excelsior Steel.'

'Oh? And the reason for that?'

Father Galileo sighed. 'My son, there is much that you have to learn. Someday perhaps...' He left the sentence unfinished. 'Now you wish to ask me about your parents. Is that right?'

Gus nodded.

'You wish to find your old home.'

'I would rather know where they died. How they died.'

'Your questions are easily answered. They were shot in Prizren in Kosovo. I believe that is where they were buried.'

'Who shot them?'

'That I do not know, my son.'

You're lying, Gus thought. I can see it in your eyes. 'Why were they killed?'

The answer, when it came, was cautious. 'It was to do with his work, I believe. It was unfortunate that your poor mother had to be with him at the time. Your father had taken her with him to Kosovo, probably because he thought he would be safer with a woman at his side, and that he wouldn't be stopped.'

'Stopped?'

The priest smiled sympathetically and scratched at his bald head. 'Stopped for questioning. Our brothers in Kosovo needed guns to fight. Your father supplied them. He had crossed the border to meet a delegation in Prizren, to broker a deal. He was killed before he could return. Your father was a brave man.'

'My father was a gunrunner,' Gus remarked curtly. 'And he got my mother killed because of it.'

Galileo chose to disregard the open criticism. 'Your father had just become boss-of-bosses here in Kukes. The quarry was one of his responsibilities. He would be proud of the quarry today, I know.'

'The quarry?' Even as he asked the question, Gus recalled how his father sometimes arrived home with his black patent shoes covered with grey dust. He would always take them off at the door and pass them on to his wife to be cleaned. Gus had hated his father for that, for treating his mother like a servant or a slave. 'What quarry?'

The priest merely shrugged, as if to say, "You'll soon find out."

'My father was Cosa Nostra but he was not avenged. My mother was not avenged.' Again, Gus was surprised by the depth of his own resentment. '…Who became boss-of-bosses after my father?'

'Lucio Cimino. He is still here as Capo.'

'And he did not seek out my mother's killers? Does not the Cosa Nostra look after its own, here in Kukes?'

'Lucio Cimino is not Cosa Nostra, my son. He is from Napoli.'

'He is Camorra?' The news surprised and angered Gus.

'Yes. The mob in Kukes is Camorra, now. The Albanian mafiosi, they take orders only from Lucio Cimino.'

Was there a vague hint in the priest's words?

'What happened to the Cosa Nostra, Father?'

'After your father was killed in Kosovo, there was much killing here in Kukes.'

'Between Cosa Nostra and Camorra?'

The older man nodded. 'Many mafiosi from Napoli arrived and Lucio Cimino became boss-of-bosses.'

'So, the business in Kukes is now run by the Camorra?' Again, the priest nodded.

'No one else?'

'In name, at least, this factory still belongs to the Cosa Nostra, but Cimino has a finger in this pie as well as that of the quarry. But such things will change now that you are manager here.'

Manager? Gus thought. Who the hell said anything about me being manager? What is Maurizio up to? And why would the Camorra in Kukes be answerable to a Cosa Nostra boss-of-bosses in Rome? The questions puzzled him. Could it be that he'd been sent here by his so-distant cousin to keep an eye on Lucio Cimino? No, that didn't make sense. Had that been Maurizio's intention, then he would have sent someone more experienced than Gus to do the job. Another possibility was that Maurizio wanted him dead and was expecting the Camorra riffraff to do his dirty work for him. But that didn't make much sense either. If that had been the case, then he would have been killed well before now. Suddenly, a new possibility struck him. Had Maurizio sent him here to deal with Cimino, knowing that he, Gus, would be prepared to do the job, if …

He now looked directly into the priest's eyes and, with a slight quiver in his voice, asked, 'Tell me, Father! Was it Lucio Cimino who killed my parents?'

Father Galileo gulped at his port wine and looked away, as if he'd known that the question was bound to come. 'Maybe so, maybe not, my son. I do not know. You were too young to understand at the time but there was much bad blood in Albania when your parents were alive. Only Cosa Nostra could sell guns then. They had – how do you say – a monopoly on the trade. But things were getting much worse in Kosovo and there was much more money to be made. Which is why the Camorra came. They wanted to muscle in. Cimino wanted a stake.'

'Gang war? Vendetta?'

The priest nodded with fake sadness and refilled his own glass before tilting the bottle in Gus' direction. The offer was refused.

'But the killing in Kukes did not start until after your father, the Capo, had been killed in Prizren.'

'Could Cimino have arranged for someone to follow my parents to Prizren?'

'Yes, he could have done that.'

Gus fell silent.

'…But you must not be rash, my son. Nothing must happen until after the first of the month.'

Gus now looked at the priest through narrowing eyes. 'And why the first of the month, Father?'

'I'm sure that you will be told when the time is right, my son. Feel sure of it. Now promise me that you will wait until after the first of the month.'

Later, back in his own dingy little office, Gus mulled over what he had learnt. Father Galileo had more or less confirmed that his parents had been murdered, sixteen years ago, on the orders of – or even by the hand of – a mafioso thug called Lucio Cimino, who was still boss-of-bosses here in Kukes. The more he thought about it, the more convinced he became that the priest had deliberately leaked him choice bits of information. Why? To what purpose? And why the reference to the first of the month? What was going to happen then? And why had the priest been so anxious to extract a promise from him not to seek revenge until after that date? So many unanswered questions led inevitably to another. If he, Gus, could establish without a shadow of doubt that it was Cimino who had been responsible for his mother's death, then would he now do anything about it? Would he consider taking revenge? And if so, how?

He didn't feel comfortable with the question nor with the answer that insisted on coming.

ROMA

'Is that Sally Jeffers?'

She had just settled in her armchair with a plateful of pasta on her lap when the phone rang.

'Yes?'

'You are a tourist guide?'

'That's right.' *Tell me more,* she thought. *So, I can place your accent.* It was obviously Scottish but she wanted to be more specific. It was a game that she liked to play with herself. If the accent was Scandinavian, was it Swedish, Norwegian, or Danish? If Eastern Mediterranean, could it be Turkish or Greek? She'd become pretty adept at placing the Americans. Texans and New Yorkers were never a problem but her ear, by now, had also become attuned to the less obvious Washingtonian and Philadelphian inflections. English accents rarely gave her trouble and she could always tell north-Walian from south-Walian, Ulsterman from Dubliner. She recognised a Glaswegian when she came across one but other Scottish accents weren't so familiar, which meant that she'd have to guess on this one.

'My name is Tom Mackay. I'm researching for my next novel and I need a wee bit of help.'

'Edinburgh?'

'Pardon?'

'You come from Edinburgh, Mr Mackay?'

'Inverness, actually.' He sounded perplexed by her question. 'Does it matter?'

Sally Jeffers laughed. 'Don't mind me! How can I help you?'

'It's just that I'm here to visit the Vatican and need a guide to show me around.' The excuse sounded lame because he knew that the Vatican provided its own tours. 'Actually, I want more than just a guided tour. Um! I'm looking for someone with a lot of background information on the Holy

See. Someone I can question when I need to. That wouldn't be easy if I was one of a group.'

'How did you get my number?'

'Um! I contacted Thomas Cook before leaving home. They recommended you. Told me that you occasionally do some work for them here in Rome.'

Odd! she thought. I wouldn't expect Thomas Cook or Thompsons to volunteer that sort of information.

Mackay sensed her hesitation. 'I'll pay you well, of course.'

'When do you want the tour?'

'As soon as possible as far as I'm concerned. This afternoon?'

'Why not.' It would be a day without pay otherwise. 'Two o'clock? Piazza San Pietro?'

'How will I know you?'

'Um! Red dress, black headband.'

'Two o'clock, then!'

She quickly finished lunch and switched on her computer. The internet would provide her with information on Tom or Thomas Mackay, novelist. If she was going to spend the afternoon in the company of a well-known author, then the last thing she wanted was the embarrassment of not being able to name any of his books.

*

'So where would you like to start, Mr Mackay? What kind of information are you looking for?'

He was older than she'd expected. Certainly older than someone researching for what had to be his very first novel. She'd tried all the search engines on the internet and none of them had come up with any hits on a novelist called Tom or Thomas Mackay, born in Inverness. She also felt uncomfortable with the way that he kept looking at her, as if he was supposed to know her.

'In the first place, thanks for agreeing to show me around.' A sweep of hand indicated St Peter's Basilica and the papal state beyond it. 'And secondly, let me complement you on the way you look. Believe me, it's quite a privilege for an old man like me to be seen in the company of such a good-looking young woman.'

Sally blushed. It wasn't a dress that she usually wore on a working day. The red suited her, she knew; just as she knew that it's above-knee hemline turned men's heads. The young and the middle-aged usually ogled shamelessly at her; it was left to the older men, people like Tom Mackay, to pay the complements. Inside the Basilica, however, her shapely legs would draw nothing but disagreeing frowns, a realisation that made her now regret not having worn something more demure.

'So, what's it all about, Mr Mackay?'

'Pardon?'

'Your novel?'

'Oh! Um! I'm just in the researching stage at the moment. I probably won't start writing for another couple of months at least. Would you mind if we gave the Basilica a miss and concentrated instead on the Papal Palaces?'

'No problem.' She aimed right, out of the Piazza and towards the Via di Porta Angelica. 'Have you had many published? Novels, I mean.'

'Um! Three so far.'

Liar! 'And what will this next one be called?'

'I haven't decided yet.' Then, as the thought suddenly struck him: 'Maybe *The Schidoni Pentacle*.'

Sally Jeffers stopped in midstride, unable to hide her surprise, a fact that he quickly picked up on.

'You seem surprised.' Could it be that he'd struck lucky at his very first attempt?

Surprised? You bet I am! Third time, now! So, who the hell are you, Mr Mackay? And what's your game? 'Yes, I am surprised, seeing that you're the third person within the past few days to mention the Schidoni Pentacle, whatever it may be. Can you tell me what it is?'

The ageing Scot realised that he'd been caught out, because it was a question that he couldn't answer. 'Um!' He smiled sheepishly. 'If you don't mind, I'd rather not say at this moment in time, especially since I haven't yet settled on the final draft of my... um... plot.' His smile broadened. 'Anyway, don't you think that you're the one who should be doing the talking, young lady? Especially since I'm paying you to do so. I'd certainly like to hear what you know about the Schidoni Pentacle.'

Touché! 'Nothing much, I'm afraid. I was asked about it a few days ago and heard it again mentioned a couple of days later, that's all.'

'Who did the asking?'

'All I can tell you is that he was an Arab, and a very intense one at that.' Seeing little point in withholding the information, she then went on to relate how the man had approached her, that afternoon in the Roman Forum. 'He asked me if I knew what the Schidoni Pentacle was but, quite frankly, he was more interested in the carvings on the Arch of Titus.'

Mackay looked at her hard, as if weighing up her words. 'And the other time?'

She now told him of the two priests who'd been discussing the Schidoni Pentacle as they were leaving the Vatican Archives that day. 'Just coincidence, most likely.'

'Hm! But you've no idea what this Pentacle might be?'

'No, but you obviously do.'

'Do I?'

'Well, yes, if it's going to be the title of your next novel.'

'Ah! I see what you mean.'

They made their way towards the Sistine Chapel.

'...Anyway,' he added dismissively. 'It's not really important. I've heard a lot about the Vatican Library. Would you mind showing me that, to begin with?'

'Not the Sistina?'

'No, I've... um! Been there before.'

Liar! 'No sweat, Mr Mackay! The Vatican Library it'll be, then.'

They walked. She talked. He listened, without any great show of interest. 'You've been in Rome for some time, Miss Jeffers?'

'Sally! Please call me Sally. Miss Jeffers makes me feel old.'

'Of course. Sally it'll be, then!'

'Getting on for three years, actually. Came here straight from university.'

'Good linguist, are you?'

'I wouldn't say that. I'm relatively fluent in Italian and French and I have a smattering of German. That's all! I wouldn't have a job here otherwise.'

'And you meet a lot of interesting people, I'm sure.'

'You could say that.'

'A friend of my son came to live in Rome just a few weeks ago. I wouldn't mind calling to see him whilst I'm here but I don't have an address. It's too much to hope that you've come across him, I suppose. His name's Gus Adams. Roughly your age. Thin, long hair, dark eyes.'

'No. Afraid not. Rome's a big place, Mr Mackay!'

He returned her mischievous smile with a smile of his own. 'So it is, Sally. So, it is.' He then offered her his calling card. 'But if you should come across him, perhaps you'd be good enough to give me a ring? Or ask him to contact me himself. I'll be in Rome for a few weeks.'

The amount he paid her for the brief tour was ridiculously generous but she wasn't going to argue the point, what with funds being so low. It did arouse her suspicions though, especially since he hadn't asked many questions about the Vatican nor bothered taking notes on her answers. Tom Mackay, she decided – if that, indeed, was his real name – was definitely not what he was claiming to be.

Kukes, ALBANIA

Gus had, by now, suffered almost three weeks of boredom and growing agitation and he was painfully aware that he hadn't contacted Tom Mackay since he'd left London. A month had gone by and Vauxhall Cross had learnt absolutely nothing from him! But he took some consolation from the fact that the Scotsman had warned him not to get in touch unless he had positive information on the whereabouts of the arms depot.

'Whatever you do, don't use your cell phone.' That's what he'd said. 'And don't trust public telephones there either.' So, what was he supposed to do? The only authorised contact he'd been given was some tourist guide or other in Rome, someone called Sally Jeffers. And even she was to be used only sparingly. 'Make damn sure she isn't compromised!' had been Mackay's instructions.

By now, Gus was convinced that the massive arms cache that MI6 had been worried about – if it even existed – wouldn't be found in Kukes at all. In some other remote corner of Albania perhaps, or over the border in Kosovo even, but not here. Yes, the factory where he worked was producing replacement gun barrels and rocket launcher parts but not in the quantities that Mackay had talked about. And there was no indication whatsoever of the presence of unconventional weapons of mass destruction. *They got it wrong about WMDs in Iraq and it looks as though they haven't got it right here, either.*

He wasn't to know it then, but he was about to be proven wrong. His inactivity was about to come to an end.

*

It started when a goods train arrived unannounced in the siding that separated Excelsior Steel from its sister factory. It was a damp morning, with Mount Gjallica in the distance, hiding under a heavy cloud. Gus, for lack of anything better to do, stood by to watch the "paddling pools" from

Kukes Plastics being loaded onto some of the empty trucks. Then, fascinated, he watched the plastic "rocks" – the so-called hard-core – being loaded onto the remaining fifteen trucks. The work was being carried out by Excelsior personnel and with Excelsior lifting equipment and Gus couldn't help wondering who was running the show because he, the so-called manager, had neither been informed nor consulted.

By midday everything had been loaded and, without further delay, the train pulled out of the siding. He wanted to know where it was bound for but he was so sure that he wouldn't get a sensible answer that he didn't bother to ask. Instead, he stood there until the last truck had been swallowed up by the mist and the screech of metal grinding on metal had grown faint and muffled in the distance.

Since his initial visit, Father Galileo had made a further three appearances at the factory and on each occasion, when Gus had asked him about the significance of the first of the month, the priest had stressed the need for patience.

'Your time will come!' he kept saying, thinking that Gus was becoming impatient to avenge his parents' death. He wasn't just expecting Gus to carry out his revenge, he was even preparing him for it.

It was on his next visit that Galileo let slip the words "*la crociata finale*" and in the same breath asked: 'Tell me, my son! Do you carry a gun?'

They were again surrounded by the clutter of the little box room and the priest was yet again enjoying a glass of his favourite tipple. Gus, by now, had come to realise why the priest preferred this particular meeting place. It was one of the few places on site that wasn't covered by a security camera.

'A gun, Father? No, I don't carry a gun. There is no need for one, surely?'

The man of God lowered his voice: 'The best advice I can give you, Guiseppe, is to be prepared at all times.' At which he got off his chair, plunged an arm behind one of the filing cabinets and drew out a gun fitted with a silencer. 'Hide it!' he commanded in a hoarse whisper, obviously concerned that someone might walk in unannounced, and Gus hurriedly took the Uzi semi-automatic pistol from him and placed it inside his loose-fitting shirt. A further search produced three clips of ammunition, all of which Father Galileo hid on his own person, beneath his cassock. He then requested the gun back. 'On second thoughts I will take it out of the building for you,' he explained. 'No one will suspect me.'

Gus smiled ruefully. *Some priest!* he thought. 'But where shall I then hide it, Father? My roommates are bound to see it.'

'Come to think of it, it would be better if it were hidden in the filing cabinet in your office. Leave it to me!'

The following day was a Wednesday. A week tomorrow, Gus pondered, will be the first of July. The countdown begins! But for what?

IL VATICANO

Had the commander of the Swiss Guard known the real identity of Aiello and what he represented, then he would have done all in his power to have him brought before the Vatican judiciary and then excommunicated. As it was, however, no one in authority within the Holy See knew even of the existence of Aiello, let alone the extent of his subversive activities.

A rogue member of Opus Dei for many years and now in his late fifties, Carlo Platina, alias Aiello, was a man with a mission; a mission *"to save the Vatican from an egotistic pope who has aspirations of early sainthood and a gaggle of senile cardinals who have neither the power nor the will to see the evil, long-term effects of their actions"*. Aiello believed that the Holy See was instigating a disastrous and ill-conceived process for world peace. Catholics the world over were being encouraged to consort with Jews and Moslems by inviting them – urging them, even – in areas where no mosque or synagogue was available, to use Catholic churches for their prayers. The Holy Father, of all people, consorting with heathens! And as if that were not enough, he had more than once since taking holy office endorsed the heretic Gnostic claim of one of his predecessors, pope Jean Paul 1, on the dual nature of God; that the creator was *"not only your father, but also your mother"*. Such talk was irresponsible and could only lead to one thing—the ordination of women priests! Not only that but the pope had also asked his Cardinals for their views on birth control in the poorer African countries, as a means of tackling poverty and the problem of AIDS. He had even raised with them the question of more tolerance towards those with homosexual or lesbian tendencies.

In the face of such heresies – heresies that threatened the very roots of the Roman Catholic faith, the true faith – Aiello had become convinced that fire could only be fought with fire.

Six years ago, retired judge Carlo Platina, clever as well as devious, had vowed that he would set things right within the Holy See. The recently elected pope had years of life left in him, years of supreme command to play at will with the tenets of the Catholic faith. And play with them he would! He had already proven as much, and there was no knowing where he would strike next. Night after night, Carlo Platina had lain awake, embittered and angry, thinking of ways to frustrate the pontiff's plans. Assassination had been one option. If Jean Paul 1 had deserved to die, then this one surely did. But on second thought, assassination could prove counterproductive. There would be a purge throughout the Holy See and Roman Catholics, worldwide, would become disillusioned with the church. Too much personal risk, anyway, he decided. But something had to be done. There had to be wiser options.

His plan, once conceived, took only a few hours to formulate. If he, Carlo Platina, had not the necessary authority himself, what was to stop him from using the authority of others? He had only to approach the right people in the right way and to dangle the right carrot under their noses. There were others, whom he knew of, whose feelings were just as strong as his own; men with strong ties to the Vatican state who had devoted their adult lives to the Holy See and to the furtherance of the Roman Catholic faith but who were now equally angered and disillusioned by the pontiff's actions. What was to stop him, Carlo Platina, from becoming the catalyst for their retribution?

After careful monitoring, he had singled out three of these men and had anonymously outlined his plans to each of them in turn, over the phone. Initially, their response had been cagey but when assured that their identities would be safeguarded, even from one another, just as Aiello's own identity would also remain hidden, and when told that nothing would be expected of them other than their concerted financial influence, plus their expert advice when that was called for, then they'd warily agreed to become founder members of a new clandestine society, to be known as *Il Cavalieri della Saggezza*—The Holy Order of the Knights of Wisdom. And since they weren't aware of each other's identities, then they couldn't know what else they held in common. Not only were they all P2 members but the three of them also happened to be senior officials within the Vatican Bank hierarchy who had had past dealings with *L'onorata società*, better known as the mafia. And as if that were not enough, the names of all three of them had been amongst those on bits of paper strewn over the naked body of Pope Jean Paul 1, after he was murdered in 1978 for demanding the resignations of all P2 members who had been involved in major money laundering for the mafia through the Vatican Bank. Ultimate proof, as far as Aiello was concerned, of the three's commitment to the cause. What they probably didn't realise though was that Aiello knew each of them personally because, like them, he too had been a prominent member of P2 for many years.

By decree of the Italian Grand Masonic Lodge, Propaganda Due should have been disbanded twenty odd years ago, because of its proven neofascist ideology and its involvement with the mafia and the CIA. But that hadn't happened because P2 was still very much alive and kicking, and still involved in whatever subversive activities were deemed necessary to protect the Catholic faith. And if that meant sharing certain ideals with neo-Nazism and other fascist movements, then so be it, as long as it furthered the cause of the true faith and aspirations to reintroduce a holy Roman empire.

The next stage of Aiello's plan had been to establish a chain of command outside the Vatican. For what he had in mind, there was no option. It had to be the mafia. So, contact had been made, again by public payphone either from the Vatican state or from neighbouring Trastevere, and again on a one-to-one basis. That way, anyone wishing to check up on the call would have it confirmed that it had originated from the papal state or somewhere close by. Always the same initial approach, in a fake voice and under a fake name. 'My name is Aiello and I speak on behalf of one in high authority in the Vatican.' The emphasis on *high* was intended to suggest the Holy Father himself without actually naming him. 'One who cannot be named because of his exalted position. But first you must assure me that you are alone; that no one can hear this conversation.' Then, having received such assurance, he'd continued: 'The person I speak of, and on whose behalf I now contact you, is extremely concerned by developments in certain parts of the world and the very real risk that they pose to the future of our true faith. For that reason, he has commanded me to seek out the help of a small but dependable band of eminent men; men who will be willing to use their influence, their expertise and their intellect in the furtherance of God's work and the preservation of His church. The one for whom I speak has given me six names to contact. Yours comes first on his list.'

Aiello had invariably paused for a second or two there, to give weight to his words, before continuing.

'…I do not expect you to give me your answer now. You must take time to consider the extent of your own commitment to God and to His church. My representative will contact you in the days ahead and your decision will then be relayed back to the one whom I serve. You will, of course, receive substantial compensation for your services.'

His next call to that person, a day or two later, had been in his natural voice: 'I speak on behalf of Aiello and an even higher authority. They wish to have your reply to a certain request that was made to you.'

And on receiving confirmation, Carlo Platina, alias Aiello, had then lowered his voice to a secretive tone: 'The blessing of God be on you, as an honoured member of Il Cavalieri della Saggezza. From now on, I shall be the only contact between Aiello and yourself. When I call, I shall refer to "the wisdom of Solomon". That password will confirm to you my identity. If it is safe for you to talk, then you will tell me so. If not… if there are others present with you… then you will use the name of Our Lady and I shall know to call you back in one hour, by which time you will make sure that whoever is with you will have departed and that you will be free to talk.'

Maurizio Bonnano, Cosa Nostra boss-of-bosses in Palermo, had received one such call, offering him the position of *capo dei capi* of the new Cupola in Rome. The offer had bolstered Maurizio's ego no end and he had jumped at the chance, even cheerfully accepting the condition: *'But it will be Aiello who will choose your consigliere, your adviser and second-in-command.'*

At the time, it had seemed but a very small price to pay.

The position of second-in-command had then been offered to Salvatore Provenzano from Napoli. Unlike Maurizio, the Camorra mafioso had been reluctant to accept, because he could see unavoidable tensions arising. 'Camorra and Cosa Nostra will not mix,' he said. 'They are like the oil of the olive and sea water.'

At which, Aiello had had to throw a vague threat at him, 'Are you saying that the Camorra do not wish to work for the true faith, Salvatore? You realise that certain people will be disappointed by your decision, none more so than the Knights of Malta.' At which the Neapolitan mobster had quickly reconsidered his position. The Knights of Malta, he knew, were not to be reckoned with.

A third call had brought in the 'Ndrangheta from Calabria in the deep south. Cosa Nostra, Aiello knew, were not only good at running things but they also had important connections... influence... within the Italian government. The Camorra, on the other hand, had to be brought in simply because they already had a firm base in northern Albania. And finally, the 'Ndrangheta were there, not so much for their expertise in heroin trafficking as for their proverbial lack of respect for human life. In that respect, the Cosa Nostra of Sicily and the Camorra of Naples were mere children at play, compared to the 'Ndrangheta of Calabria,

Carlo Platina, alias Aiello, had every reason to feel pleased with himself. He had created a tinderbox that was just waiting to burst into flames.

'When the time comes, Galileo will be there to set it off.' He smiled thinly. 'And then I'll be able to give my whole attention to the Languedoc and the problems there.'

Aiello's newfound power had already gone to his head.

Countdown in ALBANIA

On the twenty-eighth of June, Gus was sitting at his desk, doing the weekly wage packets, when Luca and Tommaso, his acquaintances from Rome, walked into the office.

'Maurizio sent us,' explained Luca. 'You will need help.'

Without really knowing why, Gus felt inwardly relieved at seeing the two familiar faces. Luca's words bothered him though. 'Help? Help to do what?'

But the Sicilian ignored the question. 'Tomorrow we go to the quarry.'

Only then did Gus suspect where the arms were really being hidden and he felt a sudden rush of adrenaline coursing his veins. What he wasn't yet aware of, though, was that the arrival of the two mafiosi from Rome had stirred a hornet's nest of suspicion and concern within the local mafia, most of whom Gus had yet to meet.

*

At one o'clock the following day, Luca and Tommaso called for him at the factory. Their car, a large Mercedes, had an Albanian driver and another Albanian as front passenger.

Not a word was said by any of them during the twenty-minute journey; probably, thought Gus, because they wouldn't have understood one another anyway. As far as he knew, the Albanians had no knowledge of Italian and it was even less likely that Luca and his partner spoke Tosk. *Maybe they'd like me to interpret,* he thought with a wry smile. But judging by their stern faces he very much doubted that his offer would be appreciated.

The quarry could be approached by road and by rail, but Gus soon found that the only way of actually getting into the workings that he'd seen from the air that day when he'd first arrived in Kukes, was via the tunnel that accommodated the railway line. Now, as the car came to a halt, he noticed that the tunnel entrance could be sealed off, if need be, with a set of solid steel doors. Security was obviously a high priority here.

Their taxi now drove off and the three of them were led, on foot, into the tunnel. They had no option but to walk single file, with one armed Albanian at the front and another bringing up the rear, an arrangement that made Luca and Tommaso extremely edgy. The single formation was made necessary by the fact that the rail-track within the well-lit tunnel held a fleet of high-sided trucks laden with rocks, ready to be transported somewhere or other. Gus instinctively counted them as he went by. The eighteenth proved to be the last. Then, they were out in sunlight once again, with the quarry workings opening out around them.

He now took careful stock of his surroundings. He was standing in a place that resembled a bowl or a grand arena carved into the mountainside. Roughly oval in shape, its quarried walls rose to heights of between a hundred and two hundred feet, sheer except for one side—the left as he looked at it. Here, the rock had been worked into galleries resembling giant stairs, each gallery about thirty feet high. At the base of the bottom gallery stood a great pile of loose rocks, some idle machinery and a single truck on an otherwise empty railway siding.

Directly ahead, the rail-track continued its way across the quarry floor, to be swallowed up by a second tunnel, roughly three hundred yards away, where another pair of heavy steel doors, identical to the ones he'd already seen, hung open. Above this entrance, a large extractor fan was languidly rotating.

Despite the fact that they were now out in the open, they still maintained single file order. Gus noticed Luca's shoes as the Sicilian walked in silence ahead of him. They were coated with quarry dust and instinctively he looked at his own black trainers and the damp clay that was clinging to the rims of their soles. His flesh tingled as he recalled the state of his father's shoes, all those years ago.

The Albanian was leading them towards the second tunnel entrance and, as they approached, Gus again sensed Luca's growing concern. Maurizio's bodyguard didn't trust the Camorra any more than the Camorra trusted him.

This entrance quickly opened out into a sizeable but poorly lit cavern, where two more Albanians, toting semi-automatic weapons, stood guard. A procession of rock- filled trucks, similar to the ones they'd already seen, crossed the cavern floor into yet another tunnel about twenty metres away. Gus again made a mental note of the number.

This second tunnel ran for roughly ten metres before opening out into a second cavern, one that was much larger than the first. Here, the convoy of trucks came to an end. He had counted another twenty-two.

The place was a hive of activity. Four empty trucks stood there, tailgates down, waiting to be loaded. Forklifts whizzed around like demented hornets, transporting crates and steel drums from a stack at the far end of the cavern to where the men were waiting to handle them. As far as Gus could tell, the workers were all Albanian, the armed guards Italian.

He knew what he was looking at. Two of the trucks were being loaded with a variety of missiles—anti-tank… air-to-air… Exocets—another with rocket launchers and the fourth with drums of what could be deadly gases or chemicals. Conventional and unconventional WMDs. All of it illegal. All of it capable of causing unimaginable human destruction.

He ought to feel elated… this was, after all, what he'd been sent here to find… but he felt somewhat puzzled by the actual size of the haul. A mere four truckloads hardly matched what MI6 had been fearing.

Suddenly, he became aware of the presence of others. Four mafiosi, heavily armed and unmistakably Italian, had appeared out of the shadows to greet Luca and Tommaso. But the meeting was tense. Gus could tell that there was too much mistrust, too much restrained animosity for it to be cordial. A fifth man, when he arrived, made no show of welcoming them. He casually waved towards the trucks now being loaded.

'As you see, the work is almost finished.'

There was a sneer and an arrogance in the way he spoke.

'…You can now return to Roma and report to the Cupola. Tell them that all preparations for La Crociata Finale are now complete! Tell Maurizio Bonnano and the Cupola in Rome…'

Even though the man's face was partly in shadow, Gus saw his lips curl with undisguised contempt.

'…That I, Lucio Cimino, *capo dei capi* here in Kukes, have personally organised everything.'

The reference to La Crociata Finale had already pricked Gus' ears – it was a term that Father Galileo had let slip recently – but, to have it confirmed that the man now swaggering before them was none other than the murderer of his parents, dispelled all other thoughts. Instinctively he took half a step forward, causing the Camorra guards to look sharply in his direction; one of them even to raise his gun threateningly. But Luca seemed unperturbed by the sudden activity. He had news for Lucio Cimino, news that immediately took all interest away from Gus.

'Why not tell Maurizio yourself, Lucio? In fact, you can tell the whole Cupola brotherhood because tomorrow they will all be here with you.'

Luca would never be the brightest spark in any firework but his words couldn't have been better chosen or better timed. Cimino's jaw fell.

'Here? You say that Maurizio Bonnano and the Cupola intend coming here? Tomorrow?'

Luca, obviously glad to have ruffled Lucio's feathers, merely shrugged as if to suggest, "So what"?

'Why? Have they no faith in Lucio Cimino who is boss-of-bosses here in Kukes?'

'They will arrive tomorrow. Maurizio and Salvatore Provenzano and other members of the Cupola wish to oversee the launch of La Crociata Finale.'

That term again! Gus thought. What is this Final Crusade that they are talking about? A crusade that even Father Galileo and the Vatican seem to be involved with.

'Bah!' was Cimino's only reply before strutting away in a fit of temper, on the pretence of having to oversee the rest of the loading process.

Gus scowled at his back. That man, he told himself, put a gun to my mother's head. That man killed both my parents! If not him, personally, then one of his cronies, on his orders. Again, he was surprised to realise that he was indeed contemplating revenge; that he was actually prepared to kill this arrogant Neapolitan who had made him an orphan all those years ago. *'Patience!'* he told himself, remembering his promise to Father Galileo. *'Patience! Your time will come!'*

Because of his agitated state of mind, he almost missed what was happening right under his nose, where the loading process had come to an end and the heavy tailgates were now being lifted into place with the use of an overhead pulley system. Tower scaffolding was being rolled into place each side of the first truck and men were already climbing it. Everything so disciplined, so well-organised.

'Move!'

It was an order, not a request.

Gus and the rest of the group turned to see six men coming towards them, carrying what appeared to be a large sheet of heavy metal, but as he made way for them to pass, he recognised it as one of the shallow so-called paddling pools from Kukes Plastics, the ones that he'd seen being taken away by train on that misty morning a fortnight ago.

Intrigued, he watched it being hooked onto the overhead pulley and winched up for those perched on the tower scaffolding to manoeuvre into place. It fitted like a glove over the top of the loaded truck.

Next came the plastic rocks! Netfuls of them being released into the tray.

'What's he doing?' Gus asked, pointing towards one of the workers who was busy spraying the lumps of plastic with a thin film of clear liquid as they settled in the tray.

'Glue! We do not want them blowing off during the journey.'

Then, when the pile of sticky "rocks" was deemed high enough, grey quarry dust was scattered freely over it all, so that the truckload of "rocks" really looked authentic. Everything so methodical, so disciplined.

That was when the full impact of it all struck Gus. Good God! he thought excitedly as he stared at the four trucks. It's not just these four! Every truck I've seen since we arrived here must also be packed with weapons.

He now recalled how many there were. Eighteen in the first tunnel plus twenty-two in the second and then these four! Forty-four truckloads in all! Enough to supply an army with the deadliest of weapons.

Bingo, Gus! You've found what MI6 have been searching for.

The blare of a klaxon horn echoing through the underground chamber startled him out of his reverie. It was evidently a signal because all the workers immediately downed-tools and made for the exit, leaving just Luca, Tommaso and himself to watch them go. Cimino and his guards had also disappeared.

'Come! We will see what is happening.' And Luca led the way.

Once out into the open again, Gus was surprised to see quarrying already in full swing. Men were climbing ladders to get to the top gallery, machinery was coming to life. Soon, the noise of drilling equipment and rocks falling could be heard, and clouds of dust were forming. A hydraulic shovel was filling its scoop with rocks and preparing to disgorge them into a railway truck in the siding.

Luca and Tommaso looked just as baffled as Gus.

Before long, a Camorra mafioso came to usher them back inside the tunnel.

'We must not be seen,' he said, without bothering to explain from where or by whom. But when he saw Gus' reluctance to move, and the question in his eyes, he pointed towards the blue sky above them and then at his watch.

'American spy satellite!' he muttered. 'It will soon be passing overhead, taking photographs.'

Gus understood. The site had to be seen as a working unit. Quarrying had to be in progress and that meant men drilling, machines working, dust rising. He also knew that American technology could enhance satellite photographs a thousandfold if need be and that the CIA might become curious at the presence of a group dressed in civilian clothing rather than overalls. He also realised why the car that had brought them here hadn't parked at the quarry entrance, but had been driven away, to return at a later time. Caught on satellite photographs, a black Mercedes would surely attract unwanted CIA attention.

Twenty minutes later, the klaxon again sounded and the Albanians returned to finish the job underground. By that time, Gus was particularly anxious to leave. He had to think of a way of warning Tom Mackay about the arms shipment. But before that, he needed to find out what its destination was going to be. And he also needed to know what the Final Crusade was all about. Maurizio's arrival tomorrow might provide some answers.

'Come! We go!' Luca made for the exit. Tommaso and Gus followed him. Lucio Cimino didn't even bother to watch them leave.

*

Gus Adams wasn't to know it, but Maurizio Bonnano had already arrived in Kukes. He had actually travelled with Luca and Tommaso two days earlier, on an unscheduled flight from Rome. Suspicious of Lucio Cimino, and fearing a Camorra double-cross, he had arranged for his private Cessna to land at a small airstrip a few miles outside of town. There, thanks to combined mafia and Vatican influence, the usual checks for drugs and weapons had been waived. Aiello had also arranged for Father Galileo to have a car waiting for them. Maurizio was to be the priest's guest, whereas arrangements had been made for Luca and Tommaso to stay at a nearby hotel. The plane had then returned to Rome to pick up the other three Cosa Nostra members of the Cupola the following morning. And as extra precaution, Maurizio had recruited an extra five men—three from Tirana and two from Durres. They, too, were expected to arrive the following morning. All of it proof that Maurizio Bonnano had become a very wary, very edgy boss-of-bosses.

Salvatore Provenzano, on the other hand, felt little need for caution. Being Camorra, and second-in-command of the Cupola, he expected to be royally welcomed by his fellow Neapolitan Lucio Cimino, as would be his three Camorra henchmen, whilst the 'Ndrangheta members of the Cupola would have preferred not to have made the trip at all. For them, time was money and they would rather have returned directly from Rome to Calabria to oversee the delivery of a large consignment of heroin that was soon to arrive from Morocco. But Aiello would not hear of it. He wanted all members of the Cupola to be present in Kukes to oversee the launch of the Final Crusade. In a phone call from a Vatican public kiosk, Maurizio had been told personally by Aiello, 'The Holy See is much indebted to you, Maurizio Bonnano, *capo dei capi*, and to Salvatore Provenzano, your *consigliere*, not to mention all other members of La Nuova Alba. Your commitment to our holy cause assures you eternal salvation.'

Carlo Platina, alias Aiello, hardly expected his tongue-in-cheek promise of divine compensation to impress the mafiosi. He knew what they – Cosa Nostra, Camorra and 'Ndrangheta alike – were interested in. It was their share of the thirty million euros that they'd been promised for their collaboration in setting up the Final Crusade, not to mention the huge sums that the Iraqis and the Arabs were reportedly prepared to pay them for the weapons. And there was also the pledge of full cooperation from the Vatican Bank for future money laundering; an arrangement that had been denied the Mob ever since the P2-Roberto Calvi debacle of 1982. Having their funds deposited in the Vatican Bank, or in its Swiss counterpart, meant that Italian courts could never again demand access to the mafia's assets.

'…I, too, have a boss-of-bosses, Maurizio,' Aiello had gone on to explain. 'And it is his wish that all members of the Cupola be present in Kukes on such an auspicious occasion, for the launch of the Final Crusade. There, we shall celebrate together and you will all be generously rewarded for your efforts.'

Maurizio Bonnano wasn't to know that Aiello had had other designs all along.

La Crociata Finale

The morning of the first of the month passed without any fresh development, leaving Gus feeling inwardly frustrated. On the one hand, he wanted no part of what was going on in the quarry; on the other, he was desperate to fill in some gaps before trying to contact Tom Mackay in London.

MI6 would want to know where the shipment was destined for and, more importantly, to what purpose. He also needed to establish exactly what The Final Crusade was all about. Could it be that the Vatican – if, indeed, it was involved – was actually harking back to Medieval times, to the troubled years of earlier crusades? Was this so-called La Crociata Finale a last-gasp attempt by the Roman Catholic church to reclaim Jerusalem from the Muslims? And not just from the Muslims of course, but also from the Israelis? If so, then it was a frightening prospect.

'A harebrained plot if ever I saw one,' he muttered. Hadn't one pope, not so long ago, publicly apologised for the Catholic church's past atrocities? There was no way that the Holy See would willingly go down the same road again. So, what was the thinking behind this Final Crusade? Could it be that MI6 intelligence was flawed and that the Vatican wasn't involved after all? Wasn't it far more likely that all this was just an ambitious mafia project? But if so, then where did the priest fit into the scheme of things?

So many questions needing answers.

It was getting on for five o'clock and he was preparing to leave the factory for the day, convinced that he had been sidelined and that the Final Crusade would be launched without him, when Maurizio Bonnano, dressed in a black suit, black shirt, white tie, walked into the tiny office unannounced, accompanied by Father Galileo, and followed by Luca and Tommaso who were making no effort to conceal their Uzi SMGs.

Draped over his arm, the priest carried a pair of dark trousers and a light-blue shirt and he now urged Gus to take them.

'Wear them, my son! You need to dress formally for the auspicious occasion that awaits us.'

'Father Galileo tells me that you have done well, Guiseppe,' said Maurizio. 'Today will be a big day for us all.' He turned to the priest and asked quietly, 'He has a gun?'

'Yes.'

'Good. Then make sure that he brings it. Come! We will wait outside, in car.'

As he watched them leave the office Gus felt the knot in his stomach tighten. Things were coming to a head he realised and family ties to Maurizio would soon count for nothing. From now on he'd have to be continually on his guard, and that meant keeping a close eye on Father Galileo. The little priest was devious and not to be trusted.

Quickly, he changed into the clothes that Galileo had brought him and found both shirt and trousers to be at least one size too big. He looked and felt uncomfortable in them but the car was waiting for him. He now retrieved the cloth bag containing the gun out of the bottom drawer of his filing cabinet.

But I'm not taking all this ammunition with me, he thought as he studied what Father Galileo had left him. Three magazines, each containing twenty rounds! Anyone would think that we were going to war. Anyway, one should be more than enough. With any luck I won't have to fire the damn thing at all.

He dropped two of the magazines back in the filing cabinet and reluctantly followed the others out.

Signs were that it was going to be a murky evening. A low drizzle-carrying cloud was creeping in from the west but a freshening wind had also been forecast for later.

The journey to the quarry was tense. Father Galileo, at the wheel of his car, was uncharacteristically reticent, while Maurizio Bonnano, sitting next to him, seemed to be lacking his usual air of composed arrogance. Gus shared the back seat with Luca and Tommaso. Their car was being followed by two others, the first of which carried the other three Cosa Nostra members of the Cupola from Rome whilst the second contained the extra mafiosi assigned from Tirana and Durres at Maurizio's demand.

When they arrived at the quarry and climbed out of Father Galileo's car, they were confronted at the first entrance by four Albanian guards, armed with Uzi SMGs, all of them loyal to Lucio Cimino. They eyed Maurizio and his entourage with a great deal of suspicion as they approached, even pointing their automatic weapons in their direction. Maurizio glowered; Luca and the others visibly stiffened and threateningly revealed their own guns, in open challenge.

Little bullies posturing, Gus thought, as he gripped the linen bag more firmly. For his own part, he was content to keep to the rear, never for a second taking his eyes off the four Albanians blocking their path. If the threat became real then he was ready to take whatever evasive action was necessary.

During his brief instruction back in London, Gus knew that the Camorra's preferred weapon was the Uzi SMG and that it could be fitted with magazines carrying up to fifty rounds, and that from a closed bolt position the gun could fire a phenomenal seventeen hundred rounds per minute. Chilling, to say the least! *If I get into an argument with these guys, then my Micro Uzi with its mere twenty rounds will be little more than child's play.*

With some authority, Father Galileo waved the guards away from the tunnel entrance and Maurizio's group entered the gloom inside, to be faced with two large and ageing diesel locomotives in tandem, both churning out asphyxiating fumes within the confined space. The priest lifted the hem of his cassock to cover his mouth and nose and quickly strode towards the little crescent of light in the distance.

Coughing, Gus and the rest followed him, passing as they did the convoy of laden trucks that had now been coupled to the engines, in readiness for their journey.

As they emerged into sunlight once more, Gus heard a little gasp from those ahead of him as they witnessed the long line of trucks stretch out across the quarry floor. Forty-four trucks, close on three hundred metres long and reaching almost as far as the second tunnel. *Such a huge shipment,* he thought, *would surely draw attention to itself, once it was on the move, despite it being so cleverly disguised.* But even so, only very close inspection would reveal the duplicity.

When he saw Lucio Cimino and Salvatore Provenzano striding towards them from the direction of the second tunnel, Gus became tense and felt intimidated. Both of them were smiling ingenuously at the overdressed Maurizio. Father Galileo, he noticed, had fallen back, to watch the meeting with interest.

'Quite a sight, Father!' Gus indicated the convoy of trucks, whilst at the same time keeping himself out of Provenzano's line of vision. The Neapolitan knew who Gus was and that he was here not only to work for the Cupola but also to seek out his father's assassin. But did he suspect who Gus' target might be? Probably not, or he would have warned Cimino before now.

'Impressive indeed, my son!'

'Tell me, Father! I know about the Final Crusade... I have heard you yourself mentioning it... but no one has ever explained it to me. Is the true church going to claim back the Holy City?' Again, he was intentionally trying to sound naïve and ill-informed.

Father Galileo, smiling broadly, turned to look at him. 'Something like that, my son. Something like that.'

'But the church has no army, Father! Who will take up these weapons in the fight against Islam?'

The priest continued to smile for a second or two but then a more calculating look clouded his face. He motioned towards Maurizio's meeting with Cimino and Salvatore Provenzano. 'I will tell you what even the members of the Cupola do not know as yet, Guiseppe.' Then in little more than a whisper, he explained: 'The contents of these trucks will not be used against Islam, but rather by Islam.'

'Pardon?' Gus was sure that he'd misheard.

'This shipment is headed for the Adriatic. There it will be loaded onto La Crociata Finale.' He paused. 'But I am not at liberty to tell you its destination.'

'I don't understand.'

Father Galileo smiled benignly. 'What don't you understand? La Crociata Finale is also the name of the ship.'

'It's not that, Father. You say that these arms are going to end up in the hands of Islamic soldiers? Militants? To fight what enemy?'

The priest's smile now became Machiavellian. 'Did you not know, Guiseppe, that the Israelis are planning a surprise attack against Islam? Syria, Jordan, and Iran will be simultaneously bombed with nuclear and chemical weapons.'

Gus stared, aghast. Eventually, he found words: 'You're not serious?'

'Maybe not, but the Arabs will believe it.'

'And the Vatican is taking sides?'

'You could say that. Yes, I suppose you could say that! Which is why certain factions of Islam have been warned about Israeli intentions.'

'Good God! It will be another world war.'

'That is where you are mistaken.'

'But if Israel uses nuclear weapons!'

'Calculated strikes, at best. And the rest of the world will consider them justified.'

Gus laughed disbelievingly. 'Justified? Whatever the West does, Father, you don't imagine that China or North Korea, or Russia either, will give their blessing on Israeli unprovoked attacks?'

'Ah! But they will be provoked when Islam decides to get its strike in first.'

'Pre-emptive strike?'

'Imagine Israel being bombarded without warning from all quarters. How would they react, do you think, Guiseppe? In the war with Saddam, Israel was persuaded by the Americans not to retaliate against the occasional scud missile but there's no way they will hold back when chemical weapons...' He nodded towards the contents of the trucks. '...Start raining down on them. You are too young to remember the Bhopal tragedy in India?'

Gus nodded. What he was hearing was bizarre to say the least.

'...In 1984, a cloud of lethal gases – hydrogen cyanide, monomethylamine... stuff like that – escaped from a factory in Bhopal. By morning, thousands of men, women and children were lying dead on the streets and in their beds.' Galileo's eyes lit up. 'Just think of the mischief that one missile-load of the stuff would do in Jerusalem!'

Mischief? Gus thought. Bloody hell!

'...And sarin is even deadlier! Remember that attack in a Tokyo subway? Sarin is one of the most effective chemical warfare agents around.

Saddam Hussein would tell you that if he were still with us. It's so toxic that it disrupts the nervous system, over-stimulating the body's muscles and vital organs.'

The subject obviously appealed to the bogus priest.

'...But the beauty of sarin is this—you don't even have to inhale it. You only have to touch it and it's absorbed into your skin. After that, it's only a matter of time before it paralyses the muscles around your lungs, and you suffocate. You're dead in a matter of minutes!'

'Charming!' Gus muttered. *This guy's a nutter!*

'Sarin is five hundred times more toxic than cyanide even.'

'But if Jerusalem is gassed, many Christians will also die. What has the Vatican to gain, Father?'

The priest's face was anything but serene and holy now. 'You have heard of the Albigensian Crusade? The first crusade to have been fought outside the Holy Land?' He didn't wait for Gus to respond. 'Many years ago, the Languedoc of southern France was blighted by the heretic faith of the Cathars. Pope Innocent III – to my mind, the greatest of all Vicars of Christ – ordered his papal legate Arnaud Amaury to rid the land of all the heretics. Now, when the Crusaders reached Béziers, a town of twenty thousand inhabitants in the Languedoc, Amaury was asked by one of his men how they were supposed to distinguish between the heretic Cathars and believers of the true faith. Do you know what the legate's reply was, Guiseppe?'

'I suspect that you're about to tell me, Father.' He was now convinced that Galileo was nothing but a fraud; a heartless hoodlum impersonating a priest.

'Amaury didn't hesitate in giving his order: *"Kill them all! God will know his own."*'

Gus strove to hide his revulsion. 'And you think that that is what will happen in The Final Crusade? The killing of Christians in Jerusalem – and there are many there, I understand – will be justified by the deaths of Moslems and Jews.'

'Of course! Setting Moslems and Jews at each other's throats can only benefit the Roman Catholic church, the true faith. Don't you agree, Guiseppe?'

Gus realised that his reactions were being closely monitored. 'Yes, I think I understand now what the Final Crusade is all about. Correct me if I am wrong, Father, but as I understand it, Moslems have been conned into thinking that Israel is about to mount a nuclear attack on them. Not too difficult to do, I imagine, given the deep suspicion that has always existed between them. So, Islam must arm itself, ready to retaliate with whatever weapons are available. Israel, in turn, will become aware of the growing threat on all its borders and there'll be a bloodbath. In the meantime, the Roman Catholic church will be standing on the sidelines, watching its two old enemies eliminating one another.'

Galileo smiled. 'You are more astute than I thought you were, Guiseppe. It is a good plan?'

'Maybe. But what if it results in just a standoff, Father? What if neither side is prepared to strike the first blow and it all ends in stalemate?'

Galileo again smiled knowingly. 'Ah! Do not underestimate Aiello's cunning, my son. It will be easy to fool Islam into striking the first blow with the weapons that we are sending them.' He again indicated the laden trucks. 'Imagine what one scud missile, with a payload of sarin gas maybe, can do to the Holy City. Metaphorically speaking, the West will be up in arms. Don't you think?'

Metaphorically and literally, Gus thought. 'And Russia and the Orient will have to respect Israel's right to strike back, paying kind with kind.'

'Exactly, Guiseppe! And while West and East are sidelined, the Star of David and the Red Crescent of Islam will shoot each other out of the sky. Clever, don't you think? There have been several Crusades over the years but this will be the last. What do you say?'

'Very clever. And who is this Aiello, this architect of such great slaughter?'

'He remains faceless to us all, but he will be remembered forever as the saviour of the true faith.'

By now, Gus needed no convincing that he was dealing with fanatics of Hitlerian proportions, who were apparently operating out of the Vatican and cleverly manipulating the mafia for their own ends. What would Maurizio and the rest of them say, he wondered, if they knew the true scenario of the Final Crusade? Come to think of it, probably not a lot! Not if there were huge financial rewards to be won.

The sooner I get word to Tom Mackay in London, the better.

Suddenly, there was shouting and cheering. Maurizio Bonnano, boss-of-bosses in Rome, and Lucio Cimino, *capo dei capi* here in Kukes, had begun walking back towards them and towards the first tunnel, each of them carrying a magnum of champagne. They were being followed in procession by Salvatore Provenzano and the Calabrian Bernardo Pellegrini, also nursing their bottles of fizz. As they passed, Gus stood aside to watch Father Galileo join the leaders and be handed his own magnum. A host of gun-toting rank and file mafiosi – Cosa Nostra, Camorra, 'Ndrangheta and Albanians of all factions – then filed by. Gus counted thirty-five in all. Finally, he took his place, again at the very rear.

By the time everyone had emerged out of the first tunnel and were facing the front locomotive, a heavy drizzle had begun to fall and was threatening to put a damper on the celebrations. Maurizio spoke first, to underline his supreme authority over all others present.

'My brothers! As *capo dei capi* of the Cupola I salute you all. For the past two years it has been good for Cosa Nostra, Camorra and 'Ndrangheta to work hand in hand, in the name of the true faith. Today sees the harvest of all our efforts...' Bombastically, he pointed towards the laden train. 'Aiello wishes me to express his great disappointment at not being here today on such an auspicious occasion, but he has asked me to thank each and every one of you personally for your efforts on behalf of this most holy cause. He is particularly indebted, as Father Galileo will confirm...'

Gus saw the priest nodding sagely.

'...Not only to myself as boss-of-bosses and Salvatore Provenzano, my *consigliere*, but also to Bernardo Pellegrini and his 'Ndrangheta brothers and, of course, to Lucio Cimino, *capo dei capi* here in Kukes.'

As he named each individual, Maurizio stepped forward to lay a hand on his shoulder, as a signal for him to be applauded, and the rank and file duly obliged.

What with Father Galileo's words still ringing in his ears and the warm drizzle turning cold on his skin, Gus began to feel distinctly uncomfortable. Salvatore was now speaking, praising the efforts of his Camorra mob. When he finished, the balding Bernardo Pellegrini was offered the chance to speak but he declined and Gus felt tempted to applaud 'Ndrangheta common sense. Then came Cimino's turn and, to a lot of noisy cheering from the

Albanians, simply because he was able to address them in their own tongue, he paid tribute to what had been achieved by himself and his Kukes mafiosi. Finally, Father Galileo stepped forward. First in Italian and then Tosk, he commended all those present on the success of their mission. He was expressing not only his own gratitude and that of Aiello but also the appreciation of an even greater authority within the Vatican.

It was, Gus realised, a cleverly veiled reference to the Holy Father himself. *Crafty bugger!* he thought, realising the extent of the priest's duplicity. *He's bloody cleverer than I've given him credit for. He's no more of a priest than Stalin was. Whatever the game will be from now on, he's the one I most need to keep an eye on.*

To end the ceremony, Father Galileo beckoned the other four to pose for a group photograph.

'Smile!' he shouted, but none of them did. Maurizio and his associates obviously considered it more befitting to appear stern and imperious. Under different circumstances, Gus would have laughed at such a display of arrogant superiority.

The session ended with the bogus priest chanting a brief prayer in Latin, none of it authentic in Gus' cynical opinion. Then, dead on the stroke of six o'clock, at Maurizio's signal and with the cassocked Galileo again taking photographs, all five of them raised their magnums of champagne and, to huge applause, smashed them against the front of the locomotive, leaving trails of white fizz on the specially polished green metal. Ironic, and a source of amusement to all, was the fact that Maurizio needed a second attempt before his own bottle broke.

With deafening toots, the two locomotives took the strain of their heavy load and, as the wheels began to turn, the crowd stepped aside to cheer the momentous departure, and continued to do so as truck after truck rolled slowly by. There was laughing and euphoria, with many of the Albanians firing salvos into the air. And even after the cheering died away, they all stood there to watch until the very last truck had receded into the distance.

It was Father Galileo who finally broke the silence. 'And now to celebrate!' he shouted. 'Aiello has arranged a great feast for us all. Come, we have a lot to talk about. There are honours to be bestowed and rewards to be handed out. Come, my friends! You, also!' he called to the four guards who had again taken their positions at the tunnel entrance 'What need is there for guards at the cage door when the bird has already flown?' To which everybody laughed and followed Maurizio and the others back into the quarry.

Gus again held back. He felt a nasty foreboding and wished that he could be anywhere but here. Had he the transport, he would leave now. The thought struck him that he could walk – run, even – the distance back to town.

'Come, Guiseppe! Why do you linger, my friend?'

Father Galileo was waiting for him to join them. Everybody else had disappeared into the tunnel once more.

'I see no point in coming to the celebration, Father. After all, I haven't made any contribution to the Crusade, so I think I will return to town.'

The threat in the priest's eye appeared for only a fraction of a second but Gus noticed it, just the same.

'Nonsense, my son! Even as we speak, a great feast is being prepared for us. And we will drink to the success of La Crociata Finale. Aiello expects it. You are Cosa Nostra, so your cousin Maurizio also expects you to be there. As I, your friend, wish you to be part of our great celebration. So, you must come.'

Gus' sense of foreboding grew. There was too much urgency in Galileo's tone. 'I think not, Father! My place is not here.'

'You will come!' It was nothing less than a command, now. The pretence had gone. 'Have I not told you everything?'

By implication, what he was saying was that Gus could not now be trusted to leave. There had been a purpose to volunteering all the information about the Final Crusade.

'...Anyway, there are other things you must hear. Things you must do.'

Such as confronting my parents' killer, Gus thought. But this is hardly the time or the place.

'Come, Guiseppe! We will walk together and I will tell you everything you need to know.'

The promise was obviously meant as an extra incentive to obey.

Nothing else for it, Gus decided. I'll just have to watch my back, that's all.

The alarm bells were ringing, though.

'Would you know why Maurizio sent me here, Father?' It was a question that had bugged him from the very start.

'... You told him that I had done well here. In fact, I've done little more than the work of a wages clerk. Anyone could have done what I have been doing.'

They were into the tunnel, now.

'At the factory, you mean. Ah! But not everyone is Cosa Nostra, Guiseppe! Maurizio needed you here to look after Cosa Nostra interests. Lucio Cimino may be boss-of-bosses here in the quarry but the factory still belongs to the Cosa Nostra, as it did in your father's day.'

So, Maurizio wanted to keep a foothold in Kukes. No big deal!

'Tell me! Does Cimino know that I am the son of Giovanni Maratta?'

'No. There is no one in Kukes except me who knows that.'

Gus felt a little better then. If Cimino didn't know his identity, then the threat wasn't there to the same extent.

'The train, Father! What is to say that it won't be stopped and searched along the way? What is to say that the consignment won't be stolen? And if it reaches port, wherever that may be...' He tried to sound casual; tried not to show that he was fishing for information. '...Then how can it be transferred onto the ship without being seen by the port authorities?'

He saw the priest's teeth flash in a smile.

'You must understand, Guiseppe, that the consignment, as you call it, is the responsibility of the mafia. No one will dare question the Mob's authority, from here to the docks or from the docks to Batumi.' He stopped, giving the impression that he'd said more than he intended. 'Ah! You have extracted the secret from me, my son. Now you know La Crociata Finale's destination. But you must promise not to tell the others.'

Who the hell are you kidding, Father? Subconsciously, Gus knew why the priest was volunteering the information. He didn't expect him to be alive to tell the tale. In which case, something was going to happen very soon. The realisation sent the blood coursing through his veins and a shiver crept over his cold wet skin. *They intend to kill me here, in the quarry!*

Had he not known that Galileo was carrying a gun under his cassock, Gus would have turned and ran. As it was, he had to fight back his panic. *Batumi?* he thought, desperately trying to engage his mind on other things. *Where the hell is that? I should know!* Slowly, it came to him. *Port on the*

Black Sea! Far end. What country? Georgia? Turkey? One of the two! What then, though? A hell of a long way over land from there to Syria, or wherever the consignment was bound for. Moslem lands though! Yes, they've got everything worked out!

The open-air quarry was more deserted than Gus had seen it. The track was empty, every machine was idle and the crowd ahead of them had already been swallowed up by the second tunnel entrance. He and Father Galileo were alone, dwarfed by the intimidating quarry walls. If he wanted to, he could easily surprise the priest, now, and disarm him. But what then? Where would he run? What hope would he have of leaving Kukes, leave alone Albania, alive? Whatever the game was, it had to be played, and that meant joining the others in the awaiting rock chamber.

'The secret has been well kept, Father. I suppose the quarry workers were sworn to silence?'

'Quarry workers?' Galileo laughed out loud. 'My boy, the quarry hasn't been worked for the best part of twenty years. Not even in your father's day. It is just a front.'

'But...'

'Ah! Cimino's men go through the motions every so often, of course.' He pointed to the idle machinery and then briefly upwards to suggest an invisible American spy satellite. 'And now and then they blast the rock to create noise and dust, but otherwise...' He obviously felt no need to finish the sentence.

'But what was it used for before the start of the Final Crusade?'

'Mafia ammunition store, pure and simple!' Seeing the incredulity in Gus' eyes, he went on. 'You must understand that the Balkans have been a melting pot for hundreds of years. Things may be quieter here now than they were a few years ago but conflict is never far away, believe me.'

'What you're saying is that gunrunning is always profitable here.'

The priest smiled. 'You could say that.' He was now euphoric and in the mood to talk.

'So, the quarry is just a convenient depot, then?'

'That's right. Very convenient, in fact, being so close to the Kosovo border. Consignments of arms are brought here to be stored until certain orders can be met.'

'Orders from whom?' Despite his nagging fears about his own immediate future, Gus still wanted explanations about this place. After all, his own father had been in charge here once.

'Guerrillas... insurgents... armies even. Take your pick. As long as they have money to pay for them.'

'And enough to pay well over the odds.'

'Of course! Someone has to acknowledge the risks involved. The mafia isn't a charity, is it Guiseppe?' He laughed briefly and without humour.

'But from where does the mafia get them. Are they all made in the factory in Kukes?'

He knew how naïve the suggestion was and the priest duly laughed. 'The factory? Only a few reconditioned Uzis from there, as you know yourself.' He indicated the linen bag in Gus' hand, as much as to suggest "The sort of gun that you've got in there". 'The factory supplies just a fraction of what has been coming to the quarry over the years. Most customers expect more than just peashooters.'

Peashooters? My God! Gus thought. 'So, if not from the factory, then from where?'

Father Galileo shrugged, as if to say, "Your guess is as good as mine". 'You'd be surprised at how easy it is to get stuff on the black market, as long as you're prepared to pay. Rogue dealers – British, French, American, Russian, Chinese – will readily supply you with whatever you need. Even helicopter gunships or fighter aircraft if you have the capital!'

'But not chemical weapons, surely? You mentioned sarin gas.'

'Why not, if you know where to look? And if not through the usual channels, then it can always be stolen or manufactured.' He grinned mischievously. 'There are some highly sophisticated thieves around.'

'Wow!' Gus again wanted to sound naïve. 'They've been very clever to keep this place hidden for so long. You'd have expected the CIA or British intelligence to know about it by now.'

'Oh, they know about the factory, all right! No doubt about that. But since the level of production has been relatively low over the past few years, then they've not been too concerned, have they? But, having said that, a few more of them have been snooping around during the past few months. Israelis, some of them. And they're more of a threat, of course.'

'In what way?'

'More dogged aren't they? There have been British and CIA agents snooping around here for years, off and on, but Mossad agents are like bloody terriers. They won't let go unless you make them.'

'And how do you do that?'

The priest's face hardened. 'By eliminating them, of course.'

'Killing them, you mean?'

'How else? Any agents found noseying around the quarry were… How shall I say? Removed.'

They'd almost reached the second tunnel by now. 'How many have there been, then?'

'Let's see!' Galileo took two or three seconds to recall. 'Over the past eighteen months, four in all. Two British, two Israeli. The Americans are no longer showing an interest. Apart from up there, of course.' And he again pointed towards the sky.

Gus took a deep breath. If he hadn't fully realised it before, he certainly did now. The people he was dealing with were nothing but cold-blooded killers. As he raised his face, as if for the last time, to receive the caress of drizzle on his skin, he was aware of but three sounds: the priest's heavy breathing, the rhythmic crunching of clayey gravel beneath their feet and the steady hum of the ventilating fan above the tunnel entrance. *Dust extractor?* he wondered. *Air conditioning maybe? Probably used for both!* With a sense of foreboding, he kept step with the priest as they left the daylight behind them.

Two Albanian guards stood just inside the first chamber and Gus couldn't help but wonder why they were there. Surely not to keep anybody out, because the quarry had already delivered its secret. Therefore, they had to be there to prevent anyone leaving. His awareness was again on a knife edge. Every movement, every word spoken from now on had to be regarded as a threat, whether it was or not.

The smaller cavern, again today, echoed the drone of the generator.

If that fails, then the lights go out!

Instinctively, Gus searched the semi-darkness for the cable that supplied the power and saw it looping its way along the rock wall, running from one lit bulb to another on its way into the tunnel that led to the larger chamber. Gus took careful stock of what he was seeing. Apart from the two guards and the generator, the first cavern was now completely empty. If he had to find his way through here in the dark, then the only other hindrance would be the rail-track. He'd have to be very careful not to trip on that.

The priest paused to say something to the two Albanian guards. His instruction, whatever it was, was brief because he re-joined Gus almost immediately.

Eventually, they reached the main chamber. With the trucks gone, Gus was able to appreciate its cavernous expanse, empty now apart from a pile of used crates and a row of trestle tables that were being hurriedly assembled and set together end-to-end. Wine bottles, blinking under the artificial lights, were being passed around in plenty, with Father Galileo urging everyone to relax and to enjoy themselves.

'Drink, my friends! You have earned it,' he kept shouting. 'And soon we shall partake of the feast that Aiello in the Vatican has ordered for us in the name of the Holy Father. So come and join me at the table, my children, and let us eat, drink and be merry.' At which point he laughed out loud and looked at Gus, as if to say, "You will know how the English idiom goes".

But Gus Adams was too busy taking stock of his surroundings. Having noticed how the Albanian mafiosi were carefully laying their guns at their feet and within easy reach, he now became conscious of his own weapon, still wrapped in the linen bag that nobody, as yet, had questioned the contents of. His knuckles ached, having gripped it so hard and for so long.

Most of the rank and file had, by now, found a crate to sit on and were guzzling wine straight out of the bottle, whilst others wandered around, crate in hand, wine in the other, looking for an empty space at the table. A quick count told Gus that there were at least thirty-five of them present. All men.

Father Galileo became agitated when he noticed that one man was about to sit at the head of the table.

'Not there, my son!' he shouted. 'Can you not see that the place has been reserved for me?'

By way of proof, he picked up the card with his name on it.

'...And as you can see, places have also been reserved for our eminent guests.' At which he began pointing: 'It is only fitting that Maurizio, boss-of-bosses of the Cupola in Rome, should have pride of place in the middle, over there on my right, with Luca at his side, as always. Just as at a wedding!'

The quip brought laughter, as everyone sensed the need to relax and to celebrate the success of their mission.

'...And Lucio Cimino, who is Capo here in Kukes, will sit opposite them, between Salvatore and Bernardo. My friends, after all they have done to ensure the success of the Final Crusade, they now deserve the right to relax and to celebrate together.'

Gus realised that only he and Father Galileo were now left standing and his anxiety was mounting.

The priest was still talking. 'There will be great speeches, of course. And the drinking of toasts.'

'Alla nostra salute! '

'Cin Cin!'

'Salute!'

'Cin Cin!'

The clinking of half-empty bottles and glasses echoed throughout the chamber.

'And photographs will be taken, as at a wedding.'

To even more boisterous laughter, the priest produced a small camera and took a series of snaps, to the sound of more, '*Salute! ... Cin Cin!*' And the waving of hands.

Then, as if he'd only just realised that Gus was still standing at his side, Father Galileo pointed towards where Maurizio was sitting. 'There is a place for you, too, Guiseppe. You will sit over there, with your cousin Maurizio and Luca, opposite Lucio Cimino and Salvatore and Bernardo.'

Across the table from my parents' murderer, Gus thought, fearing the reason for it. But why will the priest be sitting apart, at the head of table, and nearest to the exit tunnel?

It hadn't escaped his notice, either, that the rank-and-file mafiosi had chosen to sit together in their respective groups, with the Albanian mob favouring the same side as Lucio Cimino, their own *capo dei capi* .

Gus' senses by now were on a knife edge.

What else should I be looking for? What else should I be taking in?

Everyone, as far as he could tell, were seated on empty crates and boxes; everyone except Father Galileo. He would be sitting on an empty drum!

Question everything, Gus! Why is he different? Why an empty drum and not a wooden box like everyone else?

Suddenly a chilling thought struck him. *What if the drum isn't empty?*

'Come, Guiseppe! Take your seat at the table, or else the wine will all be gone. Today has been thirsty work for everybody, you included.'

The priest waited until Gus was sat next to Maurizio before taking to his own seat at the head of the table.

'...It is a good job, don't you think,' he shouted for all to hear. 'That I've kept the vodka hidden until now.'

'Vodka! Vodka! Vodka!' The call became more and more insistent, as empty wine glasses and bottles were raised in half-drunken protests. At which Galileo, with a great show of relenting, produced bottle after bottle of unlabelled vodka from beneath the table at his feet.

'You see now why this has to be my seat?' he joked, as he brought more and more bottles to light. 'There is a full bottle for you all, my friends, so that we can celebrate in style.'

Despite his lack of appetite, Gus made a show of helping himself to a glass of red wine and some Parma ham with cold pasta. Father Galileo, for his part, had poured a good measure of vodka into his glass and, after urging everyone to do the same, he called for a toast: 'To the success of La Crociata Finale!'

Everyone stood. 'La Crociata Finale!' they shouted, and emptied their glasses in Russian style, before filling them again just as quickly. Gus also made a show of drinking but he only sipped through tight lips. A glance to his left told him that the priest was doing exactly the same.

After waiting for them to refill their glasses, Galileo proposed another toast. 'To Maurizio Bonnano, boss-of-bosses of the Cupola in Rome.'

The response wasn't quite so fervent from all quarters but glasses were again raised and emptied.

'Salvatore Provenzano, of Napoli!'

'Salvatore! Salvatore!'

'Bernardo Pellegrini!'

'Bernardo! Bernardo!'

Gus noticed that the priest's glass was as full now as when he'd begun calling the toasts. *He's getting them drunk more quickly on empty stomachs,* he realised.

It was obvious that many of those at table, particularly the Albanians, preferred vodka to wine.

Question—Why provide food at all? Why not just the drinks? Answer—He wants everyone seated. He wants order. He wants control.

'Lucio Cimino! Capo dei capi!'

Father Galileo had raised his glass and his voice higher for this particular toast and the Albanian mafiosi duly obliged with loud chants of 'Lu... ci... io! Lu... ci... io!'

He was obviously trying to niggle Maurizio and the Cosa Nostra. The priest was playing a mischievous and a dangerous game.

'And now, my friends, before we eat, let us toast the one who has called for this great celebration. My friends, I give you... Aiello!'

'Ai-ell-o! Ai-ell-o! Ai-ell-o!'

It had crossed Gus' mind before now that Galileo and the faceless Aiello could be one and the same, since the names were almost a perfect anagram, but he had since concluded that that couldn't be so, because Aiello, whoever he was, operated directly out of the Vatican and had far greater power and influence than Galileo would ever have. Aiello, from all accounts, had access to Vatican banking, and it stood to reason that only very few individuals had that sort of privileged authority.

By now the wine, the vodka, and the hilarity had loosened many tongues, and the conversation was becoming more rowdy and vulgar, with even Maurizio and Cimino in joking mood.

Any minute now!

Even as the thought came to him, Gus saw the priest get to his feet again.

'Friends!' he shouted above the din. 'I must apologise to one person in particular because we haven't, as yet, drunk his health.'

He looked directly at Gus and raised his glass, whilst at the same time coming to stand behind him.

'...I ask you to raise your glasses to Maurizio's cousin, Guiseppe.'

Most of them complied, 'Guis-ép-pe! Guis-ép-pe!' Because, by now, any excuse would do. Gus, however, was watching the priest who had just stepped clear of the table and was slowly reaching into his cassock. As casually as he could, Gus bent to search for the linen bag at his feet, grateful that he'd had the intuition to attach the magazine into place beforehand. He only had to release the safety clip and the Uzi pistol was ready for firing.

'You all have reason to toast him, my friends.'

Gus was hanging on his every word and realised that the bogus priest was slowly moving away again. The Albanians looked and waited; full glasses again raised.

'...Many of you don't know him. Others of you know him as Guiseppe Kadare. Only Maurizio and one or two of his friends know who he really is. My friends... Lucio, capo dei capi... I give you...' He paused somewhat dramatically, to raise his glass. '...Guiseppe Maratta, son of Giovanni Maratta.'

Gus turned and stared in horror at Galileo's treachery but the priest was already backing slowly away in the direction of the exit, keeping a semi-automatic hidden at his side. His left hand had something else clenched in it but Gus couldn't make out what that was.

'Guiseppe Maratta! Guiseppe Mara...'

Even the more drunken ones clammed up and lowered their glasses as Lucio Cimino leapt to his feet, toppling the box that he'd just been sitting on. He wasn't looking at Gus, though. He had eyes only for Maurizio.

'Cosa Nostra viper!' he snarled, sidling away towards where his Albanian mafiosi were sitting. 'And you, Salvatore? Did you know of this treachery?'

Neapolitan Salvatore Provenzano raised his shoulders and held his hands palms upwards, to suggest that he had no idea what Cimino was talking about. His eyes were glazed and his tongue couldn't get round the question that he wanted to ask. But Lucio Cimino had already lost interest in him and was staring wildly from Maurizio to Gus and back again, like a hare trapped between a fox and a weasel.

Suddenly, he bent low behind the crate that one of his men was sitting on and picked up a gun. He pointed it menacingly at Gus and his face became creased with scorn.

'So, you wheedle your way in here to avenge your father's death.' He sniggered. 'And you expect to leave Kukes alive, you spineless worm?'

Gus spoke slowly, planning not only his next reaction but also the one after that. He had to keep calm. He had to buy time. 'And was it you who killed my parents, Lucio?'

The hum of the distant generator merely emphasised the pregnant silence as everyone waited for Cimino's reply. It soon came.

'If you ask whether I pulled the trigger or not, then the answer is no.' He paused and then grinned fiendishly: 'But if you ask whether I ordered their assassination, then I must answer truthfully must I not?'

Gus was struggling to keep ahead of the game, as he fingered the pistol in his lap. Cimino was in his line of vision but the priest was not. And that worried him! He was staring down the barrel of Cimino's gun but, for all he knew, Galileo even now might be aiming a bullet at the back of his head. He, Gus, could risk taking the first shots but it would be certain suicide just the same, because the previously boisterous Albanians were now sober again and were reaching for their Uzis, as indeed were the Cosa Nostra and the 'Ndrangheta. The only ones not in possession of weapons, as far as Gus could tell, were Maurizio Bonnano, Salvatore Provenzano and Bernardo Pellegrini.

'Why, Lucio? Why did you make me an orphan?'

The mafioso laughed out loud and waved a hand around. 'For this! What else?'

'You mean the quarry?'

The significance of what was being said brought a drunken silence all around.

'Of course. It had to be either Cosa Nostra or Camorra... Giovanni Maratta, your worthless father, or me, Lucio Cimino.'

He swaggered as he uttered his own name.

'...There could not be two boss-of-bosses here in Kukes, could there?'

Then, in a condescending tone and looking first at Maurizio and then at everyone else around him, he added, 'But Lucio is not greedy, is he, my friends? Out of the goodness of his heart, did he not let the Cosa Nostra keep control of the two factories?'

Another of his drunken laughs echoed in what had now become an otherwise silent chamber.

'...Lucio, out of the goodness of his heart, agreed to Excelsior Steel and Kukes Plastics becoming two of his suppliers... His small-time suppliers, that is!'

It was only then that Gus realised the true importance of the quarry. Since his father's time, it had been used as a huge depot for arms from where the mafia had traded with the various warring factions of the Balkans. Tom Mackay, in his active days with MI6, had been keeping the factories under surveillance. As had other agents, most probably, including the Mossad and the CIA. But those who had sussed out what the quarry was all about… those who had got too close to the truth… had been duly eliminated. Which said a hell of a lot about mafia surveillance and mafia control in the area.

With gun in hand and knowing that his Camorra and Albanian mafiosi outnumbered the Cosa Nostra mob by almost three to one, Cimino felt safe to goad Maurizio, and he was now strutting like a preened turkey – three steps to his left, three back again to his right – with gun barrel waving menacingly in the direction of Maurizio and then Gus. But he hadn't reckoned on Luca's loyalty or on the fact that the man didn't know the meaning of fear, especially now, when half-drunk.

Gus caught the movement out of the corner of his eye. He saw Luca get to his feet, saw him raise the Uzi automatic, but he barely heard the splutter of bullets, nor did he wait to see the splatter of Cimino's blood, because by that time he'd thrown himself backwards off his seat and was rolling clear of the table, his own gun searching for Father Galileo.

As Lucio Cimino fell with a chest-full of bullets, pandemonium broke loose. There was loud swearing and screaming and angry shouting, and the sound of crates being kicked out of the way. In no time, streams of red-hot bullets were criss-crossing the cavern gloom.

The shooting was indiscriminate. Maurizio and Salvatore, having no guns of their own, had already scrambled under the table, praying that its wooden planks would be a thick enough shield. Bernardo Pellegrini, on the other hand, on seeing Cimino fall in a spray of bullets and blood, charged forward to pick up a gun, only to run straight into Luca's line of fire. Bullets thudded or pinged, depending on whether they found their target or not.

Gus, as he groped along the cold cavern floor, was vaguely aware of the whining ricochets all around him. He, Guiseppe Maratta, had already been forgotten because no one, now that Cimino was gone, regarded him as a threat.

The priest would remember, though. For him, Gus could still be the danger.

Frenziedly, Gus searched for him in the tunnel exit, half-hoping that he might have already gone. But no, he was still there, his black form pressed against the tunnel wall, safe from stray bullets. Watching… waiting.

Nervously, Gus fingered the Uzi pistol. He'd held a similar kind of weapon many times before, he realised. But only as a boy! His father's gun! How his mother had screamed, how his father had laughed every time he'd picked it up, needing both hands to bear the weight. But since he'd never fired a single bullet back then, he had no idea how accurate he could be now.

The priest wasn't looking for him, though. Instead, he was fiddling in the shadows, his hands covering his face and head. Then he was crouching to pick up his gun again. When he turned once more towards the light, Gus drew a sharp breath. Father Galileo was wearing a mask! A gasmask! And he was aiming his gun not at Gus, and not at anyone else left standing, but rather at the drum that he himself had been sitting on earlier.

It took but a second or two for him to realise the priest's intentions. Father Galileo wasn't going to risk any survivors. He would be the only one to get out of this alive. That had been his plan all along! Now that the arms shipment was safely on its way, Aiello and Galileo were reneging on all their promises. The mafia would receive no payment, there would be no Vatican collaboration for money laundering. The creditors had been eliminated.

Flashes appeared in the shadows and Gus heard the splutter of bullets. A few metres away, the drum shook as it was punctured and its deadly contents were released. Instinctively, he took a deep breath and held it, at the same time pulling his shirt up to cover his nose and mouth. But he was also acutely aware that the gas, if indeed it was sarin, could be just as deadly on his skin. In a crouch, he scampered towards the exit, his pistol now searching for the treacherous Galileo. But the priest, had already gone.

Gus was halfway between the two caverns before he risked taking another breath. He reckoned he could safely get away before the gas had time to creep into the tunnel and then the smaller cavern. Behind him, the sound of desperate coughing was already more audible than the chatter of guns.

He heard shouting ahead and a further salvo from the priest's gun. *The two guards!* Gus realised. They'd been there on Galileo's instructions, probably to stop certain people escaping. Now, though, they too had been deemed expendable.

When he reached the smaller cavern, he saw the steel doors slowly closing ahead of him. Unless he could reach them in time, then this place would be his tomb as well, because the gas would get to him sooner or later, just as it was getting to all those behind him, judging from the pitiful sounds of gasping coming from that direction. Wildly, he fired towards the diminishing daylight, desperately trying to prevent the priest from locking him in, but the gun kicked back so violently in his hand that the bullets flew well wide of target.

Blindly he rushed forward through the shadows, still hoping to get to the doors in time. But he only came to more grief as his toe caught the edge of one of the railway sleepers and he was sent sprawling, badly scuffing both palms as he tried to protect himself against the fall. By the time he got up again, the doors were firmly bolted into place from the outside.

Dejectedly, he groped for the gun that he'd dropped and pushed it inside his shirt, its hot barrel now searing his skin.

No sound could be heard from the inner chamber and he had to assume that the gas had finished off what Luca had begun. The eerie silence was broken only by the hum of the generator and the lazy swish of the dust extractor fan positioned in the rock face above the steel doors. With those doors now bolted against him, he instinctively realised that the fan cavity offered his only means of escape.

He studied it long and hard. How to get up there? How to stop the fan turning? Could he remove the grill casing and work his way out into the open air? The questions came at him thick and fast, as did some answers. To turn, the fan needed electricity. To stop it turning meant cutting out the generator. Doing that meant losing what little light there was and having to climb in what would then be complete darkness. But what other choice did he have? He had to get up there as quickly as possible because an extractor fan didn't just extract dust from underground workings, it also extracted foul air and, in this case, the poisonous gas as well.

His oversized shirt and trousers were now more of an impediment, so he quickly ripped them off and cast them aside. Beneath he still had his own T-shirt and shorts and he now pushed the gun beneath the scant clothing.

His search was desperate. He could see no sign of a ladder anywhere and since it was impossible to climb up smooth steel doors, he began searching the rock face to the right of them, hoping for another way up. A fan, like everything else mechanical, needed maintaining, so there had to be a safe means of getting up to it. But this wall of the cavern had no lighting at all on it and was just a blackness to him.

Several seconds of groping the rock face gave him no hope, until his hand suddenly came into contact with a rusty iron peg, jutting ten inches or so out of the rock, at head height. His heart leapt as to its possible purpose. Lower down and a couple of feet to its right he found a similar one and another lower still, roughly two feet off the ground. Now, convinced that there would be others running diagonally up towards the fan housing and, knowing that time was of the essence, he crossed the cavern floor towards the generator, having the forethought to count his steps as he did so. Once there, he again took stock of his bearings, so, when the generator fell silent and the lights went out, he at least had a fair idea of his way back in the dark.

The amount of daylight coming in through the fan housing was of little or no help to him; the aperture being nothing more than a waning moon in a black and starless sky. So now, with arms stretched out in front of him, he inched his way back across the cavern floor, counting his steps as he did so, until his hands came into contact again with the rock face and one of the rusty pegs. His palms were wet with sweat and blood and he knew they'd be very sore once he began climbing.

'Least of your worries!' he muttered.

As expected, the climb proved risky and difficult. The step-up from one peg to another was roughly two feet, which meant that in taking each one he also had to throw his hands forward to grip the peg above it. Had he the light, or had the pegs been sensibly placed one above the other like a ladder, then it would have been fairly straightforward but as it was, every step up was literally a reach into the dark and the higher he got, the greater his concern that the next handhold might not be there at all, having perhaps rusted away, and that he'd find himself plunging into an abyss from which there would be no coming back. His heart pounded as never before.

When he finally reached the vent, he let out a huge sigh of relief. The stiffest climb in Snowdonia was child's play compared to what he'd just gone through. A glance at his watch showed it was almost five past seven; a mere hour since the locomotives had trundled out of the first tunnel with their cargo of war. Sixty minutes of eternity! So much had happened since.

The vent, as far as he could make out, was about two metres in diameter and roughly twice that in length. A circular tunnel through solid rock. The sight of daylight and a glimpse of the outside world momentarily lifted his spirits but his heart sank just as quickly when he saw how solidly the fan housing was anchored into the surrounding rock.

With no tools to work with, how the hell do I deal with this? Where do I start?... Come on! Snap out of it, Gus! Think positive for God's sake, before that fucking gas gets to you! At least you now have some daylight to work with. And you have the gun.

Yes, the gun had to be his only hope. Hadn't he seen Hollywood heroes shoot locks off cell doors? So, what was to stop him doing something similar here? He reached inside his T-shirt and pulled out the Uzi.

'Twenty rounds!' he muttered. 'How many did I fire at the priest? Two?... Three? ...Five?'

He had no idea.

'...Hopefully there are enough left to do the job, as long as I don't waste any, and as long as a ricochet doesn't kill me first!'

This was not the time for caution. A quick study of the four bolts that anchored the fan housing to the rock told him that he'd be wasting his time with those. They were at least an inch thick. His only hope had to be the fan housing itself, which comprised of two metal grills bracketed together around the fan, to protect it from accidental or criminal damage. Six small brackets in all, probably of steel. If he could remove those, then the fan housing should fall apart, allowing him to crawl out between two of fan's three blades.

He didn't have time to consider any other option, so, taking careful aim, and holding the barrel as close as he dared to the first of the brackets, he closed his eyes and pulled the trigger, only to hear the bullet ricocheting off the rock beyond the grill and whining away into the distance. A complete miss! He kept his eyes open for the second attempt and did better, but even then he only succeeded in scarring the rusty steel so that it now gleamed. A third round shaved a bit more off but it took five bullets in all to remove the first bracket.

He cursed himself aloud for having left the spare magazines back in the office. 'I could do with those extra bullets now.'

Saying the words aloud helped him to focus and to think. At best he only had twelve bullets left, so, rather than shoot each round individually, might it not be better to fire an automatic salvo of say three at a time? He had to risk it.

He got as far as removing three of the six brackets and scarring a fourth before the bullets ran out, at which point he vented his frustration out loud, and felt beaten. However, the thought of the gas creeping steadily closer and of Father Galileo getting further and further away, strengthened his resolve. Since the gun was now useless, he threw it back into the cavern and heard it crashing onto the rocky floor below, the noise serving as a timely reminder of his efforts and his success thus far.

Angrily, he grabbed at the grill where the three brackets had once been, and where there was now an obvious weakness in the fan housing, and started shaking it vigorously back and forth, back and forth, until he felt his side of the mesh begin to buckle towards him. If he could bend it enough, he might then be able to squeeze his body underneath and wriggle his way between the blades of the fan and hopefully force his way under the grill on the other side.

It's your only option, Gus.

Frantically, he pulled and pushed at the grill, willing it to bend more. It was hard work because his crouched position gave him so little purchase, and the rusty steel was abrasive on his sore and bleeding palms. But he kept doggedly at it until he got his unexpected reward. With a loud crack, the bullet-scarred fourth bracket suddenly snapped, leaving just two brackets remaining.

Within seconds he was able to crawl under the grill and to work his body between the blades of the fan, whilst at the same time, pushing as hard as he could against the grill on the other side. His prone position didn't make things any easier but slowly, inch by inch, he felt the grill give way until he finally decided that he couldn't risk waiting any longer. At one stage, the short sleeve of his T-shirt got snagged on a part of the mesh and the more he struggled the more he felt the cotton being torn off his back. But then, finally, he was out. He was free.

'The benefit of being thin!' he muttered gratefully, casting aside what was left of his T-shirt. 'But now what do I do?'

About thirty-five feet below him lay the open-quarry floor that he had crossed earlier, with Galileo at his side. Climbing down was not an option! Too risky. Climbing up, although probably twice the distance, would be easier.

So, get going, Gus, before that fucking sarin gas catches up with you.

The scratched dial of his watch showed him that it was almost half past seven. Barely two and a half hours since he'd followed Maurizio and the others out of the office. The word "eternity" again crossed his mind. An eternity indeed as far as Maurizio and Luca and the others were concerned.

Climbing out onto the quarry face proved difficult but he managed it eventually, despite his bleeding hands. His fingertips were relatively unscathed, so that had to be a plus, he thought. But the fact that dynamite blasting in the past had left the rock brittle in parts, thus threatening to break away under his weight, was a definite minus. Every handhold, every foothold – and there were plenty of them – had to be tested before each move. Another plus, the rain had stopped! More drawbacks, the rock was still wet and the wind was strengthening. And he was shirtless!

He took a deep breath. It was going to be a long, exhausting effort, but he felt he was up to it and confident that he had the necessary reserve of strength in his arms and legs. All he needed was for his luck to hold out.

When climbing in North Wales, it had always been his policy not to look up or down too often, since that only led to unneeded short rests and breaks of concentration. He preferred to push himself to the limit and to be pleasantly surprised at suddenly finding himself near the top. And that's what he would do now, keeping focused and being prepared for the worst with every move.

Some holds proved to be treacherous, breaking away at the very last second, to leave him clutching for dear life. The wind didn't help, either, gusting aggressively when he least expected it to, and threatening to blow him off the rock face like a bit of quarry dust. At times, its howling echoed like a discordant church organ within the bowl of the quarry. Another interference was his ponytail being whipped back and forth across his shoulders; but that was more of an aggravation than a problem. Water ran cold down his arms, carrying with it streaks of blood off his palms. And soon, his fingertips also became badly scored. But he was oblivious to pain by now.

Eventually, the rock began sloping away from the vertical and Gus let out an audible sigh of relief. It was only then, as he scrambled up the last few feet and felt wet grass under his palms, that he knew for sure that he'd made it out of the quarry, against all the odds. And as he threw himself down onto the cool earth, to recover his breath and his composure, the rain again began to fall.

'Wonderful!' he muttered and lay on his back to receive its cooling balm. 'Lovely, lovely rain!' He relished the feeling. He was alive!

He lay there in the wind and the rain for seconds on end, unable to take in his surroundings. Twenty-five minutes past eight, according to his watch. Yes, the climb had been arduous but he could hardly believe that it had taken him the best part of an hour. Always the case though. When his concentration was heightened, time simply flew by.

Yes, he had done it! And yes he was still alive to tell the tale. Through his own efforts, and despite everything that the priest had thrown at him, he had escaped the tomb which had claimed all the others. Maurizio was down there. Luca was down there. Lucio Cimino was down there. All of them dead.

Did he regret not killing Cimino himself? Should it not have been him rather than Luca? How much did it mean to him that he hadn't personally avenged his mother's death? But it wasn't a thought that he wanted to dwell on. Whatever his feelings towards Cimino, he doubted whether he could ever have killed him or anyone else in cold blood.

But what about the priest, Gus? What will you do about him?

The question brought him out of his reverie and he quickly got to his feet. There were things to be done, important steps to be taken. He began scrambling through the coarse grass above and around the quarry workings, towards the main entrance where a pall of black smoke was now mingling with the low mist. As he hurried, a small dark shape on the quarry floor far below caught his attention. He couldn't be sure but intuition told him that it was Galileo's discarded gasmask.

If he wanted further proof that the priest had made good his escape, he soon found it, as he descended the slope beyond the main quarry entrance. Not only was Galileo's car gone but the bogus man of God had also taken the extra precaution of setting fire to the other cars, as well as bolting and padlocking the outer set of steel doors, thus making sure that the carnage wouldn't be discovered anytime soon.

*

Gus had little option now but to make his way back to his office at Excelsior Steel and there plan his escape out of Albania. Get a message to Tom Mackay in London. Warn MI6 about the shipment of arms. Tell them about the Vatican plot.

The sarin gas was still a concern though. If it escaped into the open air would it pose a threat to the people of Kukes? Being a heavy gas, would it drift down the slopes towards the town and cause illness and death? Or would the strong wind disperse it safely? With a bit of luck, it might not even escape the quarry caverns. And maybe it wasn't sarin at all, but something less lethal.

Such were his thoughts as his feet pounded the track back to his office at Excelsior Steel. Would he risk a phone call from Albania? Mackay had warned against it. Lines could be tapped, conversations could be recorded, plans could be changed at the last minute. That's what Tom Mackay had said. Maurizio, Cimino and the others were now gone, but there were probably others who could be listening in.

Best get back to Rome, Gus, and get some woman called Jeffers to send a fax. Obey orders.

He knew that he had time to play with. The shipment wouldn't be leaving port for a day or two at the earliest, and the ship *La Crociata Finale* could easily be tracked and intercepted before it reached… Reached where? That port at the eastern end of the Black Sea! What was the name of the damn place? His mind was too agitated to remember.

It'll come back to you Gus. Give it time!

The wind gusted in his face as he ran. Reaching up, he released his frizzy hair from its ponytail and smiled inwardly and with some contentment as he equated its freedom with his own liberty. Despite the carnage that he had just witnessed, he was, he decided, beginning to enjoy being a spy.

'Batumi!' he shouted out elatedly as he passed a copse of windswept scrub and stunted pine trees. 'Batumi! That's where the arms are headed for.' Little did he think that he was passing the spot where an MI6 agent and a Mossad operative had lost their lives just a few months previously.

*

When he reached the factory in Kukes, he went straight to his little office where he kept his money and passports hidden. The place was deserted, as he knew it would be. Excelsior Steel had produced its last firearm; he was convinced of that. Just as Kukes Plastics had produced its last "paddling pool" and its last lump of hollow "rock".

For a while, he sat at his desk, unnerved by the idle machinery, the empty corridors and the profound silence. A deathly silence full of ghosts! His elation at having escaped the rock tomb was quickly evaporating and the cold and the wet were slowly getting to him. He felt at a loss, not knowing what his next step should be. What he wanted to do was to get back to Rome. Better still, get back to London. Tell Mackay about the shipment to Batumi. Pass on the responsibility. Let MI6 deal with the problem. Put his own life back on track. Return to normality. Here, cold and wet in the haunting silence and the failing light, even life in Canary Wharf had a distinct appeal.

He could make his way to the landing strip on the other side of town, in the hope that Maurizio's plane and pilot were still there. He very much doubted it, though. The priest, devious bastard that he was, would have included the Cessna in his own escape plans.

'I'd be bloody stupid not to check, though,' he muttered. 'It's only a six-mile taxi ride.'

Still rather dazed and disorientated, he checked his notice board for phone numbers for cabs. There were four. He would try each in turn. He reached for the phone. The top three came with the names of cab companies but the fourth was just a number—in Gus' own handwriting! But he'd never had reason to call for a taxi since he'd been here! And yet, he'd jotted the number down! Why?

His mind was fuzzy, tired and barely able to concentrate.

'Bloody hell, Gus! Get with it! Think! You've only been here a few weeks! Who was it?' And suddenly it all came back to him. The helicopter pilot! The number he'd shouted as Gus was leaving the chopper on that first day. *'Any time you people need my services!'* he'd yelled, above the heavy throb of the rotors. *'Just call me! I can be up here in an hour or so.'*

"*You people*" could only have been a reference to the mafia, of course. And the pilot's readiness to serve suggested that he was being paid well over the odds for his services. The man's intensity and the way he'd shouted the number at him repeatedly as he'd climbed out of the chopper had stuck in Gus' head and later, when alone in his office, he'd jotted it down and pinned it on the notice board beneath the cab numbers that were already there. So, what was to stop him calling for the chopper now? He, Gus, was still employed by the mafia, at least until somebody told him otherwise. Maurizio was certainly in no position to argue, was he*? One thing's certain, Gus! In the position you're in right now, you could do with some mafia influence and mafia benefits.*

He dialled. With a bit of luck, he could be in Tirana airport by nightfall and back in Rome before daybreak.

ROMA

As his cell phone started ringing, the stocky little man in the dark suit reached into his coat pocket. The taxi had just left the confines of Aeroporto di Fiumicino and was now heading northeast towards the city. Somewhere behind him, Maurizio's Cessna was already refuelling for the return flight to Kukes.

'Maurizio wants you to take me to Rome on an important errand, first thing tomorrow morning.' The pilot had agreed without question, of course, as Father Galileo knew he would. No self-respecting Catholic, after all, would ever doubt the word of a man of God.

Now, though, his priest's cassock had been unceremoniously bundled into a plastic bag and was lying on the seat next to him in the taxi.

'Father Galileo?' The question had a rasp to it.

'*Si*. Is that you, Aiello?'

'I speak on his behalf. Have I, too, not the wisdom of Solomon?'

The bogus priest cast a glance at the driver in front of him and decided that it was safe to talk. 'You may safely speak.'

'Where are you? We have been waiting for you to call.'

The little man sensed the reproach. 'I have just arrived in Roma and I am even now on my way into the city, in a taxicab.'

'*Bene*. We expect good news from you. But first you must receive absolution.'

The little man sighed tolerantly. 'Yes, of course!' Another game of cloak and dagger had to be played, this time in a confession box in the Basilica of Santa Maria in Trastevere, within hailing distance of Vatican City.

The phone went dead, leaving the bogus priest with a growing sense of frustration. Again, there had been no mention of payment.

Reluctantly, he drew the creased cassock out of its plastic bag.

Alet-les-Bains, Languedoc, SOUTH OF FRANCE

Claude Boudet knifed through his morning baguette and reached for the cheese and the Parma ham. His TV was on. As on most mornings, he'd been listening to the national news programme and was now waiting for the regional bulletin. For once, he felt glad that he didn't have to report for work. Five consecutive days of gallivanting around the region, keeping coachloads of tourists entertained and answering their every question, had left him tired and hoarse. He needed time off to recover.

Outside, beneath his kitchen window, the River Aude crept lazily by.

'Oh, for rain!' he muttered. 'Heavy rain to bring a torrent that will sweep the rocky riverbed clean of all the litter.' He hated having to gaze out every day at plastic bags and soggy cardboard boxes… even an old car tyre … polluting what was otherwise a picturesque setting. It was the view from this very window that had attracted him to this house in the first place, all those years ago.

'Alet-les-Bains, Claude? You're not seriously considering moving there? Leaving Carcassonne?' Sympathetic colleagues had made the effort to sound horrified, but they'd understood why he was going, why he'd begun searching even before his divorce had been finalised. The house in Carcassonne, the one that he and his wife had shared for twelve years, had become a symbol of her betrayal and of his bitterness.

Claude winced as a crust of bread scraped at his sore throat and he quickly reached for coffee to wash it down.

'…Last night, a man's badly decomposed body was discovered…'

The regional news had begun without his realising it. Hurriedly, he turned up the volume.

'…There were no clues on the body as to the dead man's identity but police have confirmed that the victim had been shot through the head and that they are now investigating a murder. A post-mortem, carried out later today, will disclose how long the…'

Claude Boudet stared at the screen. He hadn't heard the presenter say where the body had been found but now he could see for himself as a short film showed the location.

'Montségur!' he gasped.

In all the time that he'd lived in the Languedoc, and that was most of his adult life, he could only recall three other murders. This one brought the total to four. The first had been in Quillan twenty years ago, the result of a marital squabble; the other two in Rennes-le-Château, just a few weeks back. He had been there that day when the bodies were discovered and the sight still haunted him now!

He and several others had been cross-examined at length by the police that day and he'd had to give a written statement about what he'd seen and heard. But he had heard nothing since, nothing other than local speculation. It seemed that the police were still in the dark.

'...Neither will they reveal the identity of the person who discovered the body but he is thought to be a visitor to the area, possibly Italian. According to a police statement, there are no apparent links between this incident and the double murder at Rennes-le-Château last month. Further statements will be issued when more information comes to light. And now for the rest of the news...'

Claude Boudet sighed. Rennes-le-Château and now Montségur! Within a matter of weeks, both his hallowed sites had been violated. On his tours from now on he would be plagued with banal questions about tasteless contemporary murders rather than ones of genuine interest in hidden treasures, romantic mysteries and historic wrongdoings. Unless of course! The idea brought on a wily smile.

ROMA

Gus wasn't to know it, but his flight from Tirana touched down at the Aeroporto di Fiumicino just fifteen minutes after Galileo's Cessna. Had he been on the lookout as his plane descended, he might even have spotted the priest climbing into his taxi. But, convinced that his would-be killer had at least a twelve-hour head start on him, he'd felt no need to be observant. He wasn't to know that whilst he himself was being flown by helicopter back to Tirana, to catch an early morning flight to Rome, Galileo had actually been spending the night in Kukes, waiting to be flown directly to the Italian capital by Maurizio's pilot the following morning.

Gus hadn't gone back to his lodgings in Kukes; there had been no need to, since he kept his passports and his money, not to mention the equivalent of about twenty-five thousand pounds worth of mafia ready cash, in the office safe. With Maurizio and Luca and the others now gone, the Cosa Nostra would have things other than missing funds to worry about.

He had waited at the factory for the helicopter to arrive, hoping for a direct flight to Rome but the pilot had scotched that idea straight away.

'There's no way I can have air space,' he'd said, shouting above the deafening throb of his rotors. 'The best I can do is to take you back to Tirana and you can catch a commercial flight from there.'

The more Gus thought about what had happened to him since five o'clock yesterday afternoon, the luckier he felt to still be alive. Had he not suspected the priest's duplicity and been ready for his treachery, then he would be no more than a rotting corpse now, lying in that dank quarry with nothing but dead mafiosi for company.

The image wasn't one that he wanted to dwell on! His concern, he told himself, should be to contact Tom Mackay in London as soon as possible, warn him about the shipment that was on its way to Batumi and, having done that, catch the first available flight back to Britain. What had been that woman's name... his contact? Sally something or other. No worry. It was bound to come back to him. No problem with her contact number though.

He'd memorised that. Just as he'd memorised Mackay's fax number in Ealing.

*

Tom Mackay was becoming restless. Back home, he had learnt, years ago, to cope with the inactivity of retirement but here in Rome the inaction was getting to him and he was becoming increasingly frustrated. Jimmy Oldcorn was relying on him for results, so what the hell was keeping Gus Adams from getting in touch? Either the lad was already dead – God forbid – or he was in Albania and unable to make contact. Up until late last night, Tom knew that no fax had arrived from Adams because Eddie, his son, had phoned to say that he'd again been to the house in Ealing to check.

'So what the hell can I do, other than hope, and sweat it out?'

At some point of every day since he'd met her, he had made sure that Sally Jeffers knew that he was still around, usually by just acknowledging her with a raised hand as he casually walked past the tourist group that she happened to be addressing at the time, half-hoping that she'd call out to him to say that a certain Gus Adams had got in touch. It was never difficult to find her. Being such a busy girl – a guide very much in demand, it seemed – then there were certain places of interest that she was bound to visit every day; if not the Colosseum or the Forum, the Capitol or the Fontana di Trevi, then the chances were that she'd be in the Vatican. So, all he had to do was to stay put at one of them and wait for a Thomsons or a Thomas Cook's coach to pull up and disgorge its passengers. Then, once he'd realised that she had nothing to report, he'd go off and do his own little bit of sleuthing.

He'd begun, as Gus himself had begun, by enquiring about a certain Giovanni Maratta who had lived in Rome some twenty years previously. Unlike Gus, though, who had deliberately drawn attention to himself, Tom had been more discreet and, as a result, had met with very little success. Today, to take up the empty hours, he would again visit the Vatican, where there had to be somebody who could tell him what the Schidoni Pentacle was all about and whether it had any connection with the Holy See's involvement with the stockpiling of arms in northern Albania.

Basilica of Santa Maria, Trastevere, ROME

'You wish to confess your sins, my son?'

Not for the first time, Galileo got the impression that the voice he was listening to belonged to Aiello himself rather than to any of his minions. He couldn't question it though, not if he valued his health. Neither would he dare peer into the grill that separated them.

'Yes, Father.'

Assuming that the person he was talking to was also dressed in a priest's cassock, he wondered how strange that would seem to anyone who might have spotted both of them entering the confession box. Did priests also seek absolution in this way, he wondered. It was a question that hadn't crossed his mind until now.

Galileo hadn't always been this submissive. During their first contact, for instance, he had been bold enough to challenge the arrangement: 'Why must we have this charade? Why must you remain faceless?'

To which Aiello's reply had been unequivocal: 'Never question your instructions again, Galileo. Not if you value your life... or your soul! Accept that the Knights of Wisdom must remain faceless. We must work from the shadows if we are to overcome the heretic evils that threaten our holy Roman church.'

The little man hadn't questioned his instructions after that, especially after being promised payment that would ensure him luxury for the rest of his life

'Good. Now what have you to report?'

'La Crociata Finale has been safely launched.'

'Excellent. Tell me more.'

Galileo now went on to describe, in hushed tones, the extent of the shipment and how it had safely begun its journey in the care of a dozen armed mafiosi dressed as railway personnel.

'It has travelled overnight and should...' He glanced at his watch. '...Have reached port about an hour or two ago. However, the transfer of the… the commodities onto the ship will not begin until tonight, when it is dark and when there will be fewer prying eyes around. Loading will be completed tomorrow night and La Crociata Finale will leave port at first light the morning after.'

'Good! And there is no danger of it being discovered for what it is, I trust?'

Galileo chuckled briefly. 'The ship's hold is full of rocks, for sea defences at Batumi. Who will question such a cargo?'

'And there will be no problems with the unloading in Batumi?'

'None. Tell Aiello that he can sleep without worry. The shipment will be well guarded all the way to its destination, first of all by the mafia and then overland from Batumi by Hamas. Only fools would try to thwart the mission now.'

'You have done well, Galileo. And the other matter? Was that dealt with also?'

'Of course. Done and dealt with!' The little man made no effort to hide his self-satisfaction.

'Tell me how it was done.'

'Good fortune made it possible. Maurizio Bonnano contacted me almost a month ago. He said he was sending his cousin over to Kukes, a young man called Gus Adams, who was wanting to avenge the death of his parents many years ago. Maurizio wanted me to help him.'

'And how would you do that?'

'By introducing him, in person, to the assassin.'

'And was it done?'

'Very easily. It has been common knowledge in Kukes for years that Cimino arranged the deaths of Giovanni and Agnesa Maratta. Giovanni, the boy's father, was in Kosovo, brokering a Cosa Nostra deal for guns, when the Camorra assassins struck. With Giovanni Maratta dead, Cimino and his mafiosi were then able to take possession of the quarry and the business without much resistance from the Cosa Nostra. As you will recall, it was a bad time in the Balkans, with Serbs on the rampage. There was much killing and the authorities weren't going to lose any sleep over the assassination of a mafia gunrunner and his woman.'

'You are well-versed in what went on there, Galileo.'

'Ah! But I made it my business to find out everything. You see, it served my purpose to do so.' His tone now became overly pompous. 'When Maurizio telephoned me with his request, I realised that I could kill many birds with one stone. Maurizio wanted Cimino dead. That was obvious. But not until the Final Crusade was safely under way, of course. If Gus Adams, his young cousin, succeeded to avenge his parents, all well and good. If he failed… if Cimino got him first… well, it would be no great tragedy to Maurizio Bonnano. The young Englishman wasn't really a cousin, just a very distant relative. Not Cosa Nostra at all, as far as Maurizio was concerned. Gus Adams… or Guiseppe Maratta as he was baptised… could either be useful or expendable. So, when Gus Adams arrived in Kukes, I pretended that I knew his parents all those years ago and that I remembered the two children, Guiseppe and Gina, who were orphaned.'

'How did you get the information?'

'I have my ways!' Again, the hint of pomposity. 'One or two of the older workers in the factory had been acquainted with the family. They were able to give me names. Giovanni Maratta, his wife Agnesa Kadare from Durres and Guiseppe and Gina, their children.'

'Very clever.'

Galileo paused. Was he being complimented or sneered at? He decided on the former. 'I laid my plans very carefully. I used the boy.'

'Boy?'

'The young man. Guiseppe Maratta.'

'And?'

'All are dead. Maurizio, Cimino, Salvatore Provenzano… All of them! Cosa Nostra, Camorra, 'Ndrangheta… They all share the same tomb.'

'And Guiseppe Maratta?'

'Him too. It will be many days… weeks… months even before their bodies are found. And when they are found, it will be seen as mafia vendetta gone mad. By then, La Crociata Finale will have safely docked and its cargo taken to its destination.'

'The Holy See will not be compromised?'

'Rest assured. There is nothing there that will implicate the Vatican.'

'You have proof of all this?'

'Proof?'

'That they are all dead.'

'How can I prove it? I can show photographs of everyone at the quarry but I did not wait around to take pictures of their corpses. Do you doubt my word?' Galileo sounded aggrieved.

'Of course not. You have done well.'

The little man, sensing genuine approval in the words, curbed his annoyance. 'Thank you. I thought that Aiello would be pleased.'

The correction was immediate, 'Do not presume that I speak on behalf of Aiello in this instance. Aiello will decide for himself how satisfied he is with your work, as will others of a higher authority than Aiello.'

Fearing that the conversation was coming to an end before his financial reward could be discussed, Galileo now considered how best to bring up the matter. For two years he had been doing Aiello's work in Kukes but as yet he had received very little financial recognition. True, he had been on the mafia payroll for overseeing production at the two factories – a fact that Gus Adams never became aware of – but his paltry wages had been in Albanian lek, and that, as far as he was concerned, was *mickey mouse* money.

'Aiello has another task for you. A task of equal importance to that of the Final Crusade.'

Galileo's heart sank. 'I have served Il Vaticano well for over two years, at considerable personal risk, and my recompense, thus far, has been small. I have lived on mafia titbits. I was promised…'

'The true church is threatened and you can only talk of financial reward?'

The voice from beyond the grill had a distinct edge to it, causing the bogus priest to stammer in reply, out of frustration more than fear: 'I… I… did not say that I wouldn't take on the work, but Aiello can hardly expect me to live like a… like a pauper.'

'Don't worry, Galileo!' The voice had again softened. 'The agreed payment will be made into your Vatican Bank account and will be doubled when you complete your next task.'

'Ah! Then tell me what I must do.' The little man had been somewhat mollified.

'Have you ever heard of the Schidoni Pentacle?'

'No. Should I?'

'No. Nor will you know about the Map of the Count of Razes.'

Since this wasn't a question, Galileo merely waited for the explanation.

'…The map has been stolen from the Vatican Archives and the Holy Father is extremely concerned.'

'The Holy Father?' It had been hinted more than once before, in telephone conversations, but this was the first time that the pontiff had been directly referred to.

'It is a matter of grave consequence to the holy church. If the problem is not dealt with, then all your good work in Albania will have been in vain.'

'What must I do?'

'Even now, as we speak, a man is walking the corridors of the Papal Palace, enquiring about the Schidoni Pentacle. He came to our notice as soon as he arrived in Rome, a few days ago. His name is Thomas Mackay and we have learnt within the past few minutes that he has close links with the intelligence services of a foreign power, one that continually seeks to undermine the authority of the Vatican State; a power that has a history of persecuting the Catholic faith. This man is an immediate threat and must be removed.'

'And you wish me to do this? Are there not others for the work?'

The voice from beyond the grill sharpened again. 'As an associate you should know that the Knights of Wisdom are engaged the world over in combating the enemies of the true faith.'

Should I know? Galileo thought. Up until recently, I'd never even heard of the Knights of Wisdom. And now I am a member?

'Other of our enemies have been prying before now but they were only interested in our plans in Albania and, thanks to you, they have since been eliminated. As far as we can tell, this Thomas Mackay is working alone, but we must be vigilant. There is much work still to be done, here and in France.'

'France?'

'That is where you must go, once you have dealt with the spy Thomas Mackay. Aiello wants you to help our brothers in the Languedoc. You will be contacted as soon as you have completed your task here in Roma. In the meantime, Mackay is staying at the Hotel Gregorio on the Via Ludovisi, but before you eliminate him, find out how much he knows about the Schidoni Pentacle. There is no time to waste, Galileo. Do it quickly. I shall phone you later this evening for your report. Now go! And do not look back!'

Once outside, Galileo crossed the little square in front of the church and sidestepped into the shadow of a narrow side street. There, camera in hand and with its powerful lens zoomed-in on the church door, he waited to see who would follow him out. The tourists were easily recognisable but other than a few of those, the only other person to appear within the next ten minutes was a blind man feeling his way with a white walking stick. No sign of anyone who looked remotely like a papal representative. Galileo sighed with some resignation. Aiello… or possibly Aiello's messenger, in this case… would have to remain faceless.

THE VATICAN—L'Ufficio del Papa, Apostolic Palace,

'And you believe that these murders in the Languedoc are related, Commander?'

'Yes, Most Holy Father. I am convinced that all the victims were seeking the treasure, but perhaps for different reasons, some more mercenary than others.'

'And do we know who the unfortunates were? Have their bodies been identified?'

'The two at Rennes-le-Château were Israelis, the one at Montségur just a soldier of fortune as far as we can tell. We suspect that they were on the trail of the map and the pentacle and that they were killed because of them.'

'But the blasphemous Nag Hammadi papyrus? What of that?' The pontiff's brow was creased with worry. 'Is there still no news?'

'No, Your Holiness. As you know, we have eyes and ears everywhere and I'm sure that we would have heard by now if it had been put on the black market.'

The pope took little comfort from the words. 'Can you imagine, Commander, what harm that could do to our church if it were to fall into the hands of our enemies?'

The head of Vatican security remained silent. He had never seen the holy father so agitated or so deeply concerned. Bits of ancient manuscript that neither of them had heard of until a few weeks ago were now jeopardizing not only the Catholic faith but the very roots of Christianity itself.

'I should have been told of the manuscript's existence when I took office, Commander. Had I known, I would have ensured its safe keeping here in my own quarters rather than in an unattended corner of the Archivio.'

'But the curator has assured us, your Holiness, that the so-called *I Jesus epistle* was kept under lock and key at all times, and that until recently no one, apart from himself, was even aware of its existence, leave alone its significance. As he himself has told you, it is a secret that has been jealously guarded by the church for over sixty years, ever since it was spirited away from the rest of the Nag Hammadi collection before any biblical scholar was given the chance to lay eyes on it. From what the curator says, even the foremost biblical scholars of today know nothing of its existence.'

'That knowledge holds no comfort now, Commander. Imagine the joy our enemies will have if the papyri are sold on the open market and then fall into the public domain.' He waved a tired, dismissive hand. 'But we have considered such implications before now. Now, we can only wait and pray.' At which he made the sign of the cross.

The commander remained silent. He knew that the pontiff, since being told about the disappearance of the papyri and the map, had done little else but pray.

'…In your opinion, Commander, who could have been responsible for the deaths in the Languedoc?'

'That I don't know as yet, Your Holiness.'

'Some time ago you told me that you had men in place to guard Il Tesoro.'

The head of the Swiss guard sensed the worry behind the words. 'What I said, Most Holy Father, was that I have dispatched a number of my best men to the Languedoc, but even we do not know the exact location of Il Tesoro. According to the curator, no one does. From what I understand, not even the Map of the Count of Razes holds that information. The map and the pentacle together, if properly read, can do no more than point towards the general location of the treasure. They do not show the exact location. However, the curator informs me that ancient Vatican tradition does mention a location that is extremely well defended.'

'And, with God's blessing, long may it remain so. If only you could give me the same assurance about the Nag Hammadi document, Commander.' The pontiff's face became again disturbed as he reverted to his earlier question. 'But you can say categorically that you have no idea who the murderer in the Languedoc might be?' The concern in his voice and seen in his eyes was unmistakeable as he searched the commander's face for the truth.

'I can assure Your Holiness that these deaths cannot be laid at our door in the Vatican.'

The pope got to his feet and again made the sign of the cross. It was the commander's signal to leave.

ROMA

Jeffers! That was her name! Sally Jeffers! He dialled the number.

'Hello? Sally Jeffers speaking.'

'Ah! Miss Jeffers! My name is Gus Adams. I've been told you might be able to help me.'

Gus Adams? The name sounded familiar. Someone had mentioned it to her recently. 'Maybe I can, Mr Adams, but not until you tell me how.'

'You are a tourist guide?'

'Yeees?'

'You have a fax machine?'

'A fax machine?' The question surprised her. 'Yeees. Why do you ask?' Her tone had become wary.

'It's just that I need to send an urgent message to London.'

'You could e-mail... or send a text?'

'No. Your name was given to me, that's all. But look, if you're not willing to help, then maybe you could tell me where else I can lay my hands on a fax machine. I am willing to pay well for the favour.'

Choosing to ignore his peevishness, she asked: 'Where are you now?'

'Standing outside your flat.'

'Oh! And how did you know where I live?'

She suddenly felt anxious. First, there had been the Arab whom she'd thought was stalking her, then there was that man, Tom Mackay, who kept appearing out of nowhere every day, as if he was keeping an eye on her, and now, equally unnerving, had come this unusual request from a total stranger who had obviously gone to the trouble of finding her address.

But he's not a total stranger is he, because I've heard his name before. But where? And why? In her job, she met so many different people; heard so many different names.

She walked over to the window and saw him on the pavement below. Thin and unkempt... long, frizzy, dark hair trussed with a black bandana... badly in need of a shave... white cotton shirt and trousers... black trainers... cell phone in one hand, a black flight bag in the other. She didn't like the look of him.

'Who told you that I have a fax?'

Instinctively, he looked up and spotted her at the first-floor window, with the phone to her ear. No hint of a greeting from her, just a challenging and slightly apprehensive look that confirmed her distrust of him.

'This is important, believe me.'

As if to offer proof, he held up the two sheets of handwritten paper that had to be faxed.

'...It'll only take a couple of minutes. I'll pay. Twenty euros? More?'

'Twenty euros? Okay. But you'll have to be quick. I'm expecting my boyfriend any minute.'

The lie ended the telephone conversation.

She leant over the banister to watch him coming up the stairs, then stood aside to let him pass her into the room. She pointed. 'The fax machine is over there. Who gave you my name, anyway?' She was intentionally leaving the door wide open behind her.

'A man called Tom Mackay in London. That's where I need to send this, now.'

She gaped, then realised where she'd heard the name Gus Adams before.

'Save your money! Forget the fax! Your novelist is here in Rome.'

'Pardon?' He looked bemused. 'My novelist? I don't understand.'

'He is a novelist, isn't he?' She had reached for her purse and was now offering him Tom Mackay's calling card. 'At least that's what he told me. Also told me that you are his son's... friend?'

'Acquaintance more than friend.' Gus objected to the uncalled-for innuendo. Her emphasis had hinted a homosexual relationship.

Sally Jeffers shrugged, still suspecting that she was being used as a pawn in some game or other. 'Whatever! Anyway, there's his phone number. He wants you to contact him here in Rome. Famous novelist, is he?'

'Um! Yeah, you could say that.'

Liar! 'So, you won't need my services after all.'

Gus considered his options. What if he couldn't find Mackay? What if he'd already returned to London?

'I'll send the fax just the same if you don't mind. It is important, believe me.' At which he placed a twenty euro note on a little coffee table beside the machine. 'And then I'll make the phone call as well.'

ROME, Hotel Gregorio, Via Ludovici

Tom Mackay stirred. There were bells ringing. Church bells! Drowsily he peered at his watch on the bedside table. Six o'clock! A ten-minute nap… a late afternoon siesta… was all that he had intended but he'd slept for nearly an hour. Rome and its heat were getting to him. Drowsy by day, awake most of the night!

He'd spent the morning kicking his heels in the vicinity of the Colosseum, hoping to see a Thomas Cook or Thomsons coach pull up. The best part of the afternoon had seen him wandering aimlessly around San Pietro, enjoying the marble coolness and serenity of his surroundings but without really comprehending the significance of all that he was seeing. He'd be the first to admit that he'd never been a great admirer of the arts. Yes, he was impressed by all the gold in the famous Basilica… the magnificence of St Peter's Chair, for instance… but to be told that it was the work of a bloke called Bernini cut little ice with him. Neither had he lingered long in front of Michelangelo's *La Pieta*. Just another statue, as far as he was concerned, and Rome was full of those. He'd then gone to the souvenir shop where, after a show of studying some prints, and while paying for a couple of unwanted postcards, he had asked the assistant if there weren't any prints or photographs of the Schidoni Pentacle that he could buy. The woman had looked bemused and had turned to another assistant for help, only to get a similar reaction from her. It was obvious that the Schidoni Pentacle was something that they'd never heard of. He had then wandered outside into the hot sun and had sat on the steps overlooking the Piazza San Pietro, to watch the ebb and flow of tourists and to oblige when asked politely to take a couple of family group photographs. But Sally Jeffers hadn't appeared and so, when four o'clock came, exhausted and with a splitting back, he'd returned to his hotel, convinced that his visit to the Eternal City was turning out to be a complete waste of time.

Suddenly, he rolled off his bed and scrambled for his mobile phone. It wasn't just church bells that were ringing!

'Hello! Tom Mackay here.'

The caller had no trouble in recognising the heavy Scottish accent. 'Gus Adams, Mr Mackay.'

A quick intake of breath and then the sound of genuine relief: 'Thank God! I was getting worried, Gus.'

'Is that why you're in Rome? Because you were worried? Or were you just checking up on me?' Gus spoke tongue-in-cheek, relieved at hearing a familiar, friendly voice.

'You have something to tell me? To report?'

'Very much.'

'Then the sooner you get here, the better! Hotel Gregorio, Via Ludovisi.'

'Yes, I know. It's here on your calling card.'

'Ah! So, you've seen Sally? Good. I'll expect you within the next half hour. I'll order coffee for when you get here.'

*

The small foyer was empty and the reception desk unmanned. Father Galileo listened. All was quiet. Very little likelihood of him being caught unawares. Hurriedly, he pulled the guest book towards him, glanced at the list and found the name he was looking for. Room nine, first floor.

A loud click, as machinery was set in motion, told him that the lift had been activated. It was coming down. With surprising swiftness of foot for one of his shape and weight, the assassin priest made for the stairs.

*

Tom Mackay cursed as the door closed behind the hotel's receptionist-cum-waitress. She had brought the coffee much too early, but it had been his own fault. His Italian had become rusty and phrase books never seemed to have the exact wording for what he wanted to ask.

The gentle knock – the second in a matter of minutes – surprised him. Gus Adams had been quick, he thought. Good job, therefore, that the coffee had come early. There'd be no further interruption.

'Come in! It's not locked!'

Slowly, the door opened and a priest's bald head appeared, followed by a cassocked torso. Mackay stared. Father Galileo smiled apologetically. For a second or two, neither of them spoke.

'*Mi scusi! Sei* Thomas Mackay?'

The Scotsman continued to stare, his initial distrust and defensiveness gradually ebbing at the sight of a respected man of God.

'I'm sorry, Father, but I'm not very fluent in Italian. My name is Thomas Mackay, though.' He'd understood that much, at least. Now he hoped that the priest understood English. 'How can I help you?'

'It is perhaps I who can help you, signor.'

'Oh? Then you had better come in, Father.'

The priest duly obliged, taking care to close the door behind him. 'I understand that you have been seeking information?'

Mackay's back was again up. 'Have I? Who told you, Father?'

'You have been asking about the Schidoni Pentacle?'

The Scotsman stared. 'At the Vatican? Yeees! But who told you?'

'You were overheard. But tell me, Mr Mackay: What do you already know about the pentacle and the Map of the Count of Razes?'

Tom Mackay looked genuinely puzzled now. 'The Map of Razes? I've never heard of that. Never asked anybody about it either, Father.' He was getting increasingly uneasy, even though the priest was still smiling benignly.

'And the pentacle?'

'Just something I heard mentioned, Father, and I thought I'd write a novel based on it. I can't do that, though, not until I know the significance of the pentacle. You said you could help me?'

Galileo eyed him closely, as if trying to determine whether he was telling the truth or not. Time was of the essence. The tray with the coffee pot and the two clean cups suggested that the man was expecting company any minute. Swiftly he pulled out a Beretta fitted with a silencer and pointed it at the surprised Scotsman.

'You will tell me the truth, Mr Mackay.'

'I am telling… Ahhh!'

A carefully aimed bullet had passed straight through his left shoulder.

'I ask again.'

Wincing with pain and fear as he struggled to keep his balance, Mackay could see nothing but murder in the priest's eyes. 'I tell you; I am a novelist who... Ahhh!' The searing pain had now moved to his right shoulder.

'Wrong again, Mr Mackay. You are a spy and an enemy of the true faith. Now tell me why you have been asking about the Schidoni Pentacle.'

What with the pain and the fear, the Scotsman was having trouble to breathe and was struggling to get his words out. 'You have it wrong, priest, if that is indeed what you are. It is true that I was an MI6 agent many years ago but I have been retired for almost ten years and I am only interested now...'

'In finding the Schidoni Pentacle. Now tell me why.'

'As God is my witness, I don't even know what the Schidoni Pentacle looks like, leave alone anything else.'

Galileo seemed convinced. 'If that is your wish, Mr Mackay, then let God be your witness.'

Dispassionately, Galileo fired twice into the Scotsman's chest and watched him crumple backwards, eyes wide open and frozen with fear.

'...And may He have mercy on your heathen soul.' At which the assassin priest flippantly made the sign of the cross. 'If Aiello asks for proof this time,' he mused. 'Then he shall have it.'

Hurriedly, he produced his digital camera and took quick snapshots of the dying Scotsman from three different angles. Then, as he turned to leave the room, he noticed a wallet on the bedside table. Without breaking stride, he swept it up with his free hand, secreted it beneath his cassock and was reaching for the door handle when a knock came on the door. The guest-for-coffee had arrived, he realised. Holding his breath and, knowing that the door was unlocked and could be opened from the outside, Galileo tightened his grip on the Beretta.

A louder knock was accompanied by a hushed call of, 'Mr Mackay? It's me!'

The priest knew that he had a dilemma. The Englishman outside the door was probably Mackay's accomplice, in which case Aiello would expect to have him removed also. But if he opened the door to him, then the stranger was bound to see Mackay's dead body, which meant that he'd have to be shot where he stood, out in the corridor, and that was a risk that Galileo wasn't prepared to take. What if other hotel guests suddenly appeared? He might end up having to kill two or three other witnesses. Not that indiscriminate killing in itself bothered him, but it was such a pointless gamble. Aiello needn't be told everything, he decided.

'Mr Mackay? Are you there?'

Galileo waited, gun at the ready. Faint muttering came through from the corridor outside, as if someone was talking to himself, then came another despairing knock and the sound of footsteps retreating.

He listened for a few seconds more before slowly opening the door. The corridor was empty. He slipped out of the room.

What now? he wondered. *The fire exit or risk the stairs?* The lift was certainly not an option because it would draw attention to itself and he'd be stepping out into the foyer like an actor walking on stage under spotlight. Quickly, he considered his options. A cassocked priest clambering down a fire escape was just as likely to draw unwanted attention. No choice, therefore. It had to be the stairs.

As he descended towards the foyer, he could hear Italian voices. There was surprise in the woman's tone.

'But he is there, sir! I have only now come from his room. He had ordered coffee for two persons. Are you sure that you knocked on the right door?'

'You said room nine?'

'Yes.'

'Then I did knock on the right door but there was no answer.'

'I do not understand it, sir. Perhaps he was in the bathroom and did not hear you.'

Quite possible, Gus thought. How well did he know Mackay, anyway? Eddie's father could be harder of hearing than he had realised. 'I will try again, madam. Thank you.'

Galileo quickly retreated onto the stairs leading to the second floor and from there he listened to the stranger padding up the first flight and then along the corridor. From above came the distant sound of a door closing and the chatter of two hotel guests coming nearer. He waited, hoping that they were making for the lift rather than the stairs. Again, he heard the knocking at the door of Room nine, more urgent this time. 'Mr Mackay! Are you there? Are you all right?'

The second question sounded fainter which could only mean that the stranger had entered the room. Silently, Galileo hurried down again, past the first floor and onto the lower flight of stairs where he assumed a more-seemly pace as he reached the foyer. The middle-aged receptionist was surprised at seeing him.

'Father! I did not see you arrive.'

The bogus priest beamed. 'You were probably enjoying your siesta, signora, and I did not want to disturb you. Anyway, I knew the room I wanted on the second floor. One of your guests had asked me to visit her… But I cannot disclose why, of course,' he added, suggestively.

'Of course not, Father. I would not expect you to.'

He could hear the lift on its way down. 'God's blessing on you, my child.' With that, he made the sign of the cross, smiled piously and walked out.

'Thank you, Father.'

*

Gus stared in disbelief. His first impression was that Tom Mackay had either fainted or had had a heart attack.

'Mr Mackay! Are you all right?'

A stupid question, he realised, as he stepped closer, with so much blood around. Shaking and with his heart pounding, he bent over the body. Had the dead eyes fluttered? He couldn't be sure.

'Mr Mackay! Can you hear me?'

Slowly, the bloodied lips moved as if trying to say something. 'Who did this to you?'

There was blood in the mouth and a tell-tale bubble told Gus that Tom Mackay was exhaling in a desperate attempt to tell him something, with what looked like being his last breath. Quickly, he got down on his knees and placed his ear as close as he could to the dying man's lips.

'Who was it, Tom?'

'Tell… Sa… lly…'

Gus couldn't be sure what he'd heard. 'Tell Sally?' That didn't make sense! If it was a reference to Sally Jeffers, then what the hell had she to do with all of this?

'I don't understand, Tom. Tell me who?'

The eyes were rolling, the effort immense. 'Sally's... unc...' The breath gave out in a throaty gurgle and Gus knew that he was gone.

Slowly, he got to his feet, to gaze down at the still body, the blood-soaked shirt, the bloodied face, the blood-stained white hair. This man had probably witnessed much villainy in his time and now it had finally caught up with him. Gus glanced at his watch and thought about Tom's son back in London, the son whom he'd been so proud of. Even now, Eddie could be making his way to the KKK in Bermondsey, completely unaware that he had just lost his father in such horrible circumstances. Somebody would have to tell him.

Gus imagined a uniformed policeman knocking at his door and saying dispassionately, 'I'm sorry, Mr Mackay, but your father has been murdered in Rome.'

Suddenly, Gus Adams was gripped by an uncontrollable anger and he lashed wildly with his fist at a nearby table lamp, sending it hurtling across the room to smash into pieces against the far wall. 'What the hell am I doing in all this? All this fucking senseless killing.'

How long he stood there in a daze, oblivious of his bleeding knuckles, he couldn't tell, but suddenly his mind cleared and he considered his own situation. What if he was accused of murdering Tom Mackay? Could he disprove it? Of course, he could. He had no gun! And yet! He was bound to be taken in for questioning. They'd want to know why he was in Rome. The woman downstairs would testify that her guest had been alive a few minutes before his visitor arrived and it wouldn't be long, either, before the MI6 connection was discovered. Then there'd be hell to pay and, given time, they were bound to delve into his own mafia background as well, and maybe connect him with the deaths in Kukes which would be seen as a carefully planned revenge killing of his parents' assassins, a plan that had gone horribly wrong, resulting in multiple deaths.

It surprised Gus how quickly and how easily he was able to reason everything out, while standing there over Tom Mackay's warm dead body. Now, a desperate decision had to be made, with no time to ponder over its implications. He would leave the hotel as if nothing had happened, contact Sally Jeffers again to see whether she could explain Tom Mackay's final words and then get out of Italy posthaste. What would become of his fax-message to Tom's home in Ealing was now the least of his worries.

He tried not to run down the stairs, tried not to show any indication of panic. The woman was still at her desk, flipping through the pages of a colour magazine. She looked up and smiled as Gus reached the foyer.

'He was there after all, was he not?'

Gus attempted to smile back. 'Yes. As you guessed, he was using the bathroom when I first called.' With the lie, he knew he was burning the only bridge of hope left to him.

'You have hurt your hand.' She was staring with concern at his bleeding knuckles.

'Oh! Yes… Um!' he blurted, whilst struggling for a credible explanation. 'I tripped and scraped it against the staircase wall, that's all. You needn't worry though, signora! I didn't leave any blood-marks.' Even as he was saying the words, he was realising the damning irony of them. 'Goodbye!' he muttered hurriedly. 'And thank you.'

As he was making for the door, a thought struck him and he turned again to face her. 'Did you notice anyone else leaving the hotel during the past half hour or so?'

'No one…'

Oh well! He turned to leave.

'…Except the priest.'

Her words stopped him again in his tracks. 'The priest?'

'Yes. Didn't he pass you on the stairs as you were going up?'

'No. What did he look like?'

She laughed without humour. 'What do most priests look like, sir? Black cassock…jovial…'

'Bald? Stocky? Florid face?'

'Yes. You know him?' She was surprised at the possible coincidence.

'I think so.'

'You have finished the coffee.'

It was more of a statement than a question. She got to her feet, obviously intending to collect the tray from Room nine.

'Um! No! My friend was… was… just helping himself to a second cup, and he was going to… to take a bath straight afterwards. He'll bring the tray down with him, later. That's what he said.'

'Thank you, sir.'

As he exited the building, a couple were getting out of a taxi that had pulled up at the kerb. They were eyeing the hotel with some distaste and Gus guessed that they had chanced their luck when booking by phone.

'Good evening.' They were English and the man was stepping forward to ask him something.

Gus looked the other way. The police would be wanting a description from them as well. '*Buona sera*,' he muttered, barely audibly, and hurried away.

'I hope all Italians aren't so rude.'

The woman's shrill comment was meant for his ears but he was in no mood to dwell on it. He had to weigh up his options. Either he could take a taxi directly to the airport and catch the first available flight to London… Birmingham or Manchester even… or he could return to Sally Jeffers' flat, recount what had happened and between them try to make sense of Tom Mackay's final words. Would she believe him, though? Might she not panic and start screaming blue murder? Or maybe she'd pretend to believe his story and then shop him to the police at her very first opportunity. Or what if Tom's body was found in the meantime and the carabinieri were put on alert at the airports? He'd be well and truly done for, then.

By the time he'd considered all the possibilities, he'd become guilty even in his own mind. Even if he did get back to Britain within the next three hours, it would just be a matter of time before Scotland Yard or Interpol caught up with him. He'd be arrested and asked to explain not only Mackay's murder but also the killings in Kukes. How the hell would he do that? Who, in his right mind, would believe that the real killer was a Catholic priest? He'd be way out on a limb and there was no way that MI6 would back up his story.

Come what may, Sally Jeffers had to be his best option.

*

The safety chain rattled and she peered out at him.

'You're back! Sorry, but I've got company. I told you I was expecting my boyfriend tonight. You'll have to find another fax machine.'

His disappointment became immediately obvious to her and for a second or two he appeared to her like a lost soul, his thin face pallid and drawn.

'I need to talk to you alone, Sally. Believe me, I need your help,' he was whispering, lest anyone else should overhear.

'As I said, I've got company.'

'Can't you make some excuse, so that we can talk? Honestly, I wouldn't bother you otherwise. I must talk to you in private.'

His agitation and his intenseness were unnerving to say the least. 'Look, Mr Adams, I think you'd better go. We only met an hour ago...'

'Tom Mackay is dead!'

'Pardon? Say that again.'

At least he'd caught her interest! 'Tom Mackay is dead. Murdered.' He paused, to watch her eyes grow big with shock. 'When I got to his hotel room, I found him lying in a pool of blood. He'd been shot more than once.'

'Good God! Who did it?'

'I don't know... and yet again, maybe I do. Look, can we meet somewhere to talk properly? Or can I come back later when he's gone?' He nodded in the direction of the imaginary boyfriend behind her.

'No, Mr Adams, we can't. Whatever trouble you're in, I want no part of it. Please go away!' She sounded resolute and was about to close the door on him.

'I think you already have a part, Miss Jeffers.'

The formality between them was adding to the strained atmosphere.

'...Tom Mackay's dying words were a reference to you, or rather to your uncle, I think.'

'My uncle?'

If he didn't have her full attention before, he had it now.

'...Why, in God's name, would he mention my uncle? And which one? I've got three uncles.'

'Don't ask me! His last words were "Tell Sally's uncle." You'll have to figure that one out. I can't. All I can say is that the whole business has left me in a hell of a pickle and, as far as I can see, you're the only one who can help me get out of it.'

It was then that he noticed a change come over her, as if a penny had suddenly dropped. Her brain had seen some relevance, had made some kind of connection and, with a resigned sigh, she released the safety chain and held the door open for him.

'You'd better come in.'

'Thank you but we must speak alone.'

'We are alone. Now tell me who the hell you are, Gus Adams.' She closed the door behind him but refrained from replacing the safety chain. 'And who the hell was Tom Mackay?'

Her intenseness surprised him but she didn't wait for his answer. '…MI6! Right?'

'How the hell did you know that? Don't tell me that you're an agent as well?' *It would make sense though,* he thought. After all, she had been his contact and he had been warned by Mackay not to compromise her in any way.

Rather than answer this time, she went over to a cupboard that served as a drinks cabinet, poured a generous tot into a glass and handed it to him. 'You look as if you could do with that.'

He peered at the liquid. It was darker than whisky.

'Amaretto,' she explained. 'The best I can do under the circumstances. Now you'd better sit down and explain to me what this is all about.'

'Fair enough, but if you're an MI6 agent yourself, then you must have some idea of what's been going on.'

'Listen! The only agencies that I have anything to do with are travel agencies. I am, Mr Adams, a tourist guide, pure and simple.'

'But how…?'

She finished his question for him: 'How did I know you were MI6? Through my uncle. Who else?'

Gus was confused and waited for her to explain.

'One of my uncles keeps a pub in Greenwich. The other is disabled and confined to a wheelchair. They're my dad's brothers. Uncle Jim is my mother's brother. Guess what his job is.'

'Buggered if I know! He's the MI6 agent maybe?'

'Better than that, Mr Adams. In fact, Uncle Jim is your director of operations at Vauxhall Cross.'

'Oh! Highly placed then.'

She'd expected him to be more impressed but then she realised that he didn't fully appreciate her uncle's lofty status within the secret services.

'Highly placed, you say!' Her tone suggested incredulity. 'Uncle Jim is a little more than that, don't you think? In fact, he is none other than Sir James Oldcorn, your boss, and supreme head of MI6. Now if you didn't know that Mr Adams… if you didn't know that the director of operations is the top man of the secret service … in spy lingo, the big C himself… then I very much doubt all that you've been telling me so far. So, I think you'd better leave before I call the police.'

She reached for the phone and he knew that she had him over a barrel. His only hope of saving himself was to tell her everything, warts and all. 'Listen, Sally! What I've told you already is God's truth. I have only been working for MI6 for the past couple of months or so. If you're willing to listen, I'll tell you the full story. Then, if you still don't believe me, I promise that I'll stay here for the police to arrive.'

He waited while she considered his proposition; her dialling finger still poised over the phone. It took a full fifteen seconds for her to come to a decision.

'Okay, let's hear it! But it had better be pretty convincing because I'm not going to compromise my Uncle Jim or the security services, for you or anybody else. Why are you smiling?'

It had been a rueful smile, he realised. 'It's just that that was what I was told about you before I left London. That you weren't to be compromised.'

'And I still don't want to be. Just remember that! I love it here in Italy and the last thing I want is to be deported because of my association with a virtual stranger who also just happens to be a suspected murderer.'

Gus grimaced. She was blunt if nothing else and he respected her the better for it. 'Just hear me out.'

A good ten minutes later, Sally Jeffers was planning their next move. 'First thing is to get that report of yours off to Uncle Jim, to warn him about the shipment that's on its way to Batumi. Trouble is, I don't even have his home phone number. I'll have to ring Mum for it but she'll go through the roof if she thinks that Uncle Jim has been using me for his own ends.'

'Can I suggest an alternative? By now, my report will be lying in Tom Mackay's fax machine in Ealing, waiting for someone to pick it up. Tom lived alone, so unless his son Eddie happens to call by the house then no one except us will even know it's there. Can't you just ask your mother to phone your Uncle Jim to pick it up? Make up some cock-and-bull story. She needn't know that Mackay was an MI6 agent.'

Sally spent a minute or two considering the option, then she was talking to her mother in Reading: 'Listen Mum! Uncle Jim phoned me a few days ago. Wants to arrange a surprise holiday in Rome for Auntie Janet. Can you phone him to say that I've just faxed all the details to the Mackay Travel Agency in Ealing. That's where he wanted them sent. Will you do that now? Promise? Thanks. I'm a bit busy at the moment but I'll ring you later for a chat.'

Gus smiled appreciatively as he watched the phone being returned to its cradle.

Clever, he thought.

'And now, you'd better go.'

Go? Go where? 'Uh, yeah! I guess so. Thanks for your help.'

She couldn't but notice his dejection and the sudden droop of his narrow shoulders as he turned towards the door.

'What will you do now?'

He paused just long enough to answer her. 'Find my way back to the UK, I guess. It's not going to be easy.' Again, he turned to leave.

'What? Tonight? Hadn't you better check first on the next available flight?'

Gus shook his head. 'The airport's not an option. Tom Mackay's body will have been found by now and the airport will be watched. The police will have a good description of me already.'

Sally's mind was suffering a mini turmoil. She didn't want him here any longer than need be because she couldn't afford to become involved in any cloak and dagger activity. What if she were charged with being an accomplice to murder? Good God! She could end up in an Italian jail and then deported. Forced to leave Rome. Leave Italy. Such things didn't bear thinking about. On the other hand, if this poor sod was picked up by the carabinieri he'd be facing a life sentence. From what he'd told her, and she now believed him, there was absolutely no way he could prove his innocence in court. Could she let that happen? Wouldn't it be some kind of betrayal? High treason even? *Damn you, Uncle Jim! This is all your fault.*

He had his hand on the door.

'Look! You'd better stay here tonight. The couch isn't particularly comfortable but it'll have to do. And I can lend you a sleeping bag or something. But you're out of here first thing in the morning. Understand?' Even before she'd finished talking, she was regretting her stupid compassion. However much she believed him, there was no way she would be able to sleep tonight, not with a suspected murderer – assassin no less – in the next room.

Gus made no attempt to hide his relief. 'Thanks. I'll make damn sure that you're not compromised in any way.'

'Hm!' she muttered. 'That word again!' Then louder, as she looked at her watch, 'There should be a news bulletin soon. We'd better hear it.' At which she switched on the TV.

Neither of them paid any attention to the distant drone of Flight IB4637 as it gained altitude out of Fiumicino Airport.

*

'...Despite a slight headwind, we should be touching down in Barcelona in an hour and forty minutes, as scheduled. We hope that you have a pleasant flight...'

Father Galileo looked at his watch. Two minutes past nine. First thing tomorrow morning, he would hire a car in Barcelona and then drive over to France, to Carcassonne, to await further instructions from Aiello. He closed his eyes. It had been another long and eventful day.

Aiello

Satisfied that he had done all that he could for the time being, Aiello lay back in his reclining chair, closed his eyes to dispel the grey mist, and reached to switch on the radio, near to hand. There would be a news bulletin soon and it should confirm what Galileo had told him over the phone. The "priest" had done well, especially to find that tourist guide's calling card in the dead man's wallet. Could she be Mackay's accomplice in Rome? If so, then she too would have to be removed. That wouldn't be easy, he realised, not with Galileo now gone, but there were other ways of dealing with the problem. He would see to it personally.

Since his enforced retirement from office six years ago, Carlo Platina, alias Aiello, had grown increasingly more bitter and vindictive. Once an aspiring member of the judiciary, with an eye on reaching the very highest echelons of his profession within the Vatican State, his career had been cruelly cut short by failing eyesight brought on by acute glaucoma. Second and third opinions from various eye specialists had merely confirmed the original diagnosis that the affliction was too far advanced and the condition irreversible. His early stages of tunnel vision would eventually lead to total blindness. And now, six years later, those predictions were being substantiated. Aiello's world had become grey and obscure and full of phantoms, real and otherwise.

Born the youngest of Marco and Maria Platina's four children, with more than a decade between him and the youngest of his sisters, Carlo never got to know his father. Marco Platina had died before his son ever saw light of day, a tragedy that led Maria, an overly devout Catholic, to claim that her son had been sent to her from God, to give her comfort in her time of great tribulation, and to care for her when she grew old and infirm. Her selfish expectation was to dominate the boy's mind as he grew into manhood.

Carlo barely got to know his sisters either because by the time he was of school age they had left home, partly in protest at their mother's religious intolerance and partly because of her obsession with a son who, she openly claimed, was destined for sainthood. Little wonder therefore that Carlo Platina, from a very early age, considered himself superior to other children. For a start, was he not a true Roman, having been born in the old town of Trastevere and in the shadow of the Vatican State, just like his parents and grandparents before him? And had he not heard, with his very own ears, his mother thank the Holy Virgin, before the altar of San Pietro, for the blessed son that God had bestowed on her?

"True Roman, true faith" became young Carlo's maxim, a self-esteem that would not make him at all popular as he got older, especially on the campus of Temple Law School in Philadelphia where he went to study on a Vatican bursary.

Already accustomed to loneliness, Carlo's student days in America proved to be particularly difficult and friendless and, as it turned out, a real test of his Catholic faith. The enforced solitude did have its benefits, though, in that he could devote his whole time to his studies, so that when he eventually returned to his beloved Caput Mundi he did so with the reputation of being one of the best law students ever to have graduated at the Temple School.

Due to his failing eyesight, in recent years he'd had to accept the ignominy, as he saw it, of carrying a white stick wherever he went. At first, he had regarded the cane as a badge of imperfection, as his Achilles heel, but then, one day, it occurred to him that his mother, were she still alive, would define his physical blindness as the manifestation of God's will. The light that God had removed from his eyes would be transferred to shine with heavenly brightness in his spiritual eyes. Then, and only then, would his real purpose in life be revealed to him.

It did not take him long to determine what God had in mind for him. Weren't the heretic Jewish and Moslem faiths growing more sinister by the day, in a sinful materialistic world? And weren't they brazenly threatening the Holy Roman Catholic church, even in countries that stood on the very doorstep of Caput Mundi itself? Safeguarding the true faith, undermining the heretic faiths, had to be God's intended mission for him. Carlo Platina – True Roman, true faith – would launch his own personal crusade against all heretics and infidels. He would devise a way of striking at the very hearts of Islam and Judaism. He would succeed where many popes and many armies had failed in the past. His crusade would be a crusade to end all crusades. His crusade would forever be known as *La Crociata Finale* ... the very last crusade!

Galileo's regular reports from Albania had been sure proof that God was helping him to bring his plans to fruition. But then, just as the great day was getting nearer, disturbing news had come on a different front. Documents had been stolen from the secret archives and rumours claimed that their content would bring great humiliation to the Catholic church worldwide. At first he had viewed such claims with a high degree of scepticism but when his enquiries led him to think otherwise, the blind Carlo Platina decided that God was not yet finished with him; that He had a further mission for him to fulfil, this time in the hated, heretic Languedoc.

He first came to learn about the theft of the ancient manuscripts whilst taking a few days' rest at Castel Gandolfo, the papal retreat. At the time, he was enjoying a glass of wine in an open-air café on Liberty Square, outside the Papal Palace, when three men came to occupy the table next to his. One of them, noticing the blind man's white cane rolling off the table, respectfully picked it up and replaced it. After that, they paid him no further attention and were soon engaged in hushed and agitated conversation about how the commander of the Swiss Guard had ordered a full-scale enquiry into something or other. Since becoming blind, Carlo Platina, alias Aiello, had come to realise that people often associated blindness with defective hearing, deafness even. They seldom realised that their private conversations in the presence of blind people were never as whispered or as confidential as they believed them to be. They never seemed to grasp that a blind person's hearing could actually be more acute because of his blindness.

When he realised that the three men at the next table were actually employees of the Vatican Library, he had listened all the more intently and had heard them talk of stolen manuscripts and of unscrupulous mercenaries who now had it in their power to undermine the tenet of the true faith. Although sceptical of what he had heard, he had, nevertheless, cut short his holiday and had returned to Rome to begin his own private inquiry and to cut through the web of secrecy that had been woven by a pope whom Aiello regarded as heretic and unworthy. Once he got to the bottom of the mystery of the missing documents, he'd had no hesitation then in deciding that the matter warranted his undivided attention. Il Cavalieri di Saggezza – the

Knights of Wisdom – would become involved and he, Aiello, would send assassins to the Languedoc, to where the thief was said to have gone. The threat would be removed and the offending documents destroyed forever.

The familiar music announced the evening's news bulletin and stirred Aiello out of his reverie. But he still kept his eyes firmly shut.

*

'…Earlier tonight, an unidentified man, believed to be a foreigner, was found murdered in his hotel room on the Via Ludovisi…'

Gus and Sally sat bolt upright in their chairs, fearing the worst.

'…According to the police, it is too early to speculate on any possible motive but they are following what they refer to as "useful leads". They are anxious to interrogate an Italian man in his mid-twenties, said to be of medium height, thin with shoulder-length dark hair held in place with a black bandana. When last seen he was dressed in white cotton short-sleeved shirt and light-coloured trousers. The public are advised not to approach him as he is armed and dangerous, but rather to alert the emergency services… And now for the rest of the news…'

At least they haven't released a photofit of me, was the only consolation that Gus could think of as he finished off the rest of the pizza that Sally Jeffers had prepared for him.

She, however, was in no comforting mood. 'Matter of time, though, don't you think?'

'Where the hell do I go from here?'

'Your problem! But it'll have to be by morning. I can't afford having you here any longer than that. What if someone saw you, earlier, while you were standing on the pavement outside? What if one of the neighbours saw you coming up here? I can't afford to be involved. The last thing I want is to be drawn into your troubles.' She was already regretting her decision to let him stay.

'Yes, okay! I'll be gone by morning. But there is something else you could do for me before I go.'

'What?'

'As far as I can see, there's only one way for me to get out of Rome but I'll need to buy a few things first. Maybe you'd be willing to do that for me?'

'Such as?' Her reluctance to commit herself was obvious.

'I can't be seen in these for a start.'

'Your clothes?'

'Yes. Well, let's just say that I'll need to hide them!'

'You expect me to go out and buy clothes for you?' She made no effort to hide her incredulity. 'If you ask me, the first thing you need to do is to cut your hair? That's a dead giveaway, for a start.'

'Maybe it doesn't have to be.' Before she could interrupt, he went on to explain: 'What I need are some leathers and a biker's helmet, then I can do the rest of the shopping myself.'

Her raised eyebrow called for a fuller explanation from him.

'Look, Sally! As far as I can see, my best chance of getting out of Rome without being recognised and arrested is by motorbike.'

'But do you have one?'

'Not with me, no, but I could buy one, surely? I've seen two places, at least, close to here that sell bikes.'

'Of course, there are! Italians love their motorbikes. But what you're saying… correct me if I'm wrong… is that you want me to go out and buy you not only some new leathers but also a brand-new motorbike?'

Gus smiled wanly. 'Not quite. If you could get me the leathers and the helmet then I can go out and buy the bike for myself. Okay, so I'll probably look bloody stupid jumping in and out of a taxi with a great big helmet over my head but at least nobody will be able to recognise me.'

'And you won't need to have your hair cut!' She shook her head despairingly. 'Who says that women are conceited?'

'Will you do it? It doesn't matter if the leathers aren't a perfect fit. That would be the least of my worries.'

'I seem to recall somebody saying that I wasn't to be compromised. I'll be compromised for sure if I help a suspected murderer to escape, don't you think?'

'Suspected being the operative word. Look, Sally! You know damn well that I'm innocent. I can even tell you who the real murderer is.'

'You've already hinted as much. So, tell me.'

'Remember the bogus priest I told you about?'

'Father Galileo in Albania?'

Gus nodded. 'Yes, him! I'm convinced that he was in Tom Mackay's room just a few minutes before I got there. The receptionist actually confirmed that he left the building just a few minutes before I did.'

'So why can't you tell the police?'

'Oh, come on! The word of a foreign secret agent against that of a Catholic priest? This is Italy, for God's sake!'

'OK! I see what you mean.'

'So will you help me in the morning?'

Four or five seconds elapsed before she testily agreed, 'You're not giving me much choice, are you?'

It was then that the phone rang. 'Hello?'

'Is that you, Sally?'

The woman's voice sounded vaguely familiar. 'Yes. Who's asking?'

'Your Auntie Janet here! Are you free to talk?'

Uncle Jim's wife! No need to guess why she was calling, or on whose behalf. 'Auntie Janet! Nice to hear from you after all this time. How's Uncle Jim?'

'He sends his regards. Are you free to talk?'

'Yes.'

'Uncle Jim wants you to know that he popped over to the travel agents in Ealing and that he's picked up the brochures you sent. He wants to know whether you're likely to see your young man again or whether the affair is over.'

Sally refrained from sighing. She was being compromised on all sides and was expected to play their silly game, whether she liked it or not. 'We have a date tonight actually. I'm meeting him in a few minutes.'

A sudden intake of breath from the other end of the line betrayed Auntie Janet's concern. 'Oh, good! Then maybe you could ask him something.'

Sally's growing annoyance suddenly got the better of her. 'You can ask him yourself, Auntie. He's here now.'

As she handed over the phone, she couldn't help wondering which of the two – Auntie Janet or Gus Adams – was the more startled, but she left them to it and went into her tiny kitchenette to make some coffee. When she returned a few minutes later, Gus was still clutching the dead phone and looking stunned.

'Well? Did you get your pathetic cloak and dagger stuff over and done with?'

'Your uncle came on the phone. Wanted to know if I'd met Tom Mackay. Not that he mentioned him by name, of course.'

'Of course!' She was making no effort to conceal her cynicism.

'He got a hell of a shock when I told him that Tom had had a fatal accident.'

'I can imagine. So, what did he want you for? More secret missions I suppose now that you've settled all his problems in Albania.'

Rather than answer, Gus just looked at her long and hard.

'Well?' She expected an answer.

'He'll be sending me a fax, later tonight.'

'Nice of him not to compromise me, don't you think?'

Gus again ignored the sarcasm. 'Wants me to go to the south of France.'

'And you said yes, I suppose?'

'I haven't agreed to anything yet.'

'But you will.'

He remained silent. He didn't know what to think.

'…So, what's your brief this time around? Tell me what the great C wants you to do in the name of national security.'

There was little point in being secretive, he decided. The fact that he needed her help tomorrow morning meant that he had to humour her now. 'Wants me to make some discreet enquiries in Southern France.'

'Correct me if I'm wrong, but the South of France is a hell of a big place, is it not?'

Gus sighed. 'The Languedoc in particular. I expect he'll send me the details in the fax message but he did say that he wanted me to find out all I could about something called the… the Map of Races, I think he called it…'

'Sugar?' She had a spoonful poised over his mug of coffee.

'Yes, please! And something called the Schidoni Pentacle.'

Although quick to pull back in his chair, he still wasn't able to evade the splashes of coffee that now stained the front of his white cotton shirt. No apology, though, from an open-mouthed Sally Jeffers who had just dropped the spoon into his mug.

LONDON

Sir James Oldcorn spent a sleepless night racked by guilt and worry. Because of him, an old friend had met with a violent and untimely death in Rome. Not only that but he had also risked compromising his niece and, God forbid, might even have put her life in danger as well.

Given time, he'd get over the guilt of Tom Mackay's death – Tom, being an old pro, had known the risks – but his concern for his sister's girl was something entirely different. If she were to get caught up in this business... If she was...

It didn't bear thinking about.

As he lay there fully awake, envious of his wife's untroubled slumber, he strove to allay his fears. There was no way that Sally could have been compromised by last night's phone call, not after the precautions that he had taken. Despite his home being regularly checked for bugging devices and his private telephone line being constantly monitored in case of illegal tapping, he had still played extra safe by dragging his wife with him across London to a public kiosk on distant Ealing Common. It made sense to do so, he'd argued, since the journey had to be made anyway. Gus Adams had to be briefed and it would be done via Tom Mackay's fax machine while Sally, on the other hand, would be contacted discreetly by public telephone. Janet thought he was paranoid.

I probably am!

Before leaving Tom's house on Elm Avenue in Ealing, he had waited for confirmation that the message had been received in Rome and that Agent Gus was indeed prepared to travel to the south of France to investigate the connection... if there was any... between what was now going on in the Languedoc and what had been happening in Albania.

The lad had done very well thus far. As things had turned out, Tom Mackay – God rest his soul – had found the ideal man for the job, which meant that he, Jimmy Oldcorn, Head of MI6 Operations, now had reason to feel elated with the way things had gone. Now that he knew where the shipment of arms was headed for, and to what end, then he could take positive countermeasures and do so without having to implicate the service in an operation that could well become a major international incident.

First thing in the morning, he would set about killing a number of birds with one stone. First of all, he would contact his Mossad counterpart in Jerusalem and brief him about The Final Crusade. The Israelis would deal with the problem in their own way, without any help from Britain, but they would feel indebted, nonetheless, to MI6 for the timely warning and would know that reciprocal favours were expected. One of those favours, Sir James now decided, would be information on what was really going on in the South of France.

Obviously, the Mossad were involved somehow or other because they too had lost agents in the Languedoc and in Albania. So there had to be a connection. Up to now, his own intelligence service had had very little to go on, other than that the Languedoc, during the past few weeks, had been bristling with agents from Middle Eastern countries. There had been reports of Arab and Jewish presence in the region. But what was the Vatican connection? And what was behind all those unexplained deaths? Three months ago, a car, with one of his own agents at the wheel, had been forced off the road into a ravine in the Gorges de la Frau. But why was he there at all, when he should have been in Rome, investigating the Vatican's possible involvement in Albania? It was that agent's death, and that of others in Kukes and Rome, which had led to Agent Gus being recruited in the first place.

He now gave vent to his frustration with an audible sigh. In the name of national and international security, MI6 needed to find out why Vatican feathers were now being ruffled in the Languedoc and whether they were the same feathers as those ruffled in Kukes. In other words, could Schidoni Pentacle and Map of Razes be code words that connected, in some way, with what had been going on in the Balkans? If so, then it was imperative for him, as head of operations at Vauxhall Cross, to follow up the lead. If he failed in that, then Whitehall would again be breathing fire.

First light tomorrow, I'll call in one of the favours that the Israelis now owe me.

Languedoc, SOUTH OF FRANCE

Claude Boudet got up off his courier's seat to reach for the microphone but before switching it on he leaned over to have a quick word with the driver who then eased his foot on the accelerator. Their passengers had been relatively quiet for some time, in a mixture of awe and fright, as the road clung to the vertical rock wall above a precipitous ravine. Now that they had left the ravine behind and were on safe ground once more, sighs of relief could be heard, especially from the women on board.

'Ladies and gentlemen, please look to the left-hand side of the coach. There will be no time to disembark.'

As the coach crawled to a stop, the Frenchman began to explain: 'For the past ten minutes we have been travelling through the Gorges de la Frau and I can tell…' He caught the driver's eye and winked. '…that you have all been impressed with what you have seen so far. You will have realised, from its colour…' He indicated the cliff to their left. '…that the rock is limestone and therefore much softer than, for example, the granite of the Massif Central. It also explains why there are so many underground rivers and streams in this area and I have asked the driver to stop here for a second or two so that you can see an example of what I'm referring to.'

The coach had stopped opposite a large cave entrance out of which a sizeable stream flowed.

'…Notice the path that runs alongside the stream and into the cave. Should you wish, then it is possible to follow that path for a hundred metres or more underground.'

'Oooh yes!' exclaimed one of the group rather excitedly in a shrill voice as she spotted the neat set of stones just above the water level. 'And look! There's a handrail to hold on to, in case you fall in.'

'Fancy going in there to explore, Marjorie?' The question was from someone who obviously knew what Marjorie's reaction would be.

'Oooh, no way! You won't catch me going in there. There's no telling what's hiding in places like that.'

Many laughed, others concentrated on taking photographs through the window glass.

'You never know, do you?' Same teasing voice again. 'There might be a great big wild man lying in wait there, just waiting to have his way with you.'

Marjorie screamed. 'Chance would be a fine thing!' Then, a second later, 'On second thoughts, it might be worth the risk.'

Everyone laughed now, including the French driver who had got the gist of what the fun was all about.

'That was Fontestorbes, ladies and gentlemen.' Claude Boudet had returned to his courier's seat as the bus again began to move. 'Perhaps you weren't all that impressed with it but I guarantee that our next stop, in a few minutes' time, will take your breath away.' At which he switched off the microphone to let them resume their cacophony of idle chatter.

The minutes rolled by, with the narrow canyon again pressing in on both sides and offering very little for them to see. The road – not even classed "secondary" – had also narrowed and more than once the driver had to squeeze his bus past other coaches coming to meet them. On one occasion, he was heard to shout '*Espèce de connard!*' through his open window as a daredevil lorry driver almost took his wing mirror away.

Finally, the bus pulled into a little picnic area at the roadside and the courier was again switching on his microphone.

'Ladies and gentlemen, this will be a brief stop for photographs.'

They all piled out, cameras at the ready and stood there looking bemused for a second or two. What were they supposed to photograph? They were hemmed-in on both sides by canyon walls.

'Voila, messieurs... mesdames!'

Claude Boudet stood aside and pointed up the narrow canyon, into the distance, listening as he did so for their sharp intake of breath. They didn't disappoint him.

The distant mountain, bathed almost white by the morning sun but with wisps of early mist still clinging to its leafy lower slopes, seemed to be floating in mid-air. Against a cloudless azure sky, it had a truly surreal, almost regal quality; an impression enhanced by the crown-like ruins on its summit.

'It's like something out of a fairy tale.'

Whoever had spoken had done so in hushed tones. 'Camelot!' offered another, equally in awe.

'*Oui, monsieur!* Some do call it the Grail Castle.'

'Really?'

They were all spellbound.

Claude Boudet smiled. It was always the same. To those who'd never been this way before, the sight was indeed breathtaking.

'*Messieurs et mesdames*, I give you Le Chateau de Montségur!' The little bit of French always added drama to the occasion.

As they all gazed in solemn reverence, Marjorie's shrill voice suddenly shattered the silence: 'Blewdy 'ell, Monshewer Boo-dette! I thought you said that we were going to climb up to Mont-secure today?'

The courier grinned affectionately at her. From here, it was the reaction that he always expected and got. They had been warned to come in walking boots.

'*Oui, madame!* We will indeed be going up to the ruins of the old citadel.'

The group gasped incredulously.

'Well, you can count me out, Mister Boo-dét.'

The subdued Marjorie sounded adamant. Others made similar noises.

'…You've got as much chance of getting me up there as to the top of blewdy Everest.'

'We shall see, Madame Marjorie! We shall see!' The courier was enjoying himself, partly because the majesty of Montségur had again left its indelible impression and partly because he intended making the climb himself today, something he hadn't done for quite a while. 'You see, ladies and gentlemen, today will be the last chance to climb Montségur for some time to come. We have been told that, from tomorrow on, all visits have been cancelled because contractors will be starting on renovation work at the Chateau.'

One by one, the group boarded the bus once more, convinced that the summit of Montségur was beyond the reach of every one of them and that their courier, Claude Boudet, was off his rocker if he expected otherwise.

Fifteen minutes later, however, they were having a rethink. By then, the coach had wound its way up and out of the canyon and was now approaching the mountain from a more southerly direction and at a much higher elevation than before. From here, although still a daunting climb, Montségur did not look quite so intimidating or so inaccessible.

This was Claude Boudet's seventh visit of the tourist season. On previous occasions he'd either stayed on the coach with the driver whilst the passengers took to the narrow rocky path to the summit, or else he had ambled back down to the tiny village of Montségur, to spend time in its little museum, or relaxing in one of its welcoming cafés, always knowing that it would be at least an hour and a half before even the fittest of the passengers returned to the bus. Today, however, he would join them on the climb.

Although the roadside car park was spacious, the coach driver had difficulty finding room to park.

'God! Look at all the cars!' someone exclaimed. 'Do you reckon all these people have gone up there?'

Heads were seen to look up towards the ruins of the citadel that towered hundreds of feet above them.

'There's no way that I will!'

'Nor me!'

'Nor me!'

Claude had heard it all before. He'd use the same tactic as he always did, to get them going.

'You must go as far as the stele that commemorates the Cathars who died here. As you can see, it's only a gentle climb as far as there.'

He pointed to where a commemorative pillar stood on the upper fringe of a gently sloping meadow known as the Field of the Burned. Beyond it, the track seemed to rise more steeply as it disappeared under a canopy of stunted trees.

'…It's up to you after that. If you don't fancy going any higher, then you can always return to the coach and wait for the others to come down. But I should warn you that it will be quite a long wait, and the sun is getting hotter. It'll be cooler at the top, believe me. Those of you who intend to make the climb with me, then please be careful on the way. The path will be rocky and narrow in places and you can very easily trip or twist your ankle if you are not careful.' His eye twinkled as he added: 'I do not think I could carry you down one by one. What do you think, Madame Marjorie?'

Everyone laughed and Marjorie's 'You can take me in your arms any day, Monshewer Boo-dette,' went unheard.

Slowly, as if it were unnatural for him to do so, Claude took off his blazer, folded it and placed it on the parcel shelf in the coach. Then he slackened his tie just a little. His short sleeves revealed arms that had but the slightest of suntans.

'Here are your tickets, ladies and gentlemen. Part way up the path you will come to a little hut where you will be expected to show them to the ticket collector.'

He handed them out as if he either hadn't heard, or was choosing to ignore, their earlier protestations. No one refused a ticket.

'…I would suggest that you hold on to them afterwards, as souvenirs of your visit to Le Chateau de Montségur.'

At the gate where the path began, a large sign in French, English and German confirmed what Claude had told his group earlier, that, as from the following day, Montségur would be closed to the public for three weeks, so that work could be carried out in the interests of public safety.

Now every member of the group puffed his or her way up the Field of the Burned as far as the Cathar stele. From there on, the path could be seen to grow steeper and stonier as it disappeared into a jungle of tightly knit thorns and stunted vegetation. Claude Boudet waited for them to gather round him at the stone memorial. A young couple descending, red faced and perspiring, smiled sympathetically, as much as to say, "Rather you than us"!

'This, ladies and gentlemen, commemorates the end of the Albigensian Crusade, although official historical records say that it ended in 1229, exactly twenty years after it was first launched. Be that as it may, it was here that the last little band of Cathars finally surrendered to the bloodthirsty forces of the Roman Catholic Church.'

Because of his choice of words, one or two looked at him somewhat challengingly, but the Frenchman didn't seem to notice. As far as he was concerned, it was inevitable that there'd be some Catholics amongst them.

'…On the second of March 1244, after a year-long siege, over two hundred Cathar Perfect… records on the exact number vary between two hundred and two hundred and twenty-four… walked down the very path that we shall be climbing today, to be burnt to death here, at the stake.'

'Good God! Why?'

'Because they wouldn't revoke their faith.'

'They were devil worshippers?'

Claude Boudet smiled sadly. 'No. It was just that their interpretation of Christianity differed to that of the pope at the time.'

'What are you trying to say?'

The courier sensed the questioner's antagonism. Tough! He'd hear it anyway.

'In those days, the Cathar faith was a flourishing religion throughout Occitania and by that, I mean Southern France as we know it today, almost from the Atlantic coast in the west to Provence in the southeast and even as far as Lombardy in Northern Italy. It was because of its growing popularity and its threat to the Roman Catholic church that Pope Innocent III, in 1208, branded them as heretics and ordered a crusade against them. *Foxes in the vineyards of the Lord* was how he referred to them. Anyway, over the next twenty years, the Catholic army slaughtered over a hundred thousand Cathars, in the name of so-called Christianity.'

'Pah!'

The objector had heard enough and was now leaving the group and heading for the path to the summit, with his wife in tow. Claude Boudet pretended not to notice them go.

'What was so evil about these Cathars, then? What did they believe in?'

'The same God as the pope himself, actually, but they rejected Rome's version of Christianity. Their faith was gnostic. In other words, they believed that they were privy to unique religious knowledge. They also believed that the Kingdom of God was within each individual and could be achieved without the help of intermediaries such as the pope and his priests. They believed in the goodness of Christ but not in him as a son of God. Consequently, they repudiated the idea of the virgin birth and the salvation of the cross. They rejected its symbol and condemned all idolatry connected with it. This was probably their greatest heresy in the eyes of the Catholic church. Another anathema, as far as the church was concerned, was the Cathar belief in the dual nature of God. God, to them, was both a masculine and feminine deity, which was why they had male and female preachers. Imagine what the pope made of that, in those early days. Anyhow, as far as the Cathars were concerned, worship had to be an integral part of their everyday life, not just a ritual in a church. It was because of this virtuous life that they came to be known as *Les Bonhommes*, The Good People.'

Since quite a few of the group had begun drifting away by now, Claude Boudet ended his homily and they all made for the path to the summit. But, as so often happened, those with genuine interest – the ones that Claude regarded as the more intelligent – stayed close to him as they climbed. He knew that their questions would soon be coming.

'Why Cathar? Does it have a meaning?'

'Probably comes from the Greek "katharos" meaning pure. Their perfecti renounced all material possessions and avoided all temptations of the flesh.'

'Perfecti?'

'The Perfects! The Cathar ministers if you like. They paralleled their lives as closely as they could to that of Christ. They were the preachers and only they could give the consolamentum.'

He always enjoyed sharing his knowledge with those who showed genuine interest and he always made a point of letting one answer lead to another question.

'Consolamentum?'

'Baptism of the Holy Spirit is how some like to explain it. Not all the two-hundred-odd Cathars who were here in Montségur in 1244 were perfecti of course. Most of them were just ordinary men and women of the Cathar faith. When the siege finally took its toll and surrender became inevitable, they were offered deliverance on condition that they publicly renounced their so-called heretic faith. They were allowed fifteen days to consider the offer. Either freedom or being burnt at the stake.' He paused a second or two to catch his breath and to look into the questioner's eyes. 'Easy choice do you reckon?'

His rueful smile said it all and he didn't wait for an answer. '…When their time was up, every single one of them came down this very path, ready to make a *good end* as they called it, and *to go the way of the stars*. The perfecti had administered the consolamentum… both baptism and absolution in one… and death was to be welcomed.'

'Quite a story, Monsieur Boudet! Quite a story!'

The rest of the small group either nodded or murmured agreement as they looked again to the path ahead.

'I'm glad that you think so.' His critics might say that he was showing off but Claude Boudet got a lot of pleasure and satisfaction from sharing his knowledge with those who were genuinely interested.

'…Ah! Here we are!'

They'd reached the hut where admission tickets had either to be shown or bought. Today it was unmanned.

'…I have never known that before,' he mused.

A handwritten poster again proclaimed that the path to the summit would be closed to the public from the morrow until the end of the month.

Minutes went by and they continued to climb in the hot sun, being passed every so often by others on their way down. The growth on each side of an ever-steepening path was now so stunted that it rarely reached head height, thus offering little or no shade. And then, suddenly, they were climbing clear of the thorny trees and having to follow a zigzagging route amongst barren and rocky outcrops. It was hard work, made all the more difficult by the smooth, polished rock underfoot and by having to cling to the sides every so often to make room for those coming down.

'God! How high have we climbed do you reckon? Three hundred feet?'

They could see where their bus was parked far below. Down to the left, at least another three hundred feet lower than the car park, the little village of Montségur nestled into the hillside, dwarfed by its majestic surroundings. Claude Boudet spotted the coloured umbrellas of one of the little cafés and recognised, even from this distance, the terracotta roof of the local museum that was to be their next port of call when they got back down.

'Close enough,' he replied once he'd made a mental conversion into metric. 'But we have some way to go yet.' His ageing legs were already feeling the strain but he was determined to make it to the top.

'Couldn't the Cathars have escaped?' This came from a different questioner, from one of those behind him this time. 'There must be another way out of here?'

The Frenchman smiled. 'You can ask me that question again when you're looking down from the top. There is a story, though, that two… another account says four… of the Cathars did escape during the night. Not because they wanted to save their own skins but because they were given the task of saving the Cathar treasure.'

'Wow! That sounds interesting.'

The Frenchman forced a laugh despite his breathlessness. Again, he had to stop, but this time he found a rock to sit on, thus suggesting that he had another story to tell.

'Depends how you define interesting, I suppose. The treasure was probably nothing more than written documents on Cathar history, Cathar teachings... that sort of thing.'

'Oh well!' The initial interest had suddenly evaporated.

'Some have thought differently, mind you. The Nazis, for instance, during the war! In 1944, the Second SS Panzer Division Das Reich was sent down to this area by the SS Reichsführer Heinrich Himmler himself. For what? The Germans, after all, were supposed to have their hands full in Normandy, not to mention the Eastern Front, and yet they sent three hundred tanks and fifteen thousand men down here. No one to this day doubts what they were here for, and some say that they actually found it. The story goes that a one-word message was sent to Himmler in Berlin. "Eureka!" was all it said, and the next day, the sixteenth of March... which, coincidentally, just happened to be the seven hundredth anniversary of the fall of Montségur... a German plane circled over the citadel...' He looked up and they followed his gaze, as if expecting the aircraft to be still there. '...Skywriting a Celtic cross.'

Claude Boudet gave them a meaningful look.

'...The Celtic cross was, of course, the sacred symbol of the Cathars.'

'So there actually was treasure? And you say the Germans found it?'

'Maybe.' The Frenchman was enjoying himself. 'The story goes that when the division moved north again they were guarding a convoy that was transporting six hundred kilos of gold.'

'Wow!'

'Have you heard of a little place called Oradour-sur-Glane?'

No one had.

'But you have heard of the *Maquisards*? *Le Resistance*?'

'Of course.'

People on their way down now scowled as they had to squeeze past them on the narrow, treacherous path, obviously critical of where they'd stopped to chat. But Claude Boudet's Gallic smile disarmed them all.

'The convoy transporting the gold stayed the night at Oradour. By morning, the gold had disappeared and the soldiers guarding it had all been killed.'

'The Resistance!'

He nodded sagely. 'They were never caught and the gold was never found, but it was the people of Oradour who were punished. The Germans killed every single inhabitant and to this day the ruined village remains as a silent memorial to those who died.'

Their silence was his cue to move on.

ROME

Not for the first time that morning, Sally Jeffers cursed her unwelcome guest. She had expected to be back at the flat in under an hour, with the leathers and the helmet that would send Gus Adams on his way, but it was now eleven o'clock and she was still out shopping on his behalf. There had been no bother with the helmet – she'd bought that at her first port of call – but finding the leathers had been more of a problem. At last, though, she'd found him a set and, if they didn't fit, well tough shit!

He had given her more than enough cash to buy the stuff and to pay for the hired cab that had been kept waiting while she did the shopping. Now, at long last, she was heading for home again and with any luck he'd be out of her life within the hour.

*

With Sally gone, Gus had switched on the TV for the hourly news bulletin. Nothing at nine o'clock except a brief reference to the murder, to the fact that the dead man carried a British passport and that the police were still anxious to question a thin, long-haired Italian. Same again at ten o'clock. Now, however, on the eleven o'clock bulletin, what he dreaded most had suddenly appeared. His face – or at least a good resemblance – was staring at him out of the screen. The receptionist and the two English tourists arriving at the Hotel Gregorio on the Via Ludovici had obviously had a good look at him.

As the bulletin was coming to an end, he heard a sound that he knew to be the fax machine being activated. Inquisitively, he went over to see what the message was, half-expecting another instruction from Sally's uncle in London, but it was on the headed notepaper of Thomsons Holidays and addressed to Sally Jeffers. What he read made him curse: *We regret that your contract with Thomsons Holidays has been terminated with immediate effect.*

He was still mulling over it, ten minutes later, when a second one came through, this time from Thomas Cook's: Please note that your services as courier will no longer be required. The company cannot afford to have its high reputation in Italy undermined by the private affairs of one of its agents.

'Shit!' he muttered. 'What the hell will she say when she sees these?' He didn't have to wait long to find out.

Languedoc, SOUTH OF FRANCE
Le Chateau de Montségur

'Well? What do you think Monshewer Boo-dette? I bet you didn't expect to find me up here.'

She was sitting on a block of stone inside the ancient citadel, her face flushed by her recent effort and burnt red by the hot morning sun.

He smiled. 'I never doubted you, *madame*. Always knew that you were the strong-willed, determined type.'

'Really?' Marjorie seemed genuinely pleased with the compliment. 'Hear that, Sandra?'

'Hm!' If anything, her friend sounded jealous.

'So now that we're up here, Monshewer Boo-dette, what else can you tell us about Mont Secure? What does the name mean, anyway?'

He continued to smile. Days like this could become tedious if it weren't for the likes of Marjorie to liven them up.

'Exactly what you are calling it, Marjorie. Mont secure! Safe mountain!' His look turned roguish. 'You never told me that you understood French. You are a bit of a dark horse, I think.'

She squealed: 'Well fancy that, Sandra! I was right all the time. But there's not a lot to be seen here, is there? It's just an empty old ruin.'

Claude left them to it. He wanted to see what maintenance work needed to be carried out here. From what he'd heard, a tourist had almost fallen to his death here recently when a capstone on the wall that he was leaning on had suddenly given way.

He soon found what he was looking for. One corner of the ruins had been cordoned off with red and white tape and a sign, again in triplicate, warned members of the public not to venture beyond it onto the steps that ascended the ramparts. He could see that two of the capping stones did indeed appear to be perched rather precariously, as if they'd been moved. So someone or other must have been stupid enough to ignore the warning and had almost come to grief because of it.

On the other hand, the problem might not be that at all but something completely different. Perhaps someone had fallen into the old well, since it, too, had now been cordoned-off. But the well was hardly deep enough to be life-threatening, having filled-in with dirt over the years. Its depth nowadays was hardly more than a metre or two.

'Which one of us does he fancy, do you think? Me, I hope!'

Claude turned, half-expecting Marjorie to be referring to him but she and Sandra were looking the other way, in the direction of a muscular and handsome young man. The stranger, unaware of the attention, suddenly raised his camera to take a photograph.

'He's taken our photo, Sandra! What do you make of that, then? He must fancy us!'

Claude Boudet smiled sympathetically and exited the citadel through its north-facing doorway and out onto the Pog. Most of his party had already preceded him there, to continue their inspection of the site. Carefully, he picked his way along the well-worn path until he reached a rocky outcrop that projected over the sheer cliff face that overshadowed the village of Montségur, far below. Four members of his party were there ahead of him and were discussing in awe the way that the southeastern wall of the citadel – the wall with the disturbed capping stones – had been built on the very edge of the precipice. If anyone toppled over that, he thought with a shudder, then God help him. He would drop a hundred metres with hardly anything to break his fall.

'Amazing, monsieur! And frightening, too! Don't you think?'

Claude nodded. Although he had stood on this very spot many times before, he knew exactly how the man felt. Anyone suffering vertigo would have nightmares after being here.

'... Whoever thought of building a fort in such a place must have been mad, don't you think?'

'The well was the deciding factor, of course.'

'Yes. I see what you mean. No citadel could hold out long against a siege if they didn't have drinking water. But even so...'

'Another important consideration was that there were old foundations for them to build on. What you are looking at now are not the ruins of the original citadel. This, in fact, is the post-medieval Montségur III, built by the French Royal forces after they had totally demolished the Cathar stronghold which had been built by Raymond de Péreille during the early years of the thirteenth century and which today's historians refer to as Montségur II.'

'So, there must have been a Montségur I?'

'Of course. That could well have been a Visigothic fort, dating from the end of the fifth century or the beginning of the sixth. Same as at Rennes-le-Château, of course.'

'We visited Rennes-le-Château yesterday but weren't told that. We should have had you as guide, monsieur.'

Although the compliment pleased him, Claude Boudet made sounds of humility. 'Couriers have different interests, monsieur. You probably learnt other things yesterday that you would not have heard from me.'

He was about to turn away when his wily idea of a few days ago came back to him.

'...It's possible, though, that you weren't told about the hidden treasures of Montségur and Rennes and how, over the centuries, they have been protected by mysterious guardians?'

He waited for them to shake their heads expectantly and they didn't disappoint him.

'...There have been murders here of late but no arrests. Some people believe that...'

With a mischievous grin, he turned away, leaving them to mull over what they had just heard and knowing that he'd be plagued with questions on the coach on the way back.

ROME

'I can't believe this! I just can't fucking believe it!'

Gus could tell that she was close to tears but he didn't say anything. She was, after all, talking to herself and he didn't feel like inviting her anger by reminding her of his presence. It was just a matter of time, anyway.

'What the hell do I do now? Leave Rome? Leave Italy?'

'Perhaps I'd better go.'

Suddenly, her eyes flashed angrily through her tears. 'Yesss!' she hissed. 'I think you better had.' At which she scrunched the two fax messages into one ball and half-threw it in Gus' direction, watching it fall short at his feet. 'Compromised? Too fucking true I've been compromised, thanks to you!'

What could he say? 'Look, Sally! I'm really sorry for all this...' Agitatedly, he flicked at the ball of paper with his foot and watched it roll under a chair. '...But for the life of me, I can't see how I'm responsible. If anyone had seen me come here last night, then the police would have been here long before now to pick me up. Can't you phone Thomas Cook or Thomsons and ask them to explain?'

But she was in no mood to listen. 'Why don't you just... just leave! I've got you everything you wanted.'

Her tone was bitter but she wasn't the only one to feel hard done by.

'If that's what you want, but I'll leave you my mobile number, just in case you need to call me.'

She took the card from him and made a show of dropping it into a waste paper basket. 'Fat lot of use that'll be to me, with you hundreds of miles away in the south of France... or wherever your pathetic adventures lead you.'

Trastevere

Aiello felt only relatively satisfied. He had thought that his early morning calls to London, to Thomas Cook's and Thomsons, would see to the problem, but now, three hours later, he wasn't too sure. It wasn't like him not to play safe, and that was the reason he was back now at the same public kiosk that he'd visited earlier. *I should have done this first,* he thought, as his blind hand searched for the receiver.

The carabinieri were bound to welcome any anonymous tip off that might throw light on the Hotel Gregorio murder, and equally bound to respond immediately to information that linked the assassination victim to a tourist guide called Sally Jeffers. He dialled.

L'Ufficio del Papa, Apostolic Palace, The Vatican

'There can be no mistake, Commander?'

'None, Most Holy Father. It has been confirmed. The man has admitted.'

The pope gave a pained look. 'But why did he do it, Commander, after twelve years in our service? Has he explained? Was he paid to steal?'

'He says not, Your Holiness. He says that he did it for the sake of his brother's child, because the family was desperate.'

'You had better explain.'

'It seems, Most Holy Father, that his brother's daughter is dying from a rare genetic disease, one that can only be treated at a clinic in California… in Palo Alto, I believe he said. He claims the family is very poor and… Well, he admits that he came across the Schidoni Pentacle by chance, whilst tagging the archive exhibits, and that one of the older custodians happened to mention its significance to him in relation to the Map of the Count of Razes and hidden treasure.'

'But the curator assured us that he himself was the only one who knew of the connection.'

'It seems he was mistaken, Your Holiness.'

'But you questioned all the other custodians as well. Have none of them admitted discussing it with the thief?'

The commander gave the pontiff a rueful look. 'As chance would have it, Most Holy Father, the man in question was on the point of retiring and had done so before the theft was discovered.'

'So, the thief took a brass rubbing of the pentacle and then stole the map?'

'Yes, Your Holiness.'

'But the Nag Hammadi manuscript? Was he responsible for removing that as well?'

'I fear so.'

'And has it been recovered?'

'I fear not. The man tells us that he gave the papyrus, together with the map and the rubbing of the Schidoni Pentacle, to his brother.'

The pope looked towards heaven and crossed himself. 'To do what with them?' He was asking as if fearing the worst.

'He tells me that he extracted a promise from his brother that he would only sell the papyrus as a very last resort.'

'In other words, if he failed to find the hidden wealth of *Il Tesoro*.'

The commander nodded grimly.

'Which means that he knows the momentous significance of the Nag Hammadi document.'

The commander looked dubious. 'The man knows that collectors are always willing to pay good money for bits of old manuscripts and papyri. He had found out that the Nag Hammadi was in some way special, but having questioned him, I don't think he had any idea of its true significance.'

'Tell me how he was caught.'

'Recently, a man's body was found near Montségur in the Languedoc. It was badly decomposed but the French police were able to establish that the man had been murdered.'

The pontiff again crossed himself and muttered another Ave Maria. 'How was the poor man killed?'

The commander paused, as if unwilling to be the messenger of unsavoury details. 'I fear that he had been shot through the head, Your Holiness.'

'And?'

'French police have now established that the dead man was the brother of our archives custodian.'

Again, the pope made the sign of the cross. 'And the parchment is now in the hands of his murderers, men who seek the demise of our Holy Catholic church.'

The commander remained solemn.

Vauxhall Cross, LONDON

'Arrest her! Cross-examine her!' Sir James Oldcorn felt a mixture of anger and relief. At last, he had a suspect!

A week ago, he had taken the unprecedented step of seeking the help of Scotland Yard and since then a team of hand-picked secret branch professionals had been sifting through the private files of all Vauxhall Cross personnel, trying to make a connection with the recent deaths of MI6 agents in Albania and Italy. Did anyone have family ties in Albania or Italy? Was there perhaps a mafia connection? Could there be a Vatican tie-in? There were so many secret societies linked to the Holy See—Opus Dei, P2, Order of the Solar Temple, Knights of Malta, the Illuminati, not to mention the nebulous Priory of Sion. Could there be a covert association with one of those? The team's brief had been simple. Find the connection!

The initial results had been less than promising. No MI6 personnel with Albanian family ties; five with Italian connections but none of any significance; none with any known links to the mafia; sixteen Roman Catholics...

'We'll need special dispensation, Sir James, to check on personal bank accounts, private phone calls from home... That sort of thing.'

'Do it!'

The breakthrough had come when all seemed lost. A woman in her late fifties – Anne Corbett by name and Roman Catholic by religion – had been receiving phone calls at home direct from a kiosk in Trastevere. Checks had revealed that some of them were made just prior to the deaths of MI6 agents in Rome and Kukes and that the last call took place a few days before Tom Mackay's death. A further check on her bank account revealed regular payments over the last two years from a Swiss bank that had part-Vatican ownership.

'Find out what she knows, then make damn sure that you throw the fucking book at her. I want the bitch locked up and the bloody key thrown away!'

Not exactly the sort of language that one expected from the director of operations at Vauxhall Cross, or from a respected knight of the realm.

Out of Italy

Gus Adams was making for the A12 when he felt his cell phone vibrating in his chest pocket. There had been no problems with buying the bike. He had settled for the most powerful in the showroom – a Honda Goldwing 1800cc – and had paid for it with his Premier Gold credit card. Twenty minutes at the most was all that the transaction had taken, during which time he'd kept his helmet on, much to the salesman's amusement and curiosity.

He pulled over and reached for the mobile in his jacket pocket.

'Yes?' he barked, full of wariness.

'Gus Adams?'

Sally's voice! 'Sally! Are you all right?'

'No, I am not! Thanks to you I've just had two policemen here now, asking me a lot of questions.'

Shit! He felt immediate unease. 'Oh?'

'Wanted to know what my relationship with Thomas Mackay was.'

'And?'

'Isn't that enough?' She now sounded more worried than peeved. 'I told them that I hardly knew the man. But I know they didn't believe me. They said they were investigating a murder and that they had reason to think that I was one of the last to see Mackay alive.'

'Oh!' Gus was lost for words.

'Not only that, but they asked me about you.'

'They have my name?'

'You needn't worry, Mr Adams!' She'd picked up on his concern and was making no attempt to hide her sarcasm. 'What they asked was whether I knew someone who answered the description in the photofit.'

'And?'

'I told them that I did.'

'What?'

'Told them what my work is… was… and that I often met people who fitted that description.'

'They believed you?'

'Hardly. Told me I could expect another visit from them, soon. More of a threat than anything else.'

Gus wondered why she'd phoned him. 'Is there anything I can do?'

'I don't know.'

For the first time since he'd met her, she sounded lost and somewhat defenceless.

'Have you thought of leaving Rome?' Even as he asked the question, he knew how insensitive it sounded. She'd already told him what living in Italy meant to her. 'Perhaps if you went back home,' he suggested and then added lamely. 'Just until this blows over.'

'And that's all you can suggest?'

'But what else can I do, Sally?'

Her instinctive reply surprised them both. 'You could take me with you.'

'Pardon?' Had he heard her right?

'You could take me with you, wherever you're going… *Until this business blows over.* Your words!'

Gus was in a quandary. He had been warned not to compromise her but somehow or other it had happened anyway. Maybe it wasn't his fault. Maybe Mackay had been to blame? Or even her uncle, the great MI6 guru himself.

'Well?' She was persistent.

'Pack a few clothes. I'll come back for you.' It was, he realised, a decision that he had to take, and one that he might seriously come to regret.

Spanish—French Border (the following morning)

Galileo sighed with relief as the winding road reached its summit and began descending. He hadn't enjoyed the drive up the Spanish coast from the airport in Barcelona but now, at last, he had crossed into France and should reach Perpignan within the hour. Another hour or so would see him in Carcassonne. There he would pick up the gun that Aiello had promised him and then await his instructions.

Via Aurelia, NORTHWEST ITALY

'Have you any idea where we're headed?' She was shouting to be heard.

They had spent the night in a small family-run hotel on the outskirts of Viareggio, north of Pisa, and were now, after an early start, whizzing through tunnel after tunnel on the Via Aurelia. Road signs indicated that they were bypassing the port of Genova. Dials on the bike showed the time at ten minutes to nine and their speed a steady one hundred and seventy kilometres per hour.

As she clutched like a leech to the rider, Sally estimated that they were travelling at well over a hundred miles an hour but she was gradually getting used to her fear. Yesterday had been her first time ever on a bike's pillion and what a baptism that had been. Gus had come back for her at the flat, as he'd promised, having stopped on the way to buy her some leathers and a helmet. Then they'd headed north out of the city and, as the bike picked up speed on the A12, she had kept her eyes tightly shut in silent prayer. Today, though, there was a certain thrill to the experience.

'There are airports in Nice and Montpellier,' he shouted into his helmet and over his shoulder. 'You can catch a flight from either one of them to London. Which would you prefer?'

No answer came. Had she heard? Had she understood? Her silence worried him. She had already refused to be dropped off at Pisa airport, late yesterday afternoon.

'Your uncle will be contacting me before the day is out,' he stressed. 'And I'll have to tell him that you're safely on your way back to London. Tell me where you'd like to be dropped off.'

'I'll go where you're going.'

Gus eased the throttle, pulled up onto the hard shoulder and lifted his visor. 'I'm sorry but that's not an option.'

For the first time since he'd met her, she smiled at him; more of a calculating smile than anything else.

'Tell me this, Gus Adams! Do you speak French?'

'No.'

'And you expect people in the Languedoc to be fluent in English or Italian?'

'Probably not.'

'So how will you manage? You'll be asking questions that no one understands and getting answers to questions that you never asked.'

Despite her flippant exaggeration, he knew that she had a valid point. 'So, what are you saying?'

'Only that you need me, since I'm fluent in French. But don't start getting any ideas. I won't be doing it for you but for my Uncle Jim.'

It was Gus' turn to smile before pulling down his visor and revving the engine. 'I'm afraid you'll have to think again, young lady! Don't forget, you are not to be compromised.'

'I am bloody compromised,' she muttered. 'You've already seen to that!'

He either didn't hear her or else chose to ignore the argument and they both fell silent as the bike again ate up the miles.

LANGUEDOC Le village de Montségur

The village people were out on the narrow streets in numbers. The excitement had begun early, while many were still in their beds, when the heavy throb of Chinook twin rotors had announced the arrival of the contractors and their equipment.

A net full of scaffolding had been first to arrive. Seventy-five minutes later had come a cement mixer and a small compressor. And now, just after midday, the villagers were out again, craning their necks to watch the delivery of a small mechanical digger, dangling like a bright-orange conker beneath the transport helicopter.

Within minutes, and with a deafening roar, the Chinook was taking off again and its pulsating throb soon faded into the distance, in the direction of Toulouse. Returning indoors, the people of Montségur knew that there'd be very little tourist activity in the area for some weeks to come.

The two young men stood their ground as everyone else dispersed. They too had witnessed the deliveries and had recorded every detail through the powerful zoom lens of a camcorder. Now they became engaged in serious discussion which ended with one of them reaching for his cell phone and dialling.

'Hello Commander! Otto speaking. Erwin and I have just witnessed some suspicious developments in the Citadel and wonder whether we should alert the others… No, Brett and Christen are still keeping an eye on things in Rennes-le-Château…'

Le Château de Montségur

The huge placard was ready to be put in place, to be clearly visible from below; confirmation that the company now at work in the citadel was called *Morcon*. It didn't have the authority to prevent tourists visiting the Cathar stele, but it did have the right to deny them access to the path leading up to the Château itself. Signs erected in the name of the *Association des Sites du Pays Cathare* confirmed as much. Montségur was now officially closed to the public.

Inside the citadel a sheet of thick plywood served as a temporary desk on a roughly erected plinth over which three men were now holding discussion. They were looking at a sheet of tracing paper showing a diagram similar to a pentagram, and that, in turn, had been placed over a photocopy of an amateurish map. The discussion was becoming animated, suggesting disagreement over some of the details, and fingers were seen to point here and there within the citadel's enclosure. They were, in fact, discussing where the digging should start.

Despite representing a firm of contractors based in Narbonne, their conversation wasn't in French but Hebrew.

Le Village de Montségur

Otto and Erwin had become familiar faces around the village and by now were on first-name terms with the proprietor of the little café. They'd been staying in the area for the best part of three weeks and no one doubted that they were who they claimed to be, namely two Swiss research students studying the geology of the area; work that justified their visits to all sorts of remote locations; such as their chance appearance at the spot where the assassinated victim's body had recently been found. It also explained why they carried compasses, powerful cameras and binoculars. Their night vision scopes and guns, however, were well-hidden.

Despite their wanderings, their main centre of interest, as they would readily admit to anyone prepared to listen, was the geological structure known as the Pog, on which the Castello di Montségur – as they referred to it – stood. Their assortment of rock samples and abundance of geological notes was proof in itself.

Now sensing that the topic of their discussion was wearing thin, Jules, the café proprietor, made his excuses and retreated to his little kitchen, leaving his two customers to exchange relieved looks as they hurriedly brought their chairs closer together so that they could study the viewer on the camcorder. They needed to discuss exactly what they had seen arriving by helicopter and what could now be going on within the citadel under the pretence of "safety work".

A little research by the Vatican had given them all that they needed to know about *Morcon*. For a start, the company's estimate on the work that needed to be carried out at the citadel had been the most competitive of all tenders submitted and that, in itself, had guaranteed them the contract. Secondly, *Morcon* was a long-established and highly prestigious company, much involved in public works in the Languedoc. But even more significant, from a Vatican point of view, was the fact that *Morcon* was an abbreviated form of *Mordecai Construction*. An Israeli company!

Once that was realised, it had then been easy for the two young men to put two and two together. Enquiries about the near accident – the one that had necessitated the renovation work in the first place – revealed that the so-called "tourist visitor" who had almost been killed by falling masonry, had himself been Jewish. In other words, everything pointed to the same conclusions – *Morcon* was operating on behalf of whoever was in possession of the Vatican's missing documents and the riddle of the Schidoni Pentacle and the Map of the Count of Razes had been solved. Their commander in the Vatican had been right, all along, to send them here to the Languedoc, and to Montségur in particular.

As they viewed the scene being replayed on the camera's lens, Otto and Erwin again exchanged meaningful looks and, after making sure that there was no one within earshot, they began discussing their next move.

*

The trembling in the breast pocket of his leather jacket told him that his cell phone was ringing. They were crossing the Rhone at Arles at the time. He braked and pulled over, feeling Sally's weight pressing against him as the bike decelerated.

'Hello?'

'Is that Agent Gus?'

He recognised the voice of Sir James Oldcorn. 'That's right.'

'Where are you now?'

'We're just passing Arles, north of the Camargue.'

Silence. Then: 'What the hell are you doing there? I expected you to be in Carcassonne by now. You got my fax? And did I hear you right? Did you just say *we*?'

'Afraid so. Your niece is with me and we're going by road.'

Another lull, followed by, 'You'd better explain! And your explanation had better be good.'

Gus gave him a brief account of how and why they were where they were and then passed the phone on to Sally.

'Hi, Uncle Jim! So, it's safe for us now to talk, is it?'

The question did what it was meant to do, which was to throw MI6's director of operations onto his back foot.

'Um... yes! This is a safe line and anyway, the problem at this end has been removed.'

'Removed? Sounds ominous, Uncle!'

'I'd like you to fly back home, Sally. Today, if possible. I've got your mother to think of.'

'Sorry, Uncle! No deal! I intend going back to Rome as soon as things quieten down there, which will be in a few days' time, I hope. Last thing I did before leaving was to pay two months' rent in advance on my flat.'

'Put him back on!'

With a shrug and a roll of her eyes she passed the phone back to Gus.

'...Now listen, young man! First thing I want you to do when you get to the Languedoc is to put my niece on a plane out of there. Understood?'

'Easier said than done, sir, but I'll do my best.'

'Good. See to it! Now then, listen carefully! Now that our mutual friend is no longer with us, then I'll have to be your contact over the next few days. Highly irregular from my point of view but I prefer it that way, since I want to keep a tight rein on things for the time being... at least until I'm satisfied that there's no connection between what's going on in the Languedoc and that business that you were last involved with in that other place.' Despite knowing that the line was safe, Sir James was still wary of being too specific. 'It's not going to be easy for me because my time is hardly ever my own. It just means that I'll have to rely a lot on my wife as a go-between. So, when you have something to report, you talk to her as if you were talking to me. Understood?'

'No problem. So, what do I do now?'

'After you've sent my niece packing, you travel to Carcassonne and follow the instructions that I faxed you last night. You've read them, I hope?'

'Of course!' What do you take me for? A bloody dimwit?

'And you then destroyed them?'

'As per instructions,' Gus confirmed rather sarcastically, realising that Sir James didn't want anything in black and white that might even hint at MI6 involvement.

'Good. Now listen! I've received more information during the past couple of hours on the items that I mentioned in my fax.'

He was now referring, Gus realised, to the Schidoni Pentacle and the Map of the Count of Razes. He smiled. Razes – an area in the Languedoc – not Races, as he had first thought it to be!

'...They are not code words but the names of documents, missing... stolen... from the Vatican. And papal feathers are ruffled because of it! Apparently, the items have something to do with *Il Tesoro*—The Treasure. Now that could be a code word for what went on in Albania but I very much doubt it. We'll just have to keep an open mind on that, at least for the time being. Anyway, what we now need to know... what I want you to find out, Adams... is why the Vatican and the Israelis are now showing interest in the south of France of all places. And not just them, apparently. It's more than possible that Hamas are also in some way involved. Which is why I can't rule out a connection with that other business you were involved in.

'Either way, be very careful. Just keep an ear to the ground in case you hear something of interest. That's all you need do. You weren't meant to become so involved when we sent you out to Rome but you did damn well and I'm grateful. Now that things have been resolved at this end, then I can guarantee that you won't be operating alone from now on... The fax! I gave you names of possible contacts.'

Gus was momentarily confused. 'You gave me names and addresses of three historians! All living in or around Carcassonne! *Contact any one of them* was what you said. *See what information they can give you about the Map of the Count of Razes*. Are you now saying that they're not historians at all, but your agents?'

'Of course they're historians! Every one of them a recognised authority on the history of the Languedoc. And no, they are not my agents. Just pick one of them and pretend to be interested in the subject. If he knows anything about either of the two items... the map or the pentacle... then all well and good, but if he doesn't, then move on to the next one. How are you for ready cash? Tom was supposed to look after you in that respect.'

Gus was thrown by the sudden change of subject. 'Um! Well now that you ask...' He wanted to mention the cost of buying the bike. On the other hand, he still had that wad of mafia money from Kukes, that no one else knew anything about.

'I'll arrange it. I'll be in touch. Good luck!' And with that he was gone.

Le Château de Montségur

Otto and Erwin, the two young Swiss "geologists", waited until after lunch before setting off. Their ageing Dormobile took them up as far as the tourist car park; then, with backpacks of equipment and ignoring the warning sign, they took to the path leading up to the citadel. Not that they expected to get very far but they knew that they had to test the water at some time or other. The next few minutes, they realised, would determine their future course of action.

As they climbed in silence past the Cathar stele, they felt another shower coming on and they quickened their step to reach the comparative shelter of the trees and, beyond that, the shelter of the little hut where the ticket collector usually sat. As they neared, they broke into a run, laughing aloud as they did so, giving the impression that being drenched was in itself a joke. What they didn't want was to arrive unexpectedly and to be eyed with a lot of suspicion or possibly the barrel of a gun.

'You cannot go further!' The two men guarding the path by the ticket collector's hut had been chatting over their lunch, but now they'd stood up to confront the unwelcome visitors. 'Did you not see the sign?'

'Yes, we saw the sign, but we do not want to go all the way to the top. We are geologists and we only want to take rock samples off the upper slope. We only need to go just above the treeline.'

'Impossible!' Same spokesman as before. 'Too dangerous!'

The two young men, both of them supremely fit soldiers and members of the Vatican Guard, knew that they could take the unsuspecting guards by surprise and easily overpower them, but that wasn't the object of their visit. They were here merely to confirm what they already suspected.

'But!' Otto pretended to be at a loss. 'We must have samples or we won't be able to complete our research.'

His friend Erwin nodded agreement. 'It will affect our end-of-year grades at university.'

'Sorry, but there's nothing we can do about that. The path is closed from here up.'

Standing there in the rain, the two fake geologists made a point of looking not only vulnerable and miserable but also suitably perplexed by their predicament. Then Otto reached for his wallet.

'Perhaps we could pay?'

'Sorry, sir, but there is no way that you will be allowed to go further than this, however much you try to bribe us. Now please go!'

'We can seek permission from the tourist office perhaps. Or maybe from your bosses? As I said, we would not need to go to the citadel itself. We have been told that that is where the work is being done, not on the path. So where is the danger?'

The man's face hardened. 'Stones might roll and the two of you might be seriously injured, even killed. Such a risk cannot be taken, so please leave before…' The guard obviously felt no need to complete the threat.

Looking suitably abject, the two so-called students retraced their steps.

'At least we've confirmed our suspicions.'

They were well out of earshot now.

'…Did you see it? On the bench?'

'The gun? Yes.'

A hurriedly thrown jacket had failed to hide the end of the barrel.

'So, what do we do now?'

Carcassonne

Galileo had spent the night in Carcassonne and had met his contact, as Aiello had instructed. Now, he was on the road again – the D118 according to his road map – heading due south past the village of Alet-les-Bains towards a village or town called Quillan. There he would turn west onto the D117 and make for Lavelanét, a route that looked distinctly more promising on the map than the winding secondary road through the Gorges de la Frau, further south. He would approach Montségur from the north rather than the east.

For the third time since setting out from Carcassonne, he groped beneath his seat until he touched what he was looking for. The Beretta and its silencer were still safely lodged there and they gave him comfort.

He began whistling, unaware of how tuneless his *Sole Mio* really sounded. Fingerposts at a junction indicated *Rennes-Les-Baines* and *Arques* to his left, and soon afterwards another turn-off for somewhere called Rennes-Le-Château. The names meant nothing to him.

As the kilometres rolled by, the weather changed. The distant peaks had been under heavy cloud all morning but the wind was now getting stronger and the sky more leaden. He didn't have to know about local weather patterns to appreciate that there were heavy and prolonged showers on the way.

It had been his intention to stop for lunch at the place called Quillan but the D117 bore right before he reached the town's outskirts and he took the turning. There would be other places to stop, of which Lavelanét looked the most promising. The first drops of rain splattered against his windscreen as he gained altitude on the Col du Portel and, within seconds, his wipers were barely able to cope with the downpour.

The shower lasted a good ten minutes by which time Galileo was kicking himself for not having driven into Quillan and taking lunch there. His stomach was rumbling and he wasn't making the progress that he'd hoped for. Before driving into Lavelanét he would stop to put on his cassock. It would be *Father Galileo* from there on.

Alet-les-Baines

He picked up the phone. 'Allo? Claude Boudet *à l'appareil.*'

'Ah! Je m'appelle Sally Jeffers, monsieur. Je vous appelle de Carcassonne.'

'You are English?'

'Yes, monsieur.' She laughed briefly. 'Did my accent betray me?'

'Not your accent, madame, but your name. Sally Jeffers is hardly a French name.'

Sally could sense the smile behind the words. 'Of course. But I am not married, monsieur. It's mademoiselle, not madame.'

It was his turn to laugh. 'Then I am pleased to make your acquaintance, Mademoiselle Jeffers. How may I help you?'

'I have been told that you are an authority on the history of the Languedoc, Monsieur Boudet. Is that true?'

'Ah! That has to be a matter of opinion, mademoiselle. I wonder who gave a poor tourist guide such recommendation?'

The silence from the other end of the line suggested disappointment. Then: 'Forgive me, monsieur, but we were given to understand that you were a university lecturer on French history. It seems that I've been misinformed. Forgive me.'

She was on the point of putting the phone down, to dial the last number on her list of three. There had been no answer from the first one.

'Wait, Miss Jeffers! It is true that I am a poor tourist guide now but it is also true that I used to be a lecturer on French history. So perhaps I am in a position to help you, after all. Who knows?'

'Can we meet, monsieur?'

'It will be my pleasure, Mademoiselle Jeffers. But you will have to come to me.'

'And where is that?'

'Alet-les Baines, twenty-four kilometres south of Carcassonne.'

'We have travelled very far today, Monsieur Boudet, and we are very tired. May we call on you tomorrow morning?'

'But of course. I shall look forward to it.'

'Thank you, monsieur. And your address?'

Le Village de Montségur

'Ah, Father! I have been expecting you. Welcome to Montségur!' The local priest looked genuinely pleased to extend his hospitality. 'It is an honour to have you under my humble roof and I trust that our French mountain air will do much to improve your health whilst you are with us.'

'Thank you, Father.' Galileo coughed repeatedly. 'It is so good of you to have me.' He was the picture of piety but not of ill health.

'But you will have to excuse my poor Italian, Father.'

Galileo smiled sympathetically. 'Do not apologise, Father. Your Italian is one hundred times better than my French.' Which was a lie, of course, because Galileo's French was fluent by anyone's standard, only it now suited him better to pretend otherwise.

'The weather today is not nice but I am sure that it will improve soon for you Father, so that you can get some fresh air. I have been told that your doctor in the Vatican has recommended much exercise.'

As if proof of his chest condition were needed, Galileo got caught in another fit of harsh coughing, at the end of which he smiled wanly. 'Unfortunately for me, Father, that is what I must do.' He patted his burly torso, giving the impression that he was fat rather than muscular. 'As you can see, I am not a fitness fanatic.'

They both laughed.

'…But if I am to see many more years on this earth, then I shall have to be obedient to my doctor.'

'Of course, Father. But you are allowed the occasional glass of wine?'

Galileo smiled mischievously. 'Thank you, Father Francois. My doctor recommends that as well.'

They grinned at one another, having established that they had at least one thing in common.

Le Château de Montségur

It was late afternoon and tempers were becoming frayed.

The quickly erected scaffolding now displayed *Morcon* in huge red lettering above the château wall, leaving no doubt in the villagers' minds that renovation work was in progress and that the citadel was indeed closed to the public until further notice.

'The calculations must be correct, Yashar. My interpretation of the pentacle must be right. How else do you explain the connection between it and the map?'

They were sheltering under a tarpaulin cover on which the rain drummed incessantly. It hadn't been a good day for them, what with the weather and the lack of progress. The photocopied sheets of paper that were spread out in front of them over the makeshift table were becoming increasingly soggier. 'Given that there is a connection at all, of course, bearing in mind that Vatican tradition is all that we have to go on.'

Leron, the tallest of the three Mossad agents, and clearly the one in authority, made no effort to hide his irritability or his intolerance. 'Let's not start on that again. This is only our first day. Our government has been searching for the treasure from the Temple of Solomon for three score years. Many before us have failed but we are privileged.' He prodded at the papers with his forefinger. 'We have the map and the pentacle and they will enable us to return in triumph to Jerusalem. Our people's dreams will be realised and our names will go down in history.'

Yashar and Ben-Ami remained silent, as if their scepticism needed to be appeased.

'…It's regrettable, of course it is, that we haven't got the original map, but the photocopy which was taken off the Italian must be genuine. You accept that?'

Grudgingly, the other two nodded.

'…The man did have a direct link to Vatican archives, after all!'

'But our agent should have been more patient. He should have put more pressure on him to reveal where he had hidden the original. Could he not have bribed him to part with it?'

'Maybe so, but the man was a threat. Not only that, but our enemies were closing in on him. What if they had got their hands on the map and the pentacle before we did?'

Leron knew that he was going over old ground. They'd discussed all this at length before now.

'...Our agent had little choice but to take things into his own hands.'

'Maybe so, Leron, but I still have my doubts about your interpretation. We have no guarantee that this in the right place.'

Ben-Ami grunted agreement.

The search by the *Morcon* workforce had been in progress for almost seven hours and had yielded nothing up to now, either within the citadel or in its immediate vicinity on the Pog. The old well, which had been regarded as the most promising prospect, had proved particularly disappointing, yielding nothing so far but wet earth and gravel. In an adjacent corner, the mechanical digger had been busy shifting a pile of fallen masonry to discover what lay beneath, only to hit on bedrock and another dead-end.

Leron kept prodding with his finger at each of several sheets of paper spread out in front of them. They were all damp photocopies of a faint and amateurish-looking map on which pentagrams of various sizes had been pencilled-in, at different angles and seemingly at random. Closer inspection, however, would show that the geometric design was exactly the same on every map, only that it had been enlarged or diminished, rotated or flipped over in a desperate search for a likely fit.

'If we are wrong, then so was the Italian who came here with the map and the original copy of the pentacle. But I don't think he was. Nor are we. The answer must lie in this.'

Leron now pulled towards him a map that had intricate geometric designs pencilled on to it, all of them shaded in different colours.

'...Since we know that the map was drawn sometime during the eighth century then we have to assume that these...' He pointed to each of three little towers shown on the map. '...Must be the Visigothic strongholds of Toulouse, Carcassonne and Rhedae. Now then, any of today's maps will show that Toulouse is at least twice as far from Carcassonne as Rhedae is, but according to this map they are exactly equidistant.'

'It was drawn by a layman. An amateur.'

'Maybe so, Yashar, but not even a layman could have been so far out in his calculations and if you look at it from my perspective, neither could he have been so exactly precise either.'

Leron could still sense his colleagues' lingering scepticism. From the start, Yashar and Ben-Ami had argued that Schidoni's Pentacle pointed to Rhedae (renamed Rennes-le-Château at a later date) rather than Montségur as the likely hiding place of the treasure, and Leron, even by his own calculations, had to admit that they might still be right and that he could be wrong. But a decision had had to be made and that had fallen to him, as group leader. A near accident to an Israeli tourist had been engineered, immediate safety work at the citadel had been called for, *Morcon* had tendered for the contract and had been successful. Everything had worked to plan and it was far too late now to have a change of heart. Leron's only consolation, if he was proved wrong, was that they would never have had permission to excavate in Rennes-le-Château anyway.

'Look! Bear with me while I reason it out with you just one more time. What I did was to take Carcassonne as the focal point of a circle, with the distance to Toulouse or to Rhedae as its radius, since both… on this Map of the Count of Razes, at least… are equidistant. When I marked-off those radii, I found that the angle between them was exactly one hundred and twenty degrees, forming a segment that's exactly one third of a circle. Hardly another coincidence? Then, by extending those radii to show diameters, and then bisecting all the angles, the circle becomes split into six equal segments…' With pencil in hand, he was illustrating what he meant. 'By using any five of those six diametric points it is possible to draw a geometrically perfect pentacle. But as you've both pointed out to me many times already, the Schidoni Pentacle is not a balanced pentagram because one of its points lies outside the radial distance of the other four.'

Again, they sighed. Leron was going over old ground and touching on details that they'd discussed so often before now. He persisted though.

'…Unless you can persuade me otherwise, then the only way to explain the Bartolomeo Schidoni diagram is to scale it down, as I have done, so that at least four of its points coincide with the diametric ones on our assumed map circle. The problem arises with the fifth point which must therefore lie somewhere outside that circle.'

Leron now placed a piece of tracing paper, with a pentacle drawn on it, over a clean copy of the map.

'This is the scaled-down version.'

Carefully he began to rotate the tracing paper on the map. 'As you can see, I can align its points with any four of the six segmental points on the map circle. It doesn't matter which four. The problem comes with the fifth point, which must lie somewhere outside the radius. Now the only feature on the map, that this fifth point actually touches, is the tip of the mountain marked here and to my mind that can only be Montségur.'

'But if that's the case, then that means that none of the other points of the pentacle touches Rhedae. If we accept that the three forts on the map represent Toulouse, Carcassonne and Rhedae... or Rennes-le-Château as it's now called... then it doesn't make sense to us, to Ben-Ami and me, that Rhedae isn't in some way part of the solution unless...'

'Unless it is the solution! Yes, I take your point, Yashar, but I still prefer my interpretation.'

Ben-Ami had remained silent thus far but he now chipped in with his little bit of argument: 'We know that the *Société Spéleologique de l'Ariège* systematically surveyed every part of the Pog in 1960. Records show that they explored every cave and every crevice and that they found nothing here. Not only that, but between 1964 and 1975 archaeological excavations were carried out here... and in the surrounding area... by GRAME, the *Groupe de Recherches Archeologiques de Montségur et Environs*, and they didn't find anything either. No such survey has been carried out at Rennes-le-Château and when you consider the Sauniére story, well...'

Leron sighed out loud at having to argue this point again. 'Look! As I've said before, I'm willing to concede to your argument about Rennes-le-Château if you can explain to me the significance of the pentacle point that lies outside the radius of the other four.'

Since Yashar and Ben-Ami could only shrug their shoulders, Leron continued: 'I have never claimed that the treasure from Solomon's Temple would be easy to find. Common sense tells us that it is extremely well-hidden, otherwise it would have been found hundreds of years ago. There have been so many attempts to find it. The Nazis were nothing if not efficient were they? As we Jews know to our cost! And they certainly weren't fools. So why do you think that the likes of Heinrich Himmler and Martin Bormann showed such an interest in Montségur in 1943? Why was that man Otto Rahn sent here, if not to research the area? And after he submitted his report, why were teams of German scientists and geologists, historians and archaeologists sent down here – again on the express orders of the Nazis – if not to find our Treasure?'

By again remaining silent, the other two were conceding Leron's argument.

'Even if they did find some gold in the area, there's no way that they found the Treasure of Solomon. They would have gloated publicly if they had.'

'Maybe so, maybe not,' offered Ben-Ami. 'Maybe they were secretly lining their own pockets because they knew that they were losing the war.'

Yashar nodded agreement. 'Or perhaps it wasn't here in the first place! We know that the Cathars are known to have moved a treasure from here back in 1244.'

Leron looked as if he was knocking his head against a brick wall. 'We'll continue tomorrow,' he muttered. 'Hopefully, the weather will be kinder then.'

*

Through the gathering dusk, and from behind a huge boulder, Galileo watched the *Morcon* workforce troop down past the Cathar stele towards the bus that awaited them in an almost-empty roadside car park. The only other vehicles in sight were a newly registered black Renault Laguna estate, parked close to the bus, and an old orange-and-white Dormobile, standing a good distance away, at the very top end of the roadside parking area.

Father Francois had told him all about the tourist's near accident at the château and how the *Association des Sites du Pays Cathare* had had no option but to close the citadel to the public whilst safety work was being carried out there. The local priest, when asked, had also told him all he wanted to know about the history of Montségur and about *Morcon* Construction.

'The château looks so impressive, Father Francois. It would be such a shame for me not to be able to visit it before I leave.' The words had been accompanied by credible wonder as he'd stared up, wide-eyed, at the citadel.

'If you wish, I could make enquiries on your behalf but I doubt if they will agree. Everyone in the village has been told to discourage any attempts to get up there, since the site is even less safe now than it was before, because of the work that's being carried out. The path is guarded day and night against those who would ignore the warning notices.'

'Night as well? Surely not, Father?' It had been put as a casual question.

'Indeed so! *Morcon* are taking no chances, in case someone gets injured and brings a big insurance claim against the company. That sort of thing happens all too often, these days, here in France. A sign of the times that we live in, unfortunately.'

At which, Galileo had made suitable clucking noises with his tongue to suggest righteous disapproval before adding, 'Ah! We live in such a materialistic world. Don't you agree, Father? But are you saying that those poor guards have to spend every night up there, in the mist and the rain?'

'Not at the top, Father. In fact, the site is easily guarded. There is but one way up to the summit and everyone has to pass the hut where the ticket collector usually sits. From what I understand, that is where the guards are posted.' Father Francois had then patted Galileo reassuringly on the shoulder. 'But you needn't worry too much on their behalf, Father. The mist and the rain will be gone before morning.'

It looks as though the local priest was right about the weather, Galileo now thought as he crouched behind the boulder. Already, the rain had ceased and the clouds weren't hanging quite so low over the surrounding peaks but it was still gloomy enough for him to feel the need to pull up the zip of his black anorak.

The *Morcon* workers were now boarding the bus that would take them to their lodgings in Montferrier, ten kilometres away. As yet though, there was no sign of the three company officials whom Father Francois had said were staying locally in Montségur. The Renault Laguna had to be their car. The other vehicle – the rusty orange and white Dormobile at the very top end of the car park looked as if it had been abandoned.

Ten minutes went by and the bus still stood there, engine running. Then he saw five figures emerge from beneath the canopy of trees, striding purposefully past the Cathar stele. The three *Morcon* officials and the two guards, he realised. So perhaps there wasn't overnight guard duty after all? More likely, though, was that two others had already taken the watch. Galileo shrugged inwardly. It mattered not, anyway. Tomorrow night he would pay Le Chateau de Montségur a visit. Aiello would want to know what the Israelis were up to.

He waited until the bus had taken off in one direction, towards Montferrier, and the black Renault in another, down to the little village of Montségur, a mere two kilometres away. Then, when the sound of both engines had died in the distance, he crept out from behind the boulder, climbed back up onto the road and then strolled casually in the direction that the car had taken.

*

As Galileo's solitary figure receded down the hill towards the village, to be gradually swallowed by the dip – first his short legs, then his solid torso and finally his balding head – the two young men in the orange and white Dormobile turned towards one another with puzzled looks. They'd seen the little man arrive, had noticed his furtive movements to avoid being spotted by the coach driver, had watched him choose a hiding place from where he could spy on the *Morcon* workforce and now they were seeing him returning in the direction whence he'd come.

'You saw it?'

'The dog collar?'

'Yes. A Catholic priest! So, who is he? And what's he up to?'

'Hadn't we better let the commander know?'

'Not much to tell him, so far. But we'll certainly have to keep an eye on the little man.'

Alet-les-Bains

Claud Boudet expected visitors but not ones dressed as bikers. His surprise showed.

'Bonjour, monsieur! C'est Sally Jeffers et voici Gus Adams. Je vous ai téléphoné hier après midi.'

'Oui. J'étais impatient de vous rencontrer, Ms Jeffers. Entrez, s'il vous plait.'

He took her hand and, to her delight, raised it to his lips. *How quaint,* she thought, smiling.

'Vous prendrez bien un petit café avec moi?'

'C'est très gentil de votre part.'

'Et Monsieur Adams? Est-ce qu'il parle francais?'

'J'ai bien peur que non.'

'Ah! Forgive me, monsieur. I had assumed that you both understood French. Then we shall talk in English once I have brought the coffee. The kettle has already boiled so I shall not be long. Please make yourselves comfortable and remove your hot leather clothing.'

The two welcomed the offer and soon had their biking leathers draped over the back of a surplus armchair. Gus had already noticed, over breakfast at their Carcassonne hotel, how stunning Sally looked in her white halter neck top and sky-blue cotton slacks, and with her shoulder-length auburn hair complementing the golden-brown tan of her bare shoulders, but the sight made him catch his breath again now. Instinctively, he looked away. He hadn't complimented her then and he wouldn't do so now.

In the meantime, Claude Boudet had gone through to the kitchen where he had cups and saucers and a plateful of biscuits already laid out on a tray. Whilst pouring the coffee, he cast another satisfied glance at the white waters of the River Aude as they rushed past, beneath his window, carrying with them the unwelcome litter of recent dry weeks. Yesterday's rain in the Pyrenees was doing its job.

'So, tell me how I may help you, mademoiselle.'

As he placed the tray on the coffee table between them, he raised his eyes in her direction. That was when his mouth fell open.

'...*Mon Dieu!* I am surely in the presence of a Roman goddess.' Unlike Gus Adams, the Frenchman was making no effort to hide his appreciation. He turned to Gus, 'You will allow an old man to express his admiration, monsieur! Your Mademoiselle Sally looks truly ravishing.'

Gus knew he was blushing and was about to put the Frenchman right when he noticed Sally Jeffers covering her mouth with her hand, to stifle a little laugh. Boudet's misconception wasn't being seen as an embarrassment at all by her but as a joke. He felt the humiliation.

'We are on holiday, monsieur.' Sally was answering the Frenchman's earlier question. 'And have become fascinated with a story that was told us about this part of the world. It has something to do with treasure and...'

'Ah!' The Frenchman smiled sympathetically.

'And something called the Map of Razes. What can you tell us about the map, monsieur?'

Claude Boudet looked puzzled. 'I know nothing about such a map, mademoiselle. At least, not one that is associated with any treasure.'

Sally's disappointment showed as she glanced towards Gus.

But Boudet continued: 'You are not in the *Département de Razes* now, of course. Modern-day Razes is to the northwest of the Languedoc. But I can tell you about many treasures in what would be the old Razes, which used to be much larger than today's *département*. The treasures that I know of – given that they exist, of course – are all south of here.'

'Does the Schidoni Pentacle mean anything to you then, monsieur?'

'And they are connected? The map, the pentacle, and the treasure? Where did you hear this story, monsieur... mademoiselle?" The Frenchman was showing interest as he turned to look at Gus and then Sally.

Gus suddenly recalled the exact wording of the fax that he'd received before leaving Rome. 'Mister Boudet, what if it was not called the Map of Razes but the Map of the Count of Razes. Would that mean anything to you?'

The Frenchman's face lit up. 'I know nothing about a map, monsieur Adams, but I do know a tradition that links one Count of Razes with a treasure. There were, of course, several generations of Counts of Razes.'

Since they were searching for a contemporary connection between map and treasure, and since a reference to an age-old tradition didn't sound particularly promising, neither Sally nor Gus showed undue interest but Boudet continued just the same.

'...You have heard of the Merovingian dynasty?' He waited for them to shake their heads. 'Recently, certain authors have argued that the bloodline of the Merovingians began when Jesus the Nazarene fathered a child from Mary of Magdala.'

Sally and Gus cast quick glances at one another, to suggest that their choice of Claude Boudet had been a waste of time. They would finish their coffee, make their excuses to leave and try to contact the third historian on their list.

'...You should read the book. It is called *Holy Blood Holy Grail*. Fascinating reading! As is *The Bloodline of the Holy Grail* by Laurence Gardner. You know, of course, of the Magdalene's association with the Languedoc?'

He saw them again shake their heads.

'...No? Well after Jesus was crucified, she and her brother Lazarus, together with Mary Jacobi and Mary Salome, are said to have fled the holy land by ship to Alexandria and on from there to the south of France, where they landed at a little place called Ratis in the Camargue, known today as Saintes-Maries-de-la-Mer. There are many scholars who now argue that she and Jesus were already married and that she was expecting their child when she arrived here in France. Some even argue that Jesus accompanied her; that he was taken down from the cross whilst still alive and then spirited out of Joseph of Arimathea's tomb to be nursed back to health. Some old texts even claim that Jesus was not crucified at all, that a substitute victim took his place.'

Gus sighed; Sally frowned. They had more pressing things on their minds than the ramblings of a retired academic.

'...Over the years, the Roman Catholic church has demonised the Magdalene for its own ends but to this day she is still revered by the Catholics of the Languedoc.'

'You are a Catholic, monsieur?'

The Frenchman grinned. 'Not really, Mademoiselle Sally. I have no religion now. I am not atheist, mind you. Agnostic if anything. In other words, I keep an open mind. And you?'

'Church of England but not very devout, I'm afraid.'

'And you, monsieur?'

Gus slowly shook his head. He'd been asked the same question recently but he saw no point in admitting his lapsed Catholicism a second time.

'Do you know that there are more churches dedicated to the Magdalene in the south of France than to any other saint?'

'But if there were truth to the story, then why would the Vatican refute it?' Sally had now moved to the edge of her chair, suggesting that although it was time for them to leave she still wanted to rebut Boudet's wild claims.

'Ah! That is what Americans would call the sixty-four-thousand-dollar question, is it not? The Bible tells us that Simon Peter was very hostile towards Mary of Magdala and that he often reproached Jesus for paying her too much attention. He regarded her as his adversary and saw her as some kind of threat. That was because Jesus saw the Magdalene as his *Apostola Apostolorum*, his Apostle of Apostles. The Roman Catholic church prefers to think otherwise, of course, because its allegiance is to Simon Peter. As you know, Catholics see Peter as the rock on which their church was built. They think of him as Christ's original vicar on Earth, their very first pope. And since the Magdalene was seen as Simon Peter's rival, then she became the Vatican's target for character assassination. She was made out to be a whore, whereas in fact she came from a very respectable and probably a rather wealthy family.'

Boudet saw Gus glancing at his watch. Sally, on the other hand, was all ears.

'...You know of the Dead Sea Scrolls I am sure, but have you heard of the Nag Hammadi documents? Ancient manuscripts found by a young Arab boy in a sealed earthenware jar near a place called Nag Hammadi in Upper Egypt. Although they were found in 1945, it was some years later before religious scholars came to know of their existence, by which time many of the papyri had either been sold or destroyed by fire. Those that were eventually saved are now the property of the Egyptian government. They are written in Coptic script and some of them date back to the time of Christ himself, which means that they are older than the synoptic Gospels found in your Bible. They include not only the Gospel of Mary the Magdalene but also writings called the Gospel of Thomas, the Gospel of Philip and something called the Gospel of Truth, not to mention the Secret Book of James, the Apocalypse of Peter, the Letter of Peter to Phylip and others.

'From what I understand, much of their content is at odds with the Vatican's version of things. For instance, the Gospel of Phylip ridicules ignorant Christians for taking the resurrection too literally.'

By now, Sally and Gus were convinced that Claude Boudet was just another academic who had indulged himself in a new field of interest after taking retirement.

'Does this have any bearing on the Map of the Count of Razes, *monsieur*?' Sally was trying hard not to appear impolite.

'Perhaps, perhaps not, mademoiselle, but please bear with me for a little while yet. What I wanted to say was this – some of the Nag Hammadi documents are known to have been bought by the Vatican and have since been forgotten. In other words, the Roman church has either destroyed them or kept them hidden away. Why would it do that? Could it be that their content is a threat to the Catholic faith? Just imagine the implications to the Roman Catholic church – to the true faith as they like to refer to it – if those documents showed beyond doubt that Christ had indeed married Mary of Magdala and that he had fathered a child from her. What then of the so-called virtue of celibacy? Or, even more significantly, what if there were proof that Jesus survived the cross?' The Frenchman gave them a knowing look. 'Worldwide, there are over nine hundred million who live and swear by the Catholic faith. That's ninety percent of all Christians. Just think what would happen if such revelations came to light. The church would become virtually redundant overnight and its rituals and its icons the objects of derision.'

'Not just the Roman Catholic church, monsieur. Christianity itself would be under threat.'

'Ah! You mean your version of Christianity, Sally. The one that was fashioned for you by the Catholic church.'

'Explain, please!' Despite herself, she was being caught up in the argument. Gus, for his part, looked suitably bored and anxious to leave.

'As a Christian, your book is the Bible.'

Thinking that he was trying to trap her, she began to disagree. 'Not necessarily! The Old Testament means nothing to me, only the New.'

The Frenchman smiled. 'Exactly! But who decided what was to be included in your so-called Christian Testament? Or, more importantly, what was to be left out?' He paused. 'May I tell you?'

Sally gave him a look of resignation while Gus, with an audible sigh, sank back into his chair.

'...It was, in fact, the Roman Emperor Constantine. He convened the Council of Nicaea in the year 325 to discuss which texts should be adopted by the church. But it turned out to be a pretty one-sided affair because all the bishops who dared to disagree with the emperor were exiled there and then as heretics. So you see, my dear, your Christian Testament is based purely on the autocratic whims of a dictator. And over the centuries, the Roman Catholic church has done everything in its power to justify Constantine's anthology at the expense of other, possibly more authentic, accounts of Christ's ministry.'

Sally allowed herself a smile. 'Pardon me for saying so, *monsieur*, but you do not sound like an agnostic. More like a disillusioned churchgoer I would say.'

Slowly he nodded. 'You are right. In the eyes of the church, I am probably more heretic than agnostic. We are intelligent animals, *mademoiselle*, and yet the church expects us to believe, without question, in an unlikely virgin birth and an equally implausible resurrection.'

Her astonished look made him pause.

'...My views, they shock you Mademoiselle Sally?'

She shrugged. 'More surprised than shocked, actually.'

With narrowing eyes, he looked from one to the other of them. 'The Magi story is a good example of what I mean. *Mes amis,* when you look to the heavens at night, can you honestly say which stable... which town... which country even! stands directly under a particular star? Of course not!'

'Your point, monsieur?'

'My point, as you put it *mademoiselle,* is this: the church has been conning us over the centuries. Rather than involving itself in meaningless rituals, as it has done, it should have been concentrating more on the teachings of the Master. Had it done that, then the world would be a far better place to live in today.'

Sensing that Gus had little or no interest in what he was saying, the Frenchman looked again to Sally, this time with a little apologetic and somewhat mischievous laugh.

'…Are you sure that I said that I am an agnostic, Mademoiselle Sally? Maybe you misheard. What I said, perhaps, was that I am a Gnostic! Just like the Cathars.'

Oh, oh! she thought. *I'm not going to be drawn into this any further and she made to get to her feet.* 'We shall have to be going, *monsieur*. Thank you for the coffee and for a really enlightening conversation.'

Gus, surprised at how genuine her words sounded, also got to his feet, while Claude Boudet, for his part, looked dismayed by their decision.

'But I have not yet told you about the Languedoc treasures, *mes amis*. The treasures of the Cathars and the templars, not to mention those of the Merovingians and the Visigoths.'

Suddenly, a bell started ringing in Sally's head. 'Visigoths?'

'Ah! You have heard of it?'

'You're not, by any chance, talking about the Treasure of Solomon's Temple are you?'

Claude Boudet smiled widely. 'But of course! The Visigoths took it from the Romans who, in turn, had looted it from the Temple of Solomon in Jerusalem.'

Sally, with a meaningful look towards Gus, settled back into her chair. 'Tell us more, *monsieur.*'

Le Village de Montségur

Galileo was still at breakfast when his cell phone rang. 'Father Galileo?'
He recognised the voice. 'Yes.'
'I have heard that you have the wisdom of Solomon.'
With a quick look over his shoulder, he checked that his host, Father Francois, was out of earshot. 'It's safe for you to talk,' he muttered somewhat impatiently. So much caution seemed unnecessary and childish.
'Aiello wishes to know if you have anything to report.'
In hushed tones, he gave a brief account of what he had seen since arriving in Montségur, ending with: 'I have established that *Morcon* is one of the biggest construction companies in the Languedoc but I am convinced that here, in Montségur, the contract is just a front. It's an Israeli-owned company and the entire workforce here is probably Jewish as well. That's how they're keeping such a tight lid on things. But I suspect that the three officials on site are not *Morcon* employees at all. For me, they've got *"Mossad"* stamped all over them. Tell Aiello that I have photographed them and will be e-mailing those to him for identification once I have access to a computer. Tell him also that I should have more information for him after tonight.'
'Good, but your priority now must be to find the missing manuscript. That is even more important than preventing the Israelis getting their hands on <u>the Menorah.</u> And when you do, be sure that you destroy it. Burn it without trace!'
Easier said than done, Galileo thought. But the phone was already dead.

*

Father Francois had heard the phone ringing in the other room and had vaguely wondered what the muted conversation could be about. He half-assumed that it might be Father Galileo's physician checking up on his patient's condition, making sure that he was continuing to make satisfactory progress after his recent mental breakdown.

When the Vatican had first requested convalescence for Father Galileo in Montségur, one explicit stipulation had been that he wasn't to be plagued with matters of the church, since his illness had initially been brought on by the pressures of his ministry. His recovery depended on him being allowed to enjoy "a secular holiday", free to wander at will and to enjoy the healthy Pyrenean air. Nor was his host to show surprise if his guest should occasionally prefer to dress like a tourist, or if he chose not to attend church service.

Being himself a down-to-earth country priest, Father Francois had no quibble with such preconditions. His guest could do as he pleased, without any interference from him, if only… Now, as he busied himself in his kitchen, he felt a certain frustration. There was just one matter, one little problem, that he'd dearly love to discuss with Father Galileo, especially since it involved the Vatican itself. Perhaps, in a few days' time, when his guest had had more time to himself and was looking less tense, less occupied, then he might just bring the matter to his attention.

Alet-les-Bains

'Yes, monsieur, I do know some of the Holy Treasure's history.'

She had explained it often enough whilst pointing out the bas-relief on the Arch of Titus in Rome, so why couldn't she now display a bit of her own knowledge as well, especially since Claude Boudet had done most of the showing off, thus far.

'...I know, for instance, that by 70AD, Emperor Vespasian had got fed up with the Zealots who were launching guerrilla attacks on his army in Palestine and that he sent his son, General Titus, to sort things out. The story goes that Titus' soldiers pillaged the Temple of Solomon in Jerusalem and carried a lot of gold and silver and precious stones back with them to Rome. The Copper Scroll of Qumran, for example, records that there was as much as twenty-five tons of gold and about sixty-five tons of silver in the Temple. Little wonder that Titus was given a hero's welcome in Rome, or that the Arch of Titus was erected in the Roman Forum in his honour.'

'The Arch was erected eleven years later, of course, in 81AD.' Although being genuinely pleased that Sally shared some of his recently found interest, Claude Boudet still felt the need to display the extent of his own knowledge. 'And you have heard of Josephus?' As he asked, he walked across the room towards some bookshelves.

'The historian who accompanied Titus' army. Yes, of course.'

Gus sat disinterestedly as the Frenchman thumbed through the pages of a heavy volume. Eventually, Boudet found what he was looking for and began translating choice bits into English as he read. 'I am quoting from Josephus now,' he explained. '...*They also burnt the rooms of the Temple Treasury in which were kept huge sums of silver... where all Israel's wealth had been stored... At this time, one of the priests, son of Thebuthus... having received Caesar's promise that his life would be spared, gave a list of the Temple's treasures... two candlesticks... tables, vats and urns, all made of gold and exceedingly heavy. He also gave up drapes and vestments studded* with gems and a great number of the gold lamps that were used in sacred worship.'

The Frenchman thumbed through a few more pages and continued translating, '...Here to be seen were huge amounts of silver, gold and ivory carved in all sorts of shapes, appearing not as one exhibit but as a continuous river in flow... There were also glittering precious stones set in gold crowns and other wonderful settings...When we witnessed all these splendid objects gathered together, we could scarcely believe our eyes... our imagination had never contemplated such wealth.'

He looked up. '...Then Josephus goes on to describe a huge number of garments and drapes trimmed with gold and precious gems and a great number of wonderful paintings depicting fabulous walled cities and scenes of remarkable battles and Armageddon-like disasters. As he himself admits, even the Romans, who had seen their fair share of riches in the past, were stunned by the sight of such wealth. But of all the items taken from the Temple, Josephus singles these out as the worthiest of mention...'

Again, he turned to the book to quote the Jewish-Roman historian. '*The most splendid of all were the table of gold, weighing many talents* – That was known as the Missorium, by the way – *and the candlestick, also of gold.*'

'And that would be the Menorah.'

He smiled at Sally. 'Yes. But listen to Josephus describing it: ...Attached to its stout stem were branches reaching out a great distance and curving upwards, similar in shape to a trident... each of them fashioned to hold a lantern, seven in all, and symbolising the significance to the Israelis of the numeral seven.'

'And that is why the Menorah is given such pride of place on the Arch in Rome.'

Gus was the only one not to feel any euphoria. As far as he was concerned, what Boudet and Sally were discussing was ancient history and could have nothing to do with his mission here in the Languedoc.

'We can take it for granted that the details about the temple treasure are correct.' Boudet held up the volume of *Josephus' Works*. 'It's not just a historian's account. Josephus, the author, was himself a Jew, and was actually there, seeing everything unfold. And not just that, either! He was actually with Titus and his army as they later marched victorious into Rome, along the Via Sacra, to display the Treasure, and no doubt to receive a rapturous welcome from their fellow Romans.'

Sally nodded enthusiastically. 'I know, monsieur, that the Visigoths later took the treasure, when they sacked Rome, but do we know what happened to it afterwards? Didn't they take it with them to Spain?'

'You are right again, Mademoiselle Sally. That was in the year 410, I believe. The Visigoths ... or the West Goths if you like ... looted most of Rome's wealth, including the treasure from the Temple of Solomon, before migrating westwards to Spain and then the Languedoc.'

Sally again pricked up her ears when she heard the reference to the Languedoc. Her brief conversation with the Arab at the Arch of Titus was coming back to her. It seemed that her life over the past fortnight was becoming full of unexplained coincidences.

The Frenchman continued: 'The Visigoths were noted for their metalworking skills. They fashioned exquisite jewellery and jewelled crowns and crosses and stuff like that. If you want proof, then go to Madrid's National Archaeological Museum to look at the wonderful Treasure of Guarrazar... Anyway, they settled in northern Spain and the Languedoc, forming a kingdom that straddled the Pyrenees and they built great forts where today stand Toledo, Toulouse, Carcassonne and Rhedae...'

Claude Boudet had a way with words that even Gus was now beginning to find interesting.

'Toledo is in central Spain, Toulouse and Carcassonne here in the Languedoc but where is Rhedae, *monsieur*?'

'Rhedae, Mademoiselle Sally, is today called Rennes-le-Château. Now if you and Monsieur Gus have time, then I can tell you about the Rennes treasures as well.'

Boudet was making the most of his captive audience because he wasn't now being confined to time and place as when addressing a coachload of tourists.

'Can I ask you this, *monsieur*? Apart from wanting to become immensely rich, is there any other reason why someone would wish to lay his hands on the Temple Treasure today?'

Her question obviously surprised him but he gave it thought just the same. The answer, when it came, sounded tentative.

'The obvious candidates, of course, would be the Israelis but...' He paused to consider other possibilities.

'You mean they would want to claim what was rightfully theirs?'

'It would be much more than that, Sally. Don't you think?' Seeing her bemusement, he continued: 'If you were to ask the Jews as a nation what they would most like to recover from their past, what do you think their answer would be?'

'Um! The Ark of the Covenant, surely.'

He nodded. '*Mais oui!* After all, Solomon's original purpose in building his Temple was for it to house the ark. But the ark disappeared many centuries before the Romans came on the scene, sometime during the seventh or even the eighth century BC, I believe. So, it's hardly likely that the ark will ever be found. So, what would be the Jews' second choice?'

Again, Sally paused to think. 'The Menorah, perhaps?'

Claude beamed. 'Right again, *mademoiselle*! The Menorah! Second to the ark, it is the most symbolic of all Jewish artefacts. Imagine what it would mean to them as a nation if they were able to reclaim either or both of those.'

Gus, who had been listening with more interest to the conversation, was suddenly struck by a vague thought. 'It would be a good reason for them to try and reclaim the Temple Mount, don't you think?'

The Frenchman grimaced, as much as to suggest – Now that would really be setting the cat loose amongst the pigeons!

Sally made no attempt to kerb her incredulity. 'Claiming the Al Aksa Mosque, the original site of Solomon's Temple? That's nonsense! The whole of Islam would be up in arms.'

The improbability of it made her suddenly pensive. The young Arab's impassioned face as he questioned her about the Arch of Titus bas-relief had suddenly sprung to mind.

'So theoretically,' Gus said. 'Islam would also want to find the treasure, to keep the Israelis from getting it. What do you think, monsieur?'

Claude Boudet, unable to hide his pleasure at the way the conversation was developing, laughed out loud.

'...And just as theoretically the Christian world... or better still, the Vatican... would also prefer to get to it first, to prevent the Israelis, their religious adversaries, from getting their hands on it.'

Again, the Frenchman laughed, but more dismissively now. 'So let us hope therefore, *mes amis,* that the treasure is never found… More coffee?'

Trastevere, Rome

Carlo Platina, alias Aiello, shuffled out from beneath the telephone canopy, felt for the pavement kerb with his white stick and then set off on his familiar route home. He was a very troubled man. Hearing about the theft of the map and the illicit copying of the pentacle had been bad enough but learning the true significance of the missing papyrus was something far more worrying.

It hadn't been easy for him to get to the root of the mystery. He had begun by spending time wandering the corridors of the Vatican Libraries, hoping to learn something just by listening-in on conversations between members of staff. But that had proved difficult because a blind man could hardly loiter within earshot of any group, pretending to look at statues or paintings, at least not without raising immediate suspicion. He had then tried to take advantage of his reputation within the Vatican judiciary but that had cut no ice with anyone, especially not with the curator. Which made him realise that the pope had issued a directive to all members of secret archives staff not to discuss the theft even amongst themselves, let alone with any outside agency.

As he now tapped his way homewards, Carlo Platina recalled how the breakthrough had finally come for him; how he had come to know of the archives' member of staff, recently retired, who had disclosed the secret of the map and the pentacle to one of his younger colleagues who, in turn, had passed them on to his younger brother, for mercenary reasons. That brother had since been killed in the accursed Languedoc of France and the documents then taken from him, presumably by enemies of the true faith.

He, Platina, had then visited the retired archivist at home and, under pretence of a judicial inquiry, had plied him with questions about the stolen documents. 'How precious is the Nag Hammadi papyrus? What sort of threat does it hold to the Roman Catholic faith?'

The man, obviously unaware of the papal directive, had answered fully and truthfully – 'It was bought in 1948, at considerable expense to the

Vatican. The curator at the time… I remember him well because he was the one who interviewed me, years later, when I applied for work at the library… heard how some ancient papyri were being offered for sale in Cairo. He personally went over to Egypt to see for himself and it was there that he learnt about the Nag Hammadi find. He heard how a young boy and his brothers, two or three years earlier, had found a sealed earthenware jar either in a cave or buried in the ground near Nag Hammadi in Upper Egypt and when they broke it they found thirteen leather-bound volumes of papyri inside. Had the Vatican known about the discovery from the start, then the whole collection would have been bought at any price but the boy's family hadn't realised its value. It is claimed that the mother even used some of the papyri as kindling, to light her fire! Unbelievable! But whether that is true or not, over the next few months the family sold the rest of the manuscripts piecemeal to individual collectors. The curator, from what I remember, made his purchase from a backstreet dealer in Cairo and what he bought turned out to be different to the other Nag Hammadi papyri in that it was written in Greek rather than in Coptic script.'

Despite the warmth of the Italian morning sun, Platina now shivered as he remembered the man's answer to his next question: 'In your opinion, how much of a threat is the stolen manuscript to the Roman Catholic church?'

'I take it, judge, that you know about the heretical content of the Coptic gospels of Nag Hammadi? How they give conflicting accounts of Christ's ministry to those found in our synoptic gospels? Some of them discount the virgin birth, others scorn the cross and the resurrection…'

'Yes, I am aware of such blasphemies.'

'Over the centuries, the Catholic church has successfully ridiculed such claims, but the *I, Jesus* manuscript poses a totally different kind of threat.'

The words, Carlo Platina now recalled, had struck him like a bolt out of the blue. Had he heard the man correctly?

'What did you call it? The what manuscript?'

At that point, the retired archivist had looked at him long and hard before asking: 'You do know what the missing papyrus is all about, do you judge?' And had realised straightaway how little his visitor really knew of the problem. 'In the wrong hands, it could be argued that the stolen document is the gospel according to the Christ himself, because it begins with the two words *"I, Jesus"*. Mind you, I have not read it myself because I do not have the scholarship for such a task, but I have seen the papyrus and although the writing is badly faded, I have been able to discern the Greek words *"I, Jesus"* in parts of it.'

Platina had been almost afraid to ask his next question. 'And does it contradict the synoptic version of our faith?'

Here, the retired archivist had fallen silent for several seconds, seemingly unwilling to venture further. But then he'd volunteered this: 'I can only tell you what I heard others saying at the time, and to me that merely endorses the fact that the manuscript was written by a heretic and a charlatan. First of all, the apostle who takes centre stage in the so-called *"I, Jesus"* gospel is not Simon Peter but the whore Mary Magdalene. Secondly, and even more damning, it seems that the very last section was written after the crucifixion. You can understand, therefore, why the heretical document was kept locked away in the archival vaults and why religious scholars were never even told of its existence.'

Alet-les-Bains

'I do not want to disillusion you *mademoiselle... monsieur*, but reference to pentacles, or pentagrams if you prefer the word, in connection with the mysteries of this area always makes me smile. Whole books have been written about them and hundreds, quite literally, of pentacle drawings have been offered as proof of where the various treasures have been buried. The truth, *mes amis,* is that all you need do to draw a pentacle is to choose any five places on a map – say Albi, Toulouse, Carcassonne, Rennes, Perpignan... it doesn't matter how far apart they are – and then draw lines between them in a certain pattern.'

Reaching for his notepad and, without lifting his pencil off the paper, he sketched a pentagram.

'...With more care and using a ruler it can be made to look impressive and significant but it means absolutely nothing. Unless your Monsieur Schidoni... or should it be *Signore* Schidoni? ... had secret information about a treasure, then his pentacle is mere guesswork, and worthless. Do we know anything at all about him?'

'Only what I found on the internet, and that wasn't much.' Sally sounded disillusioned. 'He is attributed with just one quote in Bartlett's book of *Famous Quotations.* Something about *"Arcadia ego",* whatever that may mean. He died in 1616, I remember that.'

Claude Boudet's eyes opened wide. '*Et in Arcadia ego*? Was that the quotation?'

Sally looked at him, somewhat surprised. 'Yes. I think that was it.'

'*I, too, have lived in Arcadia.*' There was new excitement in the Frenchman's tone.

'It means something?' It was Gus' question.

'Only that it is also the title of paintings by Guercino and Poussin, and that another work by Poussin, called *Les Bergers d'Arcadie...* the Shepherds of Arcadia... is believed to hold some clue to the Rennes-le-Château treasure. The words *Et in Arcadia ego* are incorporated in the painting.' Boudet straightened in his chair. 'My friends, you must tell me all you know.'

Le Village de Montségur

The two Swiss 'geology students' had begun their day down in Montségur village, anxious to learn more about the little priest whom they'd seen spying on the *Morcon* workforce the night before. They reckoned that, if he was staying anywhere in the village, it would have to be with Father Francois.

During the past fortnight, they had made a point of becoming acquainted with the local priest in case they had to turn to him in an emergency or needed help in getting a message to the Vatican. But they had been very careful, thus far, not to give him any inkling of who they were or of their real reason for being in the area.

Twenty minutes of observing Father Francois' home from a distance finally paid off when the priest's guest suddenly appeared in the open doorway. They watched him stand there for two or three minutes, craning his neck upwards, his obvious interest being in the citadel ruins, far above.

The camera clicked four... five times... in quick succession and the powerful zoom lens recorded each slight facial movement, ending in a full-face frontal as the dog-collared stranger turned to look in their direction. But, before his suspicions could be aroused, the camera lens had turned away and was recording other village scenes of interest.

The photographs would be e-mailed to the commander at the very first opportunity, together with an account of the priest's suspicious behaviour. The two soldiers needed to know why he was there and at whose instigation.

Alet-les-Baines

Sally looked at her watch and then at Gus for confirmation of what she was about to say. 'Can I suggest that we visit Rennes-le-Château together, Monsieur Boudet? That is, if you are willing and not too busy. I'm sure we can compensate you generously for your trouble?'

Her last question was clearly aimed at Gus, who was expected to pay for the service from an MI6 slush fund.

The Frenchman beamed, not because of the offer of payment but because he clearly enjoyed the theme of their discussion. In addition, he'd started to suspect that his young guests had something more than just casual interest in treasure stories. But he had yet to decide what that *something* could be.

'*Mais oui, mes amis.* Now is as good a time as any, don't you think?' He waited for them to show assent and then grinned roguishly. 'We will go by car, of course, because I do not think that you have room for me on your powerful motorcycle. And even if you did, I'm not sure that I would want to come with you. I have seen how you young people like to whiz from place to place.' He nodded towards their leathers: 'You can collect them when we come back. Rennes is only half an hour away.'

Once he'd left the room to get himself ready, Sally turned to Gus. 'Well? What do you think?'

'Wild goose chase, I'd say. This has nothing to do with what I'm supposed to be looking for.'

'Great goose chase though, don't you think? The old man's a mine of interesting information and you have to admit that there are one or two similarities with what you were involved in before.'

'Same people, you mean?'

'Vatican, Israelis, Arabs maybe… Similar reasons too when you think about it. That business of yours in Albania! The Vatican wanting to keep the Israelis and the Arabs in check, or rather at each other's throats. From what our friend has just told us, it could be that something similar is going on here, in the Languedoc.'

Gus was far from convinced. 'Hell of a long shot.'

But she wasn't going to let him smother her optimism. 'Uncle Jim doesn't seem to think so, does he? Or else he wouldn't have sent you here.'

He saw her grin and tried to respond with a stern look of his own. 'If I'd listened to your Uncle Jim, you wouldn't be here now, young lady. You'd be back in London.'

*

'Now let me explain why Rennes-le-Château has become the centre of so much interest over the past few years.'

The road sign showed *Montazels* three kilometres to the right. The needle on the little Citroen's speedometer, Gus had noticed, had yet to touch 60kph. Boudet, who had barely stopped talking since they'd set off from Alet, twenty minutes ago, was either a painfully slow driver or else he couldn't combine reasonably quick driving with uninterrupted commentary.

'... You'll remember that I told you earlier of the tradition that Mary the Magdalene, wife of Jesus according to some, and possibly pregnant with his child, fled from Palestine and eventually settled here in the Languedoc, where she became much revered and where many churches have since been consecrated in her name. Mind you, there was a very strong Judaic presence in this area even before she came here, which probably explains why she and her companions decided to settle in the Languedoc.'

'Judaic presence?'

The Frenchman detected the note of disbelief in her voice. 'Indeed, there was. And it remained for hundreds of years after that. You will even see signs of it to this day. Did you know, for instance, that an autonomous Jewish state called Septimania... a principality, no less, governed by a recognised descendent of the Royal House of David... was established here in 768, with Narbonne as its capital?' He paused and then laughed apologetically: 'But let me not confuse you by jumping too quickly. Let us look at things chronologically.'

At this point, Sally decided to start jotting down a few notes, to help her get a clearer picture of what the Frenchman was telling them.

'...First of all, bear in mind that the Magdalene had offspring, reputedly the child, or children even, of Jesus.'

'Allegedly!'

'*Mais oui.* But bear with me, mademoiselle. There can be little doubt that she came to the Languedoc soon after the crucifixion, and the book *Holy Blood, Holy Grail* argues a strong case that she was pregnant with Jesus' child when she arrived. Now we jump more than four hundred years, to when the Visigoths came here, bringing with them the Treasure of Solomon's Temple. Toulouse became their capital but they also set up strongholds in Carcassonne and Rhedae.'

'Rhedae being Rennes-le-Château, where we're going now.'

Boudet smiled and nodded. 'Correct! You are a good student Mademoiselle Sally. Incidentally, by that time, Rennes-le-Château had become one of the most prominent centres of the Magdalene cult. Anyway, back in the year 496 a Merovingian king called Clovis marched against the Visigoths and forced them out of Toulouse and Carcassonne, thus making Rhedae, or Rennes if you prefer, their final place of refuge. And guess what they took with them there?'

Although it was meant as a rhetorical question, Sally couldn't resist answering: 'The Treasure of Solomon's Temple!'

'Exactly that! And although some historians claim that it was later removed to another safe location, the fact is that no one knows for sure... except possibly me.'

Claude Boudet eased his foot on the pedal and signalled that his little Citroen was about to take a left turn off the main road. It was a turning that Galileo had barely noticed as he'd driven past, twenty-four hours earlier.

Boudet's claim now had Gus leaning well forward in the back seat. 'You are joking of course!'

The Frenchman smiled as if to admit as much. 'Perhaps I am, Gus.' And then, more abstractedly, he added, 'Perhaps I am but I have my theories like everyone else. Ah! Here we are! We are now climbing towards Rhedae. This is the way the Visigoths came, fifteen hundred years ago.'

For the first time since they'd set-off, Claude Boudet fell silent.

Vauxhall Cross, LONDON

'And that's the name she gave you? Aiello? Nothing more?'

'That's all she knows, sir. We're convinced of it.'

'And what reason... excuse... did she give for her... her treason?'

The special branch officer from Scotland Yard gave a twisted grin. 'Claims she was told of a plot to assassinate the pope; that Vatican security was aware that foreign agents were operating in Italy but that they couldn't be sure who was who. Since MI6 wasn't regarded as hostile, then all they needed from her were the names of British operatives in the region so that they could be eliminated from their list.'

Sir James Oldcorn's face became a picture of incredulity. 'Eliminated from their list? And that's the reason this Aiello gave her? And she actually believed him?'

The man from the Met grimaced. 'Not only is she a devout Catholic, Sir James, but in our opinion she is also extremely naïve.'

MI6's head of operations detected a certain censure in the man's tone, suggesting that such a person as Anne Corbett should never have been employed by the secret services in the first place. And Sir James knew that he was in no position to argue otherwise. Okay, so the damn woman had been nothing more than a glorified typist but she'd had access to privileged information. And not only that! Like everyone else at Vauxhall Cross, she had been subjected to the usual rigorous screening process before being employed by the service. The warnings should have been there then; the weakness should have been spotted. But it hadn't been, and agents' lives had been lost because of it.

Sir James was no fool. It didn't matter who had slipped up in the past, the buck now had to stop with him. Despite the fact that he had ordered a full-scale internal inquiry into the matter, he knew only too well that when the official report was finally collated, he could expect a call to the foreign office – Downing Street, even! – to answer for his sins. His only hope of salvation was MI6's recent success in Albania and the fact that he, as director of operations, had personally been instrumental in preventing all-out war in the Middle East. Not only that but also, by extension, instrumental in suppressing media interest in what could have been a huge embarrassment for the government. What a field day the tabloids would have if they came to know that Britain and its allies had been using contaminated nuclear material in its ammunition in both Iraq and the Balkans. The scandal would be blown up out of all proportion and heads would roll, not least those of the defence secretary and his immediate boss, the foreign secretary. But thanks to him, personally, the incriminating detail didn't appear in Vauxhall Cross' draft report and Whitehall bosses would surely realise to whom they were indebted. Sir James felt that a favour was owed him, a favour that could yet prove to be his lifeline.

Rennes-le-Château

They had been shown everything of interest – the church, consecrated to Mary Magdalene, the famous Tour Magdala and the Villa Bethanie that Berenger Sauniérè had built with his mysteriously-found wealth over a century ago, the graves of the priest and his faithful housekeeper Marie Denarnaud lying side by side in the church graveyard. The little museum in the Presbytery had been left until last.

Now they were out again in Rennes' open-air restaurant, enjoying a cold drink, courtesy of Gus' expense account. They had chosen a table shaded by a tall elm. Most of the other tables were also occupied, a sure sign that lunchtime was approaching.

During the tour, Boudet had done little more than point out the interesting features, adding that he intended testing them later on the details of what they'd seen and read. The playful threat had made Sally, at least, more attentive to everything around her.

'Quite a mystery surrounding Sauniérè,' she volunteered as she sipped at her lager. 'Poor as a church mouse when he got here in 1885 and yet, six years later, he had the money to renovate the church and after that to build a tower to house his library. From what I read in the museum, he found some ancient manuscripts in the altar rail of the church and people now believe that they led him to a treasure, whatever that might have been. What do you think, monsieur? Did he find the Treasure of Solomon's Temple?'

Boudet smiled suggestively. 'Let me tell you first about the other treasures that could be hidden here, in Rennes-le-Château. Let us begin with that of the Knights Templar. You have heard of them?'

'Of course! They fought in the Crusades.'

Gus pricked up his ears on hearing the word. Hadn't he, too, in the past few weeks, taken part in a crusade of his own? Or, rather, been instrumental in preventing one! Suddenly he was reliving his nightmare in the quarry in Kukes, oblivious now to Boudet's history lesson.

'The Order of the Knights Templar was founded in 1118, here in France, soon after the First Crusade had claimed Jerusalem back from Islam. There were only nine templars to begin with and, with the blessing of pope Gregory VIII, they were allowed to use the Al Aksa Mosque on Temple Mount, where Solomon's Temple once stood, as their headquarters. They were there, they claimed, to oversee the safe passage of Christian pilgrims to and from Jerusalem.' He cast Sally a meaningful look. 'Nine knights against the armies of Islam?'

'So what were they really there for?'

'The truth is that they spent nine years excavating under the Temple Mount, at the site of Solomon's Stables. What could they have been searching for, do you think?'

'Not for the Temple Treasure for sure. That was long gone.'

'Their objective, *mes amis,* was to discover the greatest of all biblical treasures – the Ark of the Covenant.'

'But obviously without success, or we would have heard about it.'

'You are most probably right, Mademoiselle Sally, but there are some who actually believe that the ark was found and brought here to France. I, for one, do not hold that view. Others say that they brought with them the Holy Grail. There are all sorts of romantic tales about their exploits. But this is what I wanted to tell you about the templars—during the next two hundred years they became very powerful; probably the most influential secret order throughout Europe at the time. They received untold wealth from all sorts of places – gifts of estates, gold, and silver, as well as the money they made from their banking enterprises. And guess where they chose as one of their bases?'

'Here? The Languedoc?'

'Right again, mademoiselle! But then, Philippe IV – Philippe le Bon... or Philip the Fair as he was known... king of France, became jealous of their wealth and in order to claim it for himself, since he had practically bankrupted his kingdom with so many wars, he brought charges of heresy against the Templars. I'll tell you later what those charges were. Anyway, in 1307 he ordered them all to be arrested, tried, tortured and put to death. But many of them were warned in time and managed to escape. There is documentation, for instance, which suggests that eighteen ships, laden with Templar wealth, sailed out of La Rochelle in the Charante, headed possibly for Scotland. Whether that is true or not is another matter. What is fact, however, is that a considerable amount of Templar treasure has remained hidden here, in the Languedoc, possibly under our very feet right now.' Boudet's look was again meaningful, as if he held a privileged secret.

Sally's eyes widened and she began jotting some more notes. 'Fascinating! Don't you think so, Gus?'

'Uh?' Her words had jerked him out of his reverie. His thoughts had moved on to Father Galileo and he'd been wondering what had become of the treacherous little assassin.

Boudet continued: 'Of course, the Templar Knights had to share the Languedoc with the Cathars. In fact, I firmly believe that many if not most of the Templars embraced the Cathar faith.'

'Pardon me, monsieur, but you have mentioned the Cathars more than once already. Who were they?'

'Ah! Forgive me! I take too much for granted. The Cathars were a very religious sect who populated the Languedoc during the time I have just talked about. Their brand of religion was at odds with the orthodox Roman Catholic faith. They were simple people who didn't believe in owning much personal wealth.'

'Was it a Christian faith?'

'Indeed so, mademoiselle! *Les Bonhommes* – the good people – as they were referred to. Even St Bernard of Clairvaux, who didn't suffer fools or heretics gladly, admitted as much when he said of them: *No sermons are more Christian than theirs… and their morals are pure.* But the Cathars were openly critical of the Vatican's obsession with building lavish churches and with gathering wealth, not to mention what they regarded as ridiculous rituals of pomp and ceremony. To them, all material things, including man's physical body, were the work of an evil God. The good God was only accountable for man's soul. More importantly, they based their faith on the Gnostic gospels that I mentioned earlier. Yes, they lived by Christ's teaching, but they rejected as Vatican fairy tales things like the virgin birth and the resurrection. Nor did they accept that Jesus Christ was actually the son of God. Incidentally, the Visigoths held similar views, centuries before them.'

Boudet, like Sally, became aware of Gus' distraction and he paused now as if he'd talked for too long.

'Please go on, monsieur.' She glared accusingly at Gus before smiling encouragingly at the Frenchman.

'I will be brief…' His new-found friends weren't to know that they were listening to yet another of his tourist talks.

With a dismissive wave of her hand and another glare at Gus, Sally made light of the note of apology in Claude Boudet's voice.

'… It is difficult for us, today, to comprehend the popularity of the Cathar faith. It was by far the most popular religion throughout Occitania. In those days, Occitania was a semi-autonomous state stretching right across from the Atlantic coast in the west to the plains of Lombardy in northern Italy in the east. That is where the name 'Languedoc originates, by the way—langue d'Oc, the language of Occitania. However, because the Cathar faith was gaining so much in popularity, the Vatican came to regard it as a very real threat to its own version of events. So, in 1209, Pope Innocent III… What a name for him! … launched his Albigensian Crusade against the so-called heretics, and his army of thirty thousand knights from across northern Europe, under the leadership of Simon de Montford, marched on the Languedoc, slaughtering thousands of Cathars as they did so…'

'I've heard of him! Simon de Montford.'

'You probably know of his son, mademoiselle. Same name as his father. He was the one who made a name for himself in England. Anyway, the pope realised that such slaughter had to be justified in the eyes of the Christian world and it didn't matter how. Which is why the Inquisition was set up. This turned out to be just another excuse for torturing the captives before burning them at the stake, after they had admitted to their heresies. The end for the Cathars came in 1244, when the last small band of them, about two hundred and twenty in all, finally surrendered at Montségur and, because they refused to renounce their beliefs, they too were all burned at the stake. According to the Vatican, they were being condemned to the fires of hell, but the Cathars themselves thought otherwise. They regarded it as a good end; not descending into hell at all but beginning the final journey of what they called *the way of the stars*.' Claude Boudet paused to smile somewhat abstractedly. 'Montségur is a place you should visit, *mes amis,* but I fear that the citadel is closed to the public at the moment.'

Gus had hardly taken anything in. He'd been looking vaguely around him at those occupying other tables and had sensed someone staring in their direction. At a table near the high ivy-covered perimeter wall of the open-air restaurant, three swarthy young men, obviously Middle Eastern, were huddled in what seemed to be serious conversation punctuated by flashing dark eyes and brusque hand gestures. Two of them sported neatly trimmed black beards and well-groomed hair and were dressed in clean polo shirts and jeans but the third was unkempt. His hair was long and crying out for a comb and his face looked rough with its week-old stubble. His maroon-coloured T-shirt, its tightness accentuating his chest and ample biceps, showed patches of dark sweat below the armpits. He was the one who was staring brazenly in their direction. At first, Gus thought that he was ogling Sally – most of the young men there were doing the same, only more respectfully – but then he caught a flicker of something in the man's eye that caused him to think again. Was it suspicion? Anger? Gus couldn't quite make it out. Then the man sensed that he, too, was being watched and he turned his eyes on Gus, eyes that glinted with a cold intensity that was meant as some sort of warning. Instinctively, Gus sneered back in a show of defiance at whatever the threat was meant to be and then looked away. The stranger was probably just a junkie with stupid notions.

'...During the Inquisition, some of the charges of heresy that were brought against the Cathars were these...' Boudet was still at it, reciting his tourist spiel. 'That they rejected the divinity of Christ and the worship of the Virgin Mary, that they spat at the cross and trampled on it, that they practised sodomy and other unnatural sexual practices. In fact, they were exactly the same charges of heresy that would be brought against the Templars, almost a hundred years later, when they too were also charged with homosexuality and with blasphemy. Like the Cathars, the Templars were also accused of trampling on the cross and it was said that they worshipped a severed head, thought to be that of John the Baptist.'

'And the Cathars also had treasure?'

'Indeed so, Mademoiselle Sally! Even though their religion didn't allow the accumulation of personal wealth, they still needed money, if only to finance the battles against their enemies. The Cathar faithful didn't fight. Their religion prevented that. Instead, they hired mercenaries to fight their battles for them.'

He noticed her surprise and laughed.

'…You are not the only one to see the contradiction in that.'

Gus was again looking away.

'…Anyway, it is said that the Cathars also amassed a treasure, one that was kept in Montségur. It has even been suggested, as I've already mentioned, that they had also become the guardians of the Treasure of Solomon's Temple and that before the fall of Montségur on the sixteenth of March 1244 they transferred it to another place for safe keeping. Guess where to, Mademoiselle Sally!'

'Not here?'

'*Mais oui*. Here to Rennes-le-Château.'

Sally laughed out loud, drawing another stare from the rough-looking young man in the sweat-stained T-shirt. Gus again caught his eye, questioningly, and thought he detected a snarl.

'… And finally, *mes amis,* there is the Merovingian treasure.'

Sally Jeffers threw her head back with another laugh. 'Not another one, surely?'

It was the reaction that the Frenchman had expected. '*Mais oui!* In the mid-thirteenth century, Blanche of Castille took to the throne of France whilst her son, Louis IX was away on crusade. But the French nobles got so stroppy that she was afraid they would steal from the royal treasury, so she made off with the royal treasure and brought it down here to the Languedoc. Some say it is hidden in Rennes-les-Bains, others say Blanchefort, neither of them far from here. But some historians do claim that it, too, is hidden here in the vicinity of Rennes-le-Château.' He smiled broadly. 'So, take your pick, *mes amis!* Which treasure are you interested in?'

'The one that's associated with the Count of Razes.' Gus was again attentive.

'Perhaps this is the time for me to bring it all together for you—the Magdalene cult, the Visigoths, the Counts of Razes who constitute the Merovingian dynasty, the Cathar and the Templar stories, Queen Blanche… They are all linked in one way or another.'

Sally placed her pencil on the table and sat back to take it all in. She motioned Gus to pay attention as well but Gus' eyes were again on the stranger who still had Sally in his fixed stare. His friends were preparing to leave but instead of following them towards the exit, the intense-looking young man, after putting on a pair of sunglasses, began striding menacingly towards the unsuspecting Sally. Gus sprang to his feet, to intercept, and it was only then that Sally and Claude Boudet sensed any threat.

The stranger stopped a couple of metres short of their table, ignoring Gus who was standing in his way. His two friends, in the meantime, had turned to see what he was up to and were now looking questioningly at one another.

'Why you here?' The snarled question was aimed over Gus' shoulder at Sally, in a bull-by-the-horns fashion. 'You follow me!'

'Pardon?' Sally looked totally bemused.

Gus felt it was time for him to butt in. 'The lady doesn't know you. I think you'd better go.'

For answer, the stranger swung a violent arm to brush Gus aside. The next thing, he'd been caught in a shoulder-throw and his sandaled feet were crashing down onto the edge of a nearby table where a startled elderly couple were just finishing their meal. With a loud cracking noise, the table collapsed under the weight, soup bowls went flying and pandemonium broke loose. A couple of young waiters and a waitress came rushing forward, shouting; customers stared in frightened silence, others immediately began to leave. The stranger's two Arab friends looked bewildered but made no move to contribute to the fracas.

Gus had no time to take any of it in. The angry stranger was back on his feet and charging with flailing arms as if he were completely demented. A quick duck to avoid the fists and in one move Gus again sent him over his shoulder, only this time in a different direction and without any further damage to furniture.

Everyone looked astounded, not least the muscular young gorilla who had been sent flying twice by a long-haired matchstick of a man. The last fall had badly winded him and one of his elbows was dripping blood but he was again getting up to continue the fray. This time, though, his two friends did rush forward to grapple with him and to whisper frantically in his ear until eventually, after a lot of struggling and swearing in a language that Gus didn't understand, he allowed himself to be dragged away, still shouting threats even after he had left the restaurant grounds.

'I think we had better leave as well.' A bewildered Sally made no attempt to hide her annoyance. 'The sooner the better, I'd say.'

Gus said nothing but once she and Claude Boudet had turned their backs, he reached for his wallet, quickly pulled out more than enough money to pay for the damage and for another meal for the elderly couple who were, thankfully, unscathed, muttered his apologies and followed the other two out. He didn't notice the three fair-haired young men at another table who now watched him leave. Nor did he see their questioning glances at one another. By the time he'd caught up with Boudet and Sally by the car, the Arabs had disappeared.

The Frenchman hardly spoke on the way back, more embarrassed by the uncomfortable silence between the young couple than by the events of the last few minutes. So preoccupied were the three of them with their own concerns that they didn't notice the car following them at a distance, nor see it stop some way back when they finally reached Alet-les-Bains.

'We are grateful to you, Monsieur Boudet, for all your trouble.' Sally pressed some notes as well as a piece of paper with her cell phone number on it into the Frenchman's rather reluctant palm. 'It has been very interesting and edifying for us both. I can only apologise for the way things turned out.'

His response, in French, came in barely more than a whisper: 'Do not be angry with your young man, mademoiselle. Do not risk losing his love. Believe me, I know what I am talking about.'

The bike roaring into life made her reply inaudible. Then, as a parting shot to them both, Claude Boudet shouted to be heard: 'Please call me again! We did not finish our conversation.' He sounded sincere.

Sally would have preferred not to hold on to any part of Gus on the way back to Carcassonne but the Honda's acceleration on the winding road ensured that she grabbed on to him for dear life. It also ensured that the car following, not to mention the one following that, had no hope of keeping up with them.

*

The knock on the door awoke him from his nap. Claude Boudet glanced at his watch. Less than fifteen minutes since the young couple had left. Could it be that they had returned? That maybe they had left something behind? Or, most probably, had forgotten to ask him something?

The sight of the two bearded strangers, whom he'd seen trying to calm their crazed companion up in Rennes a little earlier, caused his heart to miss a beat. They were standing there, side by side in the doorway, smiling disingenuously. The greeting came in uncertain French.

'Pardon, monsieur... Um! Vous parlez... um!'

'You can speak English, or Italian if you prefer?'

'Ah! I speak English. We come in house.' Without invitation, they pushed past him.

The ageing Frenchman suddenly felt fear and thought better of challenging the two.

'Now you tell where nice woman go.'

Boudet stared from one to the other. Their interest was in Sally Jeffers, not in the boyfriend who had dealt so effectively with their companion.

'I'm sorry but I'm unable to tell you that.'

The face darkened threateningly. 'You tell or... or we...' Either he didn't have the vocabulary to finish the threat or he was assuming no need to do so.

Claude Boudet's face turned ashen as he feared being struck with a fist. A knife even!

'I am a tourist guide. They paid me to take them around Rennes-le-Château. I only met them...' He glanced at his watch. '...Three hours ago. All I can tell you is that they are staying in a hotel in Carcassonne but I do not know which one.'

The one who had been doing all the talking looked at him long and hard, obviously weighing up what he had just heard. Then he turned towards his companion and a harsh discussion followed, in what Boudet recognised as Arabic. Finally, without a word of apology, the two of them turned on their heels and strode out of the house, leaving the door wide open behind them.

The Frenchman stood transfixed until he heard a car being driven away and the hum of its engine dying in the distance. Desperately, he searched for the piece of paper that Sally had given him. The sound of a second car going through its gears and taking the same direction went unheard.

*

'You embarrassed us! Embarrassed me! The man had obviously made a mistake.'

They had just removed their helmets and were crossing the car park towards the hotel foyer.

Well thanks a bunch, Gus thought. *I appreciate your gratitude.* 'He was threatening you, and he raised his hands to me.'

'So, you thought you'd teach him a lesson. Well good for you!'

She was being her most sarcastic, and proving yet again as far as Gus was concerned, that she hated his guts. Well to hell with her! He turned to look at her, fully aware that his eyes were also flashing with anger.

'Look! I'm sorry if I spoilt your day out but that business today with Claude Boudet had bugger all to do with my job here. Nor that business with the Arab for that matter. Look! I know that you don't like me… you've made that plain enough already… so tomorrow we go our separate ways. We'll both do what your precious Uncle Jim expects of us, which for you means catching the next fucking flight back home. I didn't invite you along, lady, so why don't you give me some space? And this…' Roughly he pushed some notes into her hand. '…Should more than cover what you paid our mutual French friend.'

With that, he left her standing there, looking stunned and lost… and beautiful.

As the revolving door swallowed him up, Gus heard the faint ringing of her phone but he felt no interest in who the caller might be.

*

'Can I come in?'

She was standing there, looking rather sheepish.

A good twenty minutes had elapsed since the episode in the car park and it had given Gus time to change from his leathers. For answer, he merely stood aside to let her into his room, assuming that she had come to offer an apology, and he wondered how he should he deal with it. Should he accept and let things continue as before or should he stick to his decision to go it alone?

'Boudet phoned me. He sounded upset.'

Tough! If he didn't like what happened either, then he too will just have to lump it. I'm past caring.

'...After we left him, he got a visit from those two we saw in Rennes. The two who stopped that ruffian beating you up.'

He looked at her and saw the shadow of a smile showing through her concern.

'The black beards? What did they want?'

'Monsieur Boudet says that their attitude was threatening. He sounded really frightened and concerned, Gus. Says they wanted to know where we were staying.'

'And he told them?'

'He couldn't, could he? Because he doesn't know. All he knew was that we were staying somewhere in Carcassonne. He said that he had to tell them that much or they would have harmed him. He thinks they're on their way here now.'

Gus felt unsure how to react to the news. Sally hadn't come to apologise after all, but rather to warn him, as a favour. 'So, they're coming after me. Fair enough!' He was trying to sound casual. 'I doubt if they'll find me tonight and I'll be gone first thing in the morning anyway.'

Tears welled in her eyes. 'It's not you they're looking for. It's me. Boudet was quite adamant about that.'

Gus felt himself becoming agitated. He glanced at his watch. 'So, where the hell have you been until now? Boudet phoned you a good twenty minutes ago.'

He was angry because her tears upset him more than he was prepared to admit.

'...Go pack your stuff while I try and arrange a flight for you! It'll have to be from either Toulouse or Perpignan. Neither of them is more than an hour away.'

Although looking totally dejected, she seemed about to object but then thought better of it. Without another word she turned and left the room. Gus felt a sudden emptiness as he reached for his phone.

Away from Carcassonne

With her few possessions in a bag strapped across her back, Sally climbed onto the pillion and, as the engine roared into life, she threw her arms firmly around Gus' thin frame. The squeeze that she gave him was purely instinctive but it made her aware of the raw strength that was in his deceptively frail-looking body. Just being this close to him made her feel less vulnerable.

Fifteen minutes earlier he had rung her in her room: 'We'll be leaving in ten minutes, but there'll have to be a change of plan because I haven't been able to get you a flight either tonight or tomorrow, so it will have to be the day after. But we can't risk you staying here, so we're leaving.'

His concern was for her rather than for himself, she'd realised. Uncle Jim's agents were conscientious if nothing else! Again, she tightened her hold on him as she shouted in his ear, 'So where do we go?'

'I haven't decided yet. Out of Carcassonne for a start.'

'Gus! Can I say something?'

He delayed putting on his helmet. 'What?'

His voice, she realised, still had an edge to it. Was he still angry? Or just hurt?

'I just want to say sorry. I shouldn't have said what I did.' A whispered apology in his ear was easier than to his face.

'Forget it!'

'It's just that I felt for Claude Boudet. Please understand! He takes coach tours to Rennes-le-Château regularly over the summer months, so he's well-known there and... well, I just didn't want his reputation to suffer, that's all.'

'He'll get over it.'

The harshness of his voice sounded unyielding.

'But he's frightened Gus. I could tell when he phoned me. Frightened that those men will get back to him if they don't find us... find me. Is there anything we can do for him?'

'I'll think about it. But you'll have to figure out why that Arab guy was so interested in you.'

'I tell you, I've no idea. I hardly saw his face because you were standing between us. Not only that but he was also wearing sunglasses. And then, when you'd finished throwing him around and those two others came to take him away, he had his back to me. As far as I know, I've never seen the man before in my... Good God! You said Arab?'

A possibility had suddenly struck her and she was now thinking aloud. 'Surely it couldn't be him?'

'Who?'

'I'll tell you later when we're far away from here. Oh, and Gus...'

'Yeah?'

'I'm glad you couldn't get a flight for me.'

His reply, as he pulled on his helmet and again revved the powerful engine, went unheard but he did feel her warm breath on his ear and the briefest of hugs from her arms.

'So have you decided on our next move?' The bike was now moving out of the hotel car park and she had to shout to be heard.

'Wait and see!'

Alet-les-Bains (20 minutes later)

'Have you no friends or family that you could stay with, monsieur? Just for a day or two?'

The Frenchman shook his head.

'Well, I'd prefer it if you didn't stay here on your own. They probably won't come back but it's better to play safe, don't you think?' Sally sounded contrite, as if she blamed herself for the way things had turned out.

Claude Boudet, for his part, was now convinced that his young friends weren't quite what they pretended to be. The incident at Rennes had proved that and he himself had unwittingly become involved. Or at least the two Arabs seemed to think so.

'I am not happy to stay here, Mademoiselle Sally, but there is nowhere I can go.'

'Can we stay with him, Gus?'

Whilst they were talking, Gus had been chewing over what Sally had told him on their way here about the Arab who had questioned her in Rome about the Treasure of Solomon's Temple. Could it possibly be that that was what all the fuss was about? The Treasure of Solomon's Temple? That the treasure that MI6 were worried about wasn't a code word at all and had nothing whatsoever to do with the business in Albania? Nothing to do with gun-running and Vatican plans to escalate unrest in the Middle East? And yet, ironically, the treasure, if it existed at all, would constitute the same sort of threat as the Final Crusade, because finding it could lead to a similar sort of scenario, judging from what Boudet and Sally had been saying earlier. If the Treasure of Solomon's Temple was still around, then Jewish aspirations to find it were quite understandable. And just as understandable would be the concerns of the Catholic church, as well as those of Islam.

The more he thought about it, the more he understood why the Vatican and especially the Arabs would be prepared to go to extreme lengths to prevent the Israelis getting their hands on the treasure.

'Can we, Gus?'

He had heard her the first time. 'Out of the question, I'm afraid. Once they find our hotel in Carcassonne and hear that we left in a hurry, then they're bound to come looking for us here, since Monsieur Boudet can be their only other lead to us. Mind you, they might just give up the chase. It just depends on how much they think you can tell them.'

Sally laughed nervously. 'I know nothing more than what I told him back in Rome…if, of course, it's the same man.'

'I think we can take that for granted now. Put yourself in his shoes. He saw you in Rome, studying the Arch of Titus, and now he sees you here, in Rennes-le-Château, where the treasure is thought to have been hidden. Any fool would make some sort of connection. So, he shared his thoughts with his two friends and now that they realise that we're on the run from them and that it was Claude who probably warned us, then they'll be even more convinced that you and he are involved. They might think that you're an agent for the Vatican, or something like that.'

'So, what do we do?' She sounded genuinely uneasy.

'Move on from here, for a start!'

'And take Monsieur Boudet with us.'

Not much option, Gus thought. 'He'll just have to follow us by car.'

He sighed inwardly as he made the suggestion, realising that it would be Boudet, therefore, who would be setting the pace. Having to limit the Honda to a steady forty miles per hour wasn't a prospect that particularly appealed to him.

'Where do we go, though? Have you any suggestions, *monsieur*?'

The Frenchman, who had been quiet but thoughtful thus far, looked from one to the other of them. 'If I knew what you are after, *mes amis,* then I might be able to help.'

Sally looked enquiringly at Gus who, after a second's thought, nodded, but not before giving her a little frown of warning. She read his mind and proceeded to give Boudet a brief résumé of why they were there. Gus, she told him, was a secret agent who was trying to foil a plan to upset the balance of power in the Middle East but the information he was working on was sketchy at best. '…All he knows is that the plan involves a search for Solomon's Treasure and that the Vatican is somehow involved, as well as the Arabs, by the looks of it.'

'And Israelis?'

'Could well be, monsieur. Why do you ask?'

'It is something that has just occurred to me, *mademoiselle*. The only other place that is associated with the treasure of the Visigoths is Montségur and I cannot help wondering whether there is a connection with what you've just told me and what is going on in Montségur at the moment.'

'And what would that be?' The question came from Gus.

'The *Chateau de Montségur* has been closed to the public. It seems that some construction work is going on there. The company involved is *Morcon,* a Jewish company based here in the Languedoc. Whether that has any significance, I wouldn't know.'

Sally and Gus looked at one another and came to an immediate decision. 'Then it's there we must go, *monsieur*. Will you take us?'

Le Château de Montségur

All work had stopped at the citadel. Those on the scaffolding, who until a few minutes ago had been going through the motions of doing safety work on the ruin walls, were now all looking down expectantly on the scene of commotion below. Others, on hearing excited cries, had rushed in to see what, if anything, had been found, and were now converging on the cordoned-off old well near the south wall, where Leron, Yashar and Ben-Ami were engaged in animated conversation, deaf to the incessant drone of the generator and the churning of the cement mixer.

'What other explanation can there be? It proves that the well was intentionally filled in. But why? And by whom, if not by the Cathars themselves?'

Much earth and gravel had now been removed from the old well, to a further depth of a metre and a half, to reveal huge boulders packed tightly together within its ancient circular walls. It was what they had been waiting for—certain proof that the waterhole had been intentionally and professionally bunged up. By whom and for what reason could only be speculated upon at present, although Leron seemed already convinced that he had the answer.

'How do we go about clearing it? From what I can see of it, that largest boulder in the centre must weigh at least two thousand kilos.'

The top face of the boulder that Ben-Ami was referring to was roughly four feet in diameter but the indications were that it was cone-shaped and that it was much wider at its base. Other boulders had been roughly chiselled into similar shapes so that they could be wedged tightly downwards between the central boulder and the circular well wall. What little space there was between them was still filled with earth.

'It's not going to be easy. Whoever did this, went to a lot of trouble and considerable effort.' Leron refrained from adding *and it just confirms what I've been arguing all along.* 'Obviously, the smaller boulders will have to be removed first before we can attempt the largest one, in the middle. But they are all wedged in so tight.'

'Even the smaller ones must weigh at least five or six hundred kilos apiece, wouldn't you say? We would need a crane to get them out.'

What Yashar was really suggesting was that they were faced with an impossible task. But Leron wasn't going to accept defeat that easily.

'We'll have to construct a derrick and winch them out, that's all. Come! We must draw up a list of what we'll need and arrange another chopper delivery tomorrow morning.' He turned towards the *Morcon* workers: 'In the meantime, do what you can to scrape as much earth as possible from between the boulders.'

Alet-les-Bains to Lavelanét

'I found what you were telling us earlier about the treasures of the Languedoc very interesting, monsieur, but I must admit that I am still rather confused by it all. Visigoths, Cathars, Templars, Merovingians. Who was who and who came when? Just before the... um!... unfortunate incident in Rennes-le-Château, you were about to simplify things for us.'

The decision that they'd eventually come to was for Sally to accompany the Frenchman in his car and for Gus to go on ahead to Lavelanét, to book rooms for them for the night. According to Boudet, the journey would take at least an hour, since the road was extremely tortuous in parts, but Gus knew that he could cover the distance in half the time.

Claude Boudet smiled. '*Mais oui, mademoiselle*, especially since I now know that you, too, are a tourist guide. In Rome, you say? That must be wonderfully challenging for you.'

'No more than the Languedoc is for you, monsieur. So, explain everything to me again, please.'

'Of course. And I will begin with the Magdalene. She arrived in the Languedoc either with Jesus for company or carrying his child. By popular belief, that would be in 33CE, although others will argue a slightly later date for Christ's birth and therefore a later date for his crucifixion and the Magdalene's subsequent voyage to France. Either way, it marked the beginning of the Merovingian bloodline, or so some authors would have us believe. The claim has yet to be authoritatively proved or disproved. However, centuries later, in the year 507 if my memory serves me right, the Merovingians, led by King Clovis who was... or was not... a direct descendant of Jesus and Mary Magdalene, defeated the Visigoths and pursued them out of Toulouse and then Carcassonne.'

'To Rennes-le-Château.'

'*Oui*, or Rhedae as it was then called.'

'And you say that the Visigoths took their treasure with them.'

Boudet again showed his pleasure. 'You are a model student, *mademoiselle*.'

'But according to you, *monsieur*, the Visigoths' treasure must have been enormous, especially if it included the Treasure from Solomon's Temple. Rennes is a small place. Where could they possibly have hidden it?'

'Since the days of the Romans, there has been much mining for gold and other ores in the region. You would not believe it, Sally, but the area is a maze of underground workings, not to mention all the underground river caverns that are here. There were more than enough hiding places, even in the early days of the Visigoths. Anyway, later there was some intermarriage between the Merovingian and Visigothic royal families, so it is possible...'

'That the secret of the treasure was passed on to subsequent kings of France.'

'*Oui*, that is indeed possible. Now, the Merovingian dynasty reigned France for almost four hundred years and only came to an end when Childeric III was deposed in 751 by Pepin – Pepin the Fat as he was called – father of Charlemagne. That marked the beginning of the Carolingian dynasty. And by the way, it was Pepin who agreed to the setting up of the Jewish kingdom of Septimania that I was telling you about earlier, a kingdom that had to have a descendant of the Royal House of David as its head.'

'A Jewish kingdom in the south of France! Whew! It's all too complicated for me, I'm afraid. But carry on just the same, monsieur, because I find it all very intriguing.'

'Another who could have laid claim to the Merovingian throne was Sigisbert IV. His father was the Merovingian Dagobert II, and his mother Giselle was descended from the Visigoths and lived in Rennes-le-Château.' Boudet paused briefly, to suggest the significance of his next words. '...Sigisbert became the *Comte de Razes*.'

'Ah! The one who drew the map.'

'Perhaps, but there were many Counts of Razes after him.'

'But in his position he would have known about the treasure.'

'Quite possibly, but what I find more intriguing than speculation about treasure even, are the claims today that the Merovingian bloodline is still alive and kicking; that it has been protected over the centuries by a covert society known as The Priory of Sion whose aspiration is to place a

Merovingian king... a king who can trace his ancestry back to Jesus himself... once more on the throne of France.'

'Seriously?' Sally didn't know whether to gape or to laugh.

Boudet switched the Citroen's lights on, to combat the light mist that was closing in on them . 'You'll be surprised to know that the idea is quite popular in certain distinguished circles even to this day. To those people, the name Merovingian is still synonymous with authority and sovereignty.'

'After more than a thousand years? Surely not!'

The Frenchman nodded. 'Why else do you think that Napoleon, early in the nineteenth century, tried to get himself crowned king by claiming Merovingian lineage?'

'Really?'

'Indeed! One of the Merovingian emblems was the *apis mellifica* – the honey bee – shaped out of pure gold. Napoleon had a magnificent cloak tailored for himself with many such golden bees stitched into it. But the plan didn't fool anyone and Buonaparte never became king of France.'

'Fascinating, monsieur! But let me get things clear. The Treasure of the Visigoths, which includes that from the Temple of Solomon, remains hidden, probably in this area that we're passing through now?' She had just spotted the fingerpost for Rennes-le-Château.

'Perhaps. There are stories that it was later moved. Also hidden here, maybe, are the treasures of the Merovingian kings themselves, plus those of the Cathars and the Templars.' Claude Boudet laughed out loud. 'And don't forget the one that Queen Blanche brought here from Paris. I think your secret agent boyfriend has a lot of searching to do, has he not?'

Sally also laughed, before adding rather sternly, 'Only he's not my boyfriend, monsieur.'

Boudet smiled knowingly, as if he didn't quite believe her.

'According to local tradition, there is a secret society that has been guarding the treasures over the years.'

'Old wives' tales, surely.'

'Maybe so and maybe not. If Bérenger Sauniére could speak to us from the grave, he might be able to tell us.'

'Why is that *monsieur*?'

'There was some suspicion about his death, you know? And there have been others.' Claude was thinking, in particular, of the two bodies that he himself had seen in Rennes, recently.

'But what secret society could possibly have survived over all the years?'

'Who can tell? The Priory of Sion, perhaps?'

'The one that's protecting the Merovingian bloodline?'

Boudet nodded. 'Protecting not only the bloodline but possibly the treasure as well.'

'So what periods are we talking about? The disappearance of the treasures of the temple and that of the Merovingians took place at roughly the same time?'

'It seems like it.'

'And the other treasures?'

'We know almost to the exact day when the Cathar treasure disappeared. Either the night of the fifteenth of March 1244 or possibly a fortnight before that, depending on which account you are prepared to believe. The Cathars were given a fifteen-day amnesty by the pope's army either to revoke their heresies or to perform their *consolamentum* before going to meet their Maker. That amnesty came to an end on the morning of March the sixteenth. History tells us that two, maybe four, of the Cathars escaped with the treasure by climbing down with it from Montségur. Highly unlikely, of course, unless the treasure was nothing more than some papers containing records of Cathar faith or Cathar history.'

Out of the corner of his eye, Boudet caught a glimpse of Sally's questioning look.

'…You will understand what I mean when you see Montségur. There is no way that anyone could climb down from there carrying anything heavy. But there has to be some truth to the story because the names of the two Cathars who disappeared that night are known to us even today. They shared the same surname, so they could have been father and son, or two brothers maybe.'

'And the Templar treasure? When did that disappear?'

'Roughly sixty to seventy years later. But in between comes the Queen Blanche incident. As I have already told you, she reigned France while her son Louis IX was away on crusade and, because she suspected the motives of some of her nobles, she carted the contents of the Royal Treasury all the way down from Paris, to hide it somewhere in this area. That has never been found either.'

'So, let me get this clear!' She consulted her notebook. 'Titus stole the Temple Treasure from Rome in 70AD, then in four-hundred-and-odd AD – or CE, Christ Era, as it's referred to these days – the Visigoths helped themselves to it and eventually brought it here to the Languedoc. Then, in 507, the Merovingians came to power and, by defeating the Visigoths, took possession of what was rightfully theirs.'

'Rightfully theirs? How do you mean, *mademoiselle*?'

'Well, from what you've told me, the Merovingians were descendants of Jesus and Mary Magdalene, so the Treasure of Solomon's Temple had to belong to them, as Jews.'

Boudet laughed. 'I see your point. But it is not I who claims the holy bloodline of the Merovingians. That is done by others.'

'Anyway, correct me if I'm wrong, the treasure was then lost for hundreds of years until the templars or the Cathars somehow or other became its guardians, either in Rennes-le-Château or in Montségur.'

'They are only theories, of course, and perhaps they shouldn't be taken too seriously.'

Sally chose to disregard the interruption. 'Also hidden somewhere in the region is the Queen Blanche treasure.'

'So, it is claimed.'

'So which treasure did the priest find in Rennes-le-Château, do you think?'

'You mean *l'abbé* Sauniérè?' The Frenchman chuckled. 'Your guess is as good as mine, young lady. We only know that Sauniérè took the secret with him to the grave.'

They travelled in silence for a kilometre or two until Sally recalled something else that Boudet had told her earlier in the day.

'Did I understand you right, monsieur, when we were in Rennes-le-Château? Didn't you say that you had your own theory about where the treasure might be hidden there?'

'*Oui*, mademoiselle. And you want me to share my secret with you?'

'Will you?'

They both laughed somewhat dismissively.

'I have seen no more than yourself, Sally. Did I not say that I would test you on what you had seen and read in Rennes? But unfortunately, the opportunity didn't come.' He grimaced as he recalled the incident between Gus and the Arab.

'So, what did I miss, monsieur?'

'In the museum, did you read everything about Sauniére and his housekeeper Marie Dénarnaud?'

'Of course.'

'And what do you know about them.'

'That he was a priest who suddenly became rich, probably through finding some old parchments in the church's altar rail. Those, presumably, led him to one of the treasures that you've just been talking about. But which one?'

He ignored her question. 'And Marie Dénarnaud? What about her?'

'She was in on it, I'd say. Didn't she claim that the people of Rennes-le-Château had untold wealth beneath their feet? She'd promised to tell about it before she died but then she had a massive stroke and couldn't tell anyone anything.'

'But there was something that she said... something that she did... that could be a clue to Sauniéré's hidden wealth.'

Sally laughed. 'But you're not going to tell me.'

'Ah! But I will, *mademoiselle*.' Boudet was truly serious now. 'I have become too old to put my theory to the test. If you and your young man don't have the chance to investigate, then maybe someone else will, before too long.'

'Gus Adams is not my young man, *monsieur*.'

'Ah! The lady doth protest too much, methinks.'

'Pardon?'

'Shakespeare! Hamlet!'

Sally shook her head with some amazement. 'You are full of surprises, Monsieur Boudet. But what of your theory? What clue did Sauniéré's housekeeper leave.'

'If you read everything that was being displayed on the museum wall then you will have seen a reference to a fire that threatened to burn down many of the houses in the village. Sauniéré was dead by then and the firefighters asked Marie Dénarnaud's permission to draw water from the well on her property but she refused point blank. Now why would she do that, do you suppose?'

'And that's the clue?'

'It is a clue to my theory, yes.'

Sally suddenly felt disenchanted. 'You think that Sauniéré's treasure is at the bottom of the well.'

'Not at the bottom, perhaps, but the water level might hide a secret passage? Don't you think? So, whenever he wanted to get to the treasure, all Sauniérè had to do would was to secretly drain some of the water in order to get to the tunnel entrance. Our Bérenger Sauniérè is known to have done stranger things in his time than climbing into wells. As boys growing up in Montazels, which is a mere five kilometres away from Rennes, he and his brother became quite obsessed with finding treasure. They used to spend a lot of their time searching the old underground workings in the area.'

Sally was far from convinced. 'But if the water level was higher than the tunnel entrance, then the treasure would be permanently drowned.'

'Not necessarily. There would be ways to overcome that problem.'

They fell silent again, with the Frenchman disappointed by Sally's scepticism. Then the road sign Lavelanét five kilometres emerged out of the mist.

Le-Château de Montsegur

'Today we break up early. The helicopter is due to arrive at half past nine tomorrow morning and I want you here waiting for it, so expect the bus to pick you up at your hotel in Montferrier at half past seven.'

There were a few grumbling sounds that brought an unwilling scowl to Leron's face. 'We are on the verge of reclaiming our people's history and all some of you can do is to complain?'

An embarrassed silence swept over the throng of faces in front of him.

'… You are being paid well for this work and that includes your loyalty, your silence and your full commitment to our homeland. Tomorrow, God willing, we will find what we are looking for and, if we do, then your names will be written on the scrolls of Jewish history. Cherish the thought, my friends, and look forward to tomorrow, for I believe it will be a thrilling day for us all. But be prepared also for it to be a long one. After tonight, there will be no respite until the job is finished. Now go and enjoy your well-earned rest. *Shalom*!'

As they watched them go, Leron and the others could barely contain their excitement and were soon slapping one another on the back.

'Let us have one last look, my friends, before we also descend for a little celebration.'

Ben-Ami and Yashar readily followed Leron up onto the scaffolding planks overlooking the old well. Much of the earth between the tightly packed boulders had been cleared away so that they were now able to peer down the narrow slits between them. It had been a slow and painstaking task to remove that earth, but a necessary one because it meant that tomorrow morning, once the equipment had been set up, hooks and chains could be lowered between the rocks for them to be winched up, one at a time. Getting the first one out would prove difficult but, once that had been removed, they would then have better access to tackle the others.

The three Mossad agents could barely suppress their excitement.

'There!' Leron was pointing downwards between two of the outer boulders. 'And there!' His finger had moved on to the next gap. 'There can be no mistake. It must have led somewhere.'

Ben-Ami and Yashar smiled agreement. What they were looking at was a row of capstones inside the curved wall of the well and below it an emptiness that suggested an underground doorway several feet wide.

Leron now raised his right hand skywards, inviting the others to grasp it in a show of restrained jubilation and solidarity.

'Come, my friends! We have earned our little celebration. There is nothing that can stop us now.'

Le Village de Montségur

When he saw his guest relaxing in the garden, Father Francois decided that it was a good time to seek the Vatican priest's advice on the little matter that had been worrying him of late. But then he heard his convalescing guest's gentle snores and reluctantly returned indoors.

The snoring continued for a while before easing off. Out of the corner of his eye Galileo had seen his host approaching and had decided that he didn't want to be disturbed, that he needed to be alone with his thoughts. He felt as tense now as he did on that final visit to the quarry in Kukes. Tonight, he intended climbing Montségur to see what the Israelis were up to. There would be guards, he knew that, and they would have to be dealt with. Which meant that his plans had to be precise and that he'd have to cover his tracks with great care. For his own safety he would have to wear his black suit and dog-collar. Timing was also important. He would have to get to the guards by daylight, so that they could see him coming. From there on, it didn't much matter. It promised to be a clear night anyway, so the Citadel would be bathed in moonlight. But he would take his flashlight just in case. More importantly, he would need the gun.

All Father Francois need know was that his ailing guest intended paying the local church a visit for silent prayers before going on a long and relaxing moonlit walk.

*

Father Galileo began his preparations early.

First on his list was the gun that had been delivered to his hotel in Carcassonne, the night he'd arrived in France. He had insisted on it being a Beretta, a weapon that he felt comfortable with and one that had served him well in the past. Tight security checks in Rome had meant having to leave his own gun back in Italy. Next, he checked the condition of his torch—light and easy to hide and with an extra set of AA batteries and spare halogen bulb. Then came the palm-sized digital camera with still-photograph and video facility. Fourth on the list were the pocket-sized night-vision glasses.

When he was finally ready, his only concern was the adequacy of his footwear. He knew that his shoes were hardly suitable for the steep stony path up to the Château but his only other pair was even less suited to the task.

Father Francois was surprised to see him emerge from his room dressed as if he was going to mass but he put it down to his guest's eccentricity.

'I shall visit your church, Father, to pray, and then take a long walk to enjoy the cool mountain air. Do not be surprised if it is late when I get back.'

*

Apart from one old woman lighting a candle by the altar, the church was empty when Galileo entered. He nodded in silence to her before getting to his knees and stayed there until he heard her leave. Then, after a quick look around the place, just to prove to Father Francois that he had, indeed, been inside his church, he hurried out.

Looking skywards and then at his watch, he decided that there was still plenty of time before it got dark but he also knew that, at his pace, the strenuous walk just to reach the tourist car park would take him a good twenty minutes and that he had to allow a further fifteen minutes from there to the hut where the guards were stationed. It was essential that he reached that hut well before dusk.

To anyone who might be watching, Galileo's stride was leisurely and unhurried as he walked through the village's narrow streets which twisted and turned as they gained height. As he passed, he spotted the little museum – now closed for the day – that Father Francois had recommended he should visit. *I might just do that before leaving,* he thought whimsically. *Once I've got the job done here.*

Straight ahead stood the little café that he had called at earlier in the day, where he'd been served with a free coffee by the proprietor. Many of the tables under their colourful umbrellas were now taken but Galileo had eyes for only the one nearest to the road, the one where the three men were enjoying a bottle of wine and enthusiastic conversation with their evening meal. As he walked by, one of them looked in his direction, smiled briefly and nodded.

'Good evening, Father!' To which the other two politely followed suit.

'Good evening, gentlemen,' Galileo responded. '*Bon appetit*!' He smiled, being tempted to add *'Shalom'* as he moved away. Little did they know that their faces were safely recorded in his little pocket camera.

Eventually, he reached the main road that wound its way up the hill in the direction of Montferrier. Now, with no one looking, he could quicken his pace a little, stopping to appreciate the view only when he heard cars approaching. By the time he finally reached the tourist car park for the Château, the sun was lower on the horizon than he would have wished it to be. He'd have to hurry.

The only vehicle in sight was the tatty old Dormobile at the very top end of the car park, a good hundred metres beyond the path to the citadel. It had been there last night as well, in exactly the same spot, which made him now suspect that it had been abandoned. *But better to check, just in case,* he thought. Quickly, he reached for his camera and allowed its powerful lens to zoom in on the orange and white vehicle in the distance. No sign of anyone inside. No time, either, to check further.

Drawing the Beretta out of his inside pocket and clipping it now onto his belt behind his back, Galileo set off on the path towards the Cathar stele, humming a little tune as he did so. He wanted the guards to know that he was coming. The last thing he wanted was to surprise them and perhaps get shot on sight.

*

The two Swiss guards posing as geology students had instinctively ducked when they spotted the little priest appearing on the road below them, only risking a quick peek every so often as he drew nearer and keeping well down again when they saw him produce the digital camera. They knew about the magnifying power of some zoom lenses. Then, when they saw that he'd lost interest in their Dormobile, they watched with great curiosity as he began tackling the slope up the Field of the Burned.

'What is he up to? The Israelis are long gone.'

'One thing's for sure! He's no priest, is he?' They had both seen the gun.

Just then, one of their cell phones began ringing and they scrambled to answer it, although there was little chance of the priest hearing the ring tone from that distance.

'I'll answer it, Erwin! You keep an eye on the priest.'

At the commemorative stele, Galileo paused to read out loud the words that were inscribed on it, then he began humming again as he took to the more-rocky path. The guards would surely have heard him by now and would be alert and expecting him.

'Halt! Who are you?'

They were both standing outside the ticket collector's hut, each holding his right hand behind his back. Galileo knew that the guns would appear at the slightest sign of trouble.

'Ah! Bon soir, messieurs!'

His panting was exaggerated, giving the impression that to get thus far had been a supreme effort for him. Then he began kneading his back to soothe an imaginary pain.

'…Did I startle you?' By way of apology, he made the sign of the cross, little caring that the practice would be anathema to the two Israelis.

'Why are you here, Father? Did you not read the sign? The path to Montségur is closed until further notice.'

'Forgive me, gentlemen, but I am only here as a favour to one of my parishioners. She visited Montségur recently and lost a piece of jewellery that was of great sentimental value to her.' He smiled innocently. 'You know what women are like about such things. Anyway, when she heard that I was paying the church at Montségur a visit, I had to promise her…' He gave them a mischievous, meaningful look. 'She is, after all, one of the wealthier members of my flock.'

'But it's getting dark, Father! You would have no hope of finding anything tonight.'

They were suspicious of him still, although a little less than at first.

'Truth is, *mes amis,* that until half an hour ago I had forgotten everything about my promise.' He grimaced as if in spiritual agony and again made a show of massaging his back. 'And since I shall have to be leaving Montségur at first light tomorrow morning, then this was my only opportunity. The woman is convinced that the brooch fell out of her purse whilst she was paying for her ticket, here.'

With exaggerated hand movements he indicated not only the hut but also its immediate surroundings.

'...It is a very precious family heirloom, from what I understand. Gold with many real diamonds encrusted in it. If I should find it... if I could only return it to her personally...'

He let his eyes and his half smile say it for him.

'She would be very grateful, I imagine.' At last, one of the guards was also smiling. 'And she would want to show her gratitude to the church... and perhaps to her priest as well?'

Galileo's smile again suggested a little roguishness. 'You are so understanding, my son.'

'But you haven't got a chance of finding it, Father. Hundreds of people have passed this way since then. Someone is bound to have found it before now.'

'I was hoping, maybe, that a Christian soul might have come across it and then handed it in to the ticket collector.' He shuffled to look past them into the hut whilst again digging his fingers into the imaginary back pain. 'And that he might have kept it in his little cupboard over there.'

With his left hand he now pointed past them, into the hut.

Instinctively, they both started looking over their shoulders and just as instinctively realised that they were letting their guard down. The fraction of a second, however, was enough for the experienced assassin. The Beretta had already come off its clip and it now erupted once... twice... and twice again to finish the job. The two Mossad agents were dead before they hit the ground.

*

As the call came to an end, Erwin looked enquiringly at his friend. 'Who was it, Otto?'

'Not good news, I'm afraid. That was Brett, calling from Carcassonne. He says that the Arab called Qusay was back in Rennes-le-Château again today and that he has now been joined by two others. Brett says that the new guys appear to be much more professional than Qusay. Anyway, it seems that Qusay came a cropper today. He tried to tackle some young chap... something to do with a girl, Brett thought... and Qusay came off the worst. Then, when the young man and his girl, together with an older gentleman, left Rennes by car, Qusay and his mates followed them, and

Brett and the others followed them, of course. It seems that the older man was driving and when he dropped them off at Alet-les-Bains, the young couple took off on a powerful motorcycle and Qusay and his mates lost them. And they are now going from hotel to hotel in Carcassonne, trying to find where the young couple are staying. Brett has no idea why Qusay and his mates are so interested in them. Not yet anyway!'

'It's just a matter of time before they make their way here, to Montségur, don't you think? Qusay and his friends, I mean.'

'Well, if they do and if they become a threat, then we'll just have to deal with them. What's bothering me more at the moment, Erwin, is what that priest could be up to.'

The two Vatican guards continued to peer into the gloom, expecting any minute to see the solitary figure reappear from under the black canopy of trees, having been turned back by the Israeli sentries.

'What's taking him so long do you think? Do you reckon the Israelis have dealt with him? And if so, how?'

'*Look!*' Otto became agitated and was pointing higher up the slope. Erwin followed his gaze but could see nothing.

'A flash of light! Keep watching! I know I saw it!'

Half a minute went by before the flickering light reappeared, only higher up the slope now than where Otto had been pointing. But it disappeared again just as quickly.

'What the hell's going on?'

'If it's him, if he has got past the sentries, then once he's out of the trees and into the open, he'll be easy enough to spot.'

'Not necessarily. Once he's out of the trees he won't be needing a torch. He'll be able to climb by moonlight. Come on!'

After hurriedly packing necessities into their little shoulder bags, the two set off at pace, guns at the ready. They raced up the Field of the Burned, pausing for breath only when they reached the Cathar memorial. From there, they would have to be more cautious. Since the canopy of leafy branches up ahead of them was blocking out the moonlight, they had no option but to put on their night-vision glasses, thus turning the daunting darkness into an eerie green. Now, taking great care with each step, to avoid kicking loose stones or stepping on tinder-dry twigs, they inched their way up the path. They knew that it was a goodish climb to reach the ticket collector's hut where the guards were stationed but they had to be wary in case they unexpectedly came face-to-face with one of them or, more likely, with the priest on his way down.

After what seemed an age of creeping through a surreal world, Otto, who was in the lead, raised a warning hand. The hut had come into view, but there was no movement to be seen. Cautiously, they edged forward, guns at the ready, all the while dreading a sudden flash out of the darkness and the searing pain of a hot bullet.

They got to within five metres before they saw the bodies, sprawled across the path. Otto rushed forward to survey the scene while Erwin scanned the shadows in case the assassin was still around. Blood was slowly congealing on the wooden platform in front of the hut and more of it collecting into pools in little hollows of rock on the step below.

'Had to be the priest! Who, in hell, can he be? Come!'

With far less caution now, they began haring up the path. The priest, if he could be called that, had shot the guards and was now making for the summit. It was the light from his torch that they'd seen earlier and he had a twenty-minute head start at least.

Even though the two were moving at a fair rate, it took several more minutes for them to emerge into the open and now they had no further need for the night-vision glasses, since the way ahead was bathed in moonlight. The path, however, was becoming much steeper and they were forced to slow down and to take greater care as they meandered their way between rocky outcrops, not knowing if the priest had reached the top or was just resting around the next corner, gun in hand.

The homely lights of Montségur, far below, belonged to another world.

Eventually, the walls of the Château came into view, towering ghostly white under the night sky. Still no sign of the killer, though. Tentatively now, and sweating profusely, they inched their way, guns at the ready, towards the steps and the platform that had been erected as a tourist entrance into the citadel, pausing only to catch their breath when startled by the doleful cooing of a wood pigeon close by. Finally, they made it to the top, to peer into the shell of the ancient fort.

Spotting the little man proved easy enough. He was perched on scaffolding overlooking the ancient well where, with the aid of the extra light from his torch, he was taking photo after photo of whatever lay below him, pausing after each flash to consult the viewer on his camera, probably to ensure that the pictures were of a good enough quality. Then, when they saw him preparing to leave, the two of them quickly retreated, to hide behind one of the many rocky outcrops, well away from where the path began its downward journey.

The minutes rolled by and still they waited for the assassin-priest to reappear.

'He has to come out the same way as he went in, so what's he up to now do you think?'

'Shall I go and check? We need to know.'

Erwin's decision almost proved to be his undoing. Another second or two and he would have been out in the open, in full view of Father Galileo who had suddenly reappeared in the ruin entrance. Otto yanked his friend back into the shadows by the seat of his pants just as a dollop of cloud dimmed out the moon.

For a minute or two the bogus priest stood leaning against the handrail, savouring the serene panorama and a silence broken only by the chirping of amorous cicadas in the thorny shrubs below.

'Looking at him, you'd think that he's at peace with the world.'

Otto didn't answer. He was willing the little assassin to leave.

Finally, the priest made his move, skipping down the steps with an agility that surprised the two who were watching. Then they saw him take to the path and even though he quickly dropped out of sight, they could still hear the clumping of his footsteps as he dropped heavily from step to rocky step on his downward journey.

They waited until he was well down the path before they ventured into the ghostly shell of the citadel.

Quickly, they took up the position that the priest had been in a few minutes earlier and, in the light of two powerful torches they peered down into the well, soon spotting what he had been photographing. Then, after a brief consultation, Otto put his own camera to use, until he was satisfied that he, too, had captured the detail that he wanted.

'So, this is what *Morcon* have been up to! Looks as if they're about to uncover some kind of entrance. To the treasure, possibly. We'll have to spoil their plans, somehow or other.'

Erwin had already been looking around. 'Can't we fill it in with concrete? The stuff is already here for us.' He was pointing towards a pile of coarse sand and a stack of cement bags, partially covered with plastic sheeting weighed down with a number of shovels. 'And I bet that tank over there has water in it that we can use for the mix.'

Otto gave it thought. 'We'll never manage to fill it all in, but if we could just pour cement between these rocks…' He indicated the tight-fitting boulders in the well. '…then that would make it damn difficult, if not impossible, for them to get any of them out.'

Erwin was nodding. 'That and a three-inch-thick layer of concrete to cap it off should do the job, I reckon.'

'Too much work for one night, Erwin. We'd never get it done and we can't risk the mixer in case the noise of it churning is heard down in the village.'

'What if we shovel a dry mix into the well and pour the water in after each mix? That would be easier and quicker for us, and it would probably be just as effective in the long run.'

Otto was nodding. 'Good idea! Then the sooner we start, the better. We'll take turns at mixing while the other keeps guard in case someone else comes up here. You never know, do you? I'll take the first stint.'

Without waiting for Erwin to reply, he stripped off his shirt and reached for a shovel. Then, after placing a nearby board of thick plywood flat on the ground, he threw a bag of cement onto it, sliced it open with his spade and in no time at all was furiously shovelling a quantity of coarse sand onto the dry cement and then churning it over and over. Four parts sand to one cement should do the trick, he thought, and in no time at all, his muscular torso was gleaming with sweat in the moonlight.

Seven or eight minutes later he was shovelling the dry mix into the well and then climbing in after it to coax it into the narrow gaps between the boulders. Finally, he carried water from the nearby tank and poured enough of it over the sand and cement to ensure that the mix would be rock-hard by morning. A quick look at his watch now told him that he had taken just twenty-four minutes.

They now changed roles, with Erwin taking to the shovel and Otto standing guard.

Three and a half hours later and after four stints apiece, two tired Swiss Guards were scampering down the path towards their parked Dormobile. Such was their hurry that they didn't expect to reach the ticket collector's hut so quickly and almost tripped over the two corpses that still lay there.

'Careful!'

It was Otto's warning as Erwin slipped and almost lost his balance.

'The blood!' Otto explained, letting the pencil-light of his halogen torch point to where Erwin's foot had slithered on the dark stain.

'Come on!'

Neither of them wanted to linger longer than was necessary in the blind stare of two sets of emotionless eyes.

'What now? Do we move the van?'

They were literally running down the Field of the Burned towards the roadside car park with its solitary orange and white vehicle.

'No. That's the last thing we do.' Otto sounded adamant. 'If we're gone by morning then we'll be the obvious suspects and who knows who'll be coming after us? We'll have to hide our stuff, though, because the police are bound to search us and the van.'

'Can I ask you something, Otto?'

They'd reached the car park and had now stopped to catch their breath.

'...Up there...' Erwin's glance indicated the ghostly citadel high above. 'During my stints with the shovel, did you feel anything whilst you were keeping watch?'

'How do you mean?'

'Did you sense anything?'

Rather than answer, Otto just grimaced.

'...I can see that you did. You felt as if we were being watched?'

'Yeah.' It was a grudging admission. 'Made me feel quite uneasy, to tell you the truth.'

'Me too! Was there someone else up there do you think?'

'Hardly likely. We were just tense, that's all. And who could blame us, after what we'd just seen?'

'Yes, you're probably right.'

The scene at the ticket collector's hut would keep them awake for the best part of the night.

Next morning

Visibly shaken, the group closed ranks around the two dead bodies and began looking at one another with shock and growing anger.

The busload of *Morcon* workers had arrived at the car park just as Leron, Ben-Ami and Yashar were getting out of their car. Many had sighed out loud as they'd contemplated yet another strength-sapping climb but Leron and the other two Mossad agents, excited by what the day might hold for them and with every intention of being up at the citadel to welcome the helicopter delivery, had eagerly led the way up the Field of the Burned.

'Who could have done this?'

'Shot them in cold blood!'

'But why?'

As the workers were getting over their initial shock, their questions and comments started coming thick and fast.

'Another murder happened near here recently. Did you know that?'

'And two bodies were found in Rennes-le-Château a few days ago.'

'There has to be a madman on the loose.'

'But they had guns, too,' one voice reasoned.

The dead guards' guns had been lying there for all to see but this revelation seemed to surprise all the others.

'Yes. Why did they have guns?'

Leron and his two agents offered nothing in reply. Although the entire *Morcon* workforce was of Jewish descent, none of them, until now, had fully realised the significance of the contract. All they'd been told initially was that they'd be answerable to the three so-called *structural engineers* and that an independent security company would be safeguarding the site. By now though, they had come to realise that the contract involved a lot more than just renovation work and that it's successful outcome would be of momentous significance, not only to the Israeli government but to the Jewish nation as a whole. The two bodies blocking their path could only be further proof that their enemies were doing all in their power to frustrate their efforts. What they didn't know, however, and what the structural engineers weren't prepared to tell them, was that the two who had recently been found dead in Rennes-le-Château had also been Mossad agents.

Leron now muttered a silent command to Yashar and Ben-Ami and they immediately set off for the summit, checking their own weapons and ammunition once they were out of sight of the workforce, and fully expecting to encounter the killer. Leron stayed where he was, desperately trying to work out how to deal with the situation.

Finally, he spoke. 'My friends, these are very disturbing developments for us all but they are not your responsibility. The situation is for me to deal with; therefore, I ask you to carry on today as though all this hadn't happened. Difficult, I know, but it's imperative that we work even quicker from now on before we are ordered to abandon the site altogether. The police are bound to question us all before the day is out and if they come to know that our two friends here were carrying guns of their own, then they are going to suspect each and every one else of us of being in some way complicit in what happened here last night. I suggest, therefore, that for our own good and the good of the company, not to mention the good name of our homeland, that I remove these guns before the police arrive and that we all forget that we ever saw them.'

He paused just long enough to see most of them nodding their heads, albeit reluctantly.

'…So please continue to the summit for when the helicopter arrives.' He glanced at his watch. 'It should be here within the hour.'

With some muttering the workers filed past the two bodies and the congealed blood, some choosing to look away, others taking in all the details of the gory scene. Then they were gone, leaving Leron in the company of the two men who had been relieved of their duties by the dead pair the night before and who had been expecting to start another day shift this morning.

'We don't carry guns,' one of them said. 'Why did they?'

'Hardly necessary during the day, don't you think? But imagine being alone here all night and in the dark…' Leron hoped the suggestion would satisfy them both. They weren't to know that the dead guards had been employed by the Mossad.

'So, what do we do now? Do we call the police?'

'Little option, have we?' Leron already had his phone in hand. 'First of all, though, we need to get rid of the guns. The police are bound to search us and they'll soon have a squad up here to search the area.'

'Leave that to us. There are plenty of good hiding places in the rocks higher up. They'll probably be concentrating their search down here for the time being.'

'Right. But wipe them clean of fingerprints first. Then I want you to join the other workers up in the château and stay there. Now go! And don't step on the blood! What?'

From a distance, the wailing claxon of a police car cut like a blade through the thin morning air.

*

It was several seconds later before Father Galileo heard the sound. 'Do I hear a police siren, Father?' he asked innocently.

Father Francois paused to listen. 'I believe you are right, Father. It is not often that we hear that sound in Montségur. The last time was when the body of that unfortunate young Italian was found up on the Pog. God forbid that anything like that has happened again.'

Galileo smiled inwardly and fingered the cell phone in his pocket; the one he'd used to anonymously call the police. He would get rid of it later. 'God forbid indeed! But the Pog, Father Francois? What would that be?'

'Ah! The Pog is the name of our hill.' The genuine priest indicated in the direction of the citadel. The hill on which the Château stands. The death of that young man was such a sad business.' Instinctively, he crossed himself. 'Can I ask you something, Father, since you have close connections with the Vatican?'

Galileo became immediately wary. He could so easily be caught out if he wasn't careful. Aiello had made it quite clear to Father Francois that his guest wasn't to be reminded of the work that had led to his so-called mental breakdown.

'I need your advice on one little matter, Father. It is something that has plagued my conscience for the past few weeks, ever since the young man's body was found.'

Galileo's look invited him to continue.

'...The young Italian, whose name I now know to be Piero Antonelli, attended my church for confession. It is something that he said.'

Galileo felt a surge of excitement. 'And something that your vows won't allow you to repeat. Is that what worries you, Father?'

'Yes. But now that the unfortunate man is dead, and since his confession involves the Vatican, then I would dearly like to be advised by someone like yourself who has close connections with the pontiff. I sincerely believe now that you were sent here by God, to counsel me.'

Galileo's encouraging smile didn't reflect what he really felt. 'I will do my best, Father Francois.'

'The young man called Piero Antonelli confessed that he had, in his possession, some ancient documents that had been removed from the Vatican Secret Archives.' He paused.

'Go on!' Galileo was all ears.

'He would not say what they were, nor would he say how he had acquired them, but the poor man's soul was extremely troubled by the fact that they belonged to the Roman Catholic church. I got the impression that he thought he was being followed. There was certainly fear in his voice and in his eyes. He wanted me to take the documents from him and to return them to the Vatican.'

'And did you, Father?'

'No. He did not have them on him at the time but he promised to bring them to me. I never saw him again.'

Galileo cursed under his breath. *So near!*

'I know of the missing papers, Father. I also know that the Holy Father is extremely worried because of their disappearance and that he would feel great gratitude towards whoever could recover them. Have you no idea at all where the documents might be? They weren't found on the body, were they?'

'No. I'm sure of that, because I attended the inquest and heard a list being read of what was found on the poor man's person. God rest his soul.'

Again, he crossed himself, with Galileo following suit, only less devoutly.

'So that was the only time you ever saw him? At confession?'

'No! I had noticed him at the church before then, once during mass, the other time to pray. He seemed particularly interested in our Black Madonna.'

'Black Madonna?'

Galileo tried not to sound too confused but the local priest had noticed his surprise. 'Yes, the shrine above our Maitre-Autel contains a Black Madonna. It is only small, perhaps thirty centimetres high. It was presented to our church about twenty years ago when our village was twinned with a town in Spanish Catalan where the Black Madonna is especially revered. There are, of course, many such shrines in Languedoc churches... churches consecrated to the Magdalene... and most of them are much older and far more imposing than ours. The one at Rennes-le-Château, for instance.'

Galileo felt the need to respond, 'You worship The Whore? You are surely not referring to her as the Madonna?'

At which the local priest gave a sad and somewhat patronising smile. 'Our Lady teaches us forgiveness, Father. The path to redemption is open to all sinners. Jesus forgave the Magdalene, did he not? And if He could, then surely the church can do so also.'

By answering the first question he was hoping to avoid having to answer the second one.

Galileo had no wish to be drawn into an argument on something that he knew little and cared even less about. 'And you say that the young man who made the confession was interested in your Black Madonna?'

'He certainly spent a lot of time in the Lady's presence, when I saw him there. I naturally assumed that he was praying to her. I became even more convinced of it when he later came to confession and said that his little daughter was dying from a rare genetic disease. Also, as I have already mentioned, I could sense a great fear in him for his own personal safety and I naturally assumed that he was beseeching the guidance of Our Lady.'

'But he never showed you the stolen documents, Father?'

'No. Have I done right in telling you all this, Father Galileo? I had wanted to mention it before now but didn't wish to trouble you with church matters.'

Galileo's mind was in turmoil. He had already done all he could to thwart the Israelis' plans at the Château. If he could now get his hands on the documents and destroy them as Aiello had instructed, then he would be free to return to Rome and to live out the rest of his days in comfort.

'Believe me, you have done well, Father Francois, and should the documents ever be found and returned to the secret archives then the Holy Father will feel greatly indebted to you.'

He was tempted to mention the possibility of future sainthood but suspected that that would be going a bit too far.

Lavelanet to Montségur

They set out from the hotel in Lavelanet together, with Sally again keeping the Frenchman company in his little Citroen. Gus had soon left them in his wake.

'You were never married, monsieur?' She hoped the question didn't sound impertinent.

His reply, when it came, was guarded. 'I lost my wife many years ago.'

'Oh! I'm so sorry.'

'I had lost her before the divorce.'

'Oh!' Sally, already regretting the question, wasn't going to ask him to explain further. Her best option, she realised, was to change the subject. 'May I ask you something else, monsieur?'

'*Mais oui!* Ask away!'

She smiled at his use of such a typically English idiom. 'You said that you are an agnostic.'

'Did I?' It was the Frenchman's turn to smile. They were passing through Montferrier at the time. 'Maybe you misheard me, mademoiselle. What I said, perhaps, was that I am a Gnostic.'

'I think, maybe, that that is what you are, monsieur. A Gnostic.'

'Indeed? And why do you think that?'

Yes, he was playing games with her, she realised. 'It's just something you said yesterday about the Cathars, that's all. I got the impression that you are very sympathetic towards their beliefs. Am I right?'

Claude Boudet remained pensive for some seconds. His words, when they came, were carefully chosen: 'My mother's maiden name was Domergue. Bruna Domergue.'

In the brief silence that followed, Sally wasn't sure how to respond. Was she supposed to recognise the name? Had Boudet's mother been a famous authoress or opera singer… actress even?

'My cousin's name is Arnaud Domergue.'

'Oh!' Another famous name that she was failing to recognise.

'They are names that have run in my family for countless generations.'

Realising that he was being deadly serious, she waited for him to explain.

'...On the thirteenth of March 1244, a husband and wife named Arnaud and Bruna Domergue received *consolamentum* at Montségur. Shortly afterwards, they willingly surrendered themselves, together with more than two hundred other Cathars, to be burnt at the stake on what is today known as the Field of the Burned, below Montségur.'

Sally gasped. Boudet smiled wistfully.

'...Their three young sons escaped death because they had been sent to Laroque d'Olmes, to be cared for by other members of the family.' His mood suddenly changed, becoming flippant once more. 'Good job that, or I wouldn't be here now to tell you all this.'

'Good job indeed, monsieur!' She laid a hand on his arm, by way of offering sympathy for the family tragedy of so many centuries ago. 'So you are, indeed, a Cathar? And you can actually trace your ancestry back that far?'

'The Cathar faith no longer exists, Sally, but I have my beliefs just the same, and in the eyes of the Roman church I, too, am a heretic.' He smiled. 'But don't tell anyone, will you? I do not fancy being cremated before I am dead.'

They both laughed. Then he became very agitated as a wailing klaxon caught up with them from behind and an ambulance thundered past, in the direction of Montségur. It was only after he had regained his composure that he continued.

'...Does it not surprise you that the Roman church brought the same charges of heresy against the Cathars and the Knights Templar? Spitting at or trampling on images of the Cross of Calvary was one of them.'

'Should it surprise me, monsieur? Why do you ask?'

'They were exaggerated charges, of course. The heresy of it all, as far as Rome was concerned, was that the Cathars and the templars did not accept the resurrection of Christ, because they knew differently.'

'And how would they know something like that?' She was making no effort now to disguise her scepticism.

'Perhaps the Magdalene had something to do with it.'

Sally wasn't at all sure that she wanted to pursue the matter any further. 'You actually believe the story that Mary Magdalene settled here in the Languedoc?'

'Of course. There can be no question of it.'

'And that Jesus Christ fathered a child with her?'

He chose not to answer her directly: 'There is no question that the Templars unearthed some important secrets when they started digging under the Temple Mount in Jerusalem. Many like to think that it was the Holy Grail, the cup that Christ used during the Last Supper, others say that they found the Ark of the Covenant.'

'But you don't agree?'

'Perhaps they did, perhaps they did not, but I firmly believe that they found some important documents.'

'That proved that Christ hadn't died on the cross?'

'*Oui, mademoiselle*. I do believe that. I also believe that they came across the secrets of fine architecture.'

Sally remained silent, convinced that the Frenchman was delving in pure speculation.

'...Building the Temple of Solomon was a magnificent feat of architecture. With their great wealth, when they returned from the Holy Land, the Templars began building great cathedrals, the likes of which had never been seen before in France, or the rest of Europe for that matter. You have visited Chartres, mademoiselle?'

'No.'

'Then you must go. Chartres Cathedral typifies what I am talking about. And when you go, remember to study the carvings and the gargoyles. They will surprise you, as indeed will the labyrinth inlaid on the floor of the nave.'

'Why would they surprise me?'

'Maybe because they are so un-Christian?'

She shrugged. For the first time since they'd met, Claude Boudet was beginning to bore her. He sensed it and fell silent, pretending to concentrate on the road ahead. But only until his passion for the subject again got the better of him.

'...You know, of course, that the Templars were the forerunners of Freemasonry?'

'No, I didn't know that.' Her tone suggested the rejoinder, *'Nor do I care.'* The countryside around her was more interesting.

'The Freemasons recognise a God that they refer to as The Great Architect of the Universe. And their Masonic Halls are decked like a black and white chess board, based, I imagine, on the Beausant flag of the Templars. You remember that I mentioned to you yesterday how Napoleon tried to get himself crowned as Merovingian king of France?'

'Yes.'

'During his Egyptian Campaign, Napoleon and many of his men became very sceptical of Rome's version of Christianity. Some even converted to Islam. I personally believe this was the result of having made some important discoveries while they were in Egypt.'

Sally stretched her neck in an attempt to relieve the tedium of their journey.

'…One of them was the Rosetta Stone, which finally helped scholars to understand Egyptian hieroglyphs. And do you know who found that Stone of Rosetta?'

'No, but I suspect that you're about to tell me.'

'…A soldier by the name of Hautpoul. Now the Hautpouls were a well-known Razes family that lived at Rennes-le-Château.'

'Oh?' He had her attention again.

'And a family that had strong traditional links with the Magdalene. You'll remember that the church at Rennes is consecrated in the name of Mary of Magdala and that there is a statue there of the Black Madonna. You also saw the bas-relief of her that Sauniéré had had painted on the altar.'

'Pardon me, monsieur. All you say is very interesting but I am unable to take it in. I'm afraid that my interest in history' - *And particularly your detailed version of it!* - 'is very limited … Ah!' Her face suddenly lit up and she raised a finger to point through the windscreen. 'That must be Montségur!'

'Oui, Mademoiselle Sally. That is, indeed, le Château de Montségur.'

*

Gus heard the sirens coming from afar. He had just brought the Honda to a halt, near to where an old orange-and-white Dormobile was parked and he now sat astride his stationary bike, helmet in hand, contemplating the scene below. At the lower end of the roadside car park, some two hundred metres away, two police cars stood nose to tail, their blue lights flashing. Beyond them were parked a work-bus, with its driver still at the wheel, and a black Renault Laguna estate. Nearby, where a kissing gate and a flight of steps gave access to the path up to the Cathar stele and the citadel, a solitary gendarme stood guard.

Gus listened to the approaching klaxon and wondered what was happening.

*

'Take a couple of photos of him. Just in case.'

Erwin reached for his camera and zoomed-in, first on the stranger's face in profile, then on the bike, and finally on the bike's registration number.

'Probably just an inquisitive stranger but you never know. Better be safe than sorry.'

Otto now turned his attention back to the crumpled pieces of paper on the narrow table in front of him and, with both palms, carefully tried to smooth out the creases in them.

'…They're still damp. They'll tear very easily if I'm not careful. A pity you didn't remember about them last night. We could have dried them out properly by now.'

Erwin grimaced. 'Yes, I know! But I forgot, in all the excitement.'

He had found the scrunched ball of wet paper in amongst the bags of cement up at the citadel and had shoved it into his trouser pocket and then forgotten about it.

Otto peered at the two sheets. 'Photocopies! One is a map, the other a pentacle.'

'They're copies of what we're looking for, do you think?'

'Probably.'

'Do you reckon that they, up there, have the originals?' Erwin nodded in the direction of the citadel where the Israelis were still working

'Either that or they've had access to copies of them.'

'Will the police interrogate us, do you think?'

'Very likely. Which is why we must be doubly sure that there is nothing in here to incriminate us. You hid all the stuff last night?'

Erwin frowned. 'That's the third time this morning that you've asked me that, Otto. The guns, the night-visions… everything like that… I've hid in a hollow under a boulder, a full kilometre away from here.' He indicated in the direction of Lavelanet. 'Their search is never going to be that wide.'

'Good. Now let's clear the table and get out our notes and some rock samples. They'll have to be convinced that we actually are a couple of student geologists.'

'What about those papers?'

'The police won't know about their significance. I'll just slip them in amongst the rest of my notes.'

'That biker is still there, Otto! And look! Someone else has arrived!'

They both stared in silence as a green Alpha Romeo pulled up near the police cars at the lower end of the parking area and a man and woman climbed out, both dressed in dark blue blazers with name tags on their lapels.

*

The crime scene had been secured and two gendarmes in bulletproof vests and body armour stood guard, their semi-automatic weapons at the ready. A third stood nearby, waiting to accompany his inspector back down to the car park once he had finished interrogating the *Morcon* structural engineer.

'So, what is your role in all this, monsieur?' The police inspector was eyeing Leron closely. He had already questioned him about how the bodies had been found.

'I merely oversee the safety work that's being carried out at the Chateau, inspector.' Leron nodded towards the two corpses. 'These were my men and they had been posted here to guard the path.'

'You say guard? Explain please!'

'The citadel is dangerous to tourists and has been closed for renovation work. Even at night we could not risk having people wandering up there and getting injured or killed. You know what insurance claims are like these days.'

The inspector seemed to accept the explanation. 'And you have not touched anything? Nor removed anything from the scene?'

'Nothing at all.' The lie was convincing because Leron had been expecting the question.

'Good, but we shall need to question your workers.'

'All of them?' The Mossad agent showed his concern. 'We are awaiting a delivery by helicopter any minute. I cannot possibly call my men down now.'

'There is no hurry, *monsieur*. Our scenes-of-crime officers must investigate down here first, where the men were killed. I do not think your workers will be going anywhere soon, will they?' he added cynically, knowing that the path was the only access to and from the citadel. 'At least not without being seen by my men. And I certainly don't want them traipsing down here and perhaps disturbing what evidence there is. But you do realise that all will have to be questioned thoroughly before the morning's out?'

Leron saw another question coming.

'…But if you didn't phone us, monsieur, then who did?'

'I assure you that I have no idea, Inspector. It certainly wasn't myself or any of my men because we only arrived here a few minutes before you came.'

'But the caller knew there were bodies here. He called us on his cell phone, thirty minutes ago to report the killings.'

'Then you will have his number. Which means that you should be able to trace him.'

'That is already in hand.' Instinctively the Inspector turned a page in his notebook, to where the number had been jotted down, but showed no intention of sharing the information with Leron.

It was at that point that Ben-Ami and Yashar appeared, one behind the other, on their way back down the narrow path and they caused enough distraction for Leron to steal a glance at the policeman's notebook. What he saw stunned him because the number was one that he immediately recognised as belonging to one of the dead guards.

The inspector now ordered them to return to the car park.

'And you will stay there, *messieurs*, to be questioned more fully later.'

Once they were out of the policeman's earshot, Yashar and Ben-Ami began an agitated conversation with Leron and he, in turn, became visibly disturbed by what he was hearing. Whoever was responsible had now made their task virtually impossible, he realised.

'It will take weeks to drill out the concrete and to remove those boulders. I'm not even sure that it can be done.'

'But it must be done, Yashar! Even if it takes months... years.'

But Leron knew that Yashar was right. *Morcon* would have to be off the mountain by the end of the month. There would be no hope of doing anything after that.

They were halfway down the Field of the Burned and in sight of the car park when they noticed a man and a woman receiving clearance from the gendarme who was stationed there. The two had an officious air as they began to trek up towards them. Leron looked at his watch. It was twenty minutes to ten.

'You have been to the citadel this morning?' It was the man's question.

'No. But who's asking?' A quick glance at one of the nametags merely added to his despair. As he'd feared, they were from the office of tourism.

'What is happening there?'

'Renovation work, what else?'

'Was it you who telephoned, earlier?' There was more authority in the woman's voice.

'Telephoned about what, exactly?'

'The caller reported that unauthorised work is being carried out at the Château and we are here to investigate.'

'Who telephoned?'

'He didn't give a name.'

'But you have his number?'

'Of course!'

The man pulled a piece of paper out of the top pocket of his blazer.

'May I see it?'

The two officials deliberated for only a second or two before the woman shook her head. 'No. We have no authority to do that, *monsieur*.'

Leron shrugged. 'I think I know, anyway.' And, with that, he rattled off the number that he'd seen and recognised in the inspector's notebook.

From the look that came to their faces, he knew that he was right.

*

Sitting astride his bike, Gus watched as things developed. He saw the two officials walk up the path and stop to talk to the group of men coming down. He also saw the villagers crowd round the *gendarme* who was guarding the gate that gave access to the path, no doubt to question him about what was going on. And he was also aware of the two pairs of eyes watching everything from the back of the old Dormobile behind him.

Then, just as Claude Boudet's little Citroen finally arrived, the heavy throb of twin rotors filled the air and a Chinook loomed large in the northern sky. Dangling beneath it, a bundle of metal poles shone steel-grey in the morning sun.

Sally came to stand beside him. 'What's going on Gus?'

'Buggered if I know but, whatever it is, it's all happening at once.'

*

'I shall probably be leaving today or tomorrow Father Francois.'

'So soon, brother?' The local priest looked genuinely surprised.

'I feel so refreshed, so much better, mentally. I shall telephone the airport in Barcelona to arrange a flight. Toulouse or Perpignan would be so much more convenient but they do not fly to Rome, do they? But before that I must pay your church another visit, for I must thank Our Lady for all the Christian love that you have shown me, Father Francois.'

As he made his way up towards the church, Galileo nonchalantly dropped something into a roadside litter bin. It was a cell phone for which its late owner would have no further use. And just as nonchalantly he glimpsed up at the Chinook as it hovered noisily over the empty shell of the citadel. *Another problem dealt with,* he thought smugly.

A few minutes later, he was standing outside the church and again thinking how unimpressive the Eglisé de Montségur really was. Had it not been for the black iron cross nailed to the wall, then he would never have thought it to be a place of worship. What didn't register for him, even now, was that the cross had a Cathar design.

As he pushed at it, the heavy door creaked on its hinges and the coolness of the nave kissed his skin as he stepped inside. Carefully, he peered into the gloom, half-expecting to encounter the cleaning lady whom he'd seen here before. But the church was empty and he uttered a little sigh of relief. With luck, his search would be uninterrupted.

'Try and put yourself in his shoes,' he told himself. 'If you had priceless documents to hide in a hurry, where would you put them?'

For answer, he sat in the rearmost pew and began looking around him. 'If they're here, I'll find them,' he muttered resolutely.

Twenty minutes later he wasn't so sure. He had looked in every nook and cranny within reach; had even peered by torchlight beneath the altar and under every pew in case they had been taped to the underside. But without success. Now he was sitting in the front pew, under the penitent gaze of the Madonna from her little shrine above the Maitre-Autel. The Black Madonna! According to Father Francois, the young thief had come here to pray to her. Fat lot of good it did him, though, because within a couple of days he was dead and the stolen documents gone. So where could those be? Had they fallen into the hands of his assassin or had they been safely hidden before then? And if so, where?

Galileo's pessimism returned. The tiredness that he felt now was more than just aching limbs from last night's climb. This weariness sprang from mental despair. Slowly he got to his feet and made for the door, shivering slightly as he went. The pleasant coolness of the church had suddenly become a chilly gloom.

Halfway back down the aisle, he paused. The Black Madonna! What if the thief hadn't been praying at all? What if he had merely been searching for a place to hide the documents? Could he have reached up into the shrine and hidden them there?

Excitedly, he returned to the altar and, using Father Francois' kneeling-stool as a step, he irreverently climbed up onto the high altar, the Maitre-Autel, from where he could easily reach into the shrine, behind the effigy of the Madonna.

*

Gus watched the three men climb into their black Renault and remain there, deep in conversation.

'They are Israelis and they don't look too happy, do they, *mes amis?*' Boudet had now joined them but rather than wait for a response he turned his attention to the Chinook that was hovering above the citadel. 'The helicopter is making a delivery. I shall make enquiries.' And with that, he began strolling down at a leisurely pace, to join the little crowd of villagers who had gathered around the solitary gendarme.

'Look!' Sally had seen sudden movement near the Cathar stele and was now pointing to where a police inspector, with a gendarme in tow, was emerging out of the tree cover and making his way down onto the sloping meadow that was called The Field of the Burned.

She and Gus watched them until they reached the car park and there they saw the inspector look towards the Renault Laguna, as if intending to question its occupants, but then change his mind and point, instead, towards the orange and white dormobile at the top end of the parking area and close to where they, Gus and Sally, were standing.

'He's not coming to question us, is he Gus?' She sounded concerned.

'No. Why would he?'

A minute later, as they walked past, the inspector and the gendarme scrutinized the biker and his partner before deciding that they had probably only just arrived and that they could be nothing other than inquisitive tourists.

An ashen-faced Boudet now rejoined his friends. 'I fear that more horrible murders have been committed.' He was visibly upset. 'There is talk of multiple deaths at the Château. I have been able to learn that much. The gendarme would not confirm it, of course, but he did not dispute it either. But you know what village gossip is like. Should we wait a little longer?'

Gus nodded but Sally seemed unsure.

They now watched the inspector flash his warrant card to the occupants of the rusty camper van and he was heard to give them orders.

'He wants proof of their identities,' Sally explained to Gus. 'And he wants to search their van, to eliminate them from his enquiries.'

Gus heard the reply for himself as the two young men climbed out of the vehicle and responded in English: 'Enquiries into what, Inspector? We have seen the commotion but we have no idea what has happened. You are, of course, welcome to search our van. We are Swiss geology students and we have nothing to hide.'

*

Galileo could barely contain his euphoria as he made his way back to the local priest's residence. He would telephone Barcelona Airport, book the first available flight to Roma and then take his leave of Father Francois. Yet another mission successfully accomplished! Aiello would be more than pleased. And overly generous, surely.

He got back to his room without being seen and, having found the number, dialled the Spanish airport. Next available flight – *'Twenty-one hundred hours'.* Barcelona was no more than three and a half hours away. He could stay for lunch with Father Francois and then take a leisurely drive down to Perpignan and on from there onto the tortuous coast road. That was the bit he didn't fancy but today he didn't care. He couldn't wait to get back to Rome.

First, however, he needed to inspect the contents of the sealed plastic bag, the one that had been hidden in the church, behind the effigy of the Black Madonna. With excited and trembling fingers, he pulled out a package, loosely wrapped in what he suspected was old camel hide, and impatiently unfolded the dry cracked leather.

The first item to appear was a single sheet of parchment, timeworn and frayed around the edges and on it several faded lines and symbols that suggested the work of an amateurish hand. He stared at it long and hard until the penny finally dropped.

'This has to be the map of the Count of Razes!' he muttered excitedly. 'The one that Aiello wants destroyed.'

Next came a sheet of modern-day drawing paper that had on it a geometric diagram comprising of what looked like a number of intertwined triangles forming a skewed star shape.

'And this must be The *Schidoni* Pentacle. Or at least a brass rubbing of it. Also, to be destroyed.'

He hadn't felt such elation since his brilliant coup in Kukes where, with great cunning and bravery, he had rid Aiello of his debts to the mafia, and rid Rome of many of its scoundrels. How long ago had that been? He counted the days and shook his head in disbelief. Barely a week! He reached for a glass and his bottle of port wine. Didn't he have every reason to feel contented? *And here in the Languedoc, I have achieved so much more.*

He now turned his attention to the third item on the table before him. Pieces of ancient papyri, amateurishly sewn together, probably by a more recent hand. He counted three pages in all, roughly ten centimetres wide by fifteen in length. From the way the top and bottom edges of those pages curled inwards, Galileo suspected that they had originally been part of a larger scroll which, when discovered, had then been cut and sold individually, probably at extortionate prices in a Cairo market.

So, what would their worth be today?

The possibilities excited him as he closely scrutinized the bits of papyri. Sadly, most of the writing was badly faded and, in Galileo's inexpert opinion, totally illegible. 'No scholar, however good he is, can decipher what is no longer there,' he mused. 'All that fuss for just this! But it does look extremely old and, to some collectors, is probably worth a fortune.'

But Aiello had instructed him to destroy all the documents. So how would he do it? Burning them was the only effective way. But why would he do that, especially if they were as valuable as he, Galileo, suspected? Hadn't Aiello already shown his suspicious nature and how ungrateful he could be? Would he believe that the documents had been found and then destroyed? What if he didn't? Might he take it as an excuse for not honouring his promise? *I shall take photographs to prove that I have recovered them, but I will not destroy them, for now. Who knows what they could be worth.*

He raised his glass and drank another toast to his own success. Then he carefully laid each document out on a table near the window, where the light was good, and proceeded to take photograph after photograph of each page, as well as of the map of the Count of Razes and the so-called Schidoni Pentacle. Finally, he checked in the camera viewer that they were of a good enough quality.

And now I am expected to burn them?

His smirk said it all.

*

After he'd packed his few belongings, he found that he still had a couple of hours to spare so he went looking for his host.

'I shall be leaving for Barcelona straight after lunch, Father, from where I have booked a flight back to Roma. I shall now go out and buy us a bottle of good wine, to celebrate.'

Father Francois didn't question his guest's sudden good humour nor his choice of the word *celebrate*. 'I am glad that you are feeling so much better, Father,' was all he could say.

Once out into the open air, Galileo made for the road up to the tourist car park. It was a goodish walk, though nothing to compare with last night's climb.

They say that the murderer always returns to the scene of his crime. The thought, as he left the narrow village streets behind him, brought on a smile that was almost satanic.

*

Although he hadn't expected to find anything of note on the two students or in their vehicle, the inspector still felt somewhat disappointed. He would so dearly love to solve this case before Interpol became involved.

'And now I must ask for all your footwear, *messieurs*.'

'Our footwear, Inspector? I don't understand.' Otto could barely hide his concern.

'Forensics will need to check for traces of blood. Whoever was up there last night left his footmark on one of the steps. We will need to check your footwear before we can finally eliminate you from our enquiries. Don't worry, it shouldn't take long.'

As he looked to his minion to carry out his instructions, the inspector failed to notice the worried look that passed between Otto and Erwin.

*

'Is there any point in us staying here any longer? We're not likely to be told anything, are we?' Sally looked from Gus to Claude Boudet. 'There must be somewhere where we can get a cold drink?'

'There is a nice café down in the village, *mademoiselle*. We could park in the village car park and walk the short distance from there.'

'What do you think, Gus?'

'Fine. I'll follow you down.'

He watched as Sally and the Frenchman set off in Boudet's Citroen and, after putting his helmet back on, he sat astride the Honda to watch another carload of *gendarmes* arriving from the direction of Lavelanet and soon after that an ARV full of municipal police who were escorting a large white van that looked like a mobile forensic lab. Other traffic, although light, was also coming to a stop, everyone wanting to know what the commotion was all about. The scene, Gus realised, was rapidly becoming a hive of inquisitive activity, and policemen had begun diverting traffic away from the parking area. One of them waved his arms at him: 'You as well, sir. Move on please!'

The wide meander of the road down to Montségur was littered with pedestrians – dozens of inquisitive villagers on their way to investigate the strange activity at the citadel – many of them puffing and panting in their hurry to reach the scene, others pausing briefly to catch their breath.

Had he been travelling at his usual pace, rather than the one being set by Claude Boudet in the Citroen ahead of him, then Gus would almost certainly have driven past, without recognising him. It was the walk – that purposeful stride for one so burly – that drew his attention.

Father Galileo! Gus could barely believe his eyes. The very last person he expected to see here. In Albania, the little man had worn a cassock. As he had in Rome, that day that Tom Mackay had been murdered. Here, though, he was dressed in a respectable black suit and dog collar.

Could he be mistaken? By pure coincidence, might it not be a look-alike? Surprised and shaken, Gus braked and turned to watch the little priest continue his way up. No! No doubt about it! It was Galileo. So, what the hell was he doing here? A few minutes ago, Boudet had reported that bodies had been found on the path up to the citadel and the huge police presence gave credence to the story. And who should now appear on the scene? None other than the arch-assassin himself, looking as innocent and as pious as ever! Death and the little man were inseparable, it seemed.

When Galileo momentarily stopped for breath and to look back at the way he'd come, Gus hurriedly lowered his visor and looked away, pretending that he'd only stopped to adjust his helmet. There was little likelihood of the bogus priest recognising him, of course. Only a few days days ago, Galileo had left him for dead in an Albanian quarry.

With a rev of the Honda's engine, Gus took off again to catch up with Sally and Claude Boudet but with every intention of returning in two or three minutes time, to keep an eye on the bogus priest. Sally and the Frenchman needn't be told why he wouldn't be joining them at the café, nor would he tell them about this latest development in a catalogue of astonishing coincidences.

*

'Do you see what I see?'

'Yes. They're here!'

'They?' It was only then that Otto realised that Erwin wasn't looking in the same direction as he was.

'Ah! You mean Qusay and company? So, Hamas have finally decided that this, rather than Rennes-le-Château, is where the action lies. There's nothing they can do about the temple treasure now... we've seen to that... but we'll have to make sure that they, nor the Israelis, get their hands on the precious papyri either... You see who else is here?'

'The priest!'

'Bit late for him to offer the last rights.' Otto's tone was bitter.

'That motorcyclist is back as well. It seems that we're not the only ones who are interested in the angel of death.'

'What? You think he's also here to keep an eye on the priest?'

'Hard to tell. But he's got him in his sights, hasn't he? When he was here a few minutes ago, he had his helmet off. Now, he prefers to keep it on. Why would that be, unless?"

'Perhaps you're right. And look who's now arriving! Brett and the others, having tailed Qusay and his mates from Rennes. We'll have to brief them on what's been going on here because as soon as those forensic guys find traces of blood on your trainers, then the two of us are going to be in deep shit. As sure as anything, that police inspector will be coming back here to arrest us. Brett will have to get word to the commander in the Vatican, for him to get us out of this mess and also to warn him about the priest. We'll give Brett the camera so that he can send those photographs of him back to the Vatican. Then either Brett or one of the others will have to tail him... see what he does, where he goes.'

*

Leron and the other two Israelis sat watching from their black Renault as the two officials from the tourism board emerged out of the trees and trudged their way down the Field of the Burned. Totally exhausted and sweating profusely, they had their jackets slung over one shoulder. The woman looked particularly uncomfortable, as if she was hobbling barefoot on hot coals or broken glass. Her feet had obviously become badly blistered.

'Wait for it! Here they come!'

Leron, as he got out of the car to face them, seemed totally resigned to what was about to happen and Yashar and Ben-Ami looked similarly dejected. They watched as the two officials donned their blazers to reveal their nametags and then make an angry beeline towards them, with the woman leading the way and looking particularly annoyed.

'The *Morcon* contract here is cancelled as from now!' she said, thrice prodding the dial of her watch to stress the exact second in time. 'Your workers have been ordered to pack up and leave, but only after the police are done with them.'

The woman's pique had as much to do with her aching feet as with her dissatisfaction at what she and her colleague had witnessed up at the citadel.

'...Do you realise what you have done? You have filled in with concrete an old well that dates back at least a thousand years. That work was never stipulated in your contract. All that was required of you was to carry out minor renovation work on the walls of the citadel but when we got up there, what did we find? A mechanical digger of all things! And an ancient well destroyed! Believe me, our report to *Le Comité Départemental de Tourisme* and to *Le Association des Sites du Pays Cathare* will hold *Morcon* responsible.'

Leron was in no mood to argue or to plead innocence. 'You do that! In our opinion, the well was a danger to tourists. If you think differently, then say so in your report.'

And with that he returned to the car and slammed the door shut.

The two officials scowled before strutting away in the direction of their green Alfa Romeo.

*

Galileo looked on, innocently. Inwardly, however, he was smiling. Then, fascinated, he watched as four gendarmes marched up to the orange and white Dormobile in the distance and, at gunpoint, handcuff its two young occupants.

Bizarre! he thought. Good time for me to leave, I think.

In his euphoria, he barely noticed the Honda roaring past him. Nor was he aware of the young Swiss guard called Christen who had begun to follow him on foot, but at a distance.

Le Village de Montségur

Despite the Château being such a popular tourist attraction over the years, the village itself had barely grown. It remained no more than a cluster of houses nestling into the hillslope, in the shadow of the towering Pog; its population barely more than a hundred.

Gus had no trouble finding the café where Sally and Claude Boudet were now enjoying a cold beer under a colourful sunshade. He took off his helmet and left it at his feet where he could get to it at short notice, should Galileo suddenly appear. The little man could come this way and the last thing that Gus wanted was to be recognised by him.

'The café proprietor says there'll be rain later.' Boudet volunteered the information as his attention was drawn to the strengthening wind flapping the sunshade above their heads.

'Where shall we stay tonight?' Sally looked at each of them in turn. 'I doubt if there's anywhere available here, in the village.'

'It depends on what your plans are, *mademoiselle*. Whether you intend spending more time in this area or not. If so, then I suggest that we use the same hotel as last night, in Lavelanét. It is not far.'

They turned to Gus for an answer but he, oblivious to the question, was gazing up at the grey wall of the Chateau high above them. Then, they saw him produce a small but powerful pair of binoculars to examine the sheer cliff below the citadel; a rock face that ended in a scree slope overgrown with stunted trees and bushes that ran steeply down towards the village.

'What do you say, Gus? Will we be staying in this area tonight?'

'Mm? Yes, of course.'

'So, we go back to the hotel in Lavelanét, as Monsieur Boudet suggests?' she again asked.

'Yes, you do that.'

'What do you mean, you do that? You're coming as well?'

'Maybe. I've got something to do first.'

'Such as?'

'I have to see what's up there.'

He was obviously referring to the citadel.

'Impossible, Gus! The police will not allow you access whilst their investigations are ongoing.'

'Perhaps I won't need their permission, *Monsieur*.'

Sally and the Frenchman noticed his wry smile and looked mystified.

*

With Otto and Erwin being held on suspicion of murder, the onus was now on Brett to make all the decisions. He had already dispatched Christen to keep an eye on the priest. Now, he and Alain were left to watch the Arabs.

From what Otto and Erwin had told him before they were arrested, the Treasure of Solomon's Temple was now safely beyond the reach of everybody. That was good! It meant that the Map of the Count of Razes was no longer of any great significance. But the Nag Hammadi papyrus stolen from the secret archives was an entirely different matter. It was still out there somewhere and, according to the commander, if it fell into the wrong hands then it could pose a very real threat to the Roman Catholic church. The Holy Father, he'd told them, was seriously concerned by its loss.

'Wrong hands' stood for Israelis and Arabs; Brett told himself. That meant that Qusay and company would still have to be closely watched. As would the Mossad agents who even now were waiting in their Renault estate car to be interviewed by the police. Should either of those two groups succeed in getting hold of the stolen papyrus, then he knew that he would have no option but to deal with them permanently, without the pontiff or even the commander, being told.

Brett suddenly felt the full weight of the responsibility on his young shoulders.

*

It was the phone call that put Gus off guard. Sally and Boudet were chatting in French.

'Is that Gus?'

He recognised the voice. Sally's Aunt Janet! 'Yes.'

'My husband is worried about his niece and wants to know what you have to tell him.'

Was it a genuine enquiry about Sally or just a veiled request for information about the way things were going?

'Sally is here with me now. We're enjoying our time here in the Languedoc. We've just arrived at a little place called Montségur and there's a lot going on here at the moment. The rumour amongst the villagers is that some Israeli workers were killed here during the night. The police are certainly treating it as murder. Not only that but we've also met a few old friends here. Otherwise, things have been pretty uneventful. I'll put Sally on for you now.'

As he passed her the phone, Gus sensed that he was being watched. He turned to look. In the road, no more than five metres away, with eyes wide open and mouth gaping, stood Father Galileo: his face a picture of incredulity. He was staring at what could only be a ghost!

Gus, for his part, cursed his own carelessness for not having seen him coming, but his brain was already in overdrive, desperately considering a plan of action should the priest suddenly produce a gun.

How long they remained staring at one another was difficult to gauge. A lifetime of probably no more than four or five seconds. And then, Galileo's face broke out in a genuine little smile that was followed by a sharp look of warning, as if to say, "I'm glad that you're still alive Guiseppe but don't mess with me". Then, with the slightest of nods, he continued on his way down the narrow street.

Boudet had been studying the menu, Sally was still chatting to her aunt. Neither had noticed the incident.

*

Qusay and his friends watched from their car as the bodies of the Mossad agents were brought down off the mountain to be whisked away by ambulance to a pathology lab in Carcassonne for immediate post-mortem. They also waited to see the *Morcon* workforce trooping down to be questioned and then being herded into their work-bus and driven away. Then it was the turn of the two young men from the orange and white Dormobile. Handcuffed and bundled into the back of a police car they were now being taken to Carcassonne police cells. The Israelis in the Renault would be the last to leave.

Now that most of the onlookers had left, their curiosity satisfied, the Arabs felt exposed. Apart from the Renault, the police vehicles, and the abandoned Dormobile, their own car was now the only one still around and it was beginning to draw inquiring glances from some of the gendarmes.

'We go!' The command was in Arabic.

'Where?'

'To the village. I think the danger is over but we must make sure.'

'How will we do that?'

'We must find out what has been going on here.'

Qusay pointed towards those in the Renault. 'They have not found their Menorah, that is for sure, or they would not be wearing such long faces.' His laugh was nothing if not bitter.

*

'You mean to *what?*' Sally Jeffers made no effort to keep her voice down or to temper her disbelief. 'You... are... not... serious? Tell me that you are not serious.'

Claude Boudet looked equally stunned.

'How do I get up there otherwise? But keep your voice down!'

She now realised that he was indeed being deadly serious. 'You say that you're going to climb *that?*' The words were being hissed through clenched teeth as she pointed at the rock face, sheer in parts, below the Chateau. 'Not even you can be that bloody mad, surely? And anyway, you'd soon be seen and they'd be waiting for you when you come down... provided, that is, that you won't have broken your stupid neck before then.'

Gus ignored her scorn as he glanced up at the sky. 'I'll wait until late afternoon. It looks as if it's going to cloud over. If there's no sun... if it's grey overhead... then there's less chance of anybody spotting me. Anyway, these people...' He indicated towards a couple of villagers who happened to be walking by. '... don't go around all day looking up at the Château, do they? They'd all have permanent stiff necks if they did.'

He smiled but Sally didn't. Neither did Boudet.

'But why, Gus? What's the point? There's nothing up there, is there, or the police would have found it by now.'

He could sense her growing desperation.

'...Nobody in his right mind would attempt what you're thinking of doing.'

'Yeah! I am a bit mad; I suppose. You'll just have to trust me, though. Anyway, I've done a bit of rock climbing in the past.'

'A bit of rock climbing! Good God! This is ridiculous! Not even my Uncle Jim would expect you to do such a stupid thing. I'll ring him and you can tell him to stuff his fucking job.'

The intensity of her concern surprised him but he chose to make light of it. 'Forget it, Sally. What's it to you, anyway?'

'What's it... to me?' There was a distinct crack in her voice. 'I'll tell you what it is to me! I don't fancy being sat here, watching you bouncing like a fucking rag doll down that rock face. That's what!' She was bordering on panic. 'And neither does Claude, I'm sure!'

'That's why I want you to leave now. Rather than going back to Lavelanét, why don't you both go back to Monsieur Boudet's home in Alet-les-Baines? You will let her stay the night, monsieur?'

'So that's how much you care about us? It doesn't matter if those Arabs come looking, as long as you don't have to be there to face the music.'

Was her sneer one of genuine contempt or just a desperate attempt to get him to change his mind?

'The reverse, actually! The men we saw in Rennes-le-Château are here in Montségur. I saw them arrive a few minutes ago.' He nodded in the direction of the top car park. 'In fact, everyone is here, as far as I can see! The Jews, the Arabs, not to mention a couple of young Swiss or Italian guys who have just been arrested and who have links to the Vatican, I suspect.' He attempted a smile before adding, 'Not to mention yours truly, of course, here to represent your Uncle James and MI6.'

He ignored her glare and his tone again became serious.

'...And guess who else is here?' *She might as well know,* he thought. If he could frighten her enough then she'd be more likely to do as she was told, for once. 'None other than Tom Mackay's killer! So that's why you have to leave.'

'You're lying, Gus! I know you are.' But she sensed that he wasn't. 'You're just trying to scare us, that's all.'

'I only wish I was. He actually walked past us here just a few minutes ago, while you were on the phone.'

'And he recognised you?'

Gus nodded with a wry smile. 'He did that, all right! So, you see why you'd both better leave?'

*

Gus Adams wasn't to know it but Father Galileo had already ceased to be a threat to him. Even as they spoke, the priest's rented Seat Leon was making its way out of Montségur and heading east towards the Gorges de la Frau. Eventually, it would get him on to the D117, a decent route all the way to Perpignan. Two hours should see him cross the border into Spain. The flight back to Roma was beckoning.

*

'Brett? Christen here. The priest has made his move and I'm in tow. We've just passed a village called Fougax something or other, travelling east. I'll keep you posted. Can I suggest that you question Father Francois, the local priest, about him? Hold on! I've just seen him throw something out of the car window into the river. Could be a gun! ... Water level isn't all that high. Can you come and check it out? Look for the bridge where the road crosses the stream.'

*

For the next two and a half hours, Gus kept a low profile. His priority was to avoid another encounter with Father Galileo and he didn't particularly want to come across the angry young Arab and his mates either. But their presence in the area, together with that of the Israelis, fuelled the theory that there was a connection between what was going on here and what had been happening in Albania. Same protagonists! Even the mafia were here, courtesy of Father Galileo.

The more he thought about it, however, the less likely it seemed that there was any stockpiling of arms here in the Languedoc. Not only was the area a popular tourist attraction but French local government was also too well structured for any gun-running to be remotely possible here. This wasn't the Balkans. So why all the interested parties? Could they be after real treasure, after all? One of those treasures that Boudet had ranted on about. If that was the case, then only the Treasure of Solomon's Temple fitted the bill and, in particular, the important historical artefacts that were supposed to be part of it.

Gus mulled over the idea. It would certainly explain the trouble that the Israelis had gone to thus far. Reclaiming the gold candelabrum... what Boudet and Sally had called the Menorah... and returning it to the Temple Mount would be of huge significance to the Jews. What a stir it would cause in Jerusalem! And what a provocation to Islam! He winced at the thought of it. A provocation that might well threaten the current run of peace talks in the Middle East. Didn't the al Aksa Mosque on Temple Mount stand on the original site of Solomon's Temple, where the Ark and the Menorah had once been kept? What if the Jews ...?

Better not think it, Gus!

However, if that was indeed the Israeli agenda, then it would also explain the Arab presence here. According to Sally, the angry young man who had caused the bother at Rennes-le-Château and who had now turned up here, in Montségur, had shown unusual interest in the bas-relief on some arch or other in Rome, one that related to Solomon's Treasure and to the Menorah in particular. Could it be that he and his friends – the ones with him in the café in Rennes – were here to claim the Treasure for themselves, so that Islam could flaunt it under Jewish noses? Hardly! Far more likely that they were here to prevent the Israelis from getting their hands on it in the first place.

Hamas agents more than likely!

But where did the Vatican fit in all of it? That day at the quarry in Kukes, barely a week ago, the little assassin-priest had made a point of explaining to him what the Final Crusade was all about. Promoting the cause of Catholicism by igniting all-out war between Israel and Islam. Official Vatican policy? Hardly! Especially since the current Pontiff was known to be actively promoting greater understanding between world religions. So who did Galileo represent? Who was setting his agenda? And what in hell was he up to, here in Montségur?

Over the past half hour, low cloud had been drifting in from the west, casting a gloomy shadow on the scene above him and making the citadel of Montségur look more like a sinister Colditz prison. And judging by an even darker sky in the distance, rain wouldn't be long in coming either, so the sooner he got going, the better.

From what he could see through his binoculars, the climb didn't hold any particular terrors. The cliff face, pocked with stunted bushes here and there, had plenty of cracks and fissures in it, and that meant plenty of handholds and footholds. What he couldn't be sure of – at least not until he got going – was how brittle the rock itself was and how safe, therefore, those holds would be.

No worse, for sure, than that climb to get out of the quarry, a few days ago.

He again looked at his watch. Sally and Boudet would have reached Alet-les-Baines long before now and he couldn't help wondering whether he'd see either of them ever again. With any luck, Sally would catch a flight back to London tomorrow. There, she'd be safe... Would he miss her?

Don't answer that, Gus! Why should you care, anyway? You're better off with her gone. What with Galileo still around, you've got enough to worry about as it is, without having to watch her back as well. What if something happened to her whilst she was still in your care? Bloody hell! Just think! Her uncle, head of MI6, no less, would have your guts for garters.

Slowly, he got to his feet. So, let's get this over and done with!

Barcelona Airport

'You have the wisdom of Solomon?' The question had a distinct edge to it.

Galileo sighed audibly. 'Don't worry! I'm alone.' He was sitting in the reception lounge, sipping at the glass of Rioja that he'd bought at a nearby bar. In a seat, somewhere behind him, sat whoever it was who had followed him from France.

Galileo had noticed the silver Peugeot long before they'd reached Perpignan and had undertaken a manoeuvre or two just to confirm his suspicions. He had taken the slip road off the N9 at Junction forty-three, south of Perpignan, and after driving twice around a traffic island, giving the impression that he was looking for direction signs, he had then re-joined the motorway. The silver Peugeot had done exactly the same.

'There are developments?' The question from the public telephone in Trastevere sounded curt.

'Of course!' He had a right to sound smug.

'Then tell me!'

Galileo scowled. The man was being abrupt and arrogant. 'I will only speak with Aiello. In other words, the Holy Father's personal emissary.'

The sharp intake of breath at the other end of the line told him that he had crossed a line and that he shouldn't have made the reference to the pontiff, of all people.

'It matters not who you are talking to. It is enough for you to know that Aiello will receive your message.'

'Then tell him that I have completed my mission. I have recovered the stolen manuscripts and have done with them as Aiello requested.'

'They are destroyed?'

'Yes. I have burnt them.'

'And you are able to prove that?'

Galileo again scowled. 'Prove what? That I recovered them? Or that they have been destroyed?'

'Both.'

'Tell Aiello that it does not please me that my word is being doubted. When I return to Roma, I will show Aiello photographs of the documents. I did not think of taking pictures of them being destroyed, simply because I thought that Aiello would respect my word. The word of a man-of-the-cloth.'

The sharp intake of breath at the other end of the line told him that his sense of humour wasn't appreciated.

'…Anyway, the documents were not as important as Aiello would have me believe.'

'Explain.'

'The map looked like something that a child might have drawn. And it was badly faded. And as for the other items – the bits of papyri with the writing on them – only a few words were legible on those. Most of the writing had faded away completely. Not even the best scholars in the world could have made anything of them.'

'You are a fool, Galileo! Are you not aware of the infrared technology that is now available to solve such problems? These days, scientists can use multispectral imaging techniques to show ink that is otherwise invisible to the naked eye. But you, of course, cannot be expected to understand these things.' The added comment was intentionally offensive. 'Now assure me that every single centimetre of the document has been destroyed.'

Galileo had little doubt by now that the person on the other end of the line was Aiello himself and that he was in a bad mood.

'I'm telling you! All the documents have been thoroughly destroyed and I expect to be well rewarded, not only for completing my mission here but also in Albania.'

'Do not speak to me of your mission in Albania.'

Now there was added acrimony in the voice and Galileo's heart missed a beat. 'What do you mean?'

'La Crociata Finale left port five days ago. It has not been heard of since.'

Silence and then, 'You think it has sunk?'

'I pray not but it is what is feared. All I know is that it has suddenly disappeared off the radar.'

Another brief silence. 'Do we know where? Do we know why?' The bogus priest sounded genuinely aggrieved.

'It does not take much imagination. I suspect that information about the mission was leaked to the Mossad. You swore to me that no one, except yourself, escaped alive from the quarry in Kukes. So who leaked the information about the shipment? It could only have been you, Galileo.'

'That is nothing short of nonsense!'

Even as he raised his voice to protest, Guiseppe Maratta's face in the little Montségur café a few hours ago was coming back to haunt him. Not only that, but he also sensed that Aiello was about to renege on their deal.

'...I have completed both missions thoroughly,' he protested, 'and deserve full recognition for my efforts.' He wanted to add a vague threat but thought better of it.

'We shall see!' Aiello's voice held a threat of its own. 'You will be contacted again when you are back in Rome.'

Le Château de Montségur

The citadel lay hidden in low cloud and a fine drizzle had begun to fall. Far below, the tiled rooftops of Montségur were but a puddle of dull brown in the gloom.

Gus paused for breath and to rest his tired arms. He had passed the halfway point of the climb and knew that the south wall of the Chateau was directly above him. Up to now he had encountered very few difficulties but the rain meant that conditions were quickly deteriorating.

By making the most of a good foothold, he was now able to free one hand in order to check that his torch, binoculars and cell phone were still safely zipped inside the money-wallet behind his back. Whether he would need them was another matter. With so many Mossad and Arab agents around, not to mention a bloodthirsty little assassin-priest lurking in the wings, a gun would probably have been a far better option for him on reaching the summit.

The next twenty feet of the climb proved to be much more arduous. There were fewer handholds and he found himself having to traverse to his right to begin with and then left again, up a different fissure, a manoeuvre made all the more difficult by a sudden shower of heavier rain. His hair and his clothes, already damp, now became sodden and the water streaming down the rock and splashing into his eyes was making it extremely difficult to find new holds. And as if that weren't bad enough, now that the rock was so wet, the rubber soles of his trainers weren't getting the purchase that he would have wished and he was having to rely more and more on the raw strength of his fingers and arms.

The zigzag route was taking such a toll on his tiring limbs that when he eventually reached a narrow ledge running diagonally up the cliff face, he gratefully scrambled onto it and took up a semi-reclining position. Not only did he need to rest but the little overhang above him provided some shelter at least from the pelting rain.

'Some evening drizzle with localized heavy showers. Clearer skies later.' As he inched himself upwards along the ledge, towards a little bush that seemed to be rooted in bare rock, Gus prayed that the forecaster had got the last bit right as well and that conditions would improve before long. He needed that hope to allay his growing frustration and discomfort.

Eventually, he reached the bush and was glad to grasp its thick stem and trust to its roots. He glanced at his watch. Five to eight! He could hardly believe his eyes. He'd been up here for almost three hours! And, with an overhang yet to tackle, he was looking at another half hour, at least, before he could reach the top. Few climbs had ever taken him this long and, to make matters worse, the heavy cloud cover meant that an early dusk was closing in. He sighed. The last thing he'd bargained for was to be groping up here in the dark.

At great pains, he crept along the ledge and squeezed past the bush, catching his breath as he felt its creaking stem yield a little under his weight. The niche at the very top end of the crevice was now within reach. If he could just cram his slender form into that, then he'd be out of the worst of the weather. A glance over his shoulder lifted his spirits a little. The dark clouds were being sent scurrying by a strengthening wind and the sky was clearing from the west. All he had to do was to sit tight until the weather improved.

*

He wasn't to know it but until now he had been watched anxiously from below. Having travelled only a few miles as far as Montferrier, Sally had made an excuse to stop for a meal, but what she had really wanted was time to think because she knew that once they'd left Montferrier and then Lavelanét behind, then the next stop would be Alet-les-Baines and there'd be little or no chance after that of returning to Montségur.

'We must go back, *monsieur*. I feel in some way responsible for him.'

In return, the Frenchman had nodded sympathetically and given her a knowing look, a look that she had recognised and protested against: 'You don't understand, Claude. Gus is doing this because my uncle expects it of him. You've seen for yourself how stupid and how stubborn he can be. I may not particularly like the man but that doesn't mean that I want to see him breaking his neck on a fool's errand. So do you mind taking me back there so I can at least have one more try at persuading him not to be such a bloody idiot?'

'Methinks the lady...'

She hadn't even bothered to protest this time.

They were now standing under the eaves of Montségur's little museum, peering up into the gloom. Their return to the village had been too late. Gus had already gone. They had then searched and searched the cliff face until they finally saw him, dark grey against the grey rock.

'He was up there a minute ago but now I can't see him at all. Damn it! I wish I had a pair of binoculars... The bloody fool!'

Her concern was bordering on panic and Boudet realised it. He gently squeezed her arm by way of sympathy.

'...He said that he wouldn't be setting off until late afternoon. You heard him say so, Claude. We were back here well before then and he was nowhere to be seen, was he? Which means that he must have been hiding from us.'

'Or from someone else!' the Frenchman suggested.

They'd first spotted Gus about an hour ago, when he was almost a third of the way up the climb. Since then, they'd been watching his progress, as best they could, through the worsening weather. Boudet's reassuring comment: 'Your Gus seems to know what he is doing, *mademoiselle*,' had provided her with very little comfort and had gone unanswered.

'Where's the sense in it? Climbing in such weather! God! I hope he hasn't fallen. I can't see him anywhere. Try and find him, Claude!'

'Unfortunately, Sally, my eyesight isn't what it used to be.'

'I'm telling you! He was there a moment ago. Now I can't see him anywhere.' She couldn't control the tremor in her voice.

Barcelona Airport

When the call to board the nine o'clock flight to Rome was announced, Father Galileo passed belatedly through passport control and into the departure lounge. Once there, he waited to make sure that the driver of the silver Peugeot hadn't followed him. In fact, he waited much longer than that, because he was still there twenty minutes later, long after Flight IB2828 had disappeared into the night sky.

Confident that the coast was now clear and, feigning priestly innocence and pious embarrassment, he returned to passport control to explain that he had missed his flight because he had been fast asleep when the call to board the plane had been made. Reference to his convalescence following a nervous breakdown and to the strong medication that he'd been prescribed by his Vatican doctor gave further credence to his story and he was eventually allowed to return to the reception lounge, to arrange another flight for himself. Once there, he made a beeline for the Swiss Airlines desk, knowing that a flight to Zurich was due in fifty minutes. Hopefully, there'd be a vacant seat available.

The Pog of Montségur

The rain had stopped but he remained crouched and shivering in his little hollow, watching the clouds slowly dispersing overhead. Night was closing in but he argued that it made more sense for him to wait, because a moonlit sky would show up every nook and cranny, every possible handhold and foothold. A glance at his watch, now told him that he had been inactive for almost twenty minutes.

Five minutes later, the moon made its appearance and he finally ventured to move, knowing that climbing off the ledge and onto the cliff face would be tricky at best. Despite it being a warm evening, he couldn't stop shivering. His joints had stiffened, his muscles were cramped, and he wondered whether his cold hands would be up to the task ahead.

There was only one way to find out. A firm hold with his left hand now helped him into a crouching position, then a good hold with his right hand allowed him to swing a leg out onto the rock face. A brief upward glance confirmed that he was within twenty feet of the citadel wall that was looming large and white above his head. Climbing that would be a physical impossibility; he'd have no option other than to traverse to the right, away from the Chateau wall towards a nasty-looking overhang.

Once I negotiate that, I'll be home and dry. But the thought gave him no comfort because he would first have to successfully negotiate the crevice that he was now in, where handholds were hidden by stunted bushes that seemed to grow out of the bare rock.

He was now spreadeagled against the rock when something flitted past his head, causing his heart to miss a beat. And as he hung there over the abyss, the same thing happened again and again. His first impression was that someone was throwing things at him from above but then a flutter of wings made him realise that what he had for company was a cloud of bats, dozens of them laying claim to what was now a clear night sky. He had chilling visions of them clinging to his hair and clutching at his face and he shivered at the thought. Where the hell had they come from, so unexpectedly?

He took stock of what was going on. More and more pipistrelles were darting out of what seemed to be solid rock, just above his head. Again, he shuddered. *The sooner that I get across to that overhang and away from their bat cave, then the better it'll be,* he thought.

It took some seconds for him to compose himself and to realise the significance of what had just crossed his mind. If, indeed, there was a cave just above him, then now, surely, was the time to check it out. *I don't think you'll be passing this way again any time soon, will you Gus?* The improbability brought on a cynical smile.

He clung to the rock until he was satisfied that all the bats were airborne, then he pulled himself up to investigate, only to find that their exit hole was just a fissure in the rock, roughly two and a half feet long by about eighteen inches in height. Hardly a cave! Cautiously, he released his grip on one hold and, with the free hand, unzipped his money-wallet at the back of his waist and reached for the torch.

The thin shaft of halogen light revealed more. Yes there was a small cave inside, its floor covered with foul-smelling bat droppings. The roof, no higher than four feet at its highest he reckoned, sloped away into dark corners. Nothing of interest, as far as he could tell, but he still let the pencil of light do its searching, especially since one of the recesses looked darker and deeper than the others. Then, as his eyes grew accustomed to the shadows, he became convinced that he could see a narrow tunnel leading further into the rock.

He was torn by indecision. For some instinctive reason, he wanted to investigate. He knew that he could squeeze in easily enough but the prospect of climbing out again onto the cliff face would be daunting, to say the least. Was it a risk worth taking? Of one thing he was certain; it would be one of the most difficult manoeuvres that he had ever attempted.

A quick inspection of the rock face around the entrance made his mind up for him. Convinced that there were a number of good handholds to help him climb back out again onto the rock face, he slipped his head and narrow shoulders into the aperture and pulled himself inside the cave, immediately regretting his decision as his hands and then his torso slithered through a thickness of foul-smelling bat-droppings.

*

'I saw him, monsieur! I'm sure of it! There was definitely some movement up there but now he's gone again.'

Despite the failing light, Sally was convinced that she'd spotted a dark form clinging to the rock face high above them and even a brief flash of torchlight, but Claude Boudet was unable to confirm it. Even though the sky had now cleared and the air was warm again, the cold and the dampness had already gotten to the ageing Frenchman. All he wanted was to retire to somewhere that was warm and comfortable.

*

Gus wiped his hands on the seat of his wet pants and cursed his stupid decision to investigate. What the hell was he doing here? If the weather outside suddenly got worse, if the rain returned, then all those pipistrelles would be coming back to roost and his very worst fears would be realised.

But he hadn't been mistaken though. There was a tunnel leading on from the outer cave but to use it meant crawling on his belly under a rock arch that was again no higher than two feet or so. He sighed. *I've ventured this far, so why not go the whole hog?*

Gripping the now foul-tasting torch between his teeth, and resisting the urge to puke, he got down on his wet belly and, in the narrow beam of light, pulled himself through the aperture into a much larger cavern; one that hadn't – thank God – been much-favoured by the bats. *Still scary, though! Scary and bloody cold!* he thought as his wet clothes soaked in the coolness of the surrounding rock.

Hurriedly he took the torch handle out of his mouth and spat several times in a vain effort to get rid of the foul taste that it had left there. Were bat droppings poisonous? The thought worried him, but not for long.

Whatever he expected to see, he certainly wasn't prepared for what his torch light now revealed, and his gasp was audible. In the cold halogen beam, a grey skull lay there, grinning at him and, next to it, another. Two tall skeletons lying side by side in the dank surroundings, intertwined carpal bones and jointed digits suggesting that hands had been held, up to the very point of death.

In the wavering light of his torch and with his heart still pounding, he spotted something else. On the cave wall, behind where the bones lay, he could make out faint letters scraped onto the rock face. *Bonne...* L. Or was the final letter a T? Yes, probably. Above them, in tandem, were the names *Mathew* – or possibly *Matheus* – and *Peter*. Whoever they were, they must have been related, he thought. On each side of the lettering, were drawings of a bird... probably a dove... in flight. A number of crude Celtic crosses had also been roughly carved here and there onto the rock, proof of how the two had whiled away the hours whilst awaiting a slow and merciless death. But how did they get here? And why did they have to die at all?

His torchlight desperately searched for an explanation.

Behind the bones, he could see stone steps ascending – wide and with head clearance of maybe six feet or more. But only three of them! Above that, the rest of the staircase had been blocked-off with huge boulders. These two unfortunates, whoever they were, had, at some time or other, been incarcerated here to starve and to die. The place was a dungeon, macabre and spine-chilling.

Gradually, Gus' breathing returned to normal and he was able to inspect the rest of his surroundings. It was only now, under closer inspection, that he excitedly realised that his original impression of the cave's size had been wrong and that it was, in fact, at least twice as large as he had originally thought it to be. What he had assumed was the cave wall to his left now turned out to be something entirely different. The floor space, almost to roof height, was taken up by stacks of articles of various shapes and sizes, mostly hidden beneath a fabric curtain, on which lay a thick layer of dust. Only the bottom tier was visible and in the pencil-thin beam of his torch, he could make out the legs of two heavily built tables, set edge to edge.

With curiosity and excitement now getting the better of his fear, he went over to take a closer look. The amount of dust that had accumulated left him in no doubt that the cache had been standing here for tens if not hundreds of years. And if he needed further proof, he was about to get it.

As he tried to lift what was a makeshift curtain, to reveal what lay underneath, he felt the fabric crumbling to dust between his fingers and releasing a shower of tiny stones to tinkle and dance on the cave floor at his feet. Some of the dust and two of the stones clung to the filth on his palms and he caught his breath as he now glimpsed a ruby-red gemstone winking up at him out of the muck. He let out a low whistle. The gem, and the others that were now twinkling on the bare rock around his feet, must have been woven into the once ornate and heavy fabric.

He struggled to keep his imagination and his excitement in check. What on earth had he found? Could it possibly be …?

Holding the torch again between his teeth and doing his best to ignore the revulsive taste of it, he now used both hands to support the weight of the remaining fabric, only to see more of it falling away and crumbling to the ground. And as it did so, more gemstones came to light – flashing diamonds and emeralds, dusky rubies and jet, tinkling like coloured hailstones onto the cave floor. Whatever the fabric had been designed for, it must have been a fabulous sight in its day, what with all the gold braid and the gems that were studded into it. What he was looking at had once been a heavy and truly spectacular drape.

He felt no guilt in removing the rest of the material and seeing it disintegrate at his touch. Only its motionless state and its fine original quality had kept it together for all those centuries.

The next fifteen minutes proved to be an experience that Gus Adams would never forget. What he had stumbled upon was an Aladdin's cave of wealth. There was silver and gold in abundance – carved caskets packed full of rings, bracelets, necklaces… all of them studded with fine stones of every colour, from jet black to blues, emeralds, and ambers, deep ruby reds and the glint and clear sparkle of diamonds. He could barely comprehend what he was seeing. It was like something out of *Arabian Nights*; tales he'd listened to in school, all those years ago.

By now, he was convinced that he had found the riches that Titus had removed from the Temple in Jerusalem, almost two thousand years before; the very same treasure that the Visigoths had subsequently claimed when they sacked Rome.

Quietly, he cursed himself for not paying more attention to Boudet and Sally when they were discussing the details of it. Had he done so, and had he more light to properly inspect, then he might now be able to corroborate that it was indeed the treasure from Solomon's Temple.

Carefully, and still gripping the foul-tasting torch between his teeth, he pulled some of the stacked caskets off the tables and laid them out on the uneven rock floor of the cave. Then, with the palm of his hand, he swept the dust off one of the tables and gasped aloud. The gold surface shone as if it had only just been polished.

'Good God!' A table of solid gold, encrusted with gems! It, alone, had to be worth an immense fortune.

Gus stood spellbound for seconds-on-end and then, once he'd got over his awe, he hurriedly studied what else was there. Article after article that he touched was of incredible worth and as he handled each one, he recalled some of the words that Boudet had read out loud, back at his home in Alet-les-Baines, describing the Temple Treasure as a continuous river of wealth. Yes, he was beginning to appreciate the extent of it all.

Delving further into the darkness, he brought more and more wonderful treasures into view. Stacks of heavy gold-braided vestments, their material now badly perished; huge frames, covered with gold leaf, which must once have held magnificent paintings but whose colours were now badly faded or blackened by the damp air of centuries past.

Christ himself might have looked at these very things when he visited the Temple, two thousand years ago. The thought was awe-inspiring. And then, as he continued his search in almost total darkness, Gus felt his hands come into contact with the greatest artefact of all; a treasure that confirmed without any shadow of doubt that he had indeed discovered the Temple Treasure. With beating heart, he spread his arms out to grip at the extremities of the great candelabrum.

'The Menorah!' he muttered, feeling his breath being taken away from him.

Its immense weight surprised him. He could barely move it, let alone pick it up, but he eventually succeeded in dragging it forward onto the jewel-encrusted gold table that Claude Boudet had called the Missorium. Then, after running his hands over it, to wipe away much of the dust, he stood back to appreciate the true majesty of the burnished gold as it reflected the inadequate light of his torch.

'Wow! No wonder the Jews want it back.' The thought brought a wistful look to his face. 'But they never will, not unless they can find a way of clearing those steps.

'Just as well, anyway!' he concluded as he recalled Boudet saying something about Jewish aspirations to reclaim the Temple Mount and Sally voicing her fear that the whole of Islam would then take up arms.

It now struck him that Mathew, or Matheus, and Paul Bonnet, whoever they may have been, had been left down here to guard the treasure. But guard against what? Against whom? And how long ago would that be? Boudet had talked about Cathars occupying the citadel. Had they been the custodians of all this? Gus again wished that he'd paid the Frenchman more attention.

He now realised that the light from his torch was getting very dim, so he hurriedly helped himself to a handful of different gemstones off the cave floor, at the same time resisting the temptation of helping himself to more than two of the gold rings and one amulet from one of the caskets. The stones winked up at him as if they were a source of light in themselves. Hurriedly, he took the binoculars and cell phone out of the money-wallet at the back of his waist, placed them on the priceless Missorium, beside the Menorah, and then let the gems trickle one by one out of his palm and into the bag.

He'd have to hurry if he was to make the most of the clear sky outside but since he couldn't resist a last look around the cave with its fabulous, not to mention macabre, content, he sent the weakening beam of his flashlight on a final sweep of the darkness.

It was only then that he noticed a smaller pile of dust-covered objects stashed away in another rocky alcove. Despite being desperate to get away lest the bats returned, his curiosity again got the better of him and he had to investigate.

What he found was more gold, but in a different form. Bars and coins of it, obviously from a later date, but a sizeable treasure just the same. *Better take some proof of this with me as well,* he thought, as he thrust both hands into a black wooden casket, that resembled a small coffin, and stuffed handful upon handful of coins into the bag until it bulged. Some stray ones fell to the floor and, as they came into contact with hard rock, their tinkling again brought echoes from the cave's extremities.

'Now I have to go!' He said the words out loud and they came echoing back at him from all directions.

Respectfully, he then saluted the two skeletons, muttered the words, 'Rest in peace, Messieurs Bonnet,' and made for the exit.

As he climbed out again into the open air, a sudden thought made him smile: If some future Indiana Jones finds the cave, what will he make of the binoculars and the cell phone? Visigothic? Cathar? Historians will be rewriting history!

*

Sally was distraught, convinced by now that Gus Adams had fallen to his death. 'You would surely have seen it happen, mademoiselle?' Claude Boudet, also concerned for Gus' safety, was trying to offer her hope as well as some comfort.

'Too dark to tell!' she replied, fighting back the tears and unable to explain the depth of loneliness that she now felt.

'Come, my dear.' He hooked his arm under hers and began to lead in the direction of Jules' cafe. 'There is nothing we can do, at least not until we know exactly what has happened. A stiff brandy will do you good.'

'I would rather wait in the car, monsieur.' Again, she blamed herself for not having been more insistent with Gus. Not that she felt particularly attracted to the man, she reminded herself, but she should, nevertheless, have done more to prevent his stupid escapade. Damn fool that he was! Furiously, she brushed away the tears with the back of her hand. Sooner or later, she'd have to break the news to her uncle in London.

When they eventually got to the car park, the sight of Gus' silent Honda, parked next to the Citroen, with his leathers and helmet still in a neat pile beside it, made her feel an emptiness and a forlornness that she couldn't begin to comprehend and there was now no holding back the tears.

*

Unknown to Sally Jeffers and Claude Boudet, there were others also sitting in a car in that poorly lit village car park and they, too, were considering their next move. Ever since they'd arrived in the Languedoc, nothing had gone right for them. For days they'd pottered around Rennes-le-Château, hoping for some kind of lead, simply because Qusay had been convinced that that was where the Israelis would be searching for the Menorah. He had argued that the name of Rennes-le-Château was closely associated with the hidden treasure of Solomon's Temple and the presence of the two Mossad agents in the area had been further proof as far as Qusay was concerned, which was why he had lured them to the Rennes' car park after dark, when all the tourists were long gone and had shot them both dead before disposing of their bodies in the thorny undergrowth below the Belvedere.

News of the theft from the Vatican Archives and the huge significance it might hold for the Middle East, had alarmed the Hamas command. Already there was talk of the Israelis building a new temple on Mount Moriya; a temple that would tower in magnificence over Islam's ancient *al Aksa* Mosque. If the Menorah was found and given pride of place in the new temple, then it would soon become a centre of pilgrimage for Jews the world over, leading to a reversal of the centuries-old Diaspora; a situation that Islam would never tolerate. Which was why Qusay, and others like him, had been sent to investigate.

The fact that the travel guide he had questioned in Rome should suddenly turn up in Rennes-le-Château, not only proved that Rennes was the place to be but it also confirmed that the woman was herself in some way involved. Further proof, if he needed it, was the man who had protected her in the open-air restaurant yesterday. Qusay was now convinced that the escort was a trained operative, and a good one at that. But who was he? And more to the point, who did he represent? The Jews? The Vatican?

'So, what do we do now?' The language was Palestinian Arabic.

They had already discussed, at length, the events of the last few hours. All the signs suggested that the French police and the office of tourism had, between them, thwarted the Israelis' plans here at Montségur. If a serious crime had been committed, and if *Morcon* was in any way involved, then there was no likelihood of them being allowed to continue operating in the area. Chances were that there'd be a big investigation into their actions. *Morcon* would come under the media microscope and its whole organisation scrutinized. And if it could be proved that the company was acting as a front for the Mossad and the Knesset, then there would be hell to pay. With any luck, it would become a huge international embarrassment for the Jews.

'First of all, we must make an anonymous phone call to the editor of *Le Monde,* suggesting that they investigate *Morcon* because it is being manipulated by the Knesset and the Mossad. Couple that with the fact that a total of four Mossad agents have been killed in the Languedoc, two in Rennes of course and two here today by some unknown hand…'

'By Allah's hand!' Qusay was finally acceding to his colleague's reasoning. '*Allahu Akbar*!'

'… then that should really set the cat amongst the pigeons.'

'And then?'

'Then tomorrow we make a final check that nothing is going on at Rennes-le-Château and after that, we leave. Our report will state that there is no treasure, and that the cursed Israelis' attempts to retrieve the Menorah have failed dismally.'

The sound of crunching feet on gravel brought a sudden end to their discussion and Qusay was heard to catch his breath. 'It is her!' he rasped. 'The woman we saw yesterday in Rennes-le-Château! The one that I questioned in Rome!' As he spoke, he reached for the door handle with one hand, his gun with the other.

'Wait!' The command came from the one who had done most of the talking thus far.

Qusay protested. 'She is with the old man. There is no sign of the other one.'

'We wait for a few moments; in case he turns up. If he doesn't, then we ask her to explain why she is here.'

Qusay acceded and they sat in silence for several minutes.

'… You will question her now, Qusay, but you will not harm either of them.'

'She will have to be frightened, to make her talk.'

'All well and good but no more than that. We are in a foreign country and if the police come after us, then our escape will be difficult. Do nothing to cause unnecessary risk. After the way things have developed today, we have nothing to gain by it.'

*

Sally and Claude Boudet were startled when the back door of the Citroen swung open behind them. Although they'd been sitting in silence, neither of them had heard the sounds of approaching feet. Now they were aware of a huge figure, gun in hand, dropping heavily onto the back seat and Sally instinctively sought Boudet's hand, for reassurance and comfort. But the Frenchman was just as scared as she was.

'Why you here? You follow me to France.'

Sally pretended surprise. 'Followed you? From where? You are the one who threatened us in Rennes-le-Château, yesterday. We did not follow you here. You followed us!' The more she spoke, the more she regained her composure.

'You follow me from Rome.'

'Rome?' Bluffing was her only hope. 'I've never met you in my life. Never saw you before yesterday. You have mistaken me for someone else.'

'I ask you in Rome about Arch of Titus.'

Sally, still bluffing, pretended a mixture of surprise and incredulity. 'I'm a tourist guide, for God's sake! I answer thousands of questions about the Arch of Titus every year. How do you expect me to remember you?'

For a second, Qusay was at a loss. 'But why you here?'

'Why can't I be here? My boyfriend and I are on holiday.' Even in death, she was relying on Gus to help her.

'She speaks the truth, monsieur.' Claude Boudet was recovering some of his own composure by now. 'I, too, am a tourist guide and they have hired me to show them the historical sites of the Languedoc. Surely I am allowed to do that?'

'Where him now?'

Where, indeed! Sally's dejection deepened but she decided to extend her bluff. 'He was coming behind us a few minutes ago. Maybe he saw you coming into our car with a gun? Maybe he has gone for the *gendarmes*?'

The suggestion had its desired effect. Qusay, now feeling pressed for time, knew that he had little option but to take the woman and the old man at their word. Whether he believed them or not was of little consequence anyway, the way things were turning out. He had a decision to make.

'You do not follow me again!' he snarled, trying to save face.

'We didn't follow you before and we have no wish to follow you now either.'

With that, they heard the back door open and the little Citroen's suspensions groan once again as the stranger climbed out. With bated breath they listened to the retreating crunch of heavy feet on loose gravel and, seconds later, an engine being revved in anger.

It was only when they saw the car's headlights arcing upwards onto the D9, heading for Montferrier and on from there in the direction of Lavelanét and Carcassonne, that Sally and Claude Boudet felt able to breathe a meaningful sigh of relief.

*

Qusay and his friends had long gone before Gus emerged from the trees above the Cathar stele. Unlike Galileo the night before, he'd been able to descend all the way down to the ticket collector's hut without once having to use his flashlight. Not that he knew of the hut's existence beforehand but the crime-scene tape was proof in itself of where the murders had been committed. And he had also noticed the dark patches of congealed blood.

As he stepped out of tree cover into view of the Cathar stele and the moonlit Field of the Burned, he suddenly caught sight of a police car in the car park below. Cursing his own carelessness, he quickly stepped back into the shadows. He could so easily have been spotted and the last thing he wanted right now was to be caught with the diamonds in his possession. How would he explain them? And how would he explain the horrible state he was in?

A glowing light inside the car told him that at least one of its occupants was enjoying a cigarette, so hopefully they weren't as vigilant as they should be. After all, they were there to prevent anyone going up to the citadel, so they'd hardly be on the lookout for someone coming down.

He had to be careful, though. So, rather than taking the well-worn path down the Field of the Burned towards the car park, he now decided to keep to the shadow of the treeline in the direction of the village, until he was out of their sight. Then he would have some open pastureland to cross before joining the road down to where his bike was waiting for him. Once out in the open, the only risk then would be getting caught in the arcing headlights of a car coming up from Montségur. But that prospect didn't particularly worry him, since he had a good view of the road and would have time to take whatever action was needed to avoid being seen.

Having decided on this tack, he was about to make his move when a sudden unease gripped him. A sense of being watched. Watched from behind, from the path that he'd just descended. The sensation was enough to make his skin crawl and he instinctively swivelled round, ready to take evasive or protective action. But there was nothing there, nothing but the shadows that he'd become so accustomed to. And yet, the unease, the sense of a ghostly presence, remained.

Annoyed with himself for being so jumpy, he set off in a stooping run, keeping well within the tree-line shadows. He would have preferred more caution but an inexplicable sense of panic had gripped him and he kept casting quick glances over his shoulder as he ran.

Eventually, he reached the point where he had to break cover and take to the open slope. Although he was well out of sight of the police by now, he still had that premonition that hidden eyes were witnessing his retreat.

Halfway down the slope, the headlights of a car, slowly making its way up from the village, threatened to reveal his presence but he had enough time to throw himself to the ground and to lie perfectly still until they had swept over him. Little did he suspect that the whine of the engine was that of a little Citroen making its sad return to Alet-les-Baines.

Whitehall, London

Sir James Oldcorn had plenty of reason to smile as he climbed into his chauffeur-driven car. Foreign Secretary Jack Straw's grudging praise and the Israeli ambassador's sincere thanks were still ringing in his ears. Thanks to MI6 intelligence, the ship *La Crociata Finale* had been sunk by Mossad agents in the Black Sea.

The Vatican

The commander of the Swiss guard looked worried as he switched off his phone. From what he'd just been told by one of his men, the assassin dressed as a Catholic priest still hadn't arrived from Barcelona. He hadn't come off the flight that he should have boarded the night before last, nor had he been on any other subsequent flight from Spain. So where was he?

His men would continue to keep an eye on the airport. Others, carrying photographs of the bogus priest, were now making random enquiries throughout the city, in case the man had somehow slipped through the net. As Commander of the pontiff's personal guard, he couldn't afford to let ruthless killers dressed as Catholic priests roam free, to murder at will and seemingly with the consent of someone in the Vatican. This Father Galileo, as he called himself, would have to be found and made to pay for his sins.

The commander now turned to the solitary Swiss guard who had been waiting patiently for him to end his call. 'You took a risk, Christen, in bringing the gun back. How was it not spotted at the airport in Spain?'

'Security was lax, Commander, and Brett and I thought that the risk was worth taking.'

'And you are convinced that this is the assassin's gun?'

'Yes. With my own eyes I saw him throw it out through the car window into a nearby stream but because it landed on the bank and not in the water, then Brett had no trouble in retrieving it later. There was no point in handing it over to the French police. They would only see it as further proof against Otto and Erwin. Brett suggested putting it back in the priest's luggage without him knowing it. It will be difficult for him to explain when arrested.'

The commander remained silent for a second or two. 'Hm! Give to Caesar that which belongs to Caesar! Yes. It is a good plan. But first we must find this little emperor of death

Zurich Airport

Even as the commander was deliberating over what to do next, especially with regard to his two Swiss guards who were still being held on suspicion of murder in a Carcassonne jail, Father Galileo was stepping onto a plane in Zurich after having spent two nights in one of the city's cheaper hotels.

Cheerily, he greeted the stewardesses. He had every right to feel good. Hadn't he just successfully completed two missions? Wasn't he due a hefty pay packet? His only niggling fear was that Aiello might still renege on the deal because of what had happened to the arms shipment on its way to Batumi.

'But Galileo is no fool,' he muttered, as he took his seat near one of the plane's rear windows. Then, slipping his foot out of his left shoe, he quickly checked that his newly acquired safe deposit box key was still there, stuck with a piece of tape to his sweaty sole. *My insurance!* he reminded himself smugly.

He was now convinced that Aiello couldn't be trusted. Why else would someone have followed him from Montségur to the airport? Weren't the Knights of Wisdom supposed to have eyes and ears everywhere? Or so Aiello would have him believe! In which case, it was possible that someone had been keeping an eye on him throughout his stay in the Languedoc. If so, then he, whoever it was, would know of the killing of the Mossad agents. Might even have witnessed the discovery of the documents in the church. No sweat! As far as Aiello was concerned, the precious documents had been destroyed.

Casually, he switched on his cell phone to check for messages. Three on voicemail and one text message, all from the same source. The voicemails he already knew about, only the text message was new. With a cynical smile, he looked it up.

Have repeatedly tried to contact you. Why has your cell phone been switched off?

It seemed that Aiello was not a happy bunny! Tough!

'You are requested to have your phone switched off during the flight, Father.' The young stewardess looked somewhat embarrassed at having to remind him.

Galileo's smile was now all innocence. 'Bless you, my child! I was just about to do so.'

To curb his growing excitement, he now closed his eyes and tried to relax as the plane taxied onto the main runway. In less than two hours' time he would be back in his beloved Caput Mundi.

Alet-les-Baines

Sally Jeffers didn't know where to turn. She had just spent her second night in Claude Boudet's house, hoping against hope to hear from Gus. Now she was sitting at the Frenchman's breakfast table, gazing abstractedly through the window at the swirling torrent of the River Aude. Her coffee was cold, her toast untouched. Her one thought was: *What do I do now? I can't stay here forever.* Returning to Britain to be with her family seemed to be her only option, and one that she wasn't particularly averse to any more, after all that had happened. For the first time since she'd left home for university, she needed someone to turn to.

After returning from Montségur she had tried ringing Gus time and time again on his mobile but there had been no reply. Finally, and in desperation, she had asked Boudet to phone the police to report that he was missing in Montségur.

'You realise, Mademoiselle Sally, that if I tell them that your Gus was trying to climb up to the Château, then he could be in some trouble if he should turn up safe and well. The police will want to know why he was so interested in the citadel and are bound to suspect him of being involved in the murders.'

'Tell them that he went out walking and that he didn't return. Tell them about his motorbike in the village car park.'

Boudet had done just that and the police had initially shown a lot of interest. Another disappearance, in the same locality as three recent murders – and two more in Rennes, a mere fifty kilometres away – was bound to stir them. But no word had been heard from them since.

Pushing the plate, cup, and saucer away from her across the table, Sally got up and went in search of her host. She found him tidying his living room.

'Do you mind phoning the police again, monsieur? I must know what is going on. I will have to decide what I am to do.'

The Frenchman gave her a sympathetic look. He could sense how desperately lonely she felt. He wanted to comfort her but there was a limit to how much melancholy he himself could endure. The ageing Claude Boudet was already longing for his old life back again.

'Of course, my dear. I will do it now.'

Sally listened to him dialling, out in the hallway, but could make nothing of the hushed conversation that ensued. A good ten minutes later, he returned, looking somewhat bewildered.

'It is always so difficult to get hold of someone who really knows what is going on. Anyway, I was finally able to talk to the policeman whom I spoke to initially in Lavelanét but he had nothing to report except...'

'Except what, monsieur?'

'Except that when they went to look, the motorcycle wasn't there.'

It was now Sally's turn to look baffled. 'When did they go looking?'

'Early yesterday morning.'

She now became even more agitated. 'Then he must still be alive. What do you think, Claude?'

'Let us hope so, my dear.'

'Either that or... or someone could have stolen the bike, I suppose. Is that possible, do you think?'

'Yes, it is possible, I suppose, if your Gus had left the key. But that isn't likely, is it? The bike being stolen I mean. You have seen Montségur for yourself, Sally. It's a quiet, peaceful village. It doesn't harbour thieves.'

No, only killers, she thought, but refrained from saying it out loud. 'But if he is alive, then where is he? Why doesn't he come looking for me?'

Claude Boudet sensed her desperation but he didn't have to answer. That was done for him when the doorbell rang and they found a dishevelled and tired-looking Gus Adams standing there, on the doorstep.

Rome Airport

'We have him in our sights, Commander. We think that he arrived on a flight from Zurich, but we cannot confirm that yet. Should we challenge him?'

'Of course not! You are outside the jurisdiction of the Vatican State. But follow him! You can do that?'

'Yes. We have our mopeds, so it shouldn't be difficult as long as he stays within the city traffic. He's now making for the taxi rank.'

'Good. Keep me posted! I want to know what direction he takes. I am not ruling out the possibility of having him kidnapped and brought here to face Vatican law, so be prepared in case I decide on that course of action.'

Alet-les-Baines

'But where have you been? And what on earth is that horrible pong on you?' Gus, struggling to remove his leathers, was wafting stench in their direction.

Sally's initial instinct had been to rush forward to hug him, to show genuine relief that he was safe, but she now stepped back quickly and held her nose between finger and thumb.

'Long story! Sorry for the smell, *monsieur*.'

Claude Boudet smiled as if to say, "Don't let it worry you".

'I assume that you climbed it, then?' She was keeping her distance and still holding on to her nose.

Did he detect a note of derision in her question? Yes, probably, knowing her. 'I wouldn't be here, otherwise, would I?'

She in turn now felt stung. 'And how much wiser are you, would you say, after your pathetic little ego trip?' She was giving vent to her pent-up frustration and concern.

He, on the other hand, thought she was ridiculing him. 'I saw what I wanted. Not that you would be interested, even if I told you.'

Claude Boudet stood back, smiling inwardly. He knew how relieved and happy Sally really felt at having Gus back again.

'You've been sleeping rough by the looks of you.'

Rather than answer, Gus turned to the Frenchman. 'Would it be possible for me to have a bath or a shower, monsieur? It seems that my appearance is an embarrassment to your guest.'

'Of course, Gus. And may I say how glad we both are to see you safe and well.'

'Thank you, Claude. It's nice to hear someone say so. But I promise not to outstay my welcome.' A glance in Sally's direction showed what he meant. 'I'll be leaving as soon as I've washed and changed.'

'Where are we going?'

'We? I don't know about you, but I know where I'm going.'

As she watched him being led away towards the bathroom, the significance of his words struck her. She also realised that she had yet again hurt him to the quick. 'Damn!' she muttered, through silent tears. 'Why can't I keep my big mouth shut?'

Rome

'At last! Where have you been? I have been trying to contact you since yesterday morning.'

Galileo scowled and felt like reminding him that the silly question about the Wisdom of Solomon hadn't been asked. 'The battery of my phone was dead and I didn't have the chance to recharge it,' he lied.

'You will listen to confession today?'

'When? Now?'

'Yes.'

Galileo sighed. He had only just got out of a taxi and watched it leave. He hailed another that was approaching in the distance. It was pay-time, and retirement in luxury was just around the corner for him.

*

'Commander? The bird is returning to its nest. As I speak, he is entering the Basilica of Santa Maria in Trastevere.'

'He is alone?'

'Yes.'

'Does he carry any possessions?'

'Only a small valise. What should we do?'

'Watch him carefully. See if he meets someone but do not approach him until others join you. The man is not a priest... I repeat, *not* a priest... but a dangerous assassin.'

After a hurried discussion, the two Swiss guards in civilian dress entered the church as tourists and wandered around, gazing at anything and everything of interest. Sly glances told them that the bogus priest was nowhere to be seen and they began to fear that he had exited the church by another door. Using eye signals only, they split up and went their different ways, checking every possible hiding place and taking care not to attract the attention of other tourists.

Then, as one of them was passing the confession box, he heard whispered conversation. A silent nod from him signalled his friend to join him at the church door.

'It has to be him. He can't be anywhere else. You wait here and I'll take up position outside. I'll keep an eye on the priest as he leaves and you watch his accomplice. The cavalry should show at any second.'

Six minutes later, a flushed Galileo stepped out of the confession box. Whatever had been said, hadn't pleased the little man. His jaw was set and there was a determination in his step as he aimed for the exit. Being so irritated, when he walked out into the piazza he failed to notice what was going on around him. He'd barely got halfway across the little square when a dozen armed Vatican guards closed in on him from all sides, shouting threatening commands and a bewildered Galileo was handcuffed before he even realised what was happening. Tourists stood by in stunned silence. A priest being arrested?

In the kerfuffle, the commander personally took charge of the valise that the little man had been carrying and, unobserved, slipped a gun into it; a gun that had, only two days earlier, been retrieved from a river bank in the Languedoc.

The Swiss guard who had remained inside the church could hear the commotion, as could the blind man now emerging from the confession box, white cane in hand. The guard saw him pause to listen, saw the growing look of suspicion and fear on his face and watched him take a pew and kneel. *Crafty!* he thought and slipped out of the church to let his commander know what he had seen.

Alet-les-Baines

Gus, now in a clean yellow T-shirt and pair of khaki shorts, felt much more relaxed after his hot shower. He held out his hand to Claude Boudet. 'I'm grateful to you, monsieur. You have been a good friend. And thank you for taking my smelly clothes to your outside bin.'

'It is I who should thank you, Gus… you and Sally. I have seen more excitement with you in three days than in my lifetime otherwise. But why are you leaving now? Why not wait until it is all over?'

'Believe me, monsieur, it is all over. There will be no more excitement at Montségur now that the police are keeping an eye on the place and now that Interpol are involved. Yesterday, I visited Rennes-le-Château. Guess who arrived whilst I was there! Our Arab friends! Probably there for the same reason as I was.'

'Which was?'

'To make sure that there wasn't anything still going on there that we should know about.'

'And was there?'

'No. Nothing but innocent tourists. Anyway, the three of them didn't stay long and, when they left, I followed them as far as Toulouse, and watched them board a flight for Paris. No doubt they will be going on from there to wherever they came from.' Since Boudet wasn't familiar with Father Galileo, then Gus didn't bother mentioning that the priest, too, had disappeared.

'So, you are leaving me, *mes amis?*' The Frenchman smiled ruefully. Then, with tongue-in-cheek, added, 'And I had so much hoped that we could find the treasure together.'

Gus laughed, surprisingly more relaxed now. 'Ah! But which one, my friend?'

Sally remained stony-faced. She was feeling out of things, not knowing what her immediate fate was going to be. It looked as if she would have to find her own way to the nearest airport. And then where? Back to Britain was her only option.

'I will say my goodbyes then, Claude.' There was another quick handshake and Gus made for the door, leaving a dejected Sally Jeffers rooted to where she stood. The Frenchman smiled inwardly; he'd seen the wink that the young man had just given him.

Gus took his time in making himself comfortable on the Honda Goldwing and as he was about to kick-start the bike he shouted mischievously to a tearful Sally: 'If you're coming with me, then hadn't you better get your leathers on?'

Her emotions got the better of her, then, and her flood of tears made Gus regret his silly teasing.

'Sorry!' he muttered, giving her knee an apologetic squeeze as she climbed onto the pillion behind him.

She acknowledged his apology with a little tearful squeeze of her own before turning to Claude Boudet: 'Let me know when you find the treasure, monsieur.'

'Pardon?' The Frenchman looked bemused. So did Gus.

'Your theory about the well in Rennes-le-Château. I take it that you intend to check it out?'

Claude laughed. Sally laughed. Gus looked perplexed.

Il Vaticano

'Your name is Father Galileo?'

The little man felt the tension in his sinews. So far, they'd refused to say why he'd been arrested. Nor did he know anything about his interrogator, other than that the Vatican police seemed prepared to take orders from him. What option had he, therefore, but to try bluff?

'Yes. I am Father Galileo.'

'And you have just returned from the Languedoc.'

'Yes. I stayed with Father Francois at Montségur. You can easily check it out with him.'

'Ah! Do not underestimate us. We have already contacted Father Francois. He tells us that you spent a few days with him, recuperating after a nervous breakdown.'

'That's right.'

'And that the request that you be allowed to stay there came directly from here... from the Vatican.'

'Yes.'

'A personal request from the pontiff, no doubt?'

The little man gave a brief nervous laugh. 'I would not presume to say that.'

'But from someone of high authority, just the same?'

'I believe so.'

'And who was this man who is supposed to have wielded such influence?'

'I never... um!... never met him.' Galileo knew that he was digging a hole for himself. He couldn't afford to stammer.

'Surely you have a name for him?'

'Well... I... um! believe that his name is Aiello.'

By now, he was fairly convinced that Aiello had deliberately lured him to Trastevere to be arrested. So why should he, Galileo, now show loyalty at his own expense?

'...But I know no more than that. Now will you please tell me why I have been arrested and why I am being badgered like this with questions.'

'All in good time, Father. But first, tell me when was it that you first entered the priesthood? And where exactly have you served as a Catholic priest?'

More and more, he was regretting his decision to bluff his way out of trouble but he was up to his neck in it now and had no option but to try keeping afloat. 'I have served the Catholic faith... the true faith... for many years, in Albania.'

'Oh! That's interesting! But where in Albania, Father?'

'Um! My last church was in Kukes, near the Kosovo border.'

'May I see your passport?'

'Why? Do you presume to doubt my word? The word of a Catholic priest? A man of God? Who are you, anyway? And by what authority do you detain and question me?'

'For your information, I am the commander of the Swiss guard and as such have the direct authority of the Most Holy Father himself.'

Galileo felt the blood drain from his face and his devious mind began searching for an escape route. They'll find that I'm lying, that I'm not a priest at all. So what? Impersonating a priest can hardly be regarded as a serious crime. They can prove nothing else against me.

'Your passport, Father, please?' The commander held out his hand. The two policemen by the door remained alert.

'It's in my valise. You will find that it is in order. After that, you will release me or I shall take my complaint to the Italian courts. I must remind you, Commander, that I am a Roman citizen and subject therefore to Italian, not Vatican, law. You had no authority to arrest me in Trastevere.'

The commander of the pope's personal guard signalled to one of the policemen to place Galileo's valise between them on the table. With slow deliberation he unzipped it and then feigned shock and astonishment as he drew out the gun. 'One of the tools of your trade, Father?'

Galileo's own shock and amazement were anything but feigned. He stared in utter disbelief. 'That cannot be mine.'

'Cannot? Strange choice of word, Father! Are you suggesting that you own a gun but that this isn't it?'

'Of course not!' If he wasn't unduly worried before, he certainly was now. 'What I am saying is that... that horrible instrument of death... was planted in my valise.'

'Planted? Strange choice of word again, especially from a servant of the church. Don't you think?'

Galileo remained silent now as he felt himself drowning. If this was, indeed, the gun that he'd thrown away in France, then someone must have seen him doing it and that could only have been the one who had followed him out of Montségur. In other words, Aiello's spy. But even if that were so, it only explained the easier half of the puzzle. The real mystery was how the gun had found its way into his valise.

'The police will naturally want a ballistics report on it.'

The little man's mind was again in overdrive. Even if this is the gun that I used in France... although I can't see how that can possibly be... there's no way that they can link either it or me with the death of that British agent in Rome, because I used a different gun then.

' ...As will the French police, I'm sure. Interpol, even! What do you think, Father? In fact, this very weapon might help to release two of my own men who are being unjustly held in a French jail.' He paused. 'Anyway, your passport seems to be in order, Father.' The commander had put the weapon aside and was now studying the document.

'Of course, it is.'

'But we will have it checked just the same, in case it is forged.' The head of the Swiss guard smiled somewhat mischievously. 'You'd be surprised at how many forged passports there are in circulation these days. However, a man of God like yourself is hardly likely to be travelling under a false name, is he, Father?'

Again, the little man remained silent as the commander rummaged through the rest of his things. He frowned when the wallet appeared and cursed himself for having held on to it. How could he possibly explain having in his possession something that belonged to a dead British agent called Thomas Mackay?

'Careless, Father!' was the commander's only comment as he placed the wallet to one side after scanning its contents. Then: 'Ah! You have a digital camera! And a very good one at that! Expensive toy for a poor priest, I'd say. I'm into digital photography myself, you know, and the sight of this makes me feel quite envious.' Again, a wry smile. 'But I shouldn't say that in the presence of a devout man of God, should I? Envy, after all, is one of the great sins.'

The two policemen smiled as they recognised the little game that the commander was playing with his quarry. Galileo, for his part, was by now an extremely worried individual because he knew what was about to come next.

'I hear that the Languedoc is such a beautiful place to visit, Father. You won't mind my having a quick look at the pictures that you took there?'

'Yes, I do mind! They are personal!' He made to get to his feet in protest but sat down again when he saw the two policemen stepping forward to intercept him. 'Anyway, it's not my camera. It's one I found in the Languedoc. Some tourist had left it behind,' he ended lamely.

'Oh! So, whatever photographs are in it should help us trace the real owner.'

The commander now recalled what Otto had told him over the phone about seeing the priest taking photographs up at the Château de Montségur and he hoped to find evidence of that now, but what appeared on the camera's little digital screen stunned him into silence. When he next spoke, there was a distinct edge to his voice.

'I think it's about time that you started telling me the truth. To begin with, you are not a priest, are you? Never were.'

Galileo, looking like a trussed-up chicken, shrugged his shoulders. Impersonating a priest might not be a serious crime but the evidence inside the camera would prove damning for him.

'…So, what is your real name? And where are you from?' When he got no answer, the head of the pope's personal guard continued: 'Quite a celebration here! What was the occasion?'

Turning the screen towards Galileo, he showed him pictures of Maurizio Bonnano and the others breaking their magnums of champagne on the front of an old diesel locomotive.

' …Quite a party, as well.'

Photographs now showed the drinking of toasts inside the quarry cavern. Bonnano, Cimino and Salvatore Provenzano's bright faces were clearly within range of the camera's flash; other faces, further away and in the shadows, were paler and more ghostly.

A glint of surprise now appeared in the commander's eyes as he recognised the person in the next picture; the man with the white cane exiting the Basilica of Santa Maria in Trastevere. Retired Judge Carlo Platina! Could it possibly be that he was the blind man who had met Galileo in the confession box of that same church, less than an hour ago? He had ordered Galileo's accomplice to be arrested for interrogation but had yet to see him for himself. If that person was indeed Judge Carlo Platina, then the commander knew how serious the developments were going to be.

'Whom did you speak to at the Basilica of Santa Maria?'

'I spoke to no one.'

'You are doing yourself no favours by denying it. You spent time in the confession box talking to a blind man.'

Galileo's face now showed genuine incredulity. Then he laughed. 'A blind man? What game are you playing, Commander?'

'No game. I will give you one more chance to help. Was this the man?' Again, he turned the camera screen towards Galileo. 'You didn't take this picture today, did you? And yet, this morning, you met him again, in the same church.'

The little man looked confused. He could remember taking the picture but it had never crossed his mind that the blind man might have been Aiello or Aiello's accomplice.

'... Not only do we know the identity of this man but we have him waiting to be interviewed. You would do well to consider your situation.'

Rather than wait for his prisoner to respond, the commander moved on to view other photographs stored on the camera's digital card, with his face showing revulsion when the photograph of the dying Tom Mackay appeared on the screen. He was even more appalled at the sight of the twisted bodies of Mossad agents lying awkwardly on a stony and bloodied path. Otto and Erwin had already informed him about Galileo's role in the murders at Montségur. They'd also told him about the bogus priest's nocturnal photographic work up at the citadel, so he knew what the next pictures were about, as well, because he had received similar ones from his own agents. According to Otto and Erwin, the bricked-up entrance inside the well was thought to hide the Treasure of Solomon's Temple, and they had sent him similar pictures, showing how they had sealed the well with cement. Yes, his men had done extremely well to outwit the Israelis but it would be of little comfort to the pontiff because the documents removed from the secret archives were still unaccounted for. What the commander wasn't aware of, as yet, was the irony of it all. He wasn't to know that the cold-blooded assassin, facing him now, had been working towards the same end as his own men.

Whatever else he expected to find in Galileo's digital gallery, he certainly wasn't prepared for the next surprise.

'But this is! These are!' He became more and more agitated as he flicked from one picture to the next. Finally, he got to his feet, to look down at his prisoner. 'Where did you find these? And where are they now?'

Galileo knew what his interrogator was referring to. 'They have been destroyed.' The commander could barely control his angry response: '*Destroyed?*'

The little man nodded, having already decided to make as clean a breast of things as would benefit him, personally. 'I was obeying orders.'

Aiello no longer deserved his loyalty, he decided. Hadn't he used the fate of the ship La Crociata Finale as an excuse to renege on his promise of full payment? And hadn't he shown a lack of trust in him by sending spies to the Languedoc to keep an eye on him? The biggest double-cross of all, though, was having the gun brought over from France and having it planted, somehow or other, in his luggage. What confused him more than anything, however, was the attitude of this commander. As personal guard to the pontiff he should know that he, Galileo, had been indirectly employed by the pontiff himself. As, indeed, had Aiello and all other so-called Knights of Wisdom. They had all been taking their orders from the Holy Father but it had been up to him, Galileo, to rescue the precious documents from enemy hands.

'Orders from whom?'

'The man who calls himself Aiello.'

'The man you met at the Basilica of Santa Maria in Trastevere?'

'Perhaps. He could have been Aiello or, possibly, his accomplice. But I warn you, Commander, that you are meddling here with things that you do not understand... things that go far above your head.'

The head of the pope's personal guard was barely listening. He turned to the two policemen: 'Keep him here while I question the judge, in the next room.'

*

'You realise who it is that you are talking to, Commander?' The tone of the question harboured a threat.

'Of course, Judge. You are here because I believe you will be able to help us with our enquiries. You were in the Basilica of Santa Maria earlier?'

'Of course! It's where the police found me and disturbed me at my prayers.'

'Why there, Judge?'

'Why not there? The Basilica is where I usually worship. I am a Trasteverian, a true Roman, born and bred. Now what is this all about?'

'The man you met there. Who is he?'

A look of disdain came to the retired judge's face. 'I met no man!'

'In the confession box, I believe.'

'Of course, I met a man in the confession box, you fool! He was a priest! From whom else would I seek absolution?'

The commander had never liked Judge Carlo Platina. Not many did. Now he realised why. The man's contempt towards others was so offensive.

'It surprises me, Judge, that you confess your sins to a known assassin.'

The surprise that appeared on the blind face was so obviously feigned. 'What on earth are you talking about? The priest who listened to my confession...'

'Was no priest at all! Let's not play games, Judge Platina. The man we are referring to is being held in our custody. He is no priest. He is a known killer and he has told us of his association with you. Says that he was employed by you. I believe he knows you as Aiello.'

A look of some resignation came over Carlo Platina as he quickly weighed up his options. He knew that there was no likelihood of a court of law taking the word of an assassin against that of a respected former judge but what he couldn't be sure of was whether this commander had some indisputable evidence against him. If that was the case, then he would have to change his tack. And if that didn't work, then only one other option remained - his accuser would have to be silenced before he could cause further embarrassment.

'I wish to speak to you alone, Commander!'

The blind judge waited until he could hear only two of them breathing in the room, then: 'First of all, may I remind you that you, personally, have no legal right to cross-examine anyone in police custody. That right belongs to the Vatican police and judiciary. Secondly, and more importantly, there are some things that relate to Citta Vaticano that you are not meant to know about. Your responsibility is to ensure the pontiff's personal safety. The Knights of Wisdom have a far wider responsibility.'

He paused, but the commander, who knew most things about the Holy See's various factions and undercurrents, remained silent. The Knights of Malta he knew about, not to mention the Solar Templars and Opus Dei. It was no secret, either, that P2, the illicit Masonic lodge, was still meeting in secret and engaging from time to time in furtive activities. But he'd never heard of the Knights of Wisdom and that fact alone concerned him.

'...The Knights of Wisdom exist to safeguard the well-being of the Roman Catholic faith, not only here in Italy but throughout the world. I tell you this now in confidence, Commander.'

'So, what is your involvement with this assassin, Judge?'

'I have only your word that he is an assassin. It is true that I played a small part in recruiting him to our order but it is ridiculous to claim that he is in my employment. Look into his bank account if you must. You will not find there a single payment that came from me. If this man, as you claim, has taken human life, then I want to make it perfectly clear that it wasn't the Knights of Wisdom who gave him that mandate. In fact, the Knights will tell you quite unequivocally that, if guilty, he should face the full retribution of Vatican law. However, there are more important things at issue here, Commander. The man known as Galileo, whom you have in custody, was sent to the Languedoc to retrieve important documents that had been stolen from our secret archives. I take it that you know of the theft?' The blind judge assumed a nod from the head of the Swiss guard before continuing: 'The purpose of my meeting with him this morning was to receive his report.'

'And what did he tell you, Judge?'

'That he has destroyed the documents.'

'And in doing that, was he following your orders?'

'Not my orders, Commander. His brief was to recover the documents and to return them to the secret archives. However, if there was any danger of them falling into the wrong hands, then he was to destroy them. Which, I presume, is what happened.'

'The Most Holy Father will not be pleased, Judge.'

Aiello's face became contorted as it fought to suppress a fit of rage. 'The Most Holy Father must take a lot of responsibility for the loss of the documents in the first place, Commander. Have you any idea of the heretical content of one of them? You fool! Do you not realise that had it fallen into the hands of our enemies, then our faith... the true faith... would have become the subject of derision, the world over? Many would believe it to be genuine and not the work of a heretic charlatan?'

The commander looked at him long and hard. 'We will continue this conversation at a later date, Judge?'

*

In his cell, half an hour later, Galileo found some consolation in the belief that, when the time came, Aiello, blind or not, would be able to influence the court's decision in his favour. In the meantime, he needed to find a safe hiding place for his Swiss deposit box key. All his other possessions had been taken from him, but the valuable papyri were safely locked away in Zurich, for a later date.

He looked around. Prospects of finding a suitable hiding place were bleak. The tiled floor and walls didn't offer even the narrowest of cracks. His bed, the only piece of furniture other than a small table and chair, had to be his only hope. Deftly, he ran his fingers along its tubular frame, searching for any kind of hollow or recess but there was none. Then, when on the point of abandoning his search, he noticed that the upright tubes that formed the foot of his bed had rubber rather than welded capping on them. It took several minutes and considerable effort on his part to prise one of the rubbers loose and thus gain access to the hollow tubing. After removing the key from inside his sock, he dropped it into the bedframe, listened to it rattling its way down and then replaced the capping. There could be only one way of retrieving it now. The bed would have to be turned upside down, for it to fall out. His only misgiving was that he might be moved to another cell at short notice and that would mean having to leave the key behind.

Trastevere

Retired Judge Carlo Platina didn't take a direct route home. Instead, he called at Trastevere's open market and tarried at the various stalls under the pretence of doing some shopping. Being blind, there was no easy way for him to know whether the commander had had him followed or not. However, he finally convinced himself that that wasn't the case and he sought out a public telephone kiosk. There, after fingering the Braille pages of his little notebook, he dialled.

'Do you have the Wisdom of Solomon?' He waited for confirmation. 'The Knights of Wisdom have an important assignment for you... What? No, this is not Aiello! Aiello is not the one who makes such important decisions; I speak on behalf of one whom we all respect, one who is extremely concerned at recent developments. Now listen well! There is a man, a truly evil man, who is now in your custody...'

A blast from a passing lorry's klaxon drowned the rest of his sentence but the person at the other end of the line had got the gist of what had to be done.

Barton and Paul Solicitors' Offices, Marylebone

'So, I can leave it in your hands?'

'But of course, Mr Adams!' The young solicitor looked not only pleased but also a little excited by the commission that he had just been given. Once more, he perused the documents on his desk.

'...But let me be quite clear about what you expect of Barton and Paul's. You wish us to arrange the sale of your Limehouse property in the Docklands... all the luxury apartments except your own? Thirty-five in total?'

'That's right. Should be no problem for you. Many of the sitting tenants have shown plenty of interest in the past. I'll leave it to you to decide on the asking price.'

Gus knew that he and his sister could expect top dollar for the property since the agents would be claiming two percent of the final deal. Two percent of six million wasn't something to be sniffed at, not even by a prosperous firm of solicitors like Barton & Paul. Their services would include taking overall charge of the sale, leaving him, Gus, and his sister Gina, with just the final documents to sign.

'There's just one thing that I insist on. The money from the sale of each apartment must be paid into my account within fourteen days of every individual contract being signed.' His experience in banking had taught Gus about solicitors' penchant to hold on for as long as possible to their customers' capital, in order to reap every possible penny of interest-benefits for themselves.

The young solicitor smiled a knowing smile. 'I will see to it that such a clause is included in the contract which both parties – yourself and your sister on the one hand, Barton & Paul on the other – will need to sign. Expect to hear from me in three or four days' time, Mr Adams.'

As he headed back towards Limehouse on his Kawasaki, Gus felt relieved that they had taken the first step to sell. It was something that he and Gina had considered doing before now but had never got round to it.

There were other things also to be decided. Somehow or other, he needed to make it up to Sally Jeffers and the only way to do that was to first of all clear his own name in Rome. That could only mean picking up Galileo's trail and bringing him to justice. That much he owed, not only to Sally but also to Tom Mackay and his son. Eddie Mackay would expect redress for what had happened to his father.

Twice he had phoned Sally since returning from France three days ago, and she had told him of her intention to return to Rome within the week.

'I intend going there myself in a few days' time. Maybe we could meet?' He had expected a quick rebuff but it hadn't come. Encouraged, he'd then given her the number of his new cell phone. 'Perhaps you'll give me a call?' This again had been met with silence but then, just as he was about to tell her to forget the offer, 'Yes, I'd very much like that, Gus.' The unexpected sincerity of her reply had pleasantly surprised him.

Back in Canary Wharf, he called at a travel agent to book a flight to Rome, and then, after a visit to a gents' hairdresser, he made it to Carluccio's for lunch.

*

'Is that you, Sally?'

'Auntie Janet?'

'Yes. First of all, let me say how relieved we are to have you safely back in England. Your Uncle James was so worried that you'd been dragged into that business in Rome and then in the south of France. We have heard nothing from the young man who was with you. I only know him as Agent Gus. Have you seen him at all since returning to London?'

'No, Auntie, I haven't.' She didn't feel obliged to mention the call just now. 'Anyway, I'm going back to Rome tomorrow.'

'So soon?'

'I need the work. That is, if I can get it, of course!'

It took a second or two for her aunt to respond and when she did, she sounded apologetic. 'Your mother told me how Thomas Cook and Thomsons cancelled your contract with them. Uncle James blames himself for it, of course, but he intends to put things right for you… By the way, did you know that Agent Gus hasn't drawn a penny, as yet, out of the fund that your uncle set up for him?'

'I wouldn't know anything about that, Auntie, but I know that he did spend quite a lot of somebody's money on a brand-new motorbike, for us to escape out of Italy. His own money, I imagine!'

'Anyway, your uncle thinks that you are owed something out of the fund, to cover loss of earnings, personal inconvenience, that sort of thing. You could do with it, I'm sure, especially since you're going back to Rome.'

You can say that again, Sally thought. 'Who knows, Auntie, maybe this time around I'll find myself a wealthy husband while I'm there. Hopefully, a sugar daddy!'

The two of them laughed and the conversation came to an end.

L'Ufficio del Papa, Il Vaticano

'There is something that I wish you to do.'
 'Of course, Most Holy Father.'
 'The young man who was murdered in France…'
 'The one who stole from our secret archives?'
 'You forget that he was not the thief, but rather his brother was.'
 'They were accomplices, nevertheless.'
 'Maybe so, but it is time now to show mercy and forgiveness.'
 The pontiff's private secretary looked somewhat confused. 'How can we show mercy and forgiveness to a dead man, Your Holiness?'
 'You remember the reason behind the theft?'
 'Of course. It was to pay for medical treatment in America.'
 'Treatment for a little girl who will otherwise die. Whatever we think of the man's actions, his motives were honourable.'
 'And you wish me to do what, Your Holiness?'
 'All my prayers have brought me to the same decision. The church must see to it that the child receives her treatment in America. I want you therefore to make all the necessary arrangements, financial and otherwise, for her and her mother to be flown to the clinic in California. It is the least that the church can do in the circumstances.' A pensive look came over the pontiff's face. 'We have much to thank God for.'
 Rather than interrupt the Holy Father's thoughts, his secretary remained silent.
 '…Although the heretical papyrus that was taken from us has not been returned, it has, nevertheless, been destroyed. And who is to say that that was not God's will?

Rome

Gus felt a little trepidation as he stepped off the plane, half-expecting to see armed carabinieri closing in on him from all sides. But none came. It was late afternoon.

Forty minutes later and ten minutes early, he was standing on the ancient Via Sacra, gazing up at the Arch of Titus. Despite the sun beating down on him, he felt his skin tingling. There indeed, above him, was the scene that Sally and Claude Boudet had more than once referred to. The Menorah being carried in triumph into Rome! The great candelabrum from Solomon's Temple that he, himself, had found... had actually looked at and touched, less than a fortnight ago! The great Jewish artefact that no other living person had ever seen or was ever likely to see.

Over the past week, he had wrestled long and hard with his conscience. Did such a great historical treasure deserve to remain hidden forever? Why shouldn't he, Gus Adams, share its magnificence with the rest of the world? The find would be compared to the discovery of Tutankhamun's Tomb in Egypt! And the name of Gus Adams would go down in history, alongside the likes of Heinrich Schliemann and Howard Carter, adventurous archaeologists whom he'd heard about in school and read about in books.

Yes, he had been sorely tempted to reveal all. So why hadn't he? What had convinced him otherwise? It was something that Sally had mentioned in her conversation with Claude Boudet. 'If the Menorah is returned to the Temple Mount then the whole of Islam will be up in arms.' After all his efforts in Albania, he couldn't let that happen. If he did, then he'd be no better than Maurizio Bonnano and his mafia friends. No better than... than his own father... and he couldn't have that on his conscience.

'So near and yet so far!'

He turned, startled by the voice in his ear. And there she was! More attractive than ever, dark eyes laughing at him, thick shoulder-length auburn hair, golden brown skin, primrose-yellow dress with above-knee hemline drawing appreciative glances from all around.

He caught his breath and then leaned forward to kiss her formally on the cheek, painfully aware of his own unkempt look in loose polo shirt and oversized khaki shorts. Her perfume was like an opiate that made him pleasantly giddy.

'Nice to see you,' he muttered with obvious sincerity. He had looked forward to this meeting more than he cared to admit. 'What did you mean, so near and yet so far?'

For answer she nodded upwards towards the Arch. 'How near were we, Gus? Was it at Montségur, do you think?' She was pointing up at the carving of the Menorah. 'I'd have loved to have seen it. Me and countless others!' Her laugh revealed flashing white teeth. 'Mind you, Claude Boudet still maintains that it isn't at Montségur at all but rather in Rennes-le-Château. And who's to say that he's wrong?'

'Who, indeed!' And he looked away.

'If it exists at all, of course! Anyway, it was quite an adventure, don't you think?'

He smiled back at her but said nothing.

'…Do you know what? I like it.'

'Pardon?'

'The new Gus Adams! The hair! The pony tail's gone and the frizzy look suits you.'

He shrugged as if it was of little or no consequence. 'More manageable, that's all!'

'As I said, I like it!' She flashed another smile at him. 'And I very much like the trimmed beard. You don't look half as wild. And you are much nicer smelling than you were in France.'

He had to smile. She was having fun at his expense, and he liked it.

'I've booked us a table for later. My treat! In the meantime, let's go for a coffee or something because I've got quite a lot to tell you. I suggest that we stroll as far as the Piazza Venezia, opposite the Vittorio Emanuele monument, and have a coffee or a glass of wine in one of the cafés there. What do you say?' Without waiting for an answer, she hooked her arm into his and he felt the sudden thrill of her warm skin against his own. It struck him that he had never known such contentment before.

'On one condition! That I get to choose which café!'

Ten minutes later, the waiter at the Café Vittorio on the Via San Marco was taking their order for coffee, with a glass of red wine to follow.

'Any reason why you chose this one?'

'It brings back fond memories, that's why.'

'Oh? You've brought other women here, I suppose?'

Did he detect the slightest hint of jealously? He would like to think so but the very idea of Sally harbouring a romantic interest in him was ridiculous. 'Not really! The last time I was sitting here, I had two mafia gunmen for company and the barrel of a Magnum .357 in my ear. Both of them are dead now, though. Can't believe it was just a few weeks ago. All of it seems to belong to another time, another world. Anyway, you've only been back here a few days and already you've got a lot to tell me, you say?'

'Yes. But first of all, I want to ask you something. A cheque, made out in my name, was waiting for me when I arrived back at my flat. It had been sent by that garage in Toulouse. It seems that they've sold the bike that you left with them. A note accompanying the cheque said that they'd been instructed to make the payment to me, at my Rome address. Why?'

'Let's just say that it's for services rendered.'

Her smile gave way to playful suspicion. 'No services were rendered, Mr Adams. And, for your information, I cannot be bought!'

'Just think of it as a token of appreciation then.'

'A token? Good God! The cheque is for eleven and a half thousand euros.'

'Good. Should have been more, though.'

They both fell silent.

'Hm! My next question has also to do with money. My sources tell me that you haven't claimed a penny from MI6 for your services.'

'Your sources being your Auntie Janet, I take it?'

'Yes. What is it Gus? Do you have an allergy to money, or what?'

'Just slipped my mind, that's all, what with all the excitement. But we're not here to talk about money are we? You said that you had news for me.'

'I have, but first of all answer me this one question – Why are you here?'

'In Rome? You know why! To track down that damn priest if I can.'

She pouted playfully and laid her hand on his. 'And there's me thinking that you'd come here just to see me.'

His instant embarrassment made her giggle. Gus, she realised, wasn't too comfortable in female company and the idea of it appealed to her. 'Well, you can rest easy. He's already been caught. That was my exciting news for you! It seems that he's been arrested by the Vatican and that the Italian police have been supplied with indisputable proof that it was he who murdered Tom Mackay. In other words, you are off the hook and I am no longer compromised.'

Her smile was again infectious.

'I'm glad.' But he wasn't, because it meant that he had no reason now to stay on in Rome.

Vatican Prison

He was only halfway through his meal but was struggling to keep awake. A great drowsiness had gripped him and all he wanted now was to stagger over to his bed and to lie down on it. A deep sleep was beckoning. First, though, he had to get off his chair. He couldn't understand what was happening to him. It was as if he was drunk... drunk on sleep. His legs gave way, the plate was sent clattering onto the tiled floor and his heavy body soon followed.

The noise served as a signal. Silently, the cell door swung open and the figure standing there paused just long enough to make sure that the coast was still clear outside. Then, producing a small but sharp blade in his gloved hand, he bent over the prisoner's comatose body and deftly slashed both his wrists. Careful to avoid the spurting blood, he now pressed the blade into the dying man's palm. Then he was gone and the cell door had again been locked. Aiello would be pleased... and in his debt!

London, Five Months Later

'James. Your sister just phoned. You'll never guess her news.'

Sir James Oldcorn, director of operations at Vauxhall Cross, had his feet up for the evening. He'd just finished reading and was now inclined to snooze.

'Are you listening, James?'

'Yeees. What is it?'

'Your sister just phoned and guess what? We're being invited to Italy, to a housewarming party!'

'Great!' But MI6's director of operations sounded anything but excited.

'Sally's housewarming! She and her partner have just bought a large villa in Rome.'

'Hm! Bit sudden! You never told me she was even courting.' There was no rebuke in his voice, just lack of any real interest.

'That's because I didn't know myself. Anyway, it's going to be an all-expenses paid thing. We'll have to go.'

'Hm! We'll see! But who's the lucky man? And more importantly, does he come up to my sister's expectations?'

Janet laughed. 'Your sister didn't say. Couldn't, actually, because she's never met him either. All she knows is that he's Italian, that he's filthy rich and that he's given Sally a magnificent engagement ring. I just hope that the girl knows what she's doing. She told me once – as a joke, I thought then – that she wouldn't mind finding herself a sugar daddy. Seems she's found one!'

Sir James Oldcorn sighed. 'I don't like parties, Janet. You know that! You go. My sister will be glad of the company. I'll leave it to you to get them a present for the new home.'

Alet-les-Baines

For the first time in five months, Claude Boudet was finding it hard to concentrate. He had got to the penultimate chapter and now he couldn't get his mind back on track. From the start, he'd been quietly confident that the book, when it was finished, would become a best-seller.

He hadn't yet settled on a title. Had any treasure been found, then he'd have certainly opted for *The Schidoni Pentacle* but since there hadn't, then he would probably stick with his original choice. *The Treasures of the Languedoc* had an exciting ring to it and should generate a lot of interest.

Of late, he'd been having sleepless nights. One question hounded him. When the time came, how would he go about writing the epilogue to his book, since it was there, in the epilogue, that he intended leaving the realms of historical supposition and conjecture behind! It was where he would state, categorically, where he, Claude Boudet, author and respected historian, believed the treasure of Solomon's Temple and that of the Merovingian kings of France was hidden. That, in itself, should guarantee his book becoming an international best-seller.

Of late, though, he'd begun to consider the consequences of such a revelation. Once his book was published, Rennes-le-Château would be swamped with treasure hunters and that was something that the mayor and the inhabitants of Rennes would not be thanking him for. And it wasn't what he himself would wish for either. So perhaps he should be less dogmatic about it all and let the readers decide. Rennes or Montségur? It was worth remembering that he'd made a strong case for the latter, as well. Chapter nine, already written, recounted the strange events of a few months ago when he, the author, had been caught up in a web of intrigue that involved secret agents and murdered foreigners, not to mention the theft of an ancient map from the Vatican's secret archives, and ancient sites of great historical interest being ravaged by unauthorised searches.

He shrugged. 'Get the final two chapters out of the way first, Claude, and then decide on the epilogue.'

Today, he had something else to think about. Sally's invitation! It had come with the morning post and had left him feeling a little sad and deflated. During the past months, Sally had kept in touch through a couple of phone calls but at no time had she hinted at a love affair with a wealthy Italian. He'd been so convinced in his own mind that she and Gus would get over their little tiff but obviously they hadn't. In fact, it seemed that he'd been wrong about the two of them all along. *'He's not my young man, monsieur!'* How many times had she said that to him? He should have taken her at her word, rather than tease her with a silly quotation from *Hamlet.*

Would he accept the invitation? He'd be a fool not to, seeing that it wasn't going to cost him a single euro. An airline ticket had been included with the card, together with a note, in Sally's handwriting, saying that *'a room with a magnificent view'* would be his, for his extended stay in Rome. *Yes,* he thought. *Sally's new found companion had to be quite wealthy.*

Again, he looked at the card. "Sally Jeffers and Guiseppe Maratta would love to have their good friend Claude Boudet present at their housewarming party in Rome". And below it a P.S., also in Sally's handwriting, "We're looking forward so much to seeing you again, Claude".

Nice of her to write that, he thought. But it should be I not We, my dear, because I've yet to meet your lucky new beau.

Villa Tevere, Rome

'No, I'm not going to live with you unless you tell me the truth. And I mean it, Gus! Where did these come from?'

Sally's face was a mixture of curiosity and wonder as she stared at the things that she had emptied onto the verandah table in front of him.

'...And why didn't you tell me that you had them? Why did I have to find them for myself just now in that silly little bumbag of yours, hidden away amongst your biking leathers?'

He smiled wryly. She would have found them sooner or later, anyway, but did she need to know where they'd come from? And if he did tell her, would she then want the whole world to know about it? Yes, she probably would, despite the possible outcome. So, a white lie or two were now justified.

'They belonged to my mother. My real mother, that is.'

By now, Sally was holding a diamond-studded gold ring in one hand and half a dozen loose gems in the other.

'Your mother? Good God! Who was she? Anastasia? Pull the other one, Gus! This isn't your run-of-the-mill nine carat stuff. This is pure twenty-four carat gold.'

'Guiseppe, please!' he smilingly reminded her, hoping to take some of the sting out of the situation. 'My father got them for her. Don't ask me where, or how. Do I have to remind you about his line of work and about the powerful connections he used to have?'

She snorted disbelievingly and now held her new engagement ring up to the light. 'And are you saying that I should thank the mafia for this, as well?'

'More or less.'

'More or less? What does that mean?' She sounded even more aggrieved.

'I took some of those...' He pointed to the pile of old gold coins in the bag. '...And those...' He was now referring to the gemstones in her cupped hand. '...and took them to a master jeweller in Amsterdam. He fashioned it for you.'

She stared at him long and hard, her eyes still full of suspicion.

'...And I also got him to make us a couple of wedding rings. You never know! Some day you might want to make an honest man of me.' He smiled boyishly, hoping to see her smile back at him. 'But I'm not going to show you those just yet, in case it brings bad luck.'

'Why is it, Gus, that I don't believe a word of what you're telling me?' As she spoke, she dipped her fingers into the little bag and brought to light several of the gold coins and let them fall back onto the table. Then she picked one up and studied it more closely, muttering with growing excitement as she did so, 'If I'm not mistaken, the emblem on this side of the coin is the fleur-de-lis, which, according to our mutual friend Claude Boudet, was the emblem of the early Merovingian kings of France ... Around the turn of the sixth century if my memory serves me right.' She turned the coin over. 'And what we have on this other side is a flared cross - emblem, if my memory serves me right, of both the Knights Templar and the Cathars. Now how interesting is that, Gus?' Her smile and her tone became more flippant. 'So, tell me my darling, my true love, when did your dad pop over from Sicily to the Languedoc to pick these up?'

Before Gus could think of an equally flippant answer, something else in the bag caught her eye and she eagerly picked it up between finger and thumb and held it up to the sunlight, unable to hide her true excitement any longer. 'And what would you say this is, Gus?'

'Guiseppe, darling! Gus is dead.'

'Stop fooling and answer my question! What is this?'

'It's obviously a little bee. Why? What would you call it?'

'I would call it the *apis mellifica*. But it's not just any little bee, is it, Gus?'

He saw the discerning glint in her eye and wondered what was coming next.

'...This one's made of solid gold. And had you paid more attention to Claude Boudet, who is, after all, the expert on all things Merovingian, then you would realise the true significance of this little bee.'

Before he could respond, she came to sit on his lap, threw an arm around his neck and kissed him sweetly on the cheek. 'And now, my darling Gus, can I suggest that you start again, but with the truth this time.'

Epilogue

The scene was spectral, the ruined ramparts bleached eerie white by the Pyrenean moonlight. Night was once more laying claim to the ancient citadel, dispatching its demented squadron of pipistrelles to patrol a warm star-studded sky.

The tall phantom like figure, stepping out of the shadows and into the moonlight, paused but briefly to cast a final look around. Then, satisfied that all was well, he turned to depart, knowing that his vigil had ended, now that the threat had been removed.

Mysteries persisted though! The little priest for one! Had the Most Holy Father actually sent a Man of God from Rome to deal with the church's enemies? Surely not! The thin stranger was another. The one who had spirited himself in and out of the citadel that night before riding away on his powerful motorcycle. How had he fitted into the scheme of things? What had been his interest? And where had he gone?

As he silently zigzagged his way down the tortuous path, the ageing guardian of the Château's secrets reluctantly conceded that some questions would have to remain unanswered.